INTO THE UNBOUNDED NIGHT

Mitchell James Kaplan

Regal House Publishing

Published by
Regal House Publishing, LLC
Raleigh, NC 27612
All rights reserved

ISBN -13 (paperback): 9781646030026
ISBN -13 (epub): 9781646030293
Library of Congress Control Number: 2020930406

Interior and cover design by Lafayette & Greene
lafayetteandgreene.com
Cover images © by Shaiith/Shutterstock

Regal House Publishing, LLC
https://regalhousepublishing.com

Printed in the United States of America

For Annie.

For my mother.

For my long-lost brother.

PRINCIPAL CHARACTERS

Azazel: a Messenger of Heaven. (Note: Messenger translates the Hebrew word *malakh*. The English equivalent, angel, derives from the Greek term *angelos*.)

Aislin: a Daughter of Albion, the island known to the Romans as Britannia.

Titus Flavius Vespasianus: known as Vespasian, one of four Roman generals who conquered Britannia in 43 AD. Later, with his son Titus, charged with quelling the Judaean revolt and ultimately, with the destruction of Jerusalem. Emperor of Rome, 69–79 CE.

Septimus: a Roman soldier and fresco artist.

Yohanan, son of Zakkai: a Child of Israel; perhaps the man most responsible for the survival of the Rabbinic branch of Judaean monotheism following the Roman destruction of Jerusalem in 70 CE.

Saul of Tarsus: known in his time as Paulus and today as St. Paul; perhaps the man most responsible for the survival and spread of the Christian branch of Judaean monotheism following the Roman destruction of Jerusalem in 70 CE.

Praise for Into the Unbounded Night

"In *Into the Unbounded Night*, Mitchell James Kaplan offers a rich rendering of war and humanity in first century Rome — of tradition and loss, and the transformative power of healing and collective memory to find one's way home."

Nichole Bernier, Boston Globe best-selling author of *The Unfinished Work Of Elizabeth D.*

"Mitchell James Kaplan is the gloriously talented writer of this dramatic, intense story of conflicting emperors, slaves, priests and exiles in a first-century world whose roots and traditions are increasingly torn apart by the brutal rule of Rome. Men and women search for belief and reason, out of which will emerge a new Judaism after the destruction of Jerusalem's Temple as well as the early beginnings of Christianity. A writer of enormous scope, compassion and poetry, Kaplan has written several of the most compelling characters you will meet in the pages of a book. *Into the Unbounded Night* sweeps over you like a succession of huge waves. It is truly a major novel."

Stephanie Cowell, American Book Award recipient, author of *Claude and Camille: A Novel Of Monet*

"Kaplan's prose is so rich and agile I felt I was breathing the air of these ancient places, and his evocation of character is no less palpable. Fully embodied and driven by ambition, grief, the clear-eyed desire for truth, and fierce maternal love, these characters plunge, march, and stumble toward their fascinating and entangled destinies."

Marisa de los Santos, New York Times best-selling novelist of *I'll Be Your Blue Sky* and award-winning poet

"I'm a big fan of historical fiction when it's as good as Mitchell James Kaplan's *Into the Unbounded Night*. Vividly imagined, *Into the Unbounded Night* pulls the reader along with beautiful prose, strong characters and a wonderfully realized story."

Heidi W. Durrow, New York Times best-selling author of *The Girl Who Fell from the Sky*, winner of the PEN/Bellwether Prize

"A beautiful, informative book. It was gripping throughout, the research never overwhelms the story, but is always part of it. [The] writing is lyrical and evocative of time and place. All the characters are real and interesting. Loved it!"

Martin Fletcher, National Jewish Book Award winner, author of *Promised Land*

"From the mystical lore of Albion to the Roman siege and destruction of Jerusalem, Kaplan's meticulous research and evocative writing meld seamlessly to create a vivid, textured, and richly imagined story."

Beth Hoffman, New York Times and International best-selling author of *Saving Ceecee Honeycutt* and *Looking for Me*

"Set in Rome and Judea after the crucifixion of Jesus, Mitchell James Kaplan's finely crafted and intense second novel delves into the minds and hearts of truly captivating characters. An excellent read."

Eva Stachniak, winner of the Canadian First Novel Award, author of *The Chosen Maiden*

"Sensually provocative, verbally sharp and critically witted, Mitchell James Kaplan's *Into the Unbounded Night* brings to life the tumultuous birth of Judeo-Christian monotheism in this intimately woven narrative brimming with righteous and riotous characters striving for survival and transcendence across the ravished landscapes of Judea, the Roman Empire, and Britannia."

Jessica Maria Tuccelli, an Okra Pick winner of the Southern Independent Booksellers Alliance for her debut novel, *Glow*

"Kaplan weaves an intricate literary tapestry to create a poetic exploration of early Judeo-Christian and Roman history. He builds a diverse yet connected cast of characters whose encounters inspire timeless self-examination and advance the course of history. An engrossing work not easily forgotten."

Therese Walsh, critically acclaimed author of *The Last Will of Moira Leahy* and *The Moon Sisters*, founder of the literary blog, *Writer Unboxed*

In the *Scroll of the Watchers*, it is written that I taught men to fashion swords, knives, shields, and breastplates; that I instructed women in the art of grooming their eyebrows, painting their faces, and bejeweling their necks; that these teachings altered the world.

Other Messengers grumble to the Lord, "Azazel has infected the universe with strife and yearning. He has disclosed to mortals the secrets of the heavens. Behold, the souls of the dead cry out; nor can they elude the unrighteousness that envelops the earth."

The Lord replies: "We hold the teacher responsible, the students innocent. Azazel's teaching has corrupted the world. To him rather than his followers, therefore, we ascribe this entire crime. Bind Azazel hand and foot and cast him into darkness in the depth of Duda-El."

The Lord's condemnation of me, according to the *Scroll of the Watchers*, is eternal; as if It could never forgive such an offense; as if It never changed Its mind. Nor does It provide me with a means of escape. I have shown no remorse, but as the Lord well knows, time, darkness, and contemplation sometimes engender epiphanies, as when we dream.

PART ONE: Circa 40 CE

The villagers have assembled to usher a lamb into their world, the first-born of the season. They spin slowly in three concentric circles around a smoking bonfire as large as a thatch-roofed roundhouse. Flames illuminate their faces, arms, and torsos, which are painted with swirls and dots of sage-green, oxlip-yellow, and thistle-violet. Priestesses in mauve robes, with wild roses and rosemary in their tresses, cast juniper leaves onto the crackling blaze. Behind them, a line of elders blows into long bronze horns. A low wail like the bellowing of oxen reverberates through the valley. Drudwyn, the seer, in a bear's hide and a headdress of antlers, atop a block of granite, calls to unseeable Companions.

Cara, the mother ewe, lies on her side on the grass, her belly swollen—a ball of yellow fur, a black face, black shins and feet. Aislin kneels before her in a white robe, her blonde hair braided. Aislin, the maiden who has seen nothing of the squalor and cruelty of this world.

"All this," she whispers to the sheep, combing her soft, thick coat with her fingers. "All this, Cara. You. You and the little one you hold inside."

Cara bleats.

"You, and the little one," repeats Aislin. "All this." Her hands probe the dirt-caked curls on Cara's belly. Through her tone, firm and cheerful, Aislin wants to impart the confidence she lacks, to put Cara at ease. Neither Aislin nor Cara has done this before. If they should fail, the flowers will not bloom. The sheep and cattle will refuse to couple. The springs will run dry.

Her aunt Muirgheal crouches beside her. "Under her tail," she tells Aislin. "There it is. That is a foot." Muirgheal pats Cara's rump. "You're ready now, aren't you. You are ready now." She tugs Aislin closer. "Put your hand in. Go ahead, reach in."

Aislin reaches in, feeling the hot pulse of blood and muscle. "I feel…I think I feel.…"

"The hooves? Do you feel the hooves?"

"I am touching them."

"The knees?"

"The knees, yes."

"The nose? The face?" demands Muirgheal.

"The face?"

"Go in further."

Aislin pushes in almost to her elbow. Cara's back arches and stiffens. She bleats again, a long, low plaint. Her eyes implore Aislin. "I know, I know," Aislin tells her. "This will soon be over." A lock of hair falls over Aislin's eye. She shakes it away. "She's pushing! I have the head!"

"Grab its forelegs, now," Muirgheal instructs her. "Both of them. Hold tight. Now *pull*!"

Aislin yanks the lamb's feet.

"Now let go. Give her a moment. Let Cara breathe. Now pull again. Pull. Breathe. Pull."

Atop the granite cromlech, the seer's invocations wax and wane, droning and melismatic. The elders blow on their carnyces and the world shudders. Cara's laments dissolve in the ocean of slow melodies and spoken words and the crackling of the bonfire.

The two-toed hooves emerge, one then the other. As Cara whimpers, the blood-matted legs retreat into her womb. She pushes and Aislin pulls. They are working in unison now. In Cara's black eyes, which reflect the flames, Aislin perceives suffering and resignation, sadness and hope. *Cara knows she is about to be a mother*, thinks Aislin. *All the pain in the world is worth this privilege.* Aislin caresses Cara's belly. She presses her cheek into the sheep's flesh, which smells of a grazing animal's sweat, acrid and earthy. Cara pushes again. The little lamb's knees—*breathe and pull*—the head moist, reflecting the glow of the bonfire and moon and stars—*breathe, pull.* Aislin rests her face on Cara's belly while both recover. "Breathe, Cara. Push. Breathe," she whispers.

Cara releases another low sigh, shivers, and the chest emerges; another push, and the belly appears; and finally the rear legs. Aislin falls backward into her aunt Muirgheal's arms, drenched with the bloody afterbirth.

Muirgheal leaps to her feet, holding aloft the trembling, wet body. "The lamb is born! Aislin has pulled him!" She raises the lamb higher and proclaims, "Spring is here!"

The villagers dance in a circle singing:

Winter wings away.
Daffodils dapple the dale.
Blackbirds babble.
Streams sparkle.
Winter wings away.

"A white sheep, well, mostly white anyway, and a newborn black as night," marvels Muirgheal, sitting beside Aislin. "There is meaning in this." She peeks between the newborn's legs. "A boy then. Clean his nose. He has to breathe."

Aislin pulls a string of mucus from the lamb's nose as Muirgheal slices the umbilicus with a bronze knife. The blade is incised with circles and dots, the handle textured like knotted ropes. The lamb sneezes, shivers, flops, and tries to stand. Muirgheal nudges him toward his mother's teats.

"There, there," mutters Aislin, petting Cara. "You rest now. What are we going to call him?"

"You delivered him," says Muirgheal. "You name him."

The baby shakes and coos like a pigeon as he digs his nose into the flesh of his mother's belly searching for milk. "Elisedd, then," says Aislin, smoothing the baby's moist fur. "Gentle One."

Above the horizon a star appears, streaking through the black sky and fading to nothingness like a firefly at the farthest perceptible distance, so evanescent that Aislin wonders whether it was real.

❧

The villagers return to their huts but Muirgheal takes Aislin's arm and holds her back. "You and I must wait."

Aislin yawns. "For what?"

"To watch. To listen."

They sit on the grass as Cara nurses Elisedd beside them. They observe the sky and listen to the trilling of insects and frogs, the whistles of birds, and the crepitation of distant leaves. Toward dawn, other stars start falling. The single ember that fell and perished, after Elisedd emerged into the world, was a harbinger. Thousands of its brethren, sisters, and cousins follow in its path.

"What is this about?" whispers Aislin.

Muirgheal allows the chirrups and croaks of other beings to introduce her answer. "It is about your life," she says finally.

❧

The grass thickens on the hillsides below the village. Little flowers bloom in patches, hanging their white four-petaled heads as if studying the soil at their feet. Brass horns, smaller and more strident than those the elders blew on the night of Elisedd's birth, ring from distant valleys to announce skirmishes, in which the bravest warriors will battle to death.

Aislin awakes to whispers. Her aunt is sitting at a table at the far end of the roundhouse, her face and body painted. On the table rest a potted candle, flowers, a fist-sized leather pouch, a small cloth, and a human head, from which time has stripped all flesh. The skull is brown with age. Shadows fill its orbits and other cavities, shadows that linger within shadows even in daylight. Now, before the dawn, the flickering candle's flame only deepens the emptiness of these orifices. This head once wore the face of Muirgheal's father, Aislin's grandfather.

From the pouch, Muirgheal removes two stones. She drops them onto the cloth, jerks the cloth away, and drapes it across the orbits of her father's eyes. Peering at the stones, she murmurs and sighs. She replaces the stones in their pouch, pushes herself up from the table, and hides the pouch in her trunk.

Muirgheal retrieves her battle-stained corset, which she fashioned years ago from the stiffened hide of a wild bull. "Come, lace this for me," she tells Aislin as if she knew the entire time that her niece was watching her.

Lacing the leather girdle, Aislin asks her aunt, "Must you risk your life, then?"

"Must the stars wander across the sky?" Muirgheal replies. "Must the wind blow?" Her eyes fall to the table. "Must a candle flame leap about?"

"I already lost my mother. I don't want to lose my aunt."

"You mustn't think that way. Our village is worth protecting, is it not? Those we love? And those we don't? And our honor, is that worth nothing?"

Aislin helps her aunt don her *leine*, a lace-trimmed linen shirt, and her *brat*, a brown woolen blanket, which she cinches with a rope.

Muirgheal sits to tie her sandals. "Don't waste your day frolicking with the sheep. Make sure they're properly fed and watered, and that your sisters and cousins get barley gruel and plenty of supervision. You've got butter to churn and wool to comb. I'll be back before sunset, you can count on that." Muirgheal stands and fetches her bronze lance and her carved wood and leather shield.

&

Aislin weaves three thin ropes into a halter for Elisedd, embellishes it with knots and painted stones, and attaches a leash. While working, she imagines her aunt and the village warriors in battle. Their bodies painted, they leap, lunge, and lance. The victorious warrior chops off her enemies' heads and throws them into her wicker chariot.

What forces, Aislin wonders, determine whether one should survive while another must abandon dreams and family, leaving shattered the lives of everyone she loves? From what hidden well does Muirgheal imbibe the waters of invulnerability, and how long will this well sustain her?

An image floats to the surface of Aislin's mind: her mother's lifeless face, her eyes vacant, her hair tangled. The vision is blurry, as if seen through the surface of water. Aislin closes her eyes but her mother's distorted face continues to haunt her.

Muirgheal's deceased sister died of an illness that left her increasingly short of breath when Aislin was four. Aislin remembers almost nothing of that time but she does recall sitting in her mother's lap looking at the constellations as her mother reads the stories written in the sky.

"Each of those bright points: a hero or a heroine," her mother says, pointing. "Do you see that lady over there, leaning over the river of souls, washing her hair? Your great-aunt, the most renowned warrior of her time. She inhabits not just one star but a cluster. I was but a small child when she left us. And there, the man with the javelin in his chest: a fighter from a distant village, where they didn't honor the same rules that we do. He stole upon her while she was washing and thrust her head into the water until she expired, kicking and flailing."

But why? wonders Aislin. And although she does not verbalize this question, her mother, in her memory, answers. "That foreign warrior killed her because your great-aunt was charged with protecting a young woman, a distant cousin, whom he wanted. That young woman was destined to become my mother. It was your grandfather, my father," she concludes, "who avenged his sister's death and earned the love of my mother. Remember, Aislin, love grows not in the pure soil of forgiveness but from the mud of revenge."

Almost ten years have passed since that night. Aislin still recalls the smell of her mother's skin, a mélange of sweat and wild roses, and the glittering expanse of that evening's river of stars. How, she wonders, through the impenetrable fog of the intervening years, can she still hear the timbre of her mother's voice? If it is not a memory, what is it? *It is a form of hope,* she tells herself.

❧

At the end of the day, when the shadows grow long and she first feels the evening's chill, Aislin visits with Cara and Elisedd. In their pen, she watches the lamb push himself up on wobbly legs and prance clumsily, his short black fur glistening, his ears flopping. The lamb halts, feet splayed. Aislin crouches and gazes into his eyes. Elisedd capers off again. Aislin chases him.

He leads her to his mother, who grazes near the rear of the enclosure. Cara has shed some of the bulk of pregnancy but her yellow-brown thorax still seems too voluminous for her black, triangular head and spindly legs. Her offspring nestles between her feet and cocks his head upward to suck on her teats, his long tail swishing. Aislin strokes Cara's matted fur, taking pleasure in its soft curls. Cara turns her face toward Aislin's as if to acknowledge: *You were there. You assisted in the most important moment of my life, the moment when I achieved motherhood.*

A wind blows through the alders and elms and rattles the gate, which is built of branches tied with leather. Aislin looks at the valley and the stream sparkling in the distance, again envisaging the battles beyond the distant hills, praying that Muirgheal has not tested her good fortune one time too many.

When Aislin takes little Elisedd into her arms, Cara bleats loudly. "I'm not going to hurt him," Aislin tells her but Cara continues making a fuss. Aislin lowers Elisedd to the ground and he scampers back to his mother.

Aislin attaches his halter and leash and leads him out of the pen. As Aislin closes the gate, the rope leash slips out of her hands and he dashes off. Aislin runs after him but he is faster.

After a moment Elisedd returns to Aislin and stands near her, blinking, his pupils horizontal black rectangles floating in yellow-green irises. Elisedd sits, folding his legs under his belly as Aislin lies on her back, petting him and watching the clouds. Cara bleats in her far-off pen and Elisedd pules in response. Aislin rises to let him nurse and they race back.

Hearing a rattle of hooves and shields, Aislin turns to see her aunt slowing her muddy, blood-spattered horse. Aislin closes the gate and runs to greet her.

Muirgheal clambers out of her chariot, raising a warrior's head by its hair. "Imagine this bastard naked on the battlefield, painted and shouting. Riagan had the largest penis ever seen in Catavelaunia. Now look at him!" She plants Riagan's head on a stake beside other trophy-heads.

"Who is that?" Aislin asks, pointing toward Riagan's neighbor. Although Muirgheal has described her victims a dozen times, Aislin enjoys hearing her aunt boast.

"This is Brian." Muirgheal jerks her chin at Riagan's neighbor. "A poet of the sword, he'd sidle up next to you in his chariot, spring out, and attack you like a bog cat. And over there is Brenda, who fought women like a furious pine marten but refused to touch men."

Their mouths agape, jowls drooping, vines of ropy vessels dangling from their necks, these once-brave warriors glare at glades and woodlands they no longer recognize. Armies of bugs invade their ears, mouths, and brains. Exposed to the wind and sun, their skin dries and peels until only bones remain.

"Sometimes they'll whisper a word or two," says Muirgheal, "before they realize they're dead."

"What do they say?" asks Aislin.

"Perhaps someone understands their murmurs, but not I. Those that have been here a year or more no longer have anything to say."

"Why is that space empty?" Aislin points to the spot beside Brenda.

"That is for Bleiz," Muirgheal says, shoving her knotted copper hair over her shoulder. "When I catch the bastard."

Bleiz leads a band of marauders. He and his followers are *deorrad*, exiles from their tribes. No one has seen them, but when anything mysterious and disturbing occurs, the villagers attribute the crime to Bleiz. Not certain he is human, they despise him.

❧

In Muirgheal's bedtime tales, Bleiz rides wild bulls and casts spells. The clear stream of a poet's mind clouds and stills; a winsome lass breaks out in boils; a wood-carver's fingers shrivel. When it seems no one can save the village, a little girl, so young she has not yet mastered the art of speech, makes a pact with the Companions. She gives them a precious jewel, inherited from the ancients. The branches of the great yew enwrap Bleiz and squeeze until he gasps prayers of healing. The poet's verses again flow clear; the girl's furuncles dry; the wood-carver's fingers grow back.

"And what happens to Bleiz?" whispers Aislin's little sister, fighting sleep.

"He gets away," sighs Muirgheal with a wistful smile.

There is no better storyteller than Muirgheal, or more capable warrior. The two skills are intertwined: creating lives with words and taking them with the sword.

"Listen well to the stories you hear," Muirgheal advises her nieces. "They may save your life."

"How could a story save my life?" whispers Aislin.

"Suppose one day you find yourself trapped, then, with no way out except through someone's tale?"

Aislin snuggles beside her. "I hope it would be one of yours."

"Wait until you hear the bard."

"When will we hear him?"

"Oh, he'll wander this way soon enough. Now go to sleep."

Aislin's grandfather's skull peers at her through the darkness. Aislin closes her eyes but thoughts of Bleiz perturb her. Her aunt is one of the most favored warriors in the land. The Companions have helped Muirgheal triumph in nearly every struggle but she chooses her battles wisely. "The ones that will kill me, I avoid," Muirgheal admits with paradoxical pride.

"But how can you tell?" asks Aislin.

"I'll let you in on a secret," whispers Muirgheal, "if you promise to sleep."

"I promise."

"It is the divining stones."

Aislin remembers seeing her aunt drop the stones to a cloth on the table, pulling the cloth out from under them and muttering entreaties to the Companions. "Where did we get them?"

"Your mother found them long ago but they're not ours. As sure as you and I lie here, they belong not to this realm but to the Otherworld. So far, I've managed to hide them from the Companions, but they want them back. When I need their assistance badly enough, I shall return the stones. After that, I shall fight no more. But for now, they are mine."

"How do you know they want them back?"

"I have dreams, you know. Just like you."

"Let's find Bleiz," Aislin murmurs, "no matter how long it takes, no matter how far we must travel, and be done with him."

"Do you imagine you're prepared to sleep on the ground, then?" asks Muirgheal. "To eat berries, nuts, and raw bloody meat for days and weeks on end?"

"If you teach me, I will be prepared."

Murgheal sighs. "Since you refuse to sleep, and only because I have nothing better to do, I shall tell you how I caught a great leveret with my bare hands, broke its neck, and skinned it with my dagger. But you must do your part, and that begins with closing your eyes."

As Aislin floats into a poppy-strewn glen of slumber, Muirgheal describes how to live by one's wits, how to solicit the Companions, and how to survive in the wilderness. A mauve hue infuses Muirgheal's lexicon and the violence of her imagery spatters the cobalt dream-horizon. This is their secret adventure.

❧

"For those who wish to inflict death on animals or humans," Muirgheal tells her niece, "there are three secrets. They are simple, but they are not easy. The first is the secret of stillness. You lie in the grass and cover yourself with leaves. If your belly growls, you ignore it. You watch. This is a time for vigilance, not for movement. It may be brief. It may be excruciatingly long. Nor do you know what you're looking for. Perhaps a large beast, like a deer. Perhaps a bird.

"Finally you spy a pair of ears peeking through the grass. A pair of eyes. A little nose points upward, wiggling. Your belly protests. You can almost taste your dinner. Rabbit stew, with herbs and carrots. You can smell the exhilarating vapors of the boiling broth. And yet, now is not the time to move. Now is still the time for waiting. The rabbit hops forward, sniffs the air, and hops again. You must not reveal your presence. You lie low in the grass. Yet again the rabbit bounds forward. Finally, it is so close that the wild, pungent odor of its fur stings your nostrils.

"The second secret," Muirgheal tells Aislin, "is the secret of motion. When the moment arrives, and not before, you leap into action. The time for watching has passed. You must not reflect. If you think of your victim's pain, you are lost. You grab the rabbit by the neck and squeeze until the last glimmer of light dims in its eyes. You have extinguished a life, but you have provided yourself and your children with another evening's nourishment."

"And what is the third secret?" Aislin asks.

"Ah," says Muirgheal, "this one is the most important. If an opportunity arises, you do whatever you have to do. You forget about the first two secrets. In life there are guidelines, like well-worn paths, but nothing is certain and nothing is forever. A storm may come and wash out part of the trail, or grass may overrun it, and you'll have to find your way. That is when you must not lose courage."

❧

Elisedd disappears before his second year. Finding him gone and the gate open, Aislin scans the valley and hills, calling until she is hoarse. Her pleas dissolve like smoke in the chilly dawn. Elisedd, she knows, would scurry and stumble home if he could. Sometimes, Aislin tells herself, no matter how much you miss your safe little pen, there is no way back. Again she thinks of her mother, imagines hearing her voice in the distance, but it is only the low hoot of a red-breasted bullfinch that flaps away, a moment later, from the high branches of an elm.

Bleiz must have stolen Elisedd, Aislin concludes. She sprints to Muirgheal's hut. "That spot you want to fill, next to Brenda. It is time."

"I cannot be bothered with Bleiz today," says Muirgheal. "Not over a mere lamb."

"A *mere* lamb?" Aislin crosses her arms. "What could be worth more than a lamb? I shall find Bleiz myself, then, and avenge the theft of Elisedd."

"You are as brave as any girl your age," Muirgheal tells her. "But not old enough to wander through plains and glades by yourself."

Ignoring Muirgheal's warning, Aislin steps into the forest to search for footprints and lamb turds and to listen for Elisedd's bleats. Sunlight filters through the leaves, which tremble in the breeze. Shadows scuttle in all directions. Strange noises and magical entities fill the wood. Aislin begs the Companions to guide her. They dwell in the streams and trees, among the chirping crickets and belching frogs. She presses her hands to the trunk of a beech and leans forward. "Fagus, our Companion who dwells in the heart of the beech, you who see and hear all that pass your way, give my feet direction, my heart strength, my eyes acuity. Help me find Elisedd."

Whatever route Fagus may intend for her, Aislin dares not stray far from the stream. She chews berries, mushrooms, and nuts, but this meager nourishment leaves her belly demanding more. She makes a blanket of leaves and sleeps on the soil. At night she looks up at the canopy of leaves and stars, remembering her mother's stories about the constellations. Owls hoot, crickets chirp, a song thrush warbles. Something sniffs near Aislin's right ear. She imagines an animal the size of a pig, with thick, coarse bristles or quills, but when she opens her eyes she sees only the shadows of leaves, branches, stars, and blackness. She smiles. The Companions are toying with her.

By dawn of the third day, her belly twists with hunger. In a clearing, she lies in wait. A robin lands some distance away, twists its head, pecks at a worm, and flies off. A mouse scurries through the grass. Immobile, Aislin watches insects, leaves, and shadows. She listens to the wind.

A short-tailed weasel appears, raises its head, looks left and right, jumps forward. Its behavior resembles Muirgheal's description so closely that Aislin's belly rumbles. When the moment seems propitious, she lunges but the weasel darts off. Did she wait too long, or move too soon? Was she supposed to ignore her aunt's directives? Even with rules, life is confusing. You have to know when to apply them, and when not, and how.

☙

She reaches the next hamlet south, weakened by her journey but without fear. The tattoo on her arm, a green swirl with red dots, identifies her as a member of a friendly tribe. She knows a boy here, a distant relative.

The village is larger than her own and in a state of commotion. A dozen warriors stand at its center, dressed for battle. "This is not a safe place right now," a man warns her, lashing a horse to his chariot. "This will be no ordinary skirmish. You had better return home."

Aislin proceeds to the roundhouse where her cousin dwells. Inside, he too is preparing for battle. He approaches Aislin, studying her the way a man might examine a splendid war horse. "You're a brave girl, Aislin," he says at last, "to have journeyed all this way without protection."

Everything about him has lengthened since she saw him last—his fingers, his face, his black hair, his ears, his mouth. His voice has deepened but retains its delicate, youthful quality. The hue of his eyes is the hyacinth-blue she remembers. Aislin blushes as she realizes she has come not only in search of Elisedd but to see him. "Have some porridge. You must be hungry." He offers her oats and barley sweetened with honey.

She devours it so quickly he laughs. His laughter makes her think of ocean waves, which she has never seen but which her aunt, who also has never seen them, has described.

"What village are you fighting?" she asks.

"No village," he tells her, lacing his sandals. "Invaders from…we know not where. The fiercest enemy we've ever confronted, or so I hear."

"Please, stay here with me. Just one day," she implores him.

He reaches to caress her hair. "Your hair is so beautiful," he says.

Before joining the other fighters, Aislin's cousin leads her to the hut of a shepherd. "Of all the villagers," he tells her, "this shepherd is the one most likely to spot a wandering, ink-black lamb."

The shepherd shakes his blond curls. "Your little friend hasn't wandered this way," he assures Aislin.

Aislin's cousin urges her to return home promptly, to warn her village about the invaders. "Our battle will not be the last."

≈

As Aislin plods down the path from her cousin's village she feels his eyes upon her and turns to see him. She understands the sadness and longing in his gaze even though neither has mentioned their feelings. She enters the forest, closes her eyes, and reaches out with her mind to touch the invisible Companions, but feels only a gentle breeze on her skin. She opens her eyes and sees the sunlight filtering through the rustling leaves to the speckled soil. What invisible forces make the air, itself invisible, move? From where do those forces arise? What secrets does the wind, rustling through the leaves, whisper to her, like a thousand tongues? She cannot interpret that language. Perhaps one day she will learn to do so.

She glances to her right and left. One way is the direction of hope, but also of peril. Perhaps Elisedd wanders, bleating for his mother, just beyond the place where trees and vines blend into obscurity. Perhaps she will stumble upon the encampment of Bleiz and avenge her village for the slights and insults they have endured. Bleiz's body will ignite when she stabs it, as will the bodies of his followers, or so Muirgheal has told her. That would be a sight worth risking her life for.

Then again, Bleiz might kill her before anything at all ignites. And there are other dangers. Invaders, the fiercest ever, her cousin warned her.

The other direction promises comfort, hot meals, and duties; the predictable flow of time from one moon to the next; a languid, often stultifying march toward adulthood and battle.

Turning her back on her village, Aislin sets out again in search of Elisedd and Bleiz, but soon the forest's hootings grow bleak and direful, the stream burrows underground, and the path dissipates. As the day wanes and the shadows lengthen, she sits down and allows herself to weep.

❧

"As punishment for your disappearance," her aunt tells her when she returns home, "you're to drink the tears we shed during your absence."

Aislin sips tentatively from the glazed-clay cup, painted with garlands and flowers. Muirgheal tilts the vessel up and tears spill into Aislin's mouth, onto her chin: the salty tears of her younger sister, the sour tears of her deceased mother's sister, the muddy tears of the potter's nephew.

"You are fortunate you came back in time," Muirgheal tells her. "We have a visitor. Wash in the stream and dress in your best *leine* and *brat*."

The bard who has appeared at their gate, a huge man with a wild beard and untamed hair, is dressed in a yellow *leine* and a plum-colored outer garment. All sixty-seven villagers gather around him as he raises his hands and lowers them in a circular motion, creating an airy orb in which his characters will dwell while his words breathe life into them.

"Greetings from the court of King Togodumnus," he thunders, and the elders, together with their children and their children's children, listen captivated as he embarks upon a long, convoluted tale of warriors wandering, curses acquired and shed like ill-fitting garments, and princesses' hearts bursting with sadness and gratitude. He speaks of a wild man who hoards balms of healing; of a heartbroken knight who has forged a pact with the Companions, only to discover that he has been cheated; of a spinster who, after her death, contrives to burn down the castle of the prince who has spurned her. As the sun sets and a storm brews, the bard sits on a boulder, reels in the far-flung fibers of his story, and knots them into a loose net that traps his listeners' imaginations.

"Our lives are nothing but tales, my friends," he concludes. "Interlocking yarns that form a great epic whose outer edges we can never behold. Like all good stories our lives twist and turn; you think it's about this but then it's about that. Trails appear to lead one way but take you somewhere else. Patterns shift under our gaze like a stick on a bush that moves and becomes an insect.

"At night, look up at the heavens. Look at the constellations, the legends they relate. And consider this: another girl, another boy, a thousand days' journey distant, is gazing up at those same stars. They are telling him and her stories, too. Not the same stories. Entirely different ones. But they are the same stars."

He waves toward the horizon. "I must warn you. You will slog through many a muddy field before you happen upon the open, green landscape that causes your heart to soar. And I shall not hide it from you: you will see much tumult. Battles will be won and lost, loved ones will die and others be born. The sun may turn black but even in that murk, if you keep your eyes open, you will discern a glimmer." He lowers his voice. "Always keep in mind, the verities of the heart are the center, around which all revolves."

Although he has spoken these words a hundred times, he infuses them with such quiet, intimate passion that they sparkle like flecks of gold in a rushing stream. He possesses the ability to look all the children in the eyes at once.

"And now I defer to you to bring this magical afternoon we have spent together to a suitable conclusion. Form a circle under that tree yonder and thank our Companions for the inscrutable wonders of this existence that the universe has bequeathed to us for no reason we can hope to learn."

The children spread out under the gnarled, weeping trunk of the great yew, their hair unfurled, their faces upturned to the sky, and chant a prayer. Rain falls crimson in the sunset. Lightning streaks their eyes.

❧

That night, as Muirgheal serves the bard mutton chops and mead in her thatched roundhouse, he relates a grimmer tale to the village leaders, speaking in the tone that adults reserve for the most weighty subjects. "These invaders are well-armed and extraordinarily disciplined. They arrived in thousands of longboats that washed upon the shore like a forest of driftwood. At once they set about stealing livestock, raping and murdering women, men, and children, destroying entire villages with no regard for alliances or kinship relations, for they have none. Those who oppose them, they nail naked to trees. The bravest native warriors have won few skirmishes and no battles.

"They come from a place called Roma, and their general is a giant called Vespasian. Sooner or later they will reach your gate," concludes the bard. "If you don't surrender, and perhaps even if you do, you will die."

Muirgheal appoints a scout to investigate. He must leave this very night. He is to report back within a week.

❧

Long after everyone is sleeping, the skull on the table speaks to Aislin. She wakes to hear her grandfather discoursing with beings invisible to her, or perhaps play-acting in a fragmented Otherworld drama. "What a wee tadpole he was, and I clinging to his back with what little strength I had left, as he wiggled wild upstream." Or, more sternly: "If our swords clash, Kelwyn, the next time your Maeve sets eyes upon her lover, she will be peering at a dead man with a great bloody hole in his chest." Or again, enigmatically: "And down we glided; it seemed an eternity, did it not? Sliding through the darkest heavens as stars burst all around."

His inspired nonsense amuses Aislin. Occasionally, during the following nights and weeks, she catches other fragments, as if snatching leaves of the witch-wood as they scatter on a gusty autumn afternoon. Sometimes his lipless mouth and absent tongue birth whooshing winds, singing crickets, or splattering rain. Once, his eyes lock onto hers: "Our Companions, our protectors, they're going away now. Bid them farewell, little one!"

"That cannot be, Grandfather. The Companions have always been with us. How could we survive without them?"

He rolls his empty eyes toward a Companion she cannot see and resumes a conversation he began a few weeks earlier. "Wet as frogs, we howled in laughter and grief. Ah, Faolan, more than a friend, you were. And now you're gone." He punctuates his ardent folderol with a hearty guffaw.

❧

"Has the sleep fairy poisoned you, then," Muirgheal demands of her niece in the morning, "that you cannot rise with the rest of us? Your sister finished her porridge and yours as well. Rinse these bowls. I shall boil more for you."

She hands Aislin two ceramic dishes decorated with interlaced knots and flowers in white, yellow, and green and steps outside. When she is gone, Aislin finds Muirgheal's leather pouch in the trunk and hides it under her *brat*.

At the stream she kneels to rinse the bowls, calling to the Companions in the water and the wood. "Do not leave us! We are your people!" She removes the leather pouch. "Here! My mother's divining stones, inherited from the ancients. Our most precious possessions. You can have them, but please, do not abandon us!"

She pours the divining stones into her palm, kisses them, and allows them to slide through her fingers. "Please stay!" she implores the Companions.

The stream embraces the divining stones, enfolding them in its cool water, and carries them off. A breeze rises, rustling the trees.

❧

The scout, filthy and weary, returns late one night with grim news. Aislin awakes as her aunt ushers him into her roundhouse and offers him hot broth. Raising his bowl, sipping, he tells Muirgheal, "The bard was right. This is something we have never seen. It is moving in our direction."

Muirgheal responds in a mellifluous tone intended to calm and reassure the scout and, perhaps, herself. She glances back at her sleeping daughters and nieces. Aislin closes her eyes and continues to listen but her aunt's words blend into a sound like distant wind, and Aislin finds herself once again wandering in a forest. Birds screech and stars wink like night-bugs at her feet. She comes to a wide river that flows fiercely with a rushing sound, like air blowing in her ears. She yearns to go home, but her village stands beyond the river, across a wide field, and atop a distant hill. Although her friends and relatives are far away, she sees them as if they were close, but when she calls they seem not to hear.

With long, straight black hair tied back, his sandals softly slapping pavers, fourteen-year-old Yohanan, son of Zakkai, trudges up a flagstone path between walls of unmortared limestone. A scent of myrtle, cedar, and old urine suffuses the air.

A bumblebee buzzes toward a cluster of honeysuckle flowers that spills over a low wall. Yohanan stops to admire the rotund insect: its eyes, so large relative to its head; its fuzz-covered, segmented body; its drooping feet; the vibrations of its wings, by which it precisely controls its flight, hovering, inching forward, landing on one of the petals, pulling the branch groundward. What astonishes Yohanan is the knowledge of the world and the sense of purpose packed into this fingertip-sized, yellow-and-black-banded being.

Yohanan's own sense of purpose involves the contemplation of such marvels. The fulfillment of his destiny, whatever that may be, will depend upon his flair for observation and reflection. This sense of his path forward has grown over time and continues to grow—a gift of Messengers.

As he continues along his way, Yohanan corrects himself. Thought alone cannot suffice. The world of humans is rife with error. In addition to thought, action is required. Action, not thought, brings about change in the world. The trick, he muses, is to hold thought and action in balance. Men of action may achieve power and distinction but unless their activities are grounded in understanding, their accomplishments inevitably amount to palaces of sand.

He thinks of King Herod, known as Herod the Great, who died in the time of Yohanan's grandfather. Lost between identities—the Idumean identity of his ancestors, the Greco-Roman identity of his patrons, the Judaean identity of the people over whom he ruled—Herod built magnificent residences and expanded the Temple of Jerusalem but nearly destroyed the soul of Israel. Such, in any case, is the common opinion. Herod's name and legacy are cursed to this day in synagogues and private prayers, as if he alone were responsible for all that has gone awry.

Herod's mind was warped. His own family, many of whom he murdered, knew it all too well. His actions sprang from instincts of selfishness, greed, concupiscence, and jealousy. As a result, Herod suffered terribly, as did the world around him.

Contemplation and action, Yohanan tells himself, *must somehow inform one another.* A bridge must connect them, so sturdy it will survive even the abuse of tyrants like Herod and Caesar. The building of this bridge, or rather its reconstruction—this, surely, is a noble purpose.

He chuckles at his own presumption. What makes him imagine that he, of all people, could ever hope to erect such a bridge? He can almost hear his father's reproach: *Are you so very special?*

Reaching a wooden gate that fills a mossy, arched opening, he stops and peers through. A narrow garden separates the wall from a columned walkway adorned with frescoes and vines. At the back of this loggia, a shadowed doorway under a triangular lintel fronts a Roman-style villa. In the garden, Yohanan's friend Stefanos is juggling three lemons. Yohanan watches Stefanos's hands dance, his feet skipping forward and back, the fruit leaping, until Stefanos's eyes catch Yohanan's and his pace slows. Two lemons in one hand, one in the other, Stefanos pushes his wide black curls back from his face.

"How did you learn that?" asks Yohanan.

Stefanos smiles lopsidedly. "I taught myself." A hint of Greek privilege veils his Aramaic.

The concept of learning anything without a teacher—without reference to a tradition— perplexes Yohanan. But then, he and Stefanos have never claimed to be alike, which is why they so fascinate, delight, and infuriate each other.

"How long did it take?"

"A few months."

"You rascal, you're keeping secrets from your best friend."

"Well, at first there was nothing to brag about," explains Stefanos. "I dropped them more often than I caught them. But I'd seen it done—"

"Where?"

"In the Plaza of the Nations."

Yohanan nods. Stefanos's father, a money changer, manages a stall there.

"I so wanted to master this. It felt like praying for the messiah."

Again Stefanos launches the three lemons into the air, juggling even more spectacularly than before, with one hand moving from his chest to his back, the other left to right, his feet twisting and leaping. It is a fleeting dance, but Stefanos packs so much motion into the moment that Yohanan's eyes can hardly keep up. When Stefanos winds it up with a flourish, Yohanan applauds.

Stefanos tosses him a lemon. "Start with your right hand. Fling it into the air. Catch it. Good. Keep that up. Now bounce another with your left." He throws him a second.

Yohanan fumbles. "I am so clumsy."

"You're thinking too much," Stefanos tells him. "Let your hands do what they want. That's the trick."

Yohanan tries to let his hands do what they want but what they want, it seems, is to drop the lemons. Stefanos laughs. "Give it time." He places a hand on Yohanan's back and escorts him out through the gate. "You didn't come all this way to juggle. Let's have an adventure." They stroll through the pristine streets of Stefanos's quarter, where the residences hide behind towering walls.

"Do you even know your neighbors?" Yohanan asks.

"Not much. That's the idea," Stefanos replies.

Yohanan wonders: *Why do wealthy people not want to know their neighbors? Perhaps it has something to do with their sense of competition? Perhaps wealthy people dislike others?*

In the part of town where Yohanan lives, there is no privacy. Neighbors socialize in the streets. No walls surround the houses. There are no curtains to separate what goes on inside from what happens outside. If a man flirts with his wife's sister and his wife learns about it, everyone hears their dispute. And later that night, when he makes it up to her, the entire quarter rejoices with them in their pleasure.

Stefanos and Yohanan reach a hill that offers a view of Jerusalem, of Herod's palaces, the Greek amphitheater, the Temple complex, and the Mount of Olives. "Have you ever gone beyond?" asks Stefanos, looking at the wall of massive stones that surrounds the city.

Yohanan shakes his head. Although his father, a copyist and trader of manuscripts, often travels to distant lands, he never takes his son with him.

"Let me show you something," says Stefanos, taking Yohanan by the hand. He leads Yohanan through the city gate to an abandoned mine that dates, he claims, from the time of King Solomon: a cave, hewn into a hillside, beyond an apron of stones.

"Crawl in," says Stefanos.

Yohanan shakes his head.

"Wait for me, then." On all fours, Stefanos creeps inside.

Yohanan approaches the mouth of the tunnel and peeks into its throat. "What do you see?"

Stefanos's voice emerges from the darkness. "Nothing."

"What is so interesting about nothing?"

"Come in, and you will see."

Yohanan follows Stefanos into the wet, gloomy cave, all the way to a precipice. They hear soft crunching sounds, low grunts, a fluttering. "It's the *malakh ha-mavet*, the Messenger of Death," whispers Stefanos.

"I thought he lived in the heavens."

"He may live there, but he has to swoop down to earth—doesn't he?—to do his job."

"Let's leave." Yohanan pushes himself backward, away from the precipice and the *malakh ha-mavet*.

"They say he's covered with eyes."

"And he has thousands of wings."

Stefanos leans forward. "Listen."

"What do you hear?"

"Come closer."

Yohanan inches forward to hear the whispers and chirps that rise like steam from the abyss.

"There's a ledge," says Stefanos. "Not too far down. I've climbed down before."

"How far is it?"

"Six or seven feet. You can see a shadow, very faint, a smudge of blackness. You see that? Plenty of room for both of us."

Stefanos lies on his belly, feet toward the abyss. He anchors his palms on protruding rocks, lowers his legs, and releases his hold. Yohanan hears his sandals slap the stone of the ledge. Stefanos's voice floats up from the blackness: "The *malakh ha-mavet* hasn't gotten me yet."

"How will you climb back up?"

"There are footholds. Come!"

Shaking, Yohanan follows him. In this all-encompassing darkness, to let go is to trust in something he cannot see: Stefanos's words, mere breath. He has never before wagered his life on a promise. There is something awful and exhilarating in doing so now. He lands on the stone shelf. Stefanos seizes him to prevent him from falling.

Stefanos crouches and drops a pebble. It falls forever. They listen intently and hear a hiss, then a murmur. "I think we should leave," whispers Yohanan.

"Shh. Do you hear that?"

Yohanan hears his own breathing and the pounding of his heart. "What do you hear?"

"Shh."

The boys detect faint rustling noises, nearly inaudible sputterings. *Perhaps other Messengers congregate in the depth*, Yohanan thinks.

"They say the *malakh ha-mavet* never travels alone," whispers Stefanos. "The Lord will not allow it. Celestial guards accompany him to protect people like you and me, whose time has not yet come."

"Maybe, maybe not, but we should leave," Yohanan repeats urgently. "We're not meant to enter their places."

Stefanos gropes the wall for nooks and outcrops and pulls himself up. Yohanan tries to follow but the flint under his right hand gives way. He yelps as he almost loses balance. His cry reverberates.

"Reach up!"

Above him, lying on his belly, Stefanos lowers his hand. Yohanan reaches to grasp it. "I have you," gasps Stefanos. "Don't let go." Both boys know that if Yohanan slips, Stefanos will topple into the darkness with him. "Now find that place for your foot."

Yohanan searches the stone wall with his foot. Finding a spur, he pushes himself up.

"I have you," repeats Stefanos. Risking his own life, he strains to pull Yohanan back from the chasm, saving him from the embrace of the *malakh ha-mavet*.

❧

As the sun melts into the horizon, the boys dash back to Stefanos's villa. His mother is rinsing the path outside to greet the invisible Messenger of the Sabbath. Seeing them dirt-covered and out of breath, she shakes her head in amused resignation. "You must bathe at once, both of you. You're staying for dinner," she tells Yohanan.

"My mother will worry."

"We shall send word to your mother." She signals a slave, who assumes the task with a nod. "Spend the night with us," she adds, to Yohanan.

Stefanos and Yohanan wash at the garden fountain and break bread in a room off the atrium, sitting on padded stone benches. A three-branched candelabrum lights the leafy vermilion and Nile-green murals. Stefanos's father prays like other Judaeans but with a Greek accent stronger than his son's. They feast on lamb, chickpeas, and olives and sip diluted wine in the glow of oil lamps. For Yohanan, this is a rare privilege. He rarely tastes meat except during those holy days that require a journey to the Temple.

After dinner the boys lie on mattresses in the atrium. Stefanos's father, with abundant gray-tinged hair and fierce blue eyes, narrates a story unlike any Yohanan has encountered in the Scrolls of Tradition. His characters are Judaean travelers: seafarers transporting leopard skins and ivory from the land of Kush; caravan drivers, whose camel bags burst with frankincense and myrrh; itinerant prophets and slaves, chafing in their chains. They lose their way in the hanging gardens of Babylon or the lead mines of Hispania; they explore the sacred pyramids of Egypt and philosophize in Athens.

"How can you describe all these places and people?" Yohanan whispers, after Stefanos and his mother have drifted off to sleep. "Have you been there?"

"Only in my mind," chuckles Stefanos's father. "But I have read about these places."

"Where do you find such texts?" Yohanan's father, an expert in ancient manuscripts, has never shown Yohanan codices or scrolls like those that Stefanos's father has described.

"I have a friend, a scribe in the library of the Temple. They collect scrolls from Egypt, Greece, and Babylon, as well as our own ancient writings. I don't know all these languages, but I can read Homer, Xenophon, and Kallimachos in Greek."

"They have all these scrolls in the Temple library?"

"Of course they do, and much more."

"I thought that part of the Temple was off limits to all but the priests."

"Perhaps they shouldn't allow the likes of me," Stefanos's father laughs. "Let me tell you a secret. The Temple is only as pure as its high priest. In our age?" He shakes his head.

"What about him?"

"He's no less Greek than I, let us put it that way."

Greek means *foreign*. It can also mean *polytheistic*. Stefanos's father is no polytheist. But what is he implying about the high priest?

"Do you know what coin they accept for the tithe?" continues Stefanos's father. "But how would you know? You're too young. Wait here."

He walks to the back of the house and returns holding a silver coin. On one side, in the soft light of the oil-lamp sconces, Yohanan discerns a god with a human face crowned with leaves. "A graven image, you see," observes Stefanos's father. "And not just any image. It is the face of Ba'al, the chief god of the Tyrians." He flips the coin over. An eagle or a phoenix adorns the other side. "This is the Tyrian shekel, the only coin the Temple priests will accept." He hands it to Yohanan.

"Ba'al? Why?" breathes the boy, dismayed that images of a foreign deity circulate in the Holy Temple, in blatant contempt of the Second Commandment, which forbids depictions of any god. He hardly dares contemplate such sacrilege.

"They trust the silver. There are so many bad coins out there. Tyrian shekels are reliable. The rest of us, we close our eyes, do we not?"

Yohanan does not want to close his eyes. When he closes his eyes he sees emptiness, which reminds him of the *malakh ha-mavet*.

"You're not the only one who's appalled," says Stefanos's father. "A few years ago a revered teacher pushed his way into the Plaza of the Nations and raised a ruckus on account of these unholy coins. He overturned our tables, and some of his followers attacked the money changers with whips and swords. I still carry a mark on my back."

Stefanos's father lifts his tunic to reveal the ridged scar. "You wouldn't want to know what happened to that teacher," he concludes, as if warning Yohanan that in this sublunary realm, while there is a place for righteousness, righteousness must know its place.

That night, Yohanan dreams of strolling in the Temple library, a palace of gold, where celestial Messengers play ethereal music and silky scrolls whisper intimations of the knowledge of heaven.

෨

A cool morning breeze wafts over the hills of Jerusalem. It is spring, and after a restful night in the opulent home of his friend, Yohanan feels renewed. With Stefanos he ambles through affluent quarters that provide views of the Temple and Herod's palaces of marble and gold. Along the way they pass synagogues, often little more than rooms within the homes of scholars but sometimes two- or three-story buildings with columns, arches, and wide doorways under stone lintels. A young man, seated in a public square, celebrates the Sabbath by reciting the words of the prophet Micah from memory. Another, planted in the middle of a wide street, seems to fancy himself a prophet. With broad gestures he complains of the Roman temples that dot the Judaean hills. "They are sacrificing their pigs on our sacred soil. Surely this is an abomination! And I tell you, no good will come of it!"

This kind of speech could get a man crucified, Yohanan knows. Perhaps for this reason, no one stops to listen. Fortunately, the Roman soldiers who occasionally pass in groups of three or four understand not a word of Aramaic. Their Judaean sympathizers, who speak Greek and understand Aramaic, might be more dangerous to men like this preacher, but they care little about a rabble-rouser with no following.

Around another corner, two women and a man stand talking in the morning sun. The man wears a white headdress. One of the women has beads in her tresses and wears a scarf in the mottled colors of an unripe pomegranate, streaked with gold filaments. They wish the two boys a peaceful Sabbath and the boys reply in kind.

"Where are you going?" asks the woman with the scarf. "Why not come in and break bread with us? We call ourselves The Synagogue of the Way."

"How does your way differ from others?" Stefanos asks.

"Our anointed one has arrived. Our messiah. It is time to rejoice."

To Yohanan, pronouncements like this sound wildly optimistic, but Stefanos asks the woman, "Where?" He peeks inside the small building of ocher stone.

Candles burn in niches in the arched walls, illuminating a man with long hair the color of grilled bread. He sits, legs crossed, at the far edge of a circle on the floor, while others nearby nibble on nuts, figs, and braided loaves. Conversing quietly, the long-haired man raises his gray eyes.

"I can report to you with great joy," replies the woman, "he is here with us."

"Is that him?" asks Stefanos, referring to the long-haired man.

"That is his brother, Jacob of Nazareth," the man with the headdress explains.

Inside, the long-haired man beckons Stefanos to approach.

Stefanos turns to Yohanan. Seeing his friend so intrigued, Yohanan smiles and nods as if to say, *Go ahead. We shall part ways here. I can find my way alone.*

❧

In his father's workshop Yohanan asks, "Is it true, Father, our high priest is Greek?"

Setting a fresh parchment on the table, his father replies, "I do not think about such things. The Temple is the holiest place in the world. We all strive to be worthy of our involvement with it."

Yohanan dips his stylus into a pot of ink and copies a few letters. "In all the places you've visited, you've surely seen other peoples' temples."

Zakkai's eyes narrow as if to imply, *why do you wonder about such things?* "One need not go far to see other peoples' temples," he says. "The temples of the occupiers are everywhere."

"I don't mean Roman temples. I mean the temples of ancient peoples, as old as ours, or older."

"Besides Roman and Greek temples, what have I seen? I will tell you. I've seen statues of great rulers, reduced to dust, and the remnants of foreign gods, so timeworn you can't distinguish their mouths from their noses."

Father and son resume working silently. Yohanan's mind, though, remains restless. "When a nation dies, destroyed by another," he asks after a time, "what survives? When great leaders wander like shadows under the earth, when monuments stare at us silently or disintegrate, what is left?"

His father, his palms pressed to the table, turns to his son. "What is left? Written words. That is all, my son. Chronicles. Laws. Stories. Philosophies. These lines and dots, squiggles of ink on skin." He runs his fingertips over a dry manuscript. "They are the voices of the earth." He returns to his work.

Yohanan again interrupts him. "Father, do you believe all money changers are evil?"

His father pauses to wipe his forehead lest a drop of sweat smudge his work. "Their affairs lead them into dealings with our oppressors. That is enough for me." He places his hands squarely on the copying table, cocks his head, and peers at his son sideways. Yohanan has seen him assume this posture before. It is a question that is also a statement: *Have we discussed philosophy enough, for one afternoon?*

ॐ

A trumpet blasts from the Temple. Yohanan's father wipes the tip of his wooden pen with a rag. "It is nearly time for supper. In the morning, I must leave town."

"Where are you going, Father?"

"Alexandria."

"When will you be back?"

"You pose difficult questions, Yohanan."

"Mother grows weary," pursues the boy. "Will it be weeks, or months? We never know. Sometimes a courier brings a message. Other times, we're left wondering whether you're even alive."

"Enough of this."

Yohanan helps his father carry wood to the stone oven in the dusty courtyard they share with neighbors. "I have obtained a copy of *Pinkhas*," says Zakkai, "a small text that the Zealots cherish."

"The Zealots?" Yohanan has heard of this group but knows little about them.

"We have a buyer," continues his father. "While I'm gone, you are to copy this text. Take your time. Remember, the sheet of parchment on which you're writing was once a living goat. As you print holy words upon it, you again give it life. Life is holy, so do all this only after bathing, and with the utmost care."

"I know, Father." His father has uttered these instructions before.

"The Zealots are hungry for texts like this."

"Who are they, Father? What is their philosophy?"

"I don't know much about them, but I do know they prefer texts that seem to justify murder."

"Murder?"

Zakkai nods. "They advocate killing the occupiers and anyone who collaborates with them." He kneels and pours a little oil from a small jar onto the twigs. "Naturally, they distrust us Pharisees." He touches the flame of a small lamp to the soaked twigs, then leads Yohanan into the house to fetch the pot of lentils and onions that Yohanan's mother has prepared. "We distrust the Zealots as much as they distrust us, so be cautious. Do not deviate from the letters as you see them," Yohanan's father repeats. "This text, *Pinkhas*, belonged to your uncle Yohanan, after whom you were named. It fell into my hands recently, when your aunt passed away."

As they dine, Yohanan watches his father and his mother. They hardly speak to each other. She glances at him from time to time, but Zakkai seems scarcely to notice. Yohanan's younger sister, Hannah, does most of the talking. She speaks of a friend, whose mother recently gave birth to a son, and of a song this friend taught her, which recalls the yearning for freedom of Hebrew slaves in Egypt. The melody is haunting but the lyrics are subtly subversive, words to which the Roman overlords might object, not for what they express but for what they imply.

☙

The house consists of one room atop another, built of sun-dried bricks with cedar beams and glassless windows. Yohanan's family inhabits the downstairs portion. Rugs of ocher, green, and brown cover the packed earth floor. While his mother and sister sleep, Yohanan and his father lie awake. Moonlight and a cool breeze stream in.

"You know about your mother's brother, do you not?" Zakkai asks him, his voice a low rumble, his fingers combing Yohanan's hair.

Yohanan's mother rarely speaks of her departed brother but Zakkai has mentioned him more than once. "My uncle Yohanan?"

"Yes."

"A Roman soldier killed him, no?" whispers Yohanan. "Shortly before I was born?"

"A Roman killed him, yes."

"Why?"

"Years ago," says Zakkai, "your uncle was the priest in charge of guarding the Temple Treasure."

"Uncle Yohanan was Guardian of the Temple Treasure?"

"A terrible honor," confirms his father. "For a time. What could he do? Valerius Gratus, of cursed memory, sent a military commander, a *centurio*, with soldiers who carried axes and spears."

"Why?"

"To seize the Treasure, so they could pay for the widening of an aqueduct. Your uncle fought the intruders and died a martyr."

Yohanan has learned to root out unspoken intent in his father's language. His uncle bequeathed to the nephew not only the three syllables of his identity but an implicit assignment: to take up his mission, to redeem his name.

As Yohanan falls asleep, images of his uncle Yohanan fighting for his life against a Roman *centurio* tumble through his mind. Pierced by a sword-thrust, Uncle Yohanan collapses to his knees, staring at the younger Yohanan. The horror jolts Yohanan awake, but staring into the darkness he loses grasp of the specifics. He remembers only his uncle's eyes, and then, not even his eyes but merely the hint of light that played upon their surfaces.

꙳

In his father's absence, Yohanan carries wood and kindles the stone oven. After dinner he shows his younger sister Hebrew letters.

Thin, sprightly, always eager, Hannah peers at the text he is copying. "What does it say?"

Yohanan reads a few words. "This is the story of a hero named Pinkhas. He kills an Israelite and the Israelite's lover, a Midianite. The Lord rewards him with a *covenant of peace*, making him a priest in the Temple. You see this word? This is *shalom*, peace." He frowns. "There's something wrong."

"What is wrong?"

Yohanan peers at the text. "This doesn't make sense," he mutters. He squints at the text, wondering whether his eyes are deceiving him.

"What?" asks his sister.

"This letter, this *vav*. It is broken. I have never seen this."

Normally the letter vav, pronounced o in the word shalom, is written: ו. Here, though, it is written: ו. *How could any copyist make this mistake?* Yohanan wonders. *What am I to do? I was told to copy precisely what I see, yet this must be improper.* To corrupt a holy text is an act of murder, the gravest of sins.

"What does this mean?" asks Hannah.

Yohanan shakes his head. "I have never seen anything like this."

&

Yohanan sleeps again at Stefanos's house, as eager to absorb the strange wisdom of his friend's father as to receive further instruction on juggling. After another copious Sabbath meal, Yohanan begs Stefanos's father to tell another story. Again they lie on mattresses in the atrium, bathing in the flickering light of oil lamps. This time Stefanos's father speaks of a king of the east, a wild man, a ravishing Goddess, an icy mountain range, and a fatal glimpse of paradise. To Yohanan this tale seems stranger than any Stefanos's father previously narrated. "There are no Judaeans in it," he observes.

"All peoples are alike," answers Stefanos's father.

"But the Lord of Israel is nowhere in your story."

"It is present everywhere, whether we speak of It or not."

"Instead, you praise the beauty of foreign goddesses."

Stefanos's father tousles Yohanan's hair. "People imagine our great contribution is that we have one invisible Lord, while other nations have many gods in human form, or in animal form, or in the form of the wind or the sun. But I'll tell you a secret, and this is the most important secret you will ever hear, so listen well. That is not really our people's gift."

Yohanan listens without comment.

"Look at our Temple," continues Stefanos's father. "Do you think our rituals differ so much from those of the Romans? They, too, have priests and sacrifice unblemished bulls. They may have statues but their gods are not really those statues. None of those statues ever reached out to a supplicant or shed a tear for the martyred. They are mere proxies and the Romans know that. The Greeks know that. Their gods are just as invisible as ours and, in their view, just as powerful."

"What is our contribution, then?"

"It is the injunction to feed the widow, the orphan, and the stranger. It is the idea that life, our breath, belongs not to us but to the realm of the divine. That idea is far more potent than any theology. Stronger than any army. And in the end, that idea alone will save us."

❧

Stefanos leads Yohanan to the Roman garrison outside Jerusalem. They find a breach in the stone wall. Beyond, a field brightens and darkens with the passing of clouds.

The boys sprint across the field to the stables. Yohanan pushes the door. Stefanos shoves him inside and follows. The sweet odor of fresh dung greets them. Light tumbles from high windows. Motes of dust dance in the air. A horse nickers and tosses its head.

"Sit on it. You can, you know."

For those Judaeans who are not citizens of Rome, the vast majority, to mount a horse represents a crime against the empire. It is not, however, a transgression of the Law of Israel. Yohanan contemplates the horse, in awe of its size, power, and grace. Stefanos lifts him onto its back. Yohanan leans forward, queasy and elated, to clasp the beast's warm neck.

Two soldiers enter, conversing and chuckling, startling the boys. Yohanan slips off the horse and they scramble beneath a pile of hay. Yohanan's nose itches and his eyes water. He attempts to suppress a sneeze and at the muffled noise, the soldiers' steps quicken. The gate flies open and they yank the boys out from their hiding place.

The Romans ask their names and their fathers' names and lock them in a storage closet. A horse whinnies as the soldiers clatter away. The exterior door creaks closed and the bolt drops with a clang.

"We must find a way out," whispers Stefanos.

"Perhaps we can tunnel out," whispers Yohanan.

They search for a shovel or another implement. Yohanan scratches the dirt with his fingers. Stefanos tries rattling the gate.

A ladder leans against the wall. Above it they spy a narrow window, striped with metal bars.

❧

When the guards return hours later they find the boys asleep on the ground. They rouse Stefanos and inform him that he is very fortunate indeed. His father, it seems, is a close associate of the *centurio*. The guards allow the boys to go, warning them never to return.

Yohanan remembers his father speaking of the *centurio*, the man whom the Prefect Valerius Gratus sent to the Temple to seize the Treasure of the Lord, the bandit whose action offended the Lord and resulted in the ignoble death of Yohanan's uncle and namesake. That Roman oppressor, or one like him in station and function, Yohanan realizes, is a friend of Stefanos's father.

"Don't look at me like that," says Stefanos as they trudge back toward the breach in the wall.

"Like *what?*" But Yohanan knows his eyes have betrayed him.

"It isn't my fault," insists Stefanos. "Anyway, if my father *weren't* friends with the *centurio*, we'd be dead."

They climb through the breach in the wall, leaving the Roman fortress. "I'd better be getting home now," says Yohanan.

As he walks away, Stefanos stands immobile, his arms crossed on his chest, watching him go.

&

Yohanan devotes his time and energy to copying *Pinkhas*. The tale of promiscuity, murder, and reward troubles him. The Children of the Covenant, on their way from Egypt to the Land of Israel, camp among the Moabites. They fornicate with them and worship their gods, prompting the God of the Israelites to jealousy. It instructs Moses to order other leaders to execute the idolaters. Moses conveys this command to the other leaders, but the text does not state whether anyone is killed.

The focus shifts: The Children of the Covenant are weeping before the tent of the Lord. While they lament, an unnamed Child of Israel leads a Midianite woman into a tent. Another man, Pinkhas, described as a grandson of Moses's brother Aaron, pursues them into the tent and plunges his spear through their bellies, presumably while they are copulating. The Lord rewards Pinkhas *for turning It*—that is, the Lord Itself—*away from Its wrath*. It awards Pinkhas a *covenant of peace*. The broken *vav*, ‏ו‎, appears here, in the word *shalom*, peace.

Yohanan has never before encountered an imperfect letter in a holy text and hesitates to reproduce its imperfection. But he has promised his father he would transcribe each letter precisely, without editing. After much thought, Yohanan resolves to keep his promise. Perhaps there is a reason this *vav* is broken. He copies it precisely, allows the ink to dry overnight, and prepares to deliver it to its buyer.

❧

The Zealot who has paid for this text dwells in a dark, cramped, two-story house in the Lower City and wears a simple tunic, his feet bare. His breath stinks of onions, garlic, and cumin, spices used by the poor to cover the odor of rotting food. He asks Yohanan to leave the door open, allowing light to spill into the room, and spreads the goatskin on his rough-hewn cedar table.

Yohanan strives to hide his nervousness. If the broken *vav* is wrong, the text is unclean and without value, the expensive parchment and inks wasted, and his labor fruitless; perhaps he has even sinned. This client and others of his ilk, whose numbers have reputedly been growing, may never purchase another of his father's texts.

"*Ayn,*" says the man at last, moving his finger along the parchment, past the broken *vav*. He re-wraps the scroll and folds a gold coin into Yohanan's hand. "Tell your father Zakkai that I am pleased." His accent reminds Yohanan of reed whistles.

❧

Returning home, Yohanan passes the Place of the Fountain, where a stone faucet spits water into a basin. Women kneel, rinsing their husbands' and children's tunics. Few look up as they converse, for beyond the city walls looms the mountain known as Golgotha, the Place of the Skull, spiked with crucifixes and dotted with vultures.

Yohanan thinks of Stefanos's father, a man so gentle and kind, and yet a collaborator with the Romans and a traitor to Israel. He misses Stefanos but cannot abide consorting with the son of a man friendly with a Roman *centurio*, even if that friendship has saved their lives.

Sometimes Yohanan thinks of Stefanos when he awakes from dreams of whirling lemons and oriental traders in pleated vests who search for ancient marvels. Unable to sleep, he slips into the courtyard to practice juggling.

❧

One morning two months later, a dusty courier knocks at their door. He wears a cloth rope across his forehead, knotted behind his head. The courier hands Yohanan a papyrus letter, rolled and closed with Zakkai's seal. Yohanan scans his father's unmistakable Aramaic hand: *Business is brisk, the climate in Alexandria sweet. We pray for Jerusalem.*

Yohanan's mother offers the courier a bowl of lemon water. "You carried this all the way from Alexandria?"

"Alexandria? No."

Her brow furrows. "From where, then?"

"Carthage. But I have other business in Jerusalem."

"My husband is in Carthage?"

"That is where he resides."

Yohanan's mother stares at the wax tablet and the angular Aramaic writing.

❧

Yohanan awakes to a sound that resembles the muffled cry of a nocturnal bird, possibly an owl probing the oak-covered hills with enquiring murmurs. His mother sits against the wall, weeping. He scrambles from his mat and hugs her.

"It is nothing, my son," she tells him. "Go back to sleep."

In the morning, as he rises from a late breakfast of figs and water, she takes his hands in hers. "Yohanan, I cannot offer you the life you deserve with the coins your father sends. A boy to whom the Lord has given such a serious mind."

"Father's not coming back, is he?"

She does not answer but her silence, and the ravaged expression in her eyes, are all the confirmation he needs.

From the vantage point of a son, the father is a pedestal of granite on which to stand, with conviction and assurance. That pillar, Yohanan feels, is collapsing. It is as if he has been transported back to the cave of the *malakh ha-mavet*, the Messenger of Death, and has stumbled over the precipice. This time, however, it is his mother who holds him back from the brink. But her grip is weak.

"I've spoken with your teacher," she tells Yohanan. "He knows how you memorize long passages and pose intelligent questions. He's aware you descend from a line of priests, including my poor brother, who wanders in the mists of Sheol. He has spoken with *his* teacher about you, and a place has been prepared for you among the novices in the Temple." She offers him a determined smile. "You'll live far more comfortably." She hugs him, rubbing his back, as if kneading her decision into his flesh.

Four days ago Jupiter unleashed a storm the likes of which the Roman commander Vespasian has never seen. Fists of rain pounded the wild, unexplored island of Britannia. Rivers swelled, overflowing their banks, and fields sank into dreary marshes.

Now at last the storm is clearing. Dense foliage gleams under ash-gray skies. Bloodied and weary, the surviving troops of Rome's Second Legion slog through forests of hawthorn, willow, and alder along a wandering brook. In his first commission as military general, Vespasian has offered his troops no argument in favor of this course. He has none.

An augur appears, a lamb with inky black fur wandering through a clearing. Vespasian raises his palms and calls, "Invincible Jupiter, with a prayer of veneration we implore you, send a portent signifying our direction. We are lost. Help us avoid another ambush. Let us capture the next village with minimal losses. When all this is over and we return to Rome, may we be greeted with the cheers due to victorious soldiers."

He pronounces these last words loudly, for the benefit of his men as well as their god. He imagines citizens lining the streets of Rome and a triumphant general standing in a four-horse chariot. He sees the man's face as if through a haze.

Is it himself he sees, Vespasian wonders, thinner after months of grueling warfare? Is it his brother, Titus Flavius Sabinus, who leads another of the four legions slashing their way through the bowels of Britannia? *No matter*, he instructs himself, *so long as there is a victory parade, so long as Rome triumphs.*

Some part of him, though, refuses his own instruction. Of Rome's ultimate triumph in Britannia he has no doubt. His brother, though, should not be riding in the victory chariot. Sabinus secretly worships a foreign deity, Mithras. Vespasian thinks his practices reprehensible, dangerous not just for himself but for the empire.

A soldier hands him a jug of wine and Vespasian empties it over the tethered lamb's head. Drawing his dagger, he slits the lamb's throat, hoicking through fur, a tough layer of skin, sinews, and muscle. The beast collapses in a pool of blood. Vespasian heaves it onto its side, slashes the hide, and plunges his hands into the lamb's hot entrails. Though neither a priest nor a haruspex—a man trained to read animal innards—Vespasian has grown up on his grandmother's farm and knows a spotted liver from an unblemished one, a smooth gall bladder from a stony one. This lamb is clean and worthy of sacrifice.

"Find boulders," he instructs his men. "Build an altar. We shall burn the lamb's heart, liver, and lungs for an offering to the god Quirinus, and we shall implore Quirinus to intervene with Jupiter on our behalf."

None of Vespasian's men has heard of the god Quirinus, but all know better than to ask.

As the organs sizzle on the hot stone, a dash of darkness catches Vespasian's eye. He looks up and spots a peregrine falcon, its chest striped, its head black, soaring west. This is the answer he has been seeking. The legion changes course.

&

Two days further into the punishing land the natives call Albion, sunlight floods a broad valley where cattle and sheep graze. Above a crown of tree-trunk stakes, a village rises from a hilltop. A woman wearing a purple tunic and knee-length cloak, clasped at the breastbone with interlocking gold ropes, trudges down the muddy path toward Vespasian and his legion. He understands that she is a great local warrior, although she holds no axe or shield. He marches forward in the company of an aide who speaks the local dialects. Vespasian observes her weathered skin, long copper hair, and hazel eyes as if trying to read a foreign text. She seems to be a woman of thirty years or more, who has experienced hardship enough to fill fifty.

Holding herself tall, she speaks through Vespasian's translator. "We know about the towns you have razed, the casualties you have inflicted. The waters of the great river ran scarlet, they say. Unless provoked we will not fight, but neither will we surrender. Call me Muirgheal."

Muirgheal leads him and three aides to her roundhouse, where a maiden leans over a butter churn. Muirgheal offers him a cup of hot broth. Accepting the refreshment, he lowers himself to a bench, adjusting the carmine cape that fastens at his shoulder. The metal plates on his *pteruges*—the leather apron that covers his groin—jangle.

43

"We offer a partnership," he explains through his interpreter. "You are clearly a great warrior and a leader of your people. As a representative of the empire, you will inhabit a fine home with colonnades, hot baths, and marble statues. For breakfast you will dine on olives from Greece and cheese from Hispania, all served by slaves. You can hardly imagine the life Rome offers."

The translator's tongue trips over Vespasian's words like a boy skipping from stone to stone in a ford, leaving great *lacunae*. Many words—*empire, colonnades*—resemble concepts in the language of his village, which is similar to that spoken in Muirgheal's village. Other words—*marble, olives, Hispania*—have no local relatives.

"Those heads posted at your gate," Vespasian begins again. "That is what you do here, is it not? One tribe attacks another and displays proof of victory as a warning to others, as a mark of military prowess. This is true wherever you find men. All tribes wish to subjugate their neighbors." He tastes the broth. "We Romans have devised more efficient ways to separate heads from bodies. As a result, we dominate more peoples across farther lands—and not just for our own gain. The more nations we subdue, the less our subject tribes vie with each other."

At Muirgheal's blank gaze, Vespasian turns to his translator. "I am not certain she grasps the magnitude of what I'm saying."

"She does not, Commander," says the translator. "She cannot."

"After we build you a true city," resumes Vespasian, "not of wood and mud but of stone and brick, with running water, you won't have any further use for those skulls at your gate."

"How generous," remarks Muirgheal at last.

Vespasian sips again, studying Muirgheal's square chin, gold-flecked eyes, and fiery hair. "We offer wealth and security, a life you can hardly imagine," he repeats.

"A man who wishes to be a woman's partner," observes Muirgheal, "does not murder that woman's cousins."

"The towns south of here? Were they not, rather, your enemies?"

"Some of them," admits Muirgheal. "But we don't destroy entire towns, killing every man, woman, and child. We never leave our victims to die slowly and painfully, their knees broken, their wrists punctured. That is not how we do battle."

Vespasian clasps his hands on the table. "Trust and affection grow only in the soil of respect. Had they welcomed us into their homes, as you are doing now, instead of ambushing us in the fields—"

"Trust. Affection. Respect." Muirgheal chuckles.

The legion commander lowers his head and looks into her eyes at a slight upward angle. "You and I are warriors, Muirgheal," he says. "We are simple people. Simple people have simple needs." He leans back. "A good meal, a decent squealing fuck now and then, military victories, political victories. I'm not telling you anything you don't already know." His voice trails off as his gaze falls to the skull that reposes on a flower-strewn table. He rises, takes it in his hands, and peers into its shadowed orbits.

Muirgheal lowers her cup. "That is my father. I remember when there was flesh on those cheeks," she tells him. "He is gone now, but still speaks."

"Is that right."

"He was a seer. He bequeathed many of the stories we still tell, stories he learned from his father."

"And how does he speak now, a mere skull?"

"Through his granddaughter, my niece." Muirgheal turns to the girl at the churn. "Aislin, join us."

"What does he say, your grandfather?" Vespasian asks her as Aislin sits down.

"Many things, and nothing." Aislin wipes the hair from her face. "A stream of pretty words."

Vespasian studies the skull. "As I believe I mentioned, after months on his feet, a man feels the need for horizontal recreation." His eyes meet Aislin's; she lowers hers. "Your niece has beautiful hair," Vespasian tells Muirgheal as he gazes upon the flaxen tresses that tumble over the girl's shoulders. "We are offering friendship. More than friendship, consanguinity. You, however, must do your part."

Muirgheal gestures broadly at her possessions: the iron pot, the painted bowls, the carved wooden chest. "Take what you will, but not my niece and not my father. In a spirit of partnership, I beg you."

Vespasian signals to his aide. Holding the skull under one arm, he rises and strides toward the exit.

Aislin leaps to her feet. "Leave that!"

"It's not that I care about your grandfather," Vespasian says, turning.

"I never had the privilege of knowing him. But this skull...." He looks at it the way a geometer might study an intriguing new angle. "It represents your ties to the past, ties that must be severed if there's to be hope for our partnership. Besides, if your grandfather has something important to say, he might as well say it to me, since I'm going to be the one making decisions."

Aislin lunges for the skull. Vespasian shoves her to the ground, where two of his sentries hold her. "You know what to do with her," he tells them.

With his translator, Vespasian proceeds past a half-dozen huts to the village walls, past the fleshless skulls at the gate, and down the winding path as hills and valley dissolve in the crepuscular haze.

෨

A wall of tree trunks, lashed together vertically and sharpened, surrounds rows of tents and straight avenues that are lit by torches. The *praetorium*, the commander's tent, stands in the center of the Roman encampment, its walls and floor covered in felt-lined goatskins. Each skin, stamped LEG II AVG—for Second Legion, Augustus—was cut and sewn in a workshop in the city of Tarsus, near the opposite end of the world. The furnishings are minimal—a folding cot with curved legs, a hanging four-wick lamp, a chest, and a collapsible writing table with brass fittings.

A Gallic slave serves braised wild boar, caught that afternoon, and gruel for dinner. While he eats, Vespasian thinks of the other Roman leaders, butchering their way through distant corners of this accursed island and wonders whether his brother Sabinus is alive. He devours the boar, asking himself when he last tasted flesh so pungent and savage.

"The girl," he mutters to an aide. "That girl who was churning butter."

The aide nods and leaves through a flap in the tent.

That night a vision of his past unfolds in Vespasian's mind, vague and distorted through the swirling, bubbly glass of subsequent emotion. An afternoon meal with his grandmother in the Sabine country northeast of Rome, a repast he hoped to share with his parents and brother. He visualizes pigs dashing among trees and swimming in a river as he reflects upon the meal with his grandmother, the intertwined destinies of brothers, and the state of ignorance known as *youth*.

How old is he in this remembrance? Perhaps the very age of the girl with the wheat-colored hair. He strives to remember how it felt to be that young, that unknowing. Vespasian recalls his own youth as a time of fearful anticipation and unfulfilled longing.

&

He lies in bed, wakeful, as silver moonlight streams through the window. A cool breeze, unusual in July, has blown out the lamp. He has slept alone in this room for the best part of a year, since Sabinus left for Asia Minor. Their father serves as a *publicanus*, or tax collector, in the province of Cilicia. He sought to train Sabinus, six years older than Vespasian, in the art of census taking and taxation, rendering to Rome its share of silver coinage and lending the profit for interest.

Vespasian becomes aware of a snorting and snuffling outside. The dogs, confined to their pen for the night, begin to bark. Fearful, Vespasian wonders what unnatural forces churn in his grandmother's orchard.

Before Sabinus's departure, the two brothers planted a plum tree, dedicating it to the ancient god Quirinus. Vespasian promised Sabinus he would protect Quirinus's arboreal shrine and has watered the tree daily. The tree thrives, though it has yet to bear fruit, and Vespasian assumes Quirinus is pleased with his devotions. Now, however, in the dark of night, he worries for the tree.

Vespasian pads barefoot to the courtyard, and through the gate to the orchard, but comes to a sudden halt. Hundreds of tusked beasts swarm in the moonlight, specked with mud like demons who have tunneled their way out of the earth. Their muscular torsos matted with thick, chaotic fur, the wild pigs shove each other aside as they drive their fleshy snouts into the ground, grinding on roots and felling pear and almond trees as if they were children knocking over wooden pegs.

Vespasian dashes back into the villa, through the kitchen, past the servants' quarters, down the hall, and through the columned portico to his grandmother's bedroom. An oil lamp sputters in an altar on the wall. His grandmother, a stout woman, lies on her back under a rough woolen blanket, her hands folded across her belly, snoring. In the half-light her dark sockets appear to be staring at the carved-wood ceiling.

Vespasian grasps her shoulder and shakes her. "*Avia*, listen, they are tearing up the farm."

She wakes with a start, fixing him with empty eyes, then throws off her blanket and pulls herself up holding his hand. Seizing the branch that serves as her walking stick and club, she ventures outside, Vespasian close behind. Her tunic blows around her body like a loose layer of skin. She stops at the sight of the pigs and lowers her club. "Do not go further, Vespasian. They will stampede and tear you apart."

With a sigh, she leads her grandson back into the kitchen and sits him at the table, where a terracotta lamp burns through the night. She sighs, throws her walking stick to the side, folds her arms on the table, and leans forward.

"Long ago," she tells her grandson, "your great-great-uncle raised pigs on this farm. After five years of drought, he decided to travel to Rome to sacrifice his best hog at the Temple of Quirinus and to plead for water. On his way, a band of robbers attacked him and stole his pig. With nothing left to sacrifice, he returned home, only to find that his swine had gone wild, knocking over the fence, and uprooting trees before disappearing into the forest." She wipes her forehead with her fleshy hand and adds softly: "These are the descendants of those pigs. Tusks have sprouted from their cheeks, and their fur has thickened." She leans forward. "Quirinus must be appeased."

☙

The next morning the orchard is a ravaged battlefield. Trees lie scattered in all directions, one atop the other, fallen soldiers embracing in death. The pigs have dug holes in the soil and gnawed tree roots, rendering them useless for anything except construction or firewood. One tree still stands: the plum tree he and Sabinus dedicated to Quirinus. Vespasian hurries up the hill, scrambling over the jumbled trunks, and kneels before the tree, imploring Quirinus to pardon his neglect, his half-hearted devotions, the doubts that sometimes plague him. Even worse than his personal failings, he reflects, are those of his tribe, the Sabines. He begs the god to absolve them, too.

He tries to visualize Quirinus standing sternly before him, but his powers of visualization fail him. Ancient statues of Quirinus have been refashioned into representations of Mars, who has replaced him in the Roman pantheon. No one remembers the features of the original god of the State of Rome, the apotheosis of Romulus, its founder. Once the most powerful god of this region, Quirinus is now invisible and all but forgotten, except to Vespasian's clan, the Sabines.

This idea, of a God that has faded to invisibility, is maddening. The previous night's eruption of bestial violence was merely a warning. Vespasian curses himself for his fear of the night before, a fear that kept him overlong in his bed. He asks how he can prove himself worthy of manhood, how he can best represent the will of his ancestors and their gods. He promises an offering: the pig his great-great-uncle failed to deliver so many years ago.

"Our most valuable crop is lost," his grandmother mutters as she surveys the damage later that morning. She crouches beside a fallen cherry tree. Her fingers graze the base of its trunk, the place where its gnawed-off roots wormed into the soil. "If we do not kill these pigs, they will kill us."

"Suppose I trap them?" suggests the boy. "We could bring them to Rome and sacrifice them at the Quirinal and everything would be back as it was meant to be."

"Trap them?"

"At least one or two," concedes Vespasian. He knows that Sabinus and their father will soon be returning from Tarsus. Vespasian was always the hard-working tyro, Sabinus the heir of their father's skills and charm. He longs to show them an accomplishment of his own. Over a breakfast of porridge in the *triclinium*, Vespasian asks his grandmother for her blessing.

"I will not prevent you from trying, although you will fail," she says, with a wistful smile. "But you must first saw those trees into logs and help the slaves replant the orchard."

❧

That afternoon, Vespasian discusses his plans with Theron, a slave, who tells him where the feral pigs live, what they eat, and how to butcher them. "The pigs are smart," Theron warns him. "They are strong and they are vicious."

Off the muddied, spittle-smeared bases of the trunks he carves chunks of half-macerated wood and tosses them to Canis, his great black hound. Canis seizes them in his jaws and returns to Vespasian, who rewards him with a morsel of lard. After Canis thus learns to locate the lumps of wood by the smell of the pigs' saliva, Vespasian leads him to the stream where, according to Theron, pigs like to wallow, and prowls a mile of the shore. Failing to find his prey, he is about to turn back when Canis lurches ahead, growling and yapping as he disappears through the reeds. Vespasian chases him but the path is muddy and Canis has found a shortcut through the reeds.

When he reaches the water's edge, where Canis stands barking, he sees fifty or more feral pigs plunging into the river, grunting and snorting. They swim, their muscles undulating like reflections of the water that ripples under their hides, and Vespasian wonders how their short legs can propel their massive bodies against the current. He draws his sling and lobs a lead ball at one of the pigs. It strikes its flank but the animal keeps swimming. Vespasian fires another, then another, to no avail. It is clear he will never capture the marauders with a dog and a sling.

He and Canis shamble back to the farm as the sun goes down. By the time he reaches their homestead he has devised a better plan.

❧

He finds his grandmother collecting eggs in the quail coop, explains his idea, and asks her to instruct the slaves accordingly. She refuses to do so, advising Vespasian to persuade the servants himself. That evening, he calls together all thirty-eight slaves. "My parents and brother will be home in two weeks," he tells them. "We do not want them to see this devastation. We need to dig a ditch around the farm and throw food in it to lure the boars. I, for one, intend to work through the night. Those who join me will earn all the flesh they can eat from one of the hogs, but only after we sacrifice it and offer its fat and organs to the ancient God of our region, Quirinus."

The slaves—slouching, unshaved men who in former lives fell into inescapable debt or were captured in war—listen intently to the determined thirteen-year-old. Most have not tasted meat since the days of their freedom. Others have never tasted it. "*Serviemus*," they tell him in one ragged voice. *We serve you.*

Together, they work through the night.

❧

Vespasian fails to capture any pigs in his trench-trap. To keep his word to the slaves, he buys a slab of hog's loin with the silver coins that his father entrusted to him before his departure.

"You see," his grandmother explains, "there is no way to make things as they were. At least the pigs can cause no further damage."

On the morning when Sabinus is to return, Vespasian, his grandmother, and the thirty-eight slaves wait outside the wall that surrounds the house. As the sun nears the horizon, they first notice a dust puff in the distance, from which the travelers gradually emerge. Their slaves carry trunks and litters covered in exotic fabrics woven of red, blue, and gold threads. Vespasian did not expect them to arrive on litters. They had departed on foot.

His father's servants approach them, stop, and lower their burdens. Vespasian's mother steps down, bejeweled and swathed in luxurious foreign robes, followed by his father, whose wide curls have grayed. Finally Sabinus emerges, taller, his dark face thinner, his craggy nose prominent, his hazel eyes set deep within gray orbits. Sabinus studies his surroundings with detachment and tilts his head toward his father with a thin smile. The patriarch responds with a discreet nod.

Vespasian has waited for this moment with such fervent expectation that he now feels flustered. The young man before him, his brother, has not yet acknowledged him. Sabinus whispers something to his father, who nods again. Their mother seems to be evaluating the walls and the gate as she adjusts her garments. Vespasian's right hand, hanging at his side, tenses and he digs his nails into his palms.

His grandmother taps her stick on the soil and glances pointedly at Vespasian. Sabinus's eyes follow hers and he notices his brother, his face widening into a toothy smile. "Look at you! How you've grown! And those arms! Farm work will do that, eh?"

Their mother yawns. "They say farm work forges character, though perhaps not like javelin-throwing and wrestling."

"More so," says Vespasian's grandmother. "Far more so."

"What is the matter, brother?" asks Sabinus, embracing him. "Are you not happy to see me?"

"I am," replies Vespasian, aware that his brother has changed and that they will have to refamiliarize themselves.

"The slaves have prepared a meal for you," announces Vespasian's grandmother.

Vespasian's mother declines with a flourish of her hand. "I'm afraid we're too tired even to chew. A bath, maybe, and a restorative night's sleep."

❧

In bed that night Vespasian tells his older brother about the feral pigs and the shrine of Quirinus that miraculously survived their onslaught.

"Quirinus and the old gods," Sabinus yawns. "They mean little to me now."

"How can you say that?" whispers Vespasian. "Quirinus protected our ancestors."

"Our ancestors are dead," says Sabinus. "Their souls wander in the Asphodel Fields. I'm now devoted to another god."

"Which one?"

"It's been a long trip. We have time. Ah, it feels good to lie on this old mattress."

"Which god?" insists Vespasian.

"A secret god who wrestles a bull, if you must know. A bull whose blood falls from the heavens. Now please, let me sleep."

Vespasian tries to sleep but the thought that his brother has turned his back on Quirinus torments him. He longs to question Sabinus about his journey and his life in Cilicia but his brother is already asleep.

In the morning Sabinus instructs his personal slave to shave and dress him in a tunic he acquired in Cilicia, woven in threads of blue and silver, and secured with a matching rope-belt. As they dine on salads of leeks, coriander, parsley, and cheese, Vespasian's father asks his younger son whether he still has the silver coins he loaned him a year earlier. "Have they multiplied or are they diminished?" The thirteen-year-old recounts his disastrous experience with the boars and the commitment he made to the slaves.

"Instead of capturing a pig, then, and trying to recover some of our losses, you squandered yet more of our estate on a pig's loin, not to please the gods or men of any significance, but for the sake of slaves?"

Vespasian folds his hands together. Vespasian's mother chuckles. "We're taking Sabinus into the capital this evening," she tells her mother-in-law. "My brother has graciously agreed to provide further guidance."

"What kind of guidance?" asks Vespasian's grandmother.

"Why, to advance Sabinus's career, of course," she replies.

Vespasian's mother was born into an equestrian family. Her brother is a senator in the capital. Vespasian's father, from peasant stock, defied the odds and convention by earning his own wealth. But riches do not always equate with power. Of the two, power is by far the more admirable.

"If you want a central spot on the wrestling floor of Rome," Vespasian's grandmother advises Sabinus, "you will have to learn to strangle your friends."

&

That afternoon, as storm clouds mass on the horizon, Vespasian and Canis follow the riverbank, listening to the water, the birds, and the breeze. As they return home, a drizzle starts to fall. Canis leaps ahead growling and Vespasian again discovers the herd of spiral-tailed, floppy-eared monsters rising from the earth and plunging into the water. This time, one of the pigs straggles and Canis clamps his jaws around its rear leg. The pig squeals and twists, but Canis digs his paws into the wet soil, enduring bruises rather than allowing it to escape.

The pig, stocky and muscular, drags Canis to the river's edge, leaving a trail of blood and pulling his head into the water. Still, Canis clenches its leg in his jaw.

Vespasian tears his knife from its sash. He forgets his intention, to re-domesticate his great-great-uncle's swine for Quirinus, as Canis delivers a final yelp, which ends in a gurgle, and drifts downstream.

With a cry of rage, Vespasian leaps onto the pig and plunges his dagger under its jaw. A cloud of blood spreads in the water. The pig squirms. The boy thrusts his dagger into the pig's eye, its ribs, its belly, swallowing water and blood and gasping for air as the swine flails.

There can be no thought of hauling the corpse back to the farm in one piece. Instead, as tears of exhaustion mingle with rain on his cheeks, he hauls the pig's carcass to the shore, carves off chunks of flesh, and loads them into his tunic, which he slings over his shoulder.

"Not everyone knows how to kill," his grandmother suggested yesterday over lunch. But now *he* knows. At thirteen, armed with nothing but a dagger, he has vanquished a large, powerful beast. Tomorrow, his parents will feast on savage pork. He wipes his cheeks and marches toward the house, a sense of victory imbuing his stride with purpose, his bruises badges of honor.

೨

His mother, bedecked in pearls and lapis, spots him from a doorway as he trudges through the gate into the courtyard, stooping under the weighty sack.

"What is that?" she asks imperiously.

"A wild pig," Vespasian replies. Blood seeps through his tunic and drips on the polished tile floor.

"You're staining the tiles. Get that thing to the kitchen."

"Where are you going?"

"I told you. We're taking your brother to Rome. We shall be gone a week."

The boar meat will rot unless it is promptly consumed. He and his grandmother will eat some and the slaves, the rest. His parents will dine in Rome. He stares at the artlessly carved blocks and wedges of flesh that weep blood under the battering rain. His mind whirls as he remembers his promise to Quirinus. He swallows and raises his eyes.

His mother is gone. He gathers the corners of the tunic and heaves it onto his back.

೨

In the morning Vespasian, the legion commander, sits on his cot, lacing his sandals while an aide sets his breakfast table. A sentry enters, holding Aislin, who thrashes and struggles in his grip.

"She's a hell-kite, Commander."

"Tell her to make herself comfortable," the general instructs his translator. "She can start by removing her cloak."

"To be comfortable," replies the girl, "I'd have to be anywhere but here."

"That wouldn't make you comfortable," Vespasian tells her. "That would make you dead."

"My aunt offered you our village. Is that not enough?"

"Did she? Or did she mouth the necessary words to avoid a massacre?" Vespasian rises. An aide drapes a cloak over his back, while another pulls out a chair. "Possession is not merely a word," he warns Aislin. "It is an act. Now, come, see what we dine upon." He gestures toward the breakfast table. "Quinces, preserved in wine and served with fish sauce, is a delicacy in Rome. Far more so here in the wilderness, I promise you. If you allow yourself, you will have pleasure. A plate for our guest," he instructs his aide.

His aide sets a plate for Aislin, who remains standing.

"I'm not hungry." Aislin's eyes flick toward the guards at the entry.

Vespasian shrugs, swallowing a mouthful of quince. "Tell me, though. You, your aunt, your village, all the communities on this soggy, barbarian island, what is the purpose of resisting, when you know you will be vanquished? That is what I fail to understand. One way, you survive. If the gods will it, you prosper. The other way, you die. Yet in so many places, not just in Britannia but in Germania and Gallia and elsewhere, the natives make the wrong decision. Time and again. I pity them. I really do."

"I think you know," says the girl. "It is honor. Pride."

Vespasian chuckles. "So being associated with Rome is not honorable? Playing a role on the larger stage of history is not something to be proud of? Go ahead, ignore your breakfast. My dogs will be thrilled." He wipes his face with a towel and asks, "Now, how do you prefer to be fucked? With violence or tenderness? I am capable of both."

Aislin spits on the ground, trembling with fury and fear.

"As clear an answer as any." Vespasian nods to a guard, who moves to disrobe her.

Four soldiers attach Aislin to a cot in an empty tent. When she bites one of them he forces a thick rope into her mouth. Another soldier places her grandfather's skull on a table. Through his eyes her ancestors will witness her humiliation and surrender. She turns her face toward the tent wall.

Twice every day, morning and night, while Roman soldiers pound on drums outside, Vespasian forces himself upon her. Her fingernails draw blood from her palms; her teeth draw blood from her lips. She roars in rage and shame to the Companions, to the spirits of her ancestors, to the skies. It used to be, in her experience, that brutality and kindness fitted within a broader understanding, one warrior or tribe attacking another or forging a new alliance, in shifting eternal oscillations. Now, with the intrusion of these Romans, the balance has shattered. The weight of Vespasian's leather, flax, and muscle, the stench of his breath and sweat, his foreignness inside her, are a crude stake driven into the fertile soil of her girlhood, damp with tears.

He no longer exchanges greetings or offers quinces soaked in wine or even the caress he might give a dog. He knows she hates him and would murder him if she had the opportunity. Sometimes, though, he buries his face in her hair, inhaling deeply and murmuring soft words she cannot fathom.

Aislin lies uncovered at night. Any movement increases her pain. A guard yanks the rope from her mouth, twists her head to the side, and pours hot sheep's milk into her throat. She spits it back into his face. He slaps her but, to her disappointment, does not kill her. She sleeps intermittently, breathing in short, empty coughs. At dawn she hears birds chirping and tries to picture them winging through the heavens unconstrained. She closes her eyes and imagines running through a grassy field on a hot summer's day but the warmth eludes her, as does the sense of boundlessness, of the horizon's infinite distance. She is walking through a pleasant field that is dotted with delicate purple and yellow wildflowers when she comes to an immense chasm, a trench so dark and abysmal that the deepest levels elude perception. Some unseen force pushes her over the edge into the chilly darkness, where she falls and falls, whirling, dizzy.

Four nights into this ordeal she starts dreaming while awake. The Companions beckon, a chorus of voices, flutes, and harps. One night her grandfather speaks, his words dusky and hoarse. "The leather pouch. The divining stones. Look at me!"

For the first time since Vespasian's aides set his skull on the floor beside her cot, Aislin turns her head so that her eyes meet his empty orbits. "I lost them," she sobs. "I lost the stones! I wanted to return them to the Companions but the stream took them!"

"Remember. Remember...." He hums a dreary melody and in his nasal drone she hears other voices, some ancient, some young. Against the plucked and blown instruments of the Companions her ancestors chant of separation, yearning, and destruction. Behind the chant, Aislin hears the crackle of fire, the collapse of burning timbers; she smells acrid smoke. As in her previous dream, she feels she is twisting downward, disorientated and confused. The ancient voices still reach her but they sound increasingly distant, fainter, like the memory of a dream as it fades toward insubstantiality. Long afterward, she will forget their intent but not the sound of the flames, the acrid scent of smoke, or the vision of her aunt's divining stones sparkling in the rushing stream.

She hears a woodlark chirping in the forest. The same bird she has heard so many times, as she lay on her cow's hide in her aunt's home— or a different one—but the same melody.

Stars dust the crystalline spheres of the heavens. The chirp of a solitary woodlark awakes the night watchman Septimus, where he lies in thick grass on a hillside. Dew has soaked through his tunic.

He turns his head and the fog of sleep dissipates. Frogs and crickets chatter. A thick forest stretches between him and the water. Wild boars dwell there, and bears, and savages who paint their bodies and collect human skulls. Ethereal entities—spirits, zephyrs, and fear—swim through the clammy air. The lush chaos of nature stretches before him to the far end of this isle.

He looks the other way: a wall of sharpened tree trunks, the military camp of Rome's Second Legion. The camp's standard flaps in the warm breeze.

On one side, the disciplined, geometric palisades of Imperial Rome. On the other, the lush chaos of nature. A terrifying thought flits through Septimus's drowsy awareness: by dozing off, he has sentenced himself to death.

He reaches into his satchel, hoping against hope that he will not find the wooden token that Legion Commander Titus Flavius Vespasianus handed him at sunset. With dread, however, Septimus discovers it is there. Which means that when the *tessera* collector passed, he did not collect it, because he found Septimus sleeping. Which in turn means that Legion Commander Vespasian will learn of his nap. Each tessera is inscribed with a night watchman's station. Any tessera that is not collected is a death sentence.

Septimus's father fought alongside Vespasian in Thrace. The two soldiers remained friends up until the day Septimus's father died. Could fond reminiscence sway the commander? The young soldier refuses to deceive himself.

But perhaps the tessera collector has not yet passed. Septimus gazes at the token in his hand. The dim light of morning still shrouds its characters, but Septimus remembers his: the number VIII, representing his station; another number, CLXXXIV; and the night's password, *victus*.

From a field of stars to the west, Virgo, the Young Woman, gazes at him with black-marble eyes and char-brown hair strewn over her pillow like the pregnant wife he left in Rome, Psyche.

CLXXXIV: 184 days have passed since he left Rome. Their child might be entering the world this very morning. The woodlark sounds again, whistling plaintively like a distant echo of his newborn's birth-cry. Septimus knows that despite his distance Psyche's inky eyes will reflexively seek him as the contentment of motherhood laves away the anguish of delivery.

One-hundred-eighty-four days. The soldiers of the Second Legion have marched over mountainous Raetia, Vindelicia, and Germania, and across the forested plains and marshes of Belgica. They have rowed quinqueremes from one end of the *mare britannicum* to the other. They have fought, sacrificed, mourned, and prayed together.

Eight days ago three divisions of savages ambushed them. Vespasian's forces sustained heavy losses but prevailed after two days of fierce fighting. Septimus lost beloved friends and shed tears on the shoulders of men he despised. Whatever their differences, they all share Septimus's hatred of barbarians.

Following the Romans' near-defeat, Vespasian instructed his troops to teach the natives a lesson. His men ravished women and children in dirt-paved town squares, slaughtering the few husbands and brothers who tried to oppose them. They gorged themselves on mutton stew prepared in the natives' iron pots, and slurped mead from their colorful ceramic bowls. They drank themselves into oblivion and then, during a boisterous ceremony, a night of blood and revelry that Septimus will never forget, the legionnaires renewed their fealty to the goddess *Roma*.

What do those pledges mean now? wonders Septimus.

In Gaul, two months earlier, a watchman dozed off. His tessera was not collected. An officer tied him, naked, to a tree. Clothed only in pride, the soldier stared at his comrades, his killers, one after the other. Under the barrage of hurled rocks, his ribs cracked. Blood gushed from his left eye. Refusing to succumb all at once, he drooped little by little. When the commander ordered the stone throwers to cease, Septimus was not sure the watchman's soul had departed. He still twitched. It mattered little. He was incapacitated.

In Gaul, the external threat to a legionnaire's camp was minimal. How much more certain will Septimus's perdition be here, on this brutal island at the far edge of the world, where barbarians surround the Roman camp and the empire's dignity resides in the eyes of its watchmen.

He recalls a passage from Plato's *Phaedo* in which Socrates's disciples adjure him to escape from his Greek prison and avoid execution. In reply, Socrates speaks of the joy swans express before dying. Swans, he asserts, possess the gift of prophecy. They chant long, intoxicating melodies because they know they are bound for a place so magical their memories of the world will slip off like a snake's skin. Yet Septimus conjures no joy in the contemplation of his demise.

He considers flight. While he might survive, the repercussions would be grave. To abandon Rome would be to obliterate his identity, place, and purpose; he would be left in Britannia, pecking at a sapless existence like the natives. But to remain and die, where is the value in that? How would Septimus's death accrue to the honor of Rome? The birth of his child—of his son, he imagines—adds another complication. To leave his boy fatherless would be to condemn him to the uncertainty that has plagued Septimus like a curse. His son, his common-law wife, and his sister Poppaea would consider him a traitor. His friends would denounce him.

The choice is stark: to suffer humiliation and death now or to flee in shame, never to meet his son, never to tell his story. In the east, Aurora, the Goddess of Dawn, has peeled away a layer of darkness. To the west a shape flits between the trees.

"Who goes there?" Septimus calls.

Two nights earlier, a watchman surprised an enemy scout and impaled him. Vespasian praised the soldier before the entire camp. This shape, Septimus realizes, presents an opportunity. If he saves the camp, the missing *tessera* will signify nothing.

He approaches the thicket and peers within but perceives little in the dark foliage that surrounds him. The leaves obscure the starlight. He steels himself and enters. He turns right and left, disorientated.

Forging through the dew-damp branches, he is thirsty. The creek murmurs somewhere in the dark but remains elusive. Perhaps he is walking in circles? Without reference to the stars or the horizon, time stretches and twists, a cow's gut in the hands of a sausage-maker. If he fails to discover the enemy scout, his absence from his post will only exacerbate his guilt. Again, a rustle in the undergrowth startles him. Is it the enemy, observing him? Is he the hunter, or the hunted? He turns back, walks a few steps, and stops. He is lost. Dread clutches at his heart like the pitiless grasp of Libitina, goddess of death.

❧

As dawn breaks, Septimus asks himself whether he remains entirely Roman. If he is Roman—a soldier, a married citizen, very possibly a father—he is effectively dead. If a metamorphosis has begun, he is the worm yet to pierce its cocoon and flutter off on moist new wings. His non-Roman self, if such a being is destined to exist, is not yet entirely born.

Over a hill, down a steep slope, and past a grassy meadow, the brook finally shimmers into view. He trudges to its edge, kneels, cups his hands, and swallows great mouthfuls.

❧

When he hears the calls of soldiers fanning through the trees, their swords and armor clinking, he knows Vespasian has counted the tesserae. He considers fleeing across the hillside but decides that he will not die with his back to his pursuers. He sits in the grass, waiting.

Vespasian himself, a hunter blessed by the Goddess Diana with preternatural instincts, discovers him. The legion commander emerges from the thicket and plods heavily down the slope in his high-strapped sandals, his tunic swaying, his molded cuirass exaggerating the muscles of his massive torso, his scarlet cape pinned to his right shoulder and draped over his left arm.

Several legionnaires follow, until Vespasian turns and calls, "Go back. I shall handle this." To Septimus he barks, "Stand when your commander approaches."

Drained, Septimus rises to his feet.

"Why disgrace your country?" demands Vespasian. "Why commit suicide?"

"No excuse, Legion Commander Vespasian."

Vespasian slaps him. "You are a soldier. Your father was a soldier, an exceptional one, before he served Rome, and brilliantly, as a *quaestor.*

Tell me how this happened."

"I thought I saw a spy," mutters Septimus. "I searched for him and became lost."

"Who told you to abandon your station? To investigate on your own?"

"No one, Commander."

Vespasian smacks him harder. "Speak up. Tell me why you did it."

Septimus understands that Vespasian wants him to provide a justification, that he would prefer not to kill him. He searches his commander's face as if he could extract the necessary words from his eyes, nose, or mouth, but cannot find them.

"I wanted to protect the legion from a spy, Commander." Septimus mumbles at last.

"You abandoned your post and failed to apprehend an enemy scout. I shall have to kill you," says Vespasian. "Either that, or humiliate you before the entire legion, and then kill you. Any preference?"

Septimus knows better than to respond.

Vespasian notices a fawn grazing at the edge of the thicket. "Is that your spy?" He seizes Septimus's chin and twists his face in the direction of the fawn.

"Could be, sir."

Vespasian motions for Septimus to be still. Slowly, he takes an arrow and draws his bow. The deer looks. Vespasian releases the arrow, aiming low for the deer's lungs and heart. It hits its mark and the deer sprints back into the thicket, then collapses.

Blood splatters Vespasian's kilt and legs as he leans over the trembling body to drench his hands in its still-pulsing artery. Septimus watches, his heart thumping. Vespasian whirls on his heels and raises his bloody palms and dagger. "Because I owe my life to your father, I am going to spare you. In the eyes of my soldiers, this will be your blood. But if I or they ever see you again, I swear by Quirinus, the god of my ancestors, I will kill you. Nor do I ever betray a god. Do you understand?"

"Sir." Septimus salutes, his heart soaring and sinking, gliding through the heavens because he will survive, crashing to earth because he will henceforth be destined to forage like a satyr, half-man, half-animal.

"Remove your clothes."

Septimus removes his helmet and armor, unfurls his scarf, slips out of his tunic, belt, short-sword, and sandals, and offers them to his commander. Vespasian presses them into the deer's bloody neck, punctures the bloodstained armor with his dagger, and rends the leather.

"After I show the men my bloody hands, and your bloody garb, I'll come back to rinse in the river. Hide nearby. I'll leave some villager's rags." The legate marches back into the wood. Both men pray it is the last they will see of each other.

On the fifth afternoon of her captivity, war cries and clashing swords waken Aislin. She realizes that her aunt Muirgheal has made a momentous decision without the aid of her divining stones. She has organized an attack to save Aislin.

Aislin tries to call to Muirgheal: *Do not attempt this! Run, take refuge in our cousins' homes, hide in caves, but do not try to defeat them. They will destroy you.* All she can manage, though, is a sound she has never before heard herself utter, the stifled cry of a wounded animal.

The combat lasts into the night, a harrowing soundscape of steel, curses, and groans, attenuated by the fortress walls and the distance. A number of her kin, it seems, are lending their reputations and their courage to this campaign, the bravest warriors from half a dozen hamlets. Muirgheal has called upon all the resources available to her.

Aislin knows her aunt will fight until she can no longer stand. Muirgheal believes herself invulnerable. Until now, the blessings of the Companions have justified this confidence but it is misguided, an illusion, like the sense of summer's endlessness or of the horizon's infinite distance.

Little by little the attackers' battle cries wane as their certitudes dissolve. The shouts and screams, the clangor and hoof beats diminish in frequency and volume until only one voice remains. The last of their utterances to reach Aislin's ears is her aunt's, a cry shouted with all the vigor that remains in Muirgheal's chest: "*Dìoghaltas!*" Vengeance.

Aislin smells smoke and weeps. The Romans finish their business methodically. Soldiers chat and laugh as they trudge back to the fort.

❧

In the morning Aislin hears the Romans breaking camp, loading their massive carts with logs, throwing folded tent skins into piles, joking and laughing. *They have completed their task*, she reflects. *It is time to move on.* She hardly dares probe the implications of this unwelcome thought but feels the gall of complicity. Responsibility for the Romans' crimes is not only theirs. It is hers as well.

Three legionnaires step into the tent. One of them instructs the others, pointing here and there. Aislin rasps, "Please, kill me. What good is it to you, to leave me suffering?" The soldiers understand not a word. One holds her down while the other unties her ropes. A third squeezes her breasts and rubs his penis in front of her face, saying something in Latin. His friend laughs, answering, and hauls her outside as men pull up the stakes of the commander's tent and disassemble the supports; the tent deflates.

The men release her and she scampers into the forest on all fours. Apparently Vespasian has decreed she should live, perhaps as reward for his pleasure, perhaps as punishment for her inability, or unwillingness, to give him what all fighters crave—justification.

⇛

The Romans have departed, leaving the burnt bones of the sheep and pigs they have consumed, broken pot shards, splintered boards, torn leather, and a scattering of corpses. Hardly able to support her own weight, Aislin searches for her grandfather's skull. They have taken it along with the cot and the goatskin. Outside the desolate camp she stumbles upon the bodies of Muirgheal and two dozen village warriors in their helmets, still holding rectangular shields, face down in the mud.

Two dozen, no more. And they made the noise of seventy or eighty and held the Romans for hours. Aislin looks for the Roman dead—surely there are several—but their accomplices have denied her even this small pleasure. They have buried them somewhere in the forest, or immolated them. Yes, that would explain the smoke she smelled after the battle.

She cradles her aunt's fly-specked head in her palms. Muirgheal seems so small now. Death has reduced her to human dimensions. Blood has congealed in the corner of her down-turned mouth. Her eyes stare sightlessly at her niece. The echo of her battle cry—*dìoghaltas!*—still floats in the air.

Aislin drags Muirgheal into the wood and claws at the forest floor. Soil, moist with tears, fills her fingernails. The shadows of the trees shift as the sun slowly traverses the sky. Aislin pants with fatigue but continues scratching at the earth. Her fingers encounter worms, roots, and stones. Muirgheal lies on the ground staring at the heavens.

"After my mother departed, you saved me," Aislin tells her aunt, panting with fatigue. "I shall always love you. Your stories nourished me, those tales of beautiful maidens and innocent boys and…and, yes, vengeance. You promised me I would find a way out of my misery, one day, through stories like these. Where are they now, your words, your breath?"

She knows the answer. Aislin's heart and memory: that is where Muirgheal's voice resides. There, like all living beings, it may shift and mutate. But it remains.

Carefully, she lowers her aunt's body into the pit she has dug and folds Muirgheal's hands around her dagger. She cups a handful of moist soil and tosses it onto her aunt's soiled, bloody body. As she does so a memory returns to her.

It is the morning when they buried Aislin's mother, Muirgheal's sister. Certain details in this recollection are undoubtedly real while others, Aislin suspects, have shifted, filtered through subsequent dreams. The past is not solid; fantasy and reminiscence mix together like clouds in the sky. Her mother lies on a wheeled cart. A loose brown garment wraps her body. Only her face is exposed. Muirgheal, in purple and gold ceremonial robes, pulls the cart, flanked by Aislin and her three younger sisters, who wear white, their hair in braids. The entire village follows them, and their sheep, no less distressed than the villagers, walk beside them. All are weeping and bleating.

They come to the burial ground at the top of the next hill, past a fence of sharpened tree trunks. It is a village itself, the abode of the dead. A large bird with yellow and green wings flaps down to the gatepost, staring at Aislin with accusatory intent. It opens its beak and a song emerges, a haunting, extended melody ornamented with trills that slide one into another and flutter like butterflies. As Aislin and the bird watch each other, everything around them vanishes.

After Aislin covers her aunt with leaves and dirt, she lies upon the fresh, soft soil that is now her aunt's eternal shroud and gazes up at the leaves and heavens. They appear the same as a week ago: pale blue toward the horizon, darker toward the apex. Fluffy clouds extend their tentacles, which disappear at their farthest stretches and reappear elsewhere, patiently investigating their vast, deep habitat. Aislin knows that with the changing season, these clouds will darken. Rain will fall, the earth will roar, and lightning will streak across the sky. The storm will pass and days like today will return in another endless cycle. In the heavens, disturbances are transitory. This blue, these patches of white, this gentle breeze—they are the same as when Aislin was five, or seven. In the sky it is as if Aislin's mother never died and Vespasian never appeared at her village with his army.

The earth, though, is not like the sky. Here, when things change, they never return to the way they were. This is not the first time Aislin's world has changed. The first time was when her mother died. This time, the alteration is even grimmer.

She thinks again of that large, unusual bird with yellow and green wings, and the frightening beauty of its song. She does not want to hear it but knows that it will go on singing forever.

☙

Aislin climbs the path to her village. As she approaches, the stench of burned houses and putrescent flesh fills her nostrils. Her stomach rises in her throat. Beyond the gates she discovers the corpses of those she has known and loved, some dismembered in ponds of drying blood, others naked on their beds, their throats slit. Vanished are the shouts, giggles, and sobs that used to multiply in the air. Other than the buzzing of insects and the intermittent song of the woodlark, her hilltop universe is mute. She falls to her knees and retches sour bile.

She rises and stumbles inside. The Romans have removed most everything of value. But she retrieves her folded cow's-hide bed, a few garments, and, hidden in the dirt floor, one of her aunt's exquisitely wrought ceremonial daggers.

She totters to the village walls, breaking into a trot past the desolate sheep enclosure, through wide fields and into the thicket. Kneeling at the stream, she quenches her thirst and tries to rinse the stench from her skin and memory.

She lies upon the bank and closes her eyes but all she has witnessed, smelled, and felt remains with her. The awareness that she will forever revisit her destroyed village in her thoughts and dreams, and that she has been the cause of all this destruction, so compresses her heart that she manages only short breaths. She plunges her head into the water, seeking relief.

Something sparkles on the bed of round, black pebbles. She reaches for it but it vanishes. As she pulls back her hand, it flickers again like a memory of her aunt's divining stones. She raises her face from the water, coughing. In the brook's burble she hears the words of the bard: *The sun may turn black but even in that murk, if you keep your eyes open, you will see a glimmer.*

⪚

Aislin drifts through forests and fields, following the stream and avoiding settlements— those the Romans have depopulated and those they have spared—with little idea where she is heading or why she alone has survived to bear the burden of the dead, a weight that slows her journey. She no longer prays to the Companions or feels their presence. As her grandfather predicted, they have departed.

Shades of her friends and relatives accompany her. Sometimes Aislin glimpses them, or one of their sheep, in the distance, through trees. The flowers bloom but she cannot detect their scent. The stench of death clings to her like a coat of grime that cannot be scrubbed away.

She feels closer to the dead than to the living. The invisible and intangible elixir that surrounds the breathing self and those whom one loves, and flows between them and the Companions, has drained away. Why is she yet alive? Her aunt and sisters were more worthy than she. Aislin rejected her aunt's compassion after her mother died. She recalls her ingratitude with shame and regret.

"I am your mother now," Muirgheal reminded her, ladling gruel into her bowl. "This is not my doing, or yours, but we must both accept it."

"You're not my mother and never will be," shouted Aislin, hurling the bowl to the ground and bolting out.

Her protests, her refusal to accept that moment of irreversible change, lasted months. Muirgheal never lost patience but provided Aislin with attention and love. She held her at night, until Aislin fell asleep. She took her into the forest to hear the whisperings of the Companions.

Although Aislin no longer hears those whisperings, she tells herself that the Companions must subsist still, perhaps in the glimmer at the bottom of the stream. *The Companions are still out there. Somewhere. The memory of my people is not dead, so long as I survive to tell their story. Our story.*

The occasional report of living humans—a call, a yelp, a giggle, a scream—alarms her. She crawls through bushes in her search for food, surprising birds and rodents; she sleeps on her folded cow's hide under a blanket of leaves. Twenty-two cycles of the languid summer sun, she neither bathes nor washes her garments.

ॐ

At the bottom of a leafy gorge, a waterfall feeds a large pool. Thrusting her dagger into the moist soil, Aislin steps into the water, unpeels her dirt-filled *leine* and *brat*, rinses them, wrings them, and stretches them on a boulder to dry. Under the cascade of water she tilts her head to drink, abandoning herself to an instant of pleasure, a feral thrill.

This is the moment when she first sets eyes upon Septimus, or rather, when he discovers her bathing as he emerges from the trees to quench his thirst. She feels his eyes on her wet hair, open mouth, and small breasts, long before she sees him. Crouching in the water, she wades toward the center of the pond, scanning the tree line.

Gaunt, with ill-matched robes, Septimus now resembles nothing so much as the wild man of the bard's lore. He holds a blackened pigeon on a short, charred spit. He chews and spits out the bird's ribs.

Aislin longs for fire. She recollects the flavor of roast fowl and yearns to crack between her teeth those bones he tosses so thoughtlessly to the squirrels and rats.

He calls out to her, and she recognizes the vowels and rhythms of Latin. Despite his cornflower-blue *leine* and daffodil-yellow *brat*, he is one of *them*.

She moves toward the boulder where she spread her garments, cursing herself for leaving her knife behind, calculating how to seize it before this stranger, this Roman, manages to do to her what Vespasian and his men have done.

Instead, he covers his eyes with his hands—*Go ahead, dress yourself. I shall not look.*

Aislin retrieves her blade and wraps herself in wet garments.

He calls out again, hands still over his eyes. Is it possible that he, a Roman, is asking her, a native, for permission to remove his hands from his eyes, as if he were a boy playing a game? What is he doing out here in the forest, dressed and bearded like one of her people?

"Go away!" she shouts over the din of the waterfall.

His hands fall from his eyes and the two stand immobile for a moment, gazes locked across the water.

Aislin turns and scuttles up the escarpment. He throws his spit to the ground and pursues her. When she reaches the plateau, she dashes into the forest. Seizing her arm, he yanks her to the ground. She struggles to raise her knife but he restrains her, shouting. The syllables he utters mean nothing to her but something within her gives way and despite herself she begins to cry. Shame and anger possess her, shaking her like a fever.

He holds her until her tears slow. The two lie in the grass panting, her clothes wetting his. Staring at the clouds, he speaks quietly.

Still clutching her dagger, she sits up and raises it to stab him. His eyes fix on her hand; he could seize her arm and prevent her from plunging the blade into his heart. For a moment, though, neither moves. Finally, she gathers her hair, and, staring at him still, begins chopping it off.

The Pharisaic Academy of the Temple: a palace of melody, polished hardwoods, and the resolute laughter of young men who will never find their way home again. The classrooms open through painted archways onto a great hall. Yohanan shares a cedar-paneled classroom with twenty other priests-in-training.

The students have assembled on black stone benches around a rose-marble table, where one of the Scrolls of Tradition lies unfurled. Their teacher, Gamaliel, sits among them, neither at the head nor at the foot of the table, instructing them in rhetoric, history, law, and philosophy, particularly the interpretive moral philosophy developed by his revered grandfather, Hillel.

"To mortal eyes the Temple appears solid, and vast, no?" Gamaliel asks his students rhetorically. "But in the eyes of the Lord it is a dark pool. Braided streams of sin trickle into it from throughout Israel. And because most of the Children of the Covenant live in diaspora, these invisible streams also flow from all over the world, bearing the silt of surrounding cultures' sins as well.

"Sin, moral impurity," he continues, "is an essential aspect of the human condition. To try to escape it is futile. Nevertheless, our most important task, as laborers in the Temple, is to act as a conduit between the human and the divine, between impurity and purity. To reach up." He raises his arms and clutches at the air as if to grasp a pair of wide, sinewy wings.

&

The students sleep on narrow mattresses on the floor of the marble hall known as the Eastern Colonnade. To Yohanan's left lies Mattathias, son of Theophilus, the corpulent child of one of the most powerful families in Jerusalem. To his right lies Yosef, son of Matityahu, known as Josephus, with his thin face, strong, angled nose, and soft brown eyes that dart about. Yohanan and his two friends whisper late into the night, grousing about life in the Temple, their menial chores, and the scandalous behaviors of some senior priests. They sigh, too, about the pretty young women whose paths they have crossed.

What they most share, it seems to Yohanan, is a sense of having been misplaced, like half-burnt candles relegated to a cobwebbed chandlery, one day to be melted and reformed. Yohanan cannot force himself to admire this quality in his new friends, or even in himself, the way he once admired Stefanos's courage and penchant for adventure.

After Mattathias and Josephus fall asleep, when the only sounds in the Eastern Colonnade are rattling snores and slumberous moans, Yohanan lies awake, trying to make sense of the ways in which his life has changed. He remembers evenings spent with his mother and sister telling stories and laughing, afternoons working alongside his father, walking across the city with him, praying together. Were all those days really as sunny and color-drenched as in his recollection? He finds it increasingly hard to dissociate memories from dreams, while a gloomy haze suffuses the present.

He thinks occasionally, too, of the tales Stefanos's father told, which he claimed to have learned in the library of this very Temple. From somewhere deep within these stories, a voice calls to Yohanan, at first so quietly he hardly notices. The voice is foreign-accented and female.

He rises and wanders through the courtyards. Glancing at the arcades, courtyards, fountains, and buildings that surround him, the torch-lit interlacings of marble, gold, silver, and carved wood, Yohanan asks himself by what merit he has come to dwell in such a place.

He sits on a bench, watching clouds blow past the moon. No one in Judea doubts that the Temple of Jerusalem is the most magnificent edifice in the world. The few who have been chosen to study and pray there will one day assume roles of crucial importance, not just for their people but for all humanity.

Although Judea is a tiny land, its influence is enormous. This is due in part to its location at the border of the two eternally warring empires, Rome and Persia, and also to the fact that its inhabitants have been scattered across the world for hundreds of years. Judaeans reside in all the nations, but retain their identity and their conception of a universe imbued with moral purpose. This building, and the people who do the Lord's work here, are the center of that universe.

At least, that is the claim of the priestly class, and of the other

Sadducees. Ever since Judea was exiled to Babylon, six hundred years ago, another class has arisen to challenge the priests, arguing that the Temple can exist, in some hard-to-define way, in more than one place—in fact, wherever Judaeans gather to study the Scrolls of Tradition. This class of teachers, or rabbis, are known as the Pharisees.

In Yohanan's generation, Gamaliel is their leader. His popularity and power are so strong that the priests accord him a position of honor in the Temple. But tension between the rabbis and the priests subsists. Rome supports the priests, regarding the rabbis as "separatists"—which is the literal meaning of the word *Pharisees.*

What will my role be? wonders Yohanan. *Will this place ever feel like home?*

One night, after six months at the Temple, he rises, creeps out, and finds the staircase that leads forty feet down to the library, with its wide arches, dangling candelabras, and wooden niches for scrolls. Security is minimal in this area, where, in theory, only priests are allowed. He wanders from one scroll to the next touching each, breathing aromas of parchment, ink, and dust. He steps through a wooden portal into a chamber of black stone, and then another of raw marble.

He opens the door to a small chamber where a few delicate scrolls lie unrolled on stone platforms. One of them, a miniature whorl of polished parchment, begins *ki-tovim dodekha mi-yayin:* better than wine, your kisses. It describes a dark-skinned woman who compares her beloved to an apple tree in a wild forest.

> *Strengthen me with raisin cakes,*
> *refresh me with apples,*
> *for I am faint with love.*

Hovering over this poem, Yohanan eavesdrops on the intimate whisperings of its lovers. He recognizes their emotions and feels he has met them before, perhaps in dreams. The lyrics of lust and elation, without reference to time or place, enrapture him; it is a story that begins nowhere and ends nowhere. A man and a woman confide in him from the darkness.

> *My beloved is to me a sachet of myrrh*
> *that lies between my breasts.*
> *My beloved is to me a cluster of henna blossoms*
> *in the vineyards of Engedi.*

Yohanan swallows each syllable hungrily, like a lamb sucking at its mother's teat. Forgoing sleep and duty, he follows the track of letters to the end of the scroll. *This is my beloved.* The man implores his compatriots to accept his foreign lover. *This is my friend, o daughters of Jerusalem.*

The following day Yohanan thinks of little other than the words he perused and the passions they stirred, physical and emotional yearnings inextricably braided in a yarn of desire. He feels as if he were the young man of the text—as if the author, centuries ago, had plucked upon the harp-strings of the soul that was destined to become his.

That night, through the fog of sleep, the woman of the scroll strolls into the Eastern Colonnade and rouses him. Though exhausted, he waits until his friends' breathing acquires the regular, labored rhythms of deep quiescence, slips out in starlight to the library, and dives again into the scroll.

> *Arise, my love, my beautiful one, and come away,*
> *for behold the winter is past; the rain is over and gone.*
> *Flowers appear on the earth, the time of singing has come,*
> *and the voice of the turtledove is heard in our land.*
> *The fig tree ripens its fruit; the vines are in blossom.*
> *They give forth fragrance.*
> *Arise, my love, my beautiful one, and come away.*

Come away to where? wonders Yohanan.

❧

Two hundred years ago, his friend Mattathias's great-grandparents, known as Maccabees, successfully led a revolt against their Greek-speaking occupiers, the Seleucids. The Judaeans interpreted the Maccabees' victory as proof of divine favor, and Mattathias's family retains the prestige of that triumph. Although uninvolved in Temple affairs, Mattathias's father is a personal friend of the high priest and, unlike other students, Mattathias is permitted to leave the Temple to spend the Sabbath with his parents. These visits, however, fail to bring him joy or peace. He returns troubled and preoccupied. "My family has become lackeys of the degenerate Romans," he confides to his friends Yohanan and Josephus.

"Think how lucky you are, though," says Josephus. "You have opportunities the rest of us can only dream of."

"It feels more like a burden than an opportunity," insists Mattathias.

One Sabbath, Yohanan, Josephus, and others play a ball game under the direction of two Temple guards. Josephus scoops up the ball and tosses it to Yohanan. A classmate pushes Yohanan and he fumbles. The ball hits the ground and belongs now to the opposing team.

"Brilliant mind, clumsy hands," quips the boy who pushed him, as if the two qualities were always and necessarily related. Yohanan ignores the comment. He knows that this boy, and others, value alertness and physical dexterity above all else. They view Yohanan's love of language, stories, dreams, and beauty as a weakness, and perhaps it is.

A wispy-bearded man in the toga of a slave steps into the courtyard and speaks with one of the Temple guards, who signals Yohanan and Josephus. "You have been invited to the home of your friend Mattathias," the guard tells them. "All is arranged."

The servant leads them out of the Temple, through the winding streets of the Upper City to a wrought-iron gate set in a stone wall. A slave admits them. The wings of a palace stretch before the awestruck boys. The statues, fountains, and sculpted shrubbery seem a celebration of residential privilege unlike any Yohanan has seen in a private home. A large fresco adorns the far wall, a painting of a bird perched on the edge of a bowl, sipping water, before a leafy background.

"Wait here for Master Mattathias." The slave steps into a guards' building.

As the boys wait, they overhear a murmur of voices. Josephus pulls Yohanan close, gestures for silence, and leads him stealthily to a corner of the building. There they see a Roman soldier sitting close to a Hebrew slave, who holds his face tenderly in her hands. Their eyes locked, they exchange quiet words.

A hand grips Yohanan's shoulder. "Who are you? What are you doing?"

"We were invited. We were looking for the great hall and got turned around," Josephus lies.

At that moment Mattathias appears in a doorway across a peristyle and hails his two friends. "Ah, there you are! Come!" He waves Yohanan and Josephus over.

"Master, they were spying," the man tells him.

Mattathias smiles. "So? What do I care? Lunch is waiting!"

The man releases the boys, who scamper across the courtyard.

❧

Lying on his straw mattress in the Eastern Colonnade that night, Yohanan reflects on the events of the day. Mattathias and Josephus are both, in different ways, so unlike him. Mattathias has grown up in an environment where Roman soldiers consort with Hebrew slaves, a place where rules and decorum are the personal possessions of the powerful, to be used as they see fit. He knows how to command a servant with confidence and grace. And Josephus, Yohanan now knows, cares more about saving his hide than about truth. He lied easily and smoothly, without shame. Yohanan feels lonelier than ever.

He finds solace in his readings. The forbidden text he encountered in the library remains with him, and he sneaks out to read it for the third time. The text clarifies his emotions and then moves him to tears. One drop falls to the parchment, smudging the word *keramim*, vineyards.

Horrified, Yohanan realizes he has desecrated the scroll. The passions that have buoyed him on these three nights, sustaining his spirit in the absence of sleep, crash like a wave on hot, dry sands. He has destroyed a precious, holy narrative, perhaps the only copy that exists in the world of mortals.

The unexpected sound of a man clearing his throat startles Yohanan. Joseph, son of Kayafa—the high priest known simply as Kayafa and one of the most powerful men in Judea—fills the arched doorway like the human embodiment of an accusation.

"I ruined a holy scroll," admits Yohanan.

Over Yohanan's shoulder, the high priest gazes down at the stained page.

"This will have to be copied from the beginning," stammers Yohanan. "I can do it. I am the son of a copyist and a copyist myself. Please allow me to replicate this text. I hardly need look at it. I have committed it to memory."

"This text was never holy," replies Kayafa. "Its subject is the love between a man and a woman. It does not mention the Lord, or man's relation to It." He places a hand on the boy's shoulder. "I was once your age. I too, was filled with curiosity about forbidden things. And so this will remain between you and me."

"You're not going to punish me?"

"Not for ruining this text. One could even say you've done me a favor. This text would not be here at all, were it not for the resistance we've encountered from the rabbis. We don't need more unrest. But tell me, what spirit possessed you to venture into the library so late at night? What spirit beckoned you here?"

"What spirit?" Yohanan reflects. "Voices from within the stories that fill these shelves. From this text and others."

"Others?" Kayafa asks.

"Xenophon," Yohanan says. "Kallimachos."

"What do you know of Kallimachos?"

"I've heard speak of the wonders he discovered. A statue that comes alive; an old woman who regains her youth; a man who rises from the dead."

"Don't waste your mind with such tales."

"You don't believe them?"

Kayafa shakes his head. "I don't believe in miracles."

"What about Balaam's donkey, when it talks? Or Moses parting the Red Sea? Or Daniel surviving in a den of lions? You don't believe any of it?"

"As literal truth?" Kayafa again shakes his head.

"Then why do you believe in the power of the Lord, in Its laws, in anything?"

Kayafa's lips curl into a thin smile. "Go to bed. It's almost dawn. You wish to experience miracles? Then dream."

Yohanan turns to leave. "There is one other thing, however," says Kayafa in a softened voice. "Your mother was afflicted with sickness. She passed away and left you a small inheritance."

He allows Yohanan a moment, watching his face.

"And my sister?" asks the boy.

"She will live with your uncle and aunt. I'm sorry, Yohanan. Following your eight days of mourning, you are to polish the marble floors of our Royal Colonnade as punishment for your intrusion into the Temple library. There will be no further punishment. I expect you not to try this again."

"Yes, lord."

Outside the Temple library Yohanan finds a dark corner in the

Courtyard of the Priests and slumps against the wall. He prays for his mother's soul and weeps.

❧

During the eight days of mourning, Yohanan takes his meals in the Hall of Song, where harpists, cymbal-players, and drums accompany the Levitical choir, who chant hymns that echo through the Temple from dawn until dusk. He imagines his mother standing on the other side of the room, looking into a copper mirror on the wall, drawing a bone comb through her hair. She wears a brown tunic and her feet are bare. "What an honor to be here with you, my son," she says, "listening to this heavenly music. It is a privilege I never enjoyed while I journeyed among the living."

He questions her choice of words. *Journeying* is not something his mother did. She spent her life within a few blocks of the home of her birth. "How I wish, though, that you were still here among us," he tells her. "Even if you lived in the city, and I were here in the Temple, it would be a comfort."

She crosses over to him, places a warm hand on his cheek, and smiles. "Listen, Yohanan." Together they listen to the music. "Where does this song lead us? It transports us to the contemplation of something so much greater than our personal pain." She turns to leave.

"Mother," he calls.

But she is gone. He would have liked to talk with her about his father, his sister, the memories and hopes that attended her deathbed, and so much else.

On the second day of Yohanan's mourning, the foreign woman from the scroll visits him, together with her beloved. They walk through palaces and gardens, speaking in tender tones. Yohanan repeats every word of the text in which they have devised their immortality. As he does so, their souls intertwine with his.

> *Behold the winter is past; the rain is over and gone.*
> *Flowers appear on the earth, the time of singing has come,*
> *and the voice of the turtledove is heard in our land.*
> *The fig tree ripens its fruit; the vines are in blossom.*
> *They give forth fragrance.*
> *Arise, my love, my beautiful one, and come away.*

"Come away," Yohanan repeats to himself. *Away to where?*

In a long room of polished marble, open and pillared on one side, his teacher Gamaliel finds him. "Yohanan, of all my students, you pose the most resonant questions. Yet so often you seem lost in thought. What is it you think about so deeply?"

"A text I read," says Yohanan. "A text that ends with an unanswered request."

Gamaliel smiles. "And which request is that?"

"'Come away, my beloved,' Yohanan quotes, 'and be like a gazelle or like a young stag on the spice-laden mountains.' Such a strange way for a story to end, as if the character were talking not to her lover in the story, but to the reader directly."

"Ah, yes." Gamaliel smiles. "But to say the *Shir ha-Shirim* ends there is inaccurate. The *Song of Songs* has no beginning or ending. It goes on forever in the heart and mind."

"I understand it is not a holy text," says Yohanan.

Gamaliel raises an eyebrow. "And what sort of text do you imagine it is?"

"The high priest told me it is merely a song about mortal love."

"It is indeed a song about love," agrees Gamaliel. "But there are many forms of love, including the love between the Lord and Its creation."

Yohanan contemplates Gamaliel's suggestion that the text is meant as an allegory. This approach explains the foreignness of the beloved woman. The God of Israel, Gamaliel has explained, is at once infinitely distant and impossibly close, foreign and intimate. And yet, Yohanan cannot accept that the *Song of Songs* is not what it purports to be, an ingenuous portrayal of desire and a subtle defense of the passions that can arise between Children of the Covenant and foreigners.

He is about to ask Gamaliel more about this, and about the contrast between the *Song of Songs* and *Pinkhas,* which seems to advocate the murder of those whose love transcends conflicting traditions. He is about to ask Gamaliel about the meaning of the broken letter *vav* in *Pinkhas* when a trumpet blasts.

Gamaliel rises. "We look forward to seeing you in class again in two days." At the door, he turns. "If the *Song of Songs* speaks to you, Yohanan, listen to what it is telling you."

Come away, my love, thinks Yohanan. *That is what the Song of Songs is saying.*

❧

The limestone wall of a great basilica perches along the southern crest of the Temple mount. On its northern side, this building opens onto the Courtyard of the Priests. Four rows of Corinthian columns support a double roof, affording a view toward the Holy of Holies, where heaven reaches down to touch earth. A door in the rear wall of this Royal Colonnade leads to a stairway that zigzags to the city below, allowing citizens to ascend. A contingent of Roman soldiers preserves the peace. Only priests, properly cleansed, enter from the Temple side.

Clutching a linen rag, Yohanan kneels, polishing the marble floors with a linen rag, which he dips in a terracotta bowl of finely ground pumice and vinegar. He feels degraded—to polish the floors of the Colonnade is to be publicly rebuked—but also honored to be a witness to the proceedings that are taking place in this chamber.

Seated in a semicircle around a great table, the High Council of the Province of Judaea has convened to discuss which texts are sacred and which not. Kayafa and the other Sadducees maintain that only the five Books of Moses—*In The Beginning, Names, And He Called, In The Wilderness,* and *Words*—are holy. Other scrolls in the Temple library, those that hold sentimental or historical value, belong to Creation, not to the worlds of the Lord and Its Messengers.

The Pharisees disagree. They argue that the breath of the Lord inspires a wide range of texts, even contemporary writings. The gift of prophecy subsists into the present. The ancient scrolls themselves are as fluid as water.

The seventy-one sages have been struggling for years to reach a consensus on this matter, citing previous scholars' opinions and passages in the Tradition. They meander into and out of other dialogues, negotiations, and debates, occasionally shedding light on one or another facet of an issue deemed crucial for the preservation and advancement of an Israel that no longer exists, if it ever did—an Israel that surely needs their prayers.

In the midst of this debate a group of citizens storms in, pushing a prisoner. Yohanan recognizes Stefanos. He has grown. His eyes have darkened, lending him a grave dignity. His glance meets Yohanan's.

One of the intruders steps forward to speak, his eyes the color of a clear sky just after dawn, pale blue with yellow glints, his hair falling in loose ringlets, receding at the temples. "Esteemed sages," he begins, speaking in Greek, the language of aristocrats and foreigners. "I am Saul of Tarsus, a member of the Synagogue of the Freed Slaves. We have sacrificed everything, leaving our distant birthplaces to settle in Jerusalem. Two inseparable preoccupations unite us, our love of Israel and of the Lord."

"What has this man done, that you have forcibly dragged him before us?" Kayafa enquires.

"I ask you," Saul demands, "if a man preaches in public squares and synagogues that this land is like any other, that this Holy Temple is merely a pile of stones, then who are we, the Children of the Covenant? Have you ever heard of a people who claim no attachment to the earth under its feet, to its Sanctuary? Such a people cannot survive. And yet, that is precisely what this man asserts to all who will listen."

Saul yanks Stefanos forward by the scruff of his neck.

"You may disagree with this man's teaching," says Gamaliel, "but are you stating he has violated a law of Israel? And if not, once again, why have you dragged him before us?"

"We are told that whoever blasphemes the Lord shall be stoned."

These charged words elicit brisk discussion until Gamaliel raises his hand. "The crime to which you refer," he says, "is *to curse the name of the Lord*. Did this man curse the name of the Lord? Were there witnesses?"

Saul scratches his cheek. "With all due respect, lord, we do not read this prohibition as narrowly as you."

"How *you* read it is a personal matter," replies Gamaliel. "How *we* read it is public policy."

"I do not question your judgment, lord."

Another sage intervenes, his tone grave. "What you call our judgment, Saul, does not, in fact, belong to us. It is the patrimony of all the Children of the Covenant. It is the harvest of generations of scholarship."

"Perhaps you are thinking in your native tongue," adds Gamaliel. "The Greek word *blasphemia* has different implications than our Hebrew word *nakav*."

Kayafa, glancing at the Roman soldiers, speaks up. "Whether the accused is guilty of cursing the name of the Lord or not, his speech is clearly subversive. Part of our duty is to enforce the laws against subversive speech, is it not?"

As Yohanan and the others know, Kayafa is referring not to Hebrew, but to Roman laws.

"Rome acknowledges and supports the authority of our Temple," Kayafa continues. "In challenging this Temple, the suspect challenges Rome itself."

His heart pounding, Yohanan considers Kayafa's argument. It seems self-interested, twisted, even incommensurate with his duties as defined in the Scrolls of Tradition. To whom is the high priest loyal, Yohanan wonders, Israel or Rome? It is a question much bandied about among the priests-in-training, though only in whispers under cover of night.

Gamaliel asks the accused to speak for himself.

Stefanos introduces himself in a muted voice. "The war of the end times has begun," he says. "It is a conflict not between Israel and a foreign land, but within Israel's soul."

The High Council listens intently.

"We are not a nation," resumes Stefanos, gaining confidence, "we are a people."

"What is this distinction you are attempting?" asks Kayafa, his brow creased.

"A nation is defined by geographical bounds," says Stefanos. "Our ties to the land, though, have worn thin. We have been displaced and conquered so many times."

"A nation," says Gamaliel, "is not defined only by geography. It is defined by its language and the stories it tells—our Torah."

"Stories know no boundaries," Stefanos acknowledges.

"These displacements, as you call them—our exiles to Egypt and Babylon—were punishment for our sins," adds another scholar. "They were purifying torments, and we have returned to our land after each. Your argument ignores the teachings of history."

"No," protests Stefanos. "Our exiles, and the conquest of our land by Greece and Rome, were not punishment for sin, but reward for virtue. We learned from all these great nations, although we suffered—or because we suffered. The Lord has revealed Itself to us not from within but from without. It is in this respect that we are chosen."

Just as Stefanos's gaze has deepened, so has his mind, reflects Yohanan. He wonders what distress his friend has endured during the intervening years. Another glance from Stefanos partially answers his question. The loss of their friendship has been no less troubling for Stefanos than for Yohanan.

"If the Lord reveals Itself from without," interrupts Saul, "then this land is nothing more than sand and sea, and our Temple differs in no way from a pagan one. Is that not the result of your philosophy?"

"It is, indeed," Stefanos answers.

Is this what that Greek term blasphemia *means?* Yohanan wonders as the sages mutter heatedly amongst themselves.

"You see," insists Saul. "He denies the holiness of our Temple. Where, then, does holiness reside in this world?"

Still clutching the polishing rag, his voice quivering, Yohanan rises to his feet and announces his passionate convictions. "This case, lords, has no merit."

A hush falls over the chamber as the assembly sinks into shocked silence.

Yohanan turns to Saul. "On what grounds do you challenge a man's thoughts? If you dragged everyone here who held such beliefs, or other beliefs you disagree with, there would be no time for serious business."

Kayafa shakes his head, warning Yohanan.

"I know this man," Yohanan continues. "Or rather, I knew him once. I looked up to him then, and I still do now. He does not deserve to die."

Saul points a finger at him. "And who are *you* to tell us what we can or cannot do? If we feel a man's preaching endangers our faith, is it not our right, indeed our duty, to bring our complaint before the High Council?"

"What faith?" Yohanan's voice rises. "You're not referring to the faith of Israel but to your own opinions. You make the Lord seem petty and small. It is men like you, not Stefanos, who are a danger to our faith."

Saul's companions whisper their indignation.

"Enough!" demands Kayafa.

"Thank you, brother," Stefanos says, his smile lightening his ascetic face, his eyes crinkling.

Trumpets sound at the Antonia Fortress, announcing the hour for chanting Psalms. On a nod from Kayafa, two sentries seize Yohanan and lead him outside to the western wall where wayward students are flogged.

Yohanan removes his tunic, presses his palms to the stones, and spreads his feet. Clenching his teeth, he accepts the guards' stinging chastisement.

Following his whipping, two priests lead Yohanan to the purifying baths, where they pat him dry and instruct him not to wear a shirt for eight days. The exposed weals will mark him as a penitent and the sun will mend his wounds. Not until that night, as he lies on his straw mattress, does Yohanan learn of Stefanos's death.

"They stoned him," Josephus tells him.

"Your Stefanos was a troublemaker," Mattathias says, "and Kayafa cares about one thing, his own power."

❧

Yohanan does not sleep that night. Gamaliel has taught them that two principles distinguish their people from all others: their respect for the holiness of life and their insistence that right and wrong matter more than mortal power—for their invisible Lord is mightier than any man. How, Yohanan wonders, can the Temple be the holiest place on earth if its leader violates these principles, affirming mortal power and needlessly taking human lives? And yet, if the Temple is not the holiest place on earth, the very umbilicus of Israel, then what force holds Creation together?

On the morning when he realized that his father would not be coming home, it was as if a granite perch crumbled under his feet. Now the entire Temple seems to be falling asunder, block by block. He remembers the face of his friend Stefanos, in the garden of his home, and his voice: "Have you gone beyond?" Finally Yohanan rises.

"Where are you going?" asks Josephus.

"I don't know."

The guards pay no heed as he wanders through the Temple gates and down into the streets of Jerusalem, feeling keenly the absence of the boy who taught him to juggle. At length he finds himself standing before the Synagogue of the Way. He remembers this place, the man and woman who stood outside, and Stefanos's fascination with their talk of a messiah.

The room is candle-lit, filled with mourners. Yohanan steps across the threshold and sits cross-legged among them. The man who is speaking, with long, dark hair and an unkempt beard, acknowledges him with a nod as he answers the question of a congregant: "Not yet in paradise. Sleeping. When our brother Joshua returns, Stefanos will awaken with all the righteous, and blessedness will reign over the world."

Yohanan spends the night and the following morning in the Synagogue of the Way, sharing reminiscences. He learns that during the intervening years, Stefanos abandoned an apprenticeship in his father's money-changing enterprise to live with other Followers of the Way. He embraced their belief that the messiah had come and died and arisen from the dead, and would return again; that the War of the End Times had begun and that the messianic age, the World to Come, was imminent. "How else are we to explain this chaos?" asks the teacher, gesturing toward the Roman-occupied streets.

The name of this teacher is familiar to Yohanan. Widely respected for his piety and wisdom, Jacob the Just has taken vows never to allow a barber's blade to graze his scalp; nor does he drink wine, visit public baths, touch any corpses, or wear leathers or furs. Yohanan finds wisdom in much of Jacob's philosophy, which is predicated on the sense of powerlessness that Judaeans share under Roman domination and attempts to substitute hope for despair, community for family, and love for resentment. As the morning wears on, the sense of a communal friendship, of intimacy, grows as palpable as a warm coat woven of words. Wrapped in this coat, Yohanan dreams.

છ

At the end of the day, Yohanan starts back toward the Temple. Viewed from the streets that surround the Synagogue of the Way, it still glistens. The closer he approaches, however, the more the grime that is the unavoidable consequence of holy activities—the exsanguination of bulls, the smoke from their burning flesh, which blackens the walls and eaves of its marble porticoes—stains his view. Is it the unique privilege of student priests and other servants of the Temple, he wonders, to notice such filth?

He finds Gamaliel and the high priest studying a text in the Chamber of the Parhedrin, also known as the Chamber of Wood. Oil lamps illuminate six men from the Levitical Choir, who chant near the far wall. Yohanan knows that his intrusion marks yet another offense but the possible consequences no longer concern him. Kayafa looks up, his face bearing the dazed expression of a man who has been shaken from a pleasant dream.

"I'm here to claim my inheritance," Yohanan tells him.

Kayafa studies him. "Some of the proceeds have been placed in our trust, for your benefit. We can deliver it to you in the morning. The rest is being held for you by your father's brother, who resides in the town of Arav, in the Galilee. That would take more time to arrive, but it is yours for the asking."

"The high priest and I," Gamaliel says, "have been discussing your outburst in the basilica. You placed us in a delicate position."

A beetle whooshes past Yohanan's ear, as if to remind him with its low, mechanical buzz that his perspective, the human perspective, is but one of an infinite variety of ways to experience the world. He waves the beetle away.

"We cannot ignore your impulsiveness, your lack of self-control. At the same time, we cannot ignore the bright future that awaits you. A light shining. We feel its radiance, as we know you do."

"A grave injustice was done," says Yohanan, surprising even himself. "That is all I know. That, and the loss of my dearest friend."

Gamaliel nods.

"Whatever your feelings for this young man," says Kayafa in a quiet voice, studying the fingers of his left hand, "it is not just about him, or you, or any of us personally."

"I wish to leave this place," says Yohanan at last.

"Your father abandoned your family," replies the high priest. "Your mother has succumbed to illness, yet you have the opportunity to receive the finest education and to be trained for the priesthood. I would advise you not to act rashly."

"What does this mean, to act rashly?" asks Yohanan. "Are considerations of practical advantage always to be preferred over feelings for another human being? If I have knowledge of a man beyond that of anyone in the room, am I to hold my tongue?"

The two men confer quietly. Kayafa nods.

"Yom Kippur is approaching. Give your decision more time," Gamaliel urges.

"The captain of the Temple has fallen ill," says the high priest. "Can you help us?"

Yohanan hesitates.

"Go to the library," says Kayafa. "Read up on the responsibilities of the Temple captain during Yom Kippur. You know the way, do you not?"

Yohanan perceives the irony in Kayafa's question but refuses to acknowledge it. On its face the high priest's offer is an unexpected gift, an extraordinary honor. It is also a challenge of sorts: *Remain with us and we will reward you handsomely.* Yohanan accepts, not because he intends to stay in the Temple but because Yom Kippur is the holiest day of the year. He will remain one more day, not to serve men, but to honor the Lord.

From a Roman outpost, Septimus has stolen a lamp, a jar of oil, and a short spear. Together, Aislin and Septimus try to catch a squirrel but settle for the seeds and nuts the animal has been collecting. Following this meager repast, Aislin shoulders her cow's hide, trudges into the forest, and lies down far from Septimus's camp. She returns at dawn.

They hunt, vocalize, and ramble downstream in a murk of mutual incomprehension. With utterances and gestures Septimus communicates to her that he intends to follow the brook to the great river, and the great river to the sea. From there he will find a way back to Rome. He wishes to bid his wife and son farewell before dying the death of a traitor.

Aislin learns her first words of Latin—*fluvius* for stream, *ignis* for fire. Each night, Aislin sleeps a little closer to his fire. On a hilltop several weeks south of her village, they find the remnants of a large town, burned to the ground. Unable to bear the stench of charred and decomposing bodies, Aislin staggers out through the wooden gates, flies down the hill, and collapses in Septimus's embrace, sobbing.

Occasionally they catch sight of a *contubernium*, a unit of eight Roman legionnaires driving a procession of bound natives through the green, foggy landscape toward a lifetime of bondage in far-off Rome. Hiding amid the trees, too distant to discern individual faces, Aislin wonders how so few can so swiftly dominate so many. The obvious answer sickens her. Mastery of lives comes to those who master death.

At night she dreams of her grandfather's skull on the bedside table of Vespasian's tent, raving of voyages, fire, and deliverance. Aislin tries to question him but her words cluster and congeal. Her grandfather's head takes on features similar to her dead aunt Muirgheal's, his hair afire and blood pouring from his mouth, which forms garbled syllables. The scene shifts: Aislin is walking through an endless, smoldering city of death, skirting ruined dwellings and stumbling over dismembered body parts. And again: she is suddenly blind, inching through the mud like a worm, until she encounters a human corpse, and, penetrating its flesh, tunnels into its still-beating heart. Aislin wakens, gasping, and finds unwanted comfort in Septimus's nearness.

Through the lens of these dreams she perceives her destiny, to avenge the destruction of her village and the annihilation of her people. But how is she, one person alone, to succeed where all of Albion has failed? Yet she is certain this is what the Companions and her dead kin demand of her. They have left her one instruction: *dioghaltas*. Vengeance.

Weeks dissolve into months. One devastated town bleeds into another. Sometimes Septimus and Aislin sit on a hillside or beside a lake, silently contemplating the vista. Knowing nothing about one another, they come to trust each other in a rudimentary way—without language, like animals. Together and separately they forge their way through sun-drenched glens and rain-soaked forests.

On a flat stretch of granite, Septimus uses the charred end of a stick to sketch a somber landscape. Aislin wonders at his ability to capture the mood of a place. She admires his calm focus at such moments, his seeming ability to withdraw his mind from the tragedy of the present.

They avoid open fields and roads, studying the stars by night and the progress of the sun by day. Aislin and Septimus claw the damp soil for worms, grind ants and termites into paste, and raid birds' nests. Septimus knows how to distinguish edible from poisonous mushrooms. Occasionally, they catch a squirrel or a hare.

Her monthly flow ceases. Septimus recognizes the signs of pregnancy and communicates this to her, as if she did not already know. Feeling more vulnerable than ever, she allows herself to sleep beside him.

The presence of another life within her confuses and disturbs Aislin. She always assumed she would marry her cousin, and that their offspring would be born out of love. Instead, she will give birth to an unintended consequence of forced couplings. Her child's father will be the man she despises more than any other, the Roman commander, Vespasian.

As her baby grows within her, though, she reminds herself not to blame this new life for the circumstances of its conception. This child will also be the only descendant of her people, the heir of her murdered ancestors' songs and memories. Little by little she learns to love the infant developing in her womb.

They lie under the stars. Aislin chants the ancient melodies of her people. Weeks later, as the air chills and her blood thickens, she and Septimus stop in the afternoon to rest on a grassy hillside and speak to the child in Aislin's womb, to the future, and in a way, to each other. He recites passages from Homer and Ovid, and Aislin tells stories of rapacious, greedy warriors and forced sexual acts. Despite their ignorance of each other's tongues, the cadence of speech is soothing to them both.

❧

Her contractions, slow and painful, start at night. *I know how to do this,* Aislin tells herself. She remembers helping Cara give birth to Elisedd but this is terrifyingly different. She counts a thousand paces from Septimus and prepares a bed of soft grass between the forest and a stream under the full moon. She wants to reach in and find her baby's head but it is not time.

Her pains intensify and she cries out into the night. Septimus finds her. He kneels at her side and speaks softly, in a tone that is surely meant to be reassuring. She kicks out at him, wailing and pleading. In the end, exhausted and frightened, she lets him extract her baby. She pushes and screams. He pulls. She closes her eyes and dreams while awake. From a great distance, the ancestors beckon.

Her daughter emerges blue, lifeless, as small as a kitten, with the scrunched forehead of someone fighting pain, a tiny nose, and the jutting chin of her father, the Roman general. Clutching her baby to her breast, Aislin names her *Meitheamh*, Mid-Summer.

The emergence of her stillborn daughter leaves an emptiness within Aislin. The moon has disappeared from the sky. She holds her daughter's cold body through the day and night and late into the next morning. A thunderstorm breaks, rain lashes the ground, and lightning streaks across the sky, but Aislin scarcely notices. Hair dripping, raindrops mingling with tears, she rocks her baby and chants the ancient lullabies of her people.

> *Winter wings away.*
> *Blackbirds babble.*
> *Streams sparkle.*
> *Daffodils dapple the dale.*
> *Winter wings away.*

Septimus takes her arm, insisting they bury the baby. He says a great

90

deal besides, with sadness and conviction, most of it lost on Aislin. Beneath a willow by the stream, Aislin on her knees delves into the moist soil weeping and lays her little girl on her back, nose pointed at the sky. Mud will forever block her view but perhaps she will hear the whisperings of the ancients in the trees and water.

Septimus urges her to leave but Aislin resists, stretching out on the freshly turned ground three feet above her stillborn daughter, just as she recently lay on her aunt's grave. Companions surround them, dancing, and birds whistle in the forest.

On the Day of Atonement Yohanan leads an unblemished bull into the Courtyard of the Priests. The beast snorts at the thousands of gathered pilgrims, steam rising from its fur and nostrils, its horns twisting above its ears, its left eye blinking as a fly repeatedly alights upon its rim. Kayafa, resplendent in a blue robe embroidered with pomegranates and hemmed with golden bells, places his fleshy hands on the animal's head. The bull can easily kill Kayafa, dash into the crowd, and cause mayhem. The Children of the Covenant would interpret such an event as the Lord's refusal of their offerings, a further withdrawal of Its favor.

Standing near Kayafa, Yohanan alone hears the high priest's confession. Kayafa addresses the Lord, acknowledging his unworthiness; admitting that his mistakes are countless and grave, his devotion weak, his priesthood fraudulent. "Nevertheless," he concludes, his voice grave and measured. "You have designated me as the conduit for Israel's sins, an essential link in the chain of her redemption. We no longer know Your name. I cannot pronounce it, yet I am required to do so."

Is he confessing to the Lord, or to Yohanan? The student senses an unrequested complicity. *We are both trespassers,* Kayafa's glance seems to say. *You are smarter than the others, Yohanan, more curious and bold. Stay with me.* The high priest completes his confession and Yohanan cues the people in the plazas and streets. They fall prostrate, just as if Kayafa had pronounced the name of the Lord.

The priests have selected two identical fawn-colored goats—with black-striped legs, back-swept horns, and oval honey-colored eyes—from among the pilgrims' offerings. Yohanan shakes a box of olive wood and removes the lid. The high priest reaches in and withdraws two gold leaves, one inscribed with the words *for Azazel,* the other, *for the Lord.*

Kayafa winds a red wool string loosely around the neck of the goat on the right, the Goat of the Lord, and a second around the horns of the goat on the left, dedicated to the demon, the fallen Messenger Azazel.

The Goat of Azazel trembles and emits a bleating howl unlike any Yohanan has ever heard. The congregation falls silent, so silent that Yohanan can hear the languid summer breeze, which sounds like the whispering of Messengers.

❧

The sun has risen to its apex, glinting on the gold casings of the sanctuary. An assistant hands Kayafa a sharp knife. He kneels beside the bull and strokes its neck with his left hand. The animal exhales with a sound that resembles both a snort and a sigh, as if in resignation, and the high priest swiftly slices through the fur, hide, and sinew of the bull's throat, taking its life just as the Lord takes the lives of men—for that is the purpose of this ritual, to demonstrate within the terrestrial sphere the power of the Lord to cleanse sin, to take life, to renew fealties. The bull groans and collapses, its hot blood spurting into a stone bowl, which overflows into a slotted drain and drips into the basin below.

Kayafa turns toward the altar, a half-pyramid of unhewn stones, climbs the ramp, collects cinders with a red-gold scoop, and redescends toward the Great Sanctuary. He climbs the twelve steps to its porch, which stretches behind a sixty-foot-high tapestry that depicts the heavens. Priests part this curtain for Kayafa, who enters the inner sanctuary, the Holy of Holies that only he can enter, once a year.

When Kayafa steps out again he dips his hands into the golden bowl of blood that Yohanan holds for him, then re-enters the Holy of Holies to spatter the blood of the bull. Life resides in blood. Life negates death.

❧

The high priest has drained the blood of the bull, according to the Law, in repentance for his personal sins. Later, Kayafa executes the goat for the Lord, the one with the cord around its neck, in repentance for the collective sins of Israel. With the mingled blood of bull and goat, he smears the horns of the altar—horns that belong neither to bull nor to goat but resemble both. Priests attach pulleys and ropes to the front hooves of the dead beasts and hoist the two carcasses, drained of blood, into the air. Kayafa slices open their abdomens and carves away the fat, which will burn on the altar of the Lord. Spreading his right palm on the forehead of the goat for Azazel, Kayafa proclaims, "You are to carry the sins of Israel into the wilderness, to the leader of the

Watchers, Azazel. That is your holy mission." He removes the red cord from its horns.

❧

As the brass sun plunges toward the horizon, the Levitical choir stands in twelve rows along the perimeter of the Courtyard of the Priests. Their beards square-cut, their heads wrapped, they chant in one sonorous voice. Harps, cymbals, and flutes accompany their melody, which undulates and twists as if ascending mountain paths, pleading to divine Messengers.

Yohanan leads the Goat of Azazel into the Plaza of the Israelites. The crowd parts, recoiling from the sin-filled ibex. Some curse or spit upon it; others, holding short whips, flog it. Its head bowed, the scapegoat hesitates. As Yohanan tugs on the rope, a man kneels, buries his head in the goat's fur, and lays his hands on its flanks. Yohanan recognizes him as the zealot Saul, who dragged Stefanos before the Sanhedrin. He wants to seize him by the scruff of his neck, as this man seized Stefanos. He wants him to admit he wronged Stefanos, tragically. He wants this man to suffer for Stefanos's death. On this most holy of days, however, he knows better than to act upon his hatred. The man, Saul, raises his cerulean eyes, searches those of the young man who challenged him in the Royal Colonnade, and looks down.

"Forgive me, Lord," the man cries, palms outstretched. "Forgive me!"

Yohanan yanks the goat away. Saul may be sincere in his repentance but it is too late. Stefanos is dead.

❧

Yohanan and the goat advance through the throng of awed worshipers, through the towering Nicanor gate, through the Gate of Song, and into the avenues of the Upper City. They pass Mariamne's tower and Herod's palace, the great marketplace and the Roman theater with its three tiers of arches. The young man leads the goat through the narrow, winding paths of the lower city. Everywhere the hushed ocean of penitents parts to let them proceed, as if they were royalty, members of a social-military class they abhor.

Yohanan and the Goat of Azazel pass the pool of Siloam, exit Jerusalem, and advance into the chalk-white terraced hills, studded with olive trees, that fringe the city. As he progresses farther from the Temple and Jerusalem, Yohanan tastes a hint of freedom in the air and feels a burden slipping away.

In the stifling heat they travel south. The trees thin and the land descends toward an immense, craggy pit, the deepest and widest in the world, which the setting sun striates in hues of copper and straw. Every thousand steps they pass a priest who holds a red flag similar to the one belted to Yohanan's tunic.

Occasionally, in bewildered bleatings, the Goat of Azazel gives voice to disquietude. Yohanan answers him: "To be called upon to carry off the burden of Israel, to be our salvation, is that not the greatest honor, little goat? Bring our troubles to Azazel with this greeting: 'To you who gave mankind the instruments of power, war and beauty, mankind returns a year's harvest of sin.'"

They reach their destination, a cliff overlooking the vast scalded desert of Duda-El. At its base yawns a chasm so deep no one has ventured to its bottom except in death. The goat backs away. Yohanan sets his hands on its rump and as the goat's tail swishes, gives it a shove. Braying, the goat sets its front hooves into the flinty soil. Yohanan pushes harder. The goat loses its grip and tumbles with rocks into the cleft.

Yohanan catches his breath and steps back from the edge, queasy, as if he were toppling with the goat and whirling into the darkness below. He looks toward the light at the mouth of the tunnel, searching for Stefanos's hand.

He pulls the red flag from his scabbard and waves it in the air; a priest, a thousand paces away, raises his own flag in turn. A thousand paces further, the next priest brandishes his, and so forth all the way back to the Temple at the summit of Jerusalem.

Although he is far from Jerusalem, Yohanan knows from prior experience what will happen there. When the last priest brandishes his flag and people receive word that the Goat of Azazel has departed bearing their sins, they will break into cheers throughout the city. The sun, sinking beyond the western hills, will cast its soft rays on the Temple's silver and gold vestments and a new year, filled with renewed hope, will begin.

Out here in the desert, though, Yohanan hears no forgiveness, no rejoicing, only the low howl of the wind. He gazes back toward Jerusalem and forward to the sandy horizon. His heart tells him to return home. His mind asks: *Where is home?* His father and Kayafa have both proven themselves unworthy of his loyalty; his mother wanders amid the shadows of Sheol. Either he has no home or all the land is his home, and his heavenly Father his only guardian.

People who are governed by their hearts alone often make reprehensible decisions, he muses. *Men fall in love with foreign women, abandoning their wives and children. Those who adhere only to the precepts of reason or scholarship, however, lose their ability to hear the whisperings of Messengers, remember their dreams, or fall in love. Priests resort to violence to protect what they regard as their powers, as if they owned those powers—the responsibilities vested in them not for their own good but for that of their land and all nations.*

Again Yohanan looks back toward the Temple and then to the desolation of the parched, cracked, rust-and-chalk-streaked desert that lies ahead. Leaving Jerusalem would mean abandoning the mission his parents bequeathed to him, perhaps inadvertently, when they named him after his uncle: the privilege of guarding the Temple Treasure.

Or would it? There is no more Treasure. The Prefect Valerius Gratus stole it. Or perhaps there is one, but it is not gold and it does not reside in the Temple.

"Father, where are you? Are you blind to what is happening in our land, in your Holy Name? Where are your Messengers?"

In the dry wind Yohanan hears an echo of Stefanos's last words, *Thank you, brother.* And he walks away from Jerusalem, a lump in his throat, tears in his eyes.

In the depth of the chasm, the Goat of Azazel is first aware only of darkness and a distant sound of dripping water but then feels a presence, strong, cool and embracing. This presence is me, the fallen Messenger Azazel.

"I was expecting you, little goat," I tell him.

The goat blinks.

"I have spent a thousand years in this hole reflecting on my predicament, on the human condition, and on the Lord," I resume.

The goat steps backward.

"For all these years I have been a Messenger without a listener," I continue, "a communicator without an audience. I once possessed a body and yearn to own one again. Why? I would use it, this time, for the advancement not of knowledge but of innocence. In this endeavor, you can perhaps be of assistance."

The goat shuffles.

"You do not have a clue what I am talking about, do you, little goat? Or even who I am, or where I came from?"

The goat blinks, waiting. And so I begin.

❧

Because the Lord does not belong to the created universe, It fashioned intermediaries, Messengers that were neither men nor gods.

We are called Messengers because our mission is to convey information between mortals within the sublunary sphere, between humans and the Messengers who inhabit the lower celestial spheres, and between those Messengers and others who dwell in the higher celestial spheres.

How do we transmit information from one realm to the other, from the celestial to the terrestrial and back? It is like reshaping the prancing, round timbre of King David's lyre into the sweet, rich savor of a plum held by the woman he craves, Bathsheba. Even the task of sharing information between human minds and cultures, entirely within the terrestrial habitat, can be daunting. Yet this is our purpose, our fundamental urge.

We are not alone in yearning to transmit messages. Communication in any form, whether through caresses, glances, written words, or spoken prayers, is the purpose of all beings. What makes us different is that we communicate vertically, from the heavens to the earth and back again, as well as horizontally, among the created.

Often we speak to mortals through dreams or natural phenomena like falling stars. Occasionally we have no choice but to engage mortals directly. Messengers with flaming swords guard the portals of terrestrial paradise; others warn Lot prior to the destruction of Sodom and Gomorrah; a Messenger instructs Abraham not to sacrifice his son; another appears in a burning bush to deliver to Moses his historic mission.

The Lord divided Its Messengers into groups and tasked my unit with watching over mortals. It called us Watchers. We discovered, however, that the essence of humanity was *feeling*. We wanted to look not just at the outsides of people's homes but inside their lives, their stories. To observe humans, we Watchers had to experience the world as humans did, through the filter of emotion. Our sense of compassion deepened and we saw the beauty of mortal women as if through men's eyes. We fell in love. I even took it upon myself to help mortals improve their condition by providing them with tools to enhance their beauty and power, with tools of adornment and weapons of war.

This is how men and women diverged from their animal companions. In the wake of the transformation, rape and war—the perils of mortal power—swept across the earth. Our progeny devoured flesh and drank blood.

The earth bewailed this lawlessness. The Lord heard the earth's lament and unleashed floods to cleanse and renew the world, sparing one couple from each species as well as a human named Noah, his wife Emzarah, and their children.

To punish me for my ill-deed of compassion, the Lord banished me to this crevasse. In Its infinite charity, however, It allowed me to retain one power—a window, a way out—the ability to show mercy. For eight hundred years I ignored this window, fuming and raging, insisting I had acted in a spirit of magnanimity. I had sacrificed everything to offer mankind a taste of celestial power, the thrill of heaven. As the centuries passed, though, my agitation abated and I began to turn my attention to the world beyond my fury.

When you dwell at the blind end of a stone sack for a thousand years, subtle fluctuations in the degree of obscurity, from onyx to jet, become your entire spectrum. Often I have wondered: from where do they arise, these nearly imperceptible shifts? No glimmer of sunlight penetrates the depths of this pit. My faculty of vision, I decided, must be deluding me.

You grow familiar, dwelling here, with the texture of every surface within your reach, miniscule outcroppings and striations, rough patches of hard granite, smooth quartz, crumbly sandstone. The smallest alteration—the tumble of a pebble, the hundred-year creep of a half-inch patch of lichen—is a noteworthy event. A distant sound from the realm of mortals, the remote screech of a bird of prey, a whine of wind, is a voice calling you, reminding you of something you long ago determined to forget.

During the last two hundred years I have come to view my antediluvian rogueries in a different light. No, *light* is too strong a word: in a different degree of obscurity. My motive mattered not a whit to the Lord. What mattered was my act. To defy the Lord was to challenge the Law of the universe, to replace Creation, which is order, with *tohu v'bohu*, the sheer and utter chaos that preceded Creation. The Lord had fashioned mankind to be ignorant and content. First Sama-El, a Messenger in the form of a serpent, betrayed It in the Garden and then we, the Watchers, completed the perfidy. A race of giants, the *Nephilim*, the spawn of Messengers like me and mortal women, allowed their anger and lust to trample all remaining barriers.

And so I began my period of *t'shuva*, of turning toward purity. I prayed for forgiveness, for an opportunity to exchange immortality for reparation. I do not despair. I retain the ability to perceive the future as well as the past. You see, we Messengers, beings of heaven and earth, experience time both sequentially like mortals and from without, like the Lord. Visualize a moment as a teardrop suspended in the rarefied atmosphere of eternity. Now step back and picture a string of such lachrymal pearls curving, swooping, zig-zagging through others, vibrating and shimmering in the cosmic breeze. This tortuous concatenation of fragmentary experience is your life.

You slip along unconscious of destiny, one bead at a time, your mind looming these instants, culled from daylight and dreams, into a narrative that you call your self. The teardrops you pass remain after you move on. Now step back even further. Fill a universe with similar tracks, a vast, dense mist—all the moments in the lives of every being that has ever breathed or ever will.

We Messengers do not see all these trajectories in all their aspects. Only the Lord sees everything at once. Our vision is monochromatic but filled with shades. The darkness of Duda-El is merely one end of our spectrum.

This chasm is my palace. When the Lord condemned me It implicitly granted me the right, little goat, to delay your entrance. Not forever, but for as long as necessary to advance the celestial program. You have a role to play and now is the moment.

My humble request? That you obtain a mortal sheath that I can occupy, so that I may once again crawl, lumber, prance, and leap aboveground, no longer immortal perhaps but pure of heart, with the sole purpose of healing this despoiled land.

You see, little goat, I perceive the pattern traced by your life as a spiral. Enjoy your respite from causality, aging, and death until the day when a man once again leads you up the great stairway to the Temple of Jerusalem. Do not forget, however, that that day will come and when it does, you are to return here before sunset, for you will have fulfilled your duty to the Lord.

❧

The Goat of Azazel finds itself again on the cliff top. Although the night is dark, it knows where it is and steps away from the edge. Its ears flop as it shakes its head. The Goat gazes at the stars and the empty desert and thinks of home. A Man raised, fed, and cared for it. It has never foraged or wandered in wilderness. It knows, however, that hyenas and leopards prowl these plateaus. It was born with this knowledge, instilled by the Lord.

The Man brought his beloved goat to the Temple as an offering, a product of his labor, just as other farmers offered grain, wine, and olive oil. "In days of old," the Man explained during their pilgrimage from Yotapata, as they lay side by side under the stars, "men offered their children. You are taking the place of my son. It is because I love you that I offer you. If I did not love you, my offering would mean nothing.

That is why the Temple does not accept wild animals, but only grain, fruit, and animals that a man has raised with his hands and heart, and coin that he has earned with his sweat."

Despite the horrors it witnessed at the Temple, the Goat of Azazel yearns to find the Man or another who can provide an equal measure of love. And so the Goat begins its journey back toward the Galilee. On the way it will have to scamper over cliffs, hide in crevices, and find leaves to eat and water to drink.

In the fourth year of the reign of the emperor Tiberius Claudius Caesar Augustus Germanicus—known as Claudius, also known as Caesar—Aislin and Septimus enter the pulsing heart of the world's capital. She has never before seen such densely packed buildings, noisy, congested streets and plazas, foreigners in rags, prostitutes, or slaves pushing their way through the throng, bearing magnates on gilt litters. Vendors hawk amphorae of wine and olive oil, sulfur matches, hot sausages, and pork pies. Money changers trade Roman *aeses* and *sesterces* for foreign coins, hides, and urns of oil. Barbers' clients discuss news and weather while waiting to be shaved. Beggars abound. A boy whose mangled arm hangs limp at his side reaches out with his other as if to gather money from the air. Another juggles wooden balls, imploring Aislin with his eyes. A one-legged man sits on a wooden cart.

Septimus leads her along the Via Flaminia to a wide plaza, the *Campus Martius* or Field of War. "The Temple of the Divine Augustus," Septimus tells her, pausing.

"And who is that?" asks Aislin.

"Our first emperor, a son of the gods and a God himself," Septimus explains, "recognized to this day as Savior of the World. This place, Aislin, is the very heart of Rome. If you do not understand it, you cannot understand our world."

The succulent aroma of roasting pig wafts from a monument in the center of the plaza where priests are offering sacrifices, Septimus explains. Its sculpted walls depict luxuriant plants and animals, scenes of ritual sacrifice, and processions of cloaked men. "This frieze shows the fertility and peace of our era, the last age before the cosmos destroys itself and history begins anew. And this is our Goddess, Roma."

"Why is Roma lying on a heap of weapons?" Aislin asks.

"Because war is the foundation of empire and peace. Life depends upon death, just as the gods require our sacrifices. That's why this temple, the Altar of Peace, rises from the Field of War."

Aislin is uncomfortably aware that despite all that has happened to him, and to her, Septimus remains proud of his Roman identity. "Let us go," she urges him. This place makes her uneasy.

They enter smaller paths and byways. Bronze gods guard dense neighborhoods, where laundry flaps on ropes that span the streets. Homeless families sleep on stone pavers.

"Stay close," Septimus warns Aislin as they trudge up a steep incline between towering, crumbling apartment blocks. Workers hammer, saw, and chisel on edifices half-built or half-rebuilt following collapse or fire. The entire city seems not so much a *thing* as a *process*, inventing, destroying, and reinventing itself all at once.

The immensity and exuberance of Rome appall Aislin. She wonders how she alone, even given a lifetime, could despoil what thousands have constructed over hundreds of years. Yet she clings to the hope of returning to Rome the treatment it has bestowed upon her village. *Dìoghaltas.*

The two journey through a quiet quarter of private residences and cross through leafy parks and sacred woods. The home Septimus shared with his wife, Psyche, occupies most of the first floor of a large building, with a shop front that serves food. When the *taberna* owner sees Septimus, he covers his eyes and mutters an imprecation. A baby wails. A rat scurries along the base of the oil-stained wall.

Pilasters frame the double doors of Septimus's home. Inside, they remove their sandals and proceed down a narrow corridor over mosaic floors, past marble walls decorated with statues and altars lit by iron bowls, to a windowless room where Septimus's wife sits on a stone bench, reading to a little girl. As Septimus moves closer, his wife looks at him as if at a stranger and grips her daughter's hand. Her eyes dart to Aislin, who stands in a shadowed area at the end of the corridor watching them.

It seems to Aislin that she has walked into a strange dream, a place different from any other. Septimus has ushered her into the inner chamber of his heart, a palace of marble and echoes, a magnificent, cold tomb.

Smiling gently, Septimus kneels before his daughter, reaching out to touch her hair. The little girl recoils. "Do you know who I am, little one?" he asks her.

She stares blankly, bringing her thumb to her mouth and clutching her mother's robe.

"I can only imagine what you have heard," Septimus tells his wife. "I am not a phantasm."

"Vibius!" Psyche cries. A stocky man in dark linen emerges from the hallway, his bald spot painted with lamp-black. Psyche rises and her fingers seek his.

Vibius studies Septimus's face and attire. "We understood you were dead," he says. "You should leave."

Septimus turns to his daughter and brushes a black lock off her shoulder. She cowers.

"You are certainly in danger. For your own sake," Vibius urges him, "you must go."

Septimus rises and turns to leave, Aislin at his side. The woman who used to be his wife watches him exit.

They walk wordlessly to a park. Beneath a statue of Priapus, Septimus sits, his head in his hands. Sensing his despondency, Aislin wraps an arm around his waist. He reaches up and clutches her hand.

❧

Two hours later, a servant leads them through an expansive home on the Caelian Hill. The cool breeze, chirping sparrows, and exquisite murals conspire to weave an illusion of otherworldly pleasure. Slender vine-laced columns surround the garden where Septimus's sister, Poppaea, sits under a fig tree while servants attend to her makeup and hair.

The slave announces the guests. Poppaea's amber eyes wander over their faces and pilfered tunics like a gallfly crawling on excrement. Though only a few months younger than Aislin, at sixteen, Poppaea seems to her a girl dressed up as a woman.

"Oh, but my eyes surely deceive me!" Poppaea exclaims. She sets her copper mirror aside, rises, and embraces her brother, careful not to smudge her rouged cheeks or crush her citrus-oiled ringlets. She contemplates Aislin's shorn hair and soiled tunic. Her lips set into a thin smile, she turns back to her brother.

"So you have married, and well," observes Septimus. "Belated felicitations, sister."

"My husband's a brute, dear brother. But tell me, what of the reports?

I sacrificed a juicy hog to Pluto and here you are, all the way back from the underworld, a little—how shall I say? darkened?—but no less wizened."

"Pluto?" Septimus chuckles. "I've not yet had the pleasure of making that god's acquaintance."

Poppaea imperiously instructs the slaves to serve "something for our guests to gnaw on." Aislin's Latin is now sufficiently fluent that she understands the connotations of *rodere*, to gnaw in the manner of rats.

"I cannot stay in Rome," Septimus tells her, "but I wanted to visit with you, at least briefly."

"Don't be absurd. Where would you go? You must be famished. Come." Poppaea slings her arm around her brother's waist and escorts them to a semicircular room, adorned with frescoes, where slaves have laid out food.

Aislin finds the food strange and Poppaea's refusal to acknowledge her presence disconcerting. While Septimus takes unabashed pleasure in the roasted quail and figs, his sister relates the latest gossip of Roman society. "To them I am nothing but the wife of a captain of the Praetorian Guard, who is the son of a fishmonger in Egypt, a fact that does not prevent them from drooling."

"Their drool, your gain," remarks Septimus between mouthfuls.

"I am trying to be clever about that." Poppaea licks her fingers.

Midway through their meal, she calls for an ancient slave-woman, who approaches and leans down so Poppaea can whisper in her ear. The elderly slave nods, turns to Aislin, and motions for her to follow. Aislin glances at Septimus, who continues chatting with his sister, providing an ear for her vanity and grievances.

ॐ

The slave escorts Aislin to the street and bolts the gate. Aislin sits on a sun-warmed boulder, waiting for Septimus. Below, tiled roofs stretch in an urban maze all the way to the Forum. The Tiber River snakes its way through the city, gleaming in the late-afternoon sun. Aware that this capital, with all its pilfered wealth, is built upon a substrate of violence and vice, Aislin wonders how it can appear so alluring. Like Poppaea's home, Rome is an elaborate deception.

While the capital offers its high-ranking citizens pleasures and comforts beyond anything the villagers of Albion could have imagined, Aislin refuses to be seduced by its magnificence. Rome does not belong to her, nor does she belong to Rome. Her heart aches with loneliness and resentment. Septimus is a Roman who has returned to the fold, and sadness is her just reward for trusting him.

A rooster crows nearby. A buxom slave, hobbling up the street, peers at her and enters a gated property. Children laugh and shout in a court-yard. Aislin glances again at the gate of Poppaea's residence.

☙

Poppaea leads her brother to a windowless room and commands a servant to install a hay-filled mattress. "Why don't you rest? You just crossed half the empire. You've been scavenging with barbarians, my poor brother."

"Where is Aislin?" asks Septimus.

"Perhaps she decided to explore the city. She'll find a place for herself. She's just one of so many, brother. They all find their way eventually, do they not?"

Septimus turns away from her and steps outside. He walks to a van-tage point that offers a panoramic view of the city. Aislin is nowhere in sight. He calls out. He wanders a little farther, into an alley, past a gate.

He has stepped into a familiar garden filled with shrubbery and hidden paths. The enchanted playground of his childhood is now overgrown and unweeded, the vines and flowers ordinary, their colors faded, the footpaths insipid.

He hurries through side streets and down the Caelian Hill, calling Aislin. As a *peregrinus*, a subject of the empire but a non-citizen of Rome, she will not be entitled to the daily portion of ground millet that the state offers every citizen, the principal nourishment of Rome's ubiquitous paupers, nor does she possess coins to buy food.

Septimus and Aislin traveled together for more than a year. Their daily struggles resolved into a feeling of kinship, stronger now than the bond he shares with Poppaea. Longing to unwrap this tangle of sentiments, he wanders through the city. He hopes not only to find her but to flee his own diminished stature.

His choice is daunting, to meander through the cold streets of Rome as a specter, or to bow and scrape to his sister's whims in the ostentatious theater that is her domicile. On the one hand, free will with no certainty of survival; on the other, luxury with no power.

He rambles through the city well after nightfall searching for Aislin. Rome has not changed—the grandeur, the squalor—but the forests of Britannia transformed Septimus, he realizes. He slumps to the ground beside a stone bench in the *Horti Agrippae,* a public garden in the Field of Mars, and falls asleep like a man without a home, a rootless wanderer.

He awakes halfway through the night. A drunk somewhere chants of *eros* and dissipation. Septimus looks up at the stars, the same spray of emerald dust that hovers above Britannia. He recalls a moonless night spent with Aislin, perhaps two weeks after he met her, the first time she allowed him to sleep near her. They lay in a field by a river. She had learned a few words of Latin—*bear, wild boar, fire, river,* the names of gods of trees and shrubs. She pointed to the stars, tracing constellations he could not see.

For the first time he wonders who is right, Rome or Britannia? Which constellations are real and which illusory? For the first time he admits to himself that he will most likely never see Aislin again, that her absence will remain with him like a missing limb.

He returns to Poppaea's home the following afternoon, only to find his sister splayed against a wall in the atrium, naked and moaning as a muscular, dark-skinned man pumps her, his buttocks rhythmically tightening and relaxing like a bellows. Their clothes lie on the mosaic floor, his breast-plates and high-laced sandals strewn among her diaphanous wraps.

Septimus hastens to the peristyle, which although open to the sky, reeks of oil paint. An old man squats before a wall fresco, touching it up. His mural offers a glimpse into a half-built universe, or a half-decayed one. Ladders in the air lean against incomplete towers. Spider-like creatures dance across filaments dangling from narrow poles. Faces float, grimacing, guffawing, or observing in wonder the realm outside, where Septimus watches, spellbound. Floral motifs adorn the ionic-columned frame that separates the two worlds. Septimus admires the artist's delicate, precise strokes, the hard-to-place, subtly dappled background, and the luster he achieves using a blend of linseed oil and egg yolks.

The man turns to him. "You must be the new slave." The painter wipes his hands on his stained apron. "*Domina* has asked me to train you."

"I am afraid you are mistaken," says Septimus. "I am no slave. I am *Domina*'s brother."

The artist scratches his head and resumes his work.

Poppaea enters, tying her gown. "This is my home. I do as I please." Her flushed face radiates contentment. "You used to love drawing, Septimus. Leontis is the most talented fresco painter in Rome. You should regard his instruction as a privilege." Gesturing toward an empty wall-niche, she says, "Leontis, I want a portrait there. A nude Diana in my likeness."

"I shall be pleased to do so, *Domina*, assuming you can find the time to pose."

"For you, Leontis, always." Poppaea turns to her brother. "As for you, Septimus, you are free to leave and fend for yourself, if that is your preference."

❧

Septimus's mother discouraged her son's interest in drawing. Such occupations were meant for slaves, not the son of an eminent politician. Now that he is legally dead and without inheritance, he has only himself to please and the following morning he accepts Leontis's offer.

Leontis teaches him to mix paints from powdered lapis lazuli, rust, bones, and ground-up beetles; how to mix and apply linseed oil and egg yolks to add luster; how to fashion brushes out of twigs, twine, and squirrel fur; and how to prime walls with wet lime and marble powder.

While rambling through Rome in search of materials, he looks for Aislin. He wonders whether she can survive the brutality of the Roman street. One morning, finding himself near the spolarium, where cadavers are sorted, he decides to check inside. It is a cavernous, domed building, the interior one undivided room lit and ventilated by circular oculae in the ceiling. Bodies from all over Rome arrive by the cartload.

The scene inside belongs to the underworld. Hundreds of slaves in bloody tunics kneel to slit corpses' throats, strip them of garments and valuables, and route them to their final destinations. As in a public latrine, water flows through channels in the floor to wash away the blood.

An official leads visitors through the processing area. "Let me explain our operation. This will help you find the bodies of those who were dear to you." The official gestures toward one group of corpses and then another. "We separate them according to function, social class, and means of death. Gladiators," he points, "diverse pagans," he points, "victims of murder, the poor, the wealthy. Be careful here," he tells a bejeweled lady taking her hand, "we wouldn't want to stain your lovely *stola*. These are fed to dogs, useful in training them for war. Those, over there, are dumped in great pits. The criminals, that line, we expose for public instruction." He waves toward the last row, the aristocrats. "The most worthy we cremate, to liberate their souls."

Septimus wanders through aisles of naked bodies, many half-rotted or bloated and pale, fished from the river; some unrecognizable. It would take hours or days to examine them all. He asks the official whether any of the workers has seen a woman with wheat-colored short hair in the style of a boy and a tattoo on her arm, a green swirl with red dots.

The official glances at Septimus's tunic, the garb of a slave, and replies: "As you see, this is a busy workplace." He shrugs. "I may well have seen her. I may not have. Viewing time is up, I'm afraid."

Discouraged and queasy, Septimus climbs into the sunshine, only to discover that Rome itself now resembles a vast spolarium, an antechamber of Hades.

☙

One night, two months later, his sister wakes him, drunk and disheveled. "Septimus," she whispers, "Septimus, my brother, whom I always so admired. I am in love."

He opens his eyes.

"With Marcus Domitius Ahenobarbus," she enunciates, delighting in the individual syllables that together, like notches of a cricket's leg, form one elegant utterance.

"You're not in love with the emperor's great-nephew," Septimus tells her. The man is ugly and perverse; all Rome knows that. "Perhaps you're in love with his family or his power, but you cannot be in love with him."

She laughs. "What is a man but his station? What is identity but a reflection of others' esteem? You once knew that, brother, but I fear you've forgotten, perhaps because you no longer hold a place in society."

"Let me sleep," he mumbles, "if you value your walls."

Poppaea kisses his forehead. "Goodnight, sweet brother." She steps out.

I f *direction is a feature of the world*, Yohanan thinks, *it is hidden*. Goat paths spread like tentacles over forested hillsides and vanish into desert sands. Roads lead here and there. *As it is over land, so it is over time*, he reasons. Forward and backward seem meaningless, at least within the realm of all that can be seen and touched—the present. This sense of being adrift troubles him. *The past and future exist only in our minds and our literature, yet they are the source of all purpose. If there is to be hope, it must spring from the soil of history. The strongest hopes will have the deepest roots.*

He must look beyond the world of his father to the world of his father's fathers, past disappointment to the stories that imbued their lives with purpose. Their universe was not randomly devised and disordered. It was created. It was evolving.

Yohanan's eyes have deepened; his cheeks have hollowed; his skin has darkened. His feet pace through the courses of his people's memory like a reader's fingers sliding beneath words in a parchment. The earth, a mud and stone scroll that can never be read to the end, holds countless narratives, the legends of his people, the memories that *are* his people.

He quenches his thirst at the well where Hagar, the mother of Ishmael, encountered a Messenger, who announced her child's birth. He listens to a goat herder pipe a melody in the field where a scrawny, nervous shepherd boy stepped out on a misty morning to fight the warrior giant Goliath. He floats in the Sea of Sodom, his eyes closed, and visualizes cities burning on its shore. He climbs Mount Nebo to view the land as his nation's liberator first saw it, stark hills roasting under a sky of radiant sapphire. He meets farmers and craftsmen reduced from poverty to abject misery by Roman taxes and Temple tithes. He crosses paths with ragged beggars, hears whisperings of revolt, and meets scholars who preach a faith built of nostalgia and hope—for there seems little to celebrate in the present age. When he has bread, he shares it with those who have none, even though doing so makes him feel like a man spitting into a reservoir to increase his city's water supply. When he sees a peasant weeping by the road he sits down with her. Such despair reminds him of steam rising from a mineral spring; it cannot be contained.

He joins festivities in a village square. For one afternoon, the world exults. But when the music dies he again faces loneliness. He seeks comfort in conversations with the ancients. Phrases, entire chapters and books that he found in the Temple library, resonate in his mind.

> *Upon my bed at night I sought him whom my soul loves.*
> *I sought him, but found him not.*
> *I called him, but he gave no answer.*
> *I will rise now and go about the city,*
> *in the streets and in the squares.*
> *I will seek him whom my soul loves.*

🙙

He enters the broad valley of the Galilee with its cobalt sky and grassy hills, dotted with forget-me-nots, flame-red poppies, and wild roses. The Sea of Galilee sparkles in the distance. In Arav, the village of his father's youth, a girl takes Yohanan by the hand and leads him to the mud-brick home of his aunt and uncle, larger than his family's residence in Jerusalem, with chickens in front and two goats in a side garden. His aunt embraces him as if she has known him for years. The family runs in, barefoot, from surrounding rooms while his aunt places roasted barley, warm sheep's milk, and dried fruit on a low table. They speak in Galilean accents of Jerusalem, the Temple, and Yohanan's father, Zakkai: his childhood, his fortunes in the capital, his travels. The long-haired children, in dirty tunics, laugh and hug Yohanan at their parents' command, as if the differences between them meant nothing; all that matters is kinship. Overwhelmed by their welcome, Yohanan sits on the straw-covered dirt floor reflecting upon his father's life.

When he speaks of Zakkai's disappearance, however, his uncle turns serious. "It is not the first time my brother has fled," Zakkai's brother reflects, running a hand wearily over his bald scalp.

To Yohanan's recollections, he adds his own. Alone among his siblings, Zakkai took it upon himself to learn to read and write. In early adulthood he left home, trading the familiar territory of the Galilee and the comforts of kinship for life in the capital. Was Zakkai driven by ambition? A desire to be near the Temple? Was he unhappy in the Galilee?

When Yohanan speaks of his own education in the Temple, and of his disillusionment there, his cousins are puzzled. "What could be impure about the Temple?" they ask. "Is the Temple not the holiest place on earth?"

"I suppose that depends upon what you mean by *holy*," Yohanan replies cautiously. He does not want to rob them of hope, or of ideals, but he also refuses to deceive them or nourish their self-deception.

Yohanan's uncle lowers his hands to the table, leans upon them, cocks his head, and squints at his nephew—a posture that uncannily reminds Yohanan of his father, Zakkai. "Even if I cannot find words that can explain *holiness*," he tells his nephew, "every good person knows what it means."

"My father taught me that holiness is to be approached through the mind, through study and contemplation," Yohanan says.

"Yes, that is what Zakkai believes," his aunt agrees. "For us, holiness comes not through knowledge but through love."

Love, for Yohanan's kin in the Galilee, is neither earned nor qualified, but is the birthright of every member of one's *mishpakhah* or extended family. It results not from values or behaviors but from heritage, a shared region of history. Although these ideas are foreign to Yohanan he finds beauty and consolation in them.

"Is there a synagogue in Arav?" he asks them.

"What is a synagogue?" his uncle replies.

"A Greek word," says Yohanan. "It means *community meeting place*."

His uncle laughs and shakes his head, smiling, as if wondering, *Greek? Why would my nephew speak Greek?*

Yohanan eats well that afternoon, a simple repast of grains, sheep's milk, and dates. He laughs with his *mishpakha* and plays silly games with his younger cousins. Before bedtime, his uncle takes him aside. "You have come for your inheritance." He hands him a small leather box. Inside, there is enough silver to last a man a few cycles of the moon. "I am sorry it is not more," his uncle adds.

Yohanan looks him in the eyes and smiles. "You need not worry," he assures him. "It is much more."

❧

The love poem that Yohanan committed to memory in the Temple yearns to become incarnate again, to flow out from his mind and through his fingertips onto parchment so that it may be absorbed through others' eyes down through the generations to come. In search of ink, a writing implement, and skin, he walks to the market in Arav, a packed dirt square bounded by olive-brown, beige, and yellow walls and archways. Linen sheets, striped black, white, and blue, stretch over wooden poles, forming triangular and quadrilateral booths. Rugs, pheasants, and lengths of cloth dangle from overhead ropes. Bags of seeds, terracotta bowls, and jugs cover the ground outside vendors' stalls. Chickens and geese cluck and squawk. Marketeers call to passersby: "Candles! Oil! Tasty almonds, plump figs, sweet dates!" Shoppers jostle one another, chat in clusters, and haggle. A walnut dealer points Yohanan to the booth of a winemaker. "Hanina will have what you need."

A compact man with wide shoulders, a broad nose, and curly, graying hair sits in a booth, his lips moving as he reads. Rows of amphorae line the booth behind him, while smaller jars crowd the shelves.

"It is the story of Pinkhas," Hanina replies when Yohanan asks about his scroll. "Do you know of it?"

The mention of *Pinkhas* jolts Yohanan's memory. "A strange and difficult text," he remarks. "Did you notice this?" He points. "There's a broken *vav* in the word *shalom*, when the Lord confers upon Pinkhas his *covenant of peace*. Every time I come across this passage, I search for this word, and every time, this letter has been copied precisely in this manner—broken, like a man hobbling with a walking stick."

"An imperfect letter in a holy text! How about that?" Hanina exclaims. "And in every copy? How can it be?" He smiles broadly, evidently delighted with Yohanan's discovery.

❧

Hanina, son of Dosa, lives with his wife, Shoshana, and their helper, Shlomo, in a stone hut surrounded with vines, where sunlight and warm breezes drift through open windows and doors. There they break bread and discuss the past and the future.

"You have been wandering for years, Yohanan, son of Zakkai. What is it you are seeking?"

"I left the Temple in search of authenticity," Yohanan replies, "but now I seek engagement. A woman. A child or two. A stable life. What do I want? What everyone wants."

Hanina laughs, the hearty guffaw of a man who delights in sharing his enthusiasm. "Your path mirrors mine, Yohanan. I, too, lost my father in childhood. A tax collector strangled him. We had to sell much of our property to repay his debts. This caused me to despise Roman silver and the struggle for standing in the world of men and to seek answers in the Holy Scrolls. Now, though, I wish to produce the best wine I can and to sell it at an advantageous price. Advantageous to me, that is." He grins. "Men like you and me, Yohanan, it takes us years of study and disappointment to learn what others already know."

Despite Hanina's established network of cousins and friends who purchase his wine, he has not fared well in the village marketplace.

"Shoshana, Shlomo, and I can only do so much." Hanina pats his elderly assistant's shoulder. "Shlomo used to be a brilliant scholar, before a man attacked him over a difference of textual interpretation—in *Pinkhas*, as a matter of fact. Since that day, he does not remember much, and can no longer read."

"That is true," confirms Shlomo, spittle bubbling on his lips. "I can no longer tell the difference between what comes before and what comes after. I cannot tell *Noah* from *Grace*."

Yohanan smiles, knowing that the name of the patriarch Noah, spelled with the letters *nun-khet*, means "Grace" when spelled backward, *khet-nun*. "Perhaps there is meaning in your confusion," he consoles Shlomo.

"Of course," says Hanina. "Noah, the man of righteousness, is spared not by virtue but by the Lord's grace."

Shlomo nods, as if that was what he meant all along.

"Shlomo may not be quite himself anymore," says Shoshana. "But we love him like a brother."

༒

Hanina teaches Yohanan to plant and nurture vines and cull their fruit into mule bags in the summer dawn. They empty their sacks of grapes into a stone basin, large enough to hold six men, adding apples and sprigs of galbanum. Barefoot, they tread upon the cushion of soft fruit, their feet sinking, their calves and thighs purpling. Juice begins flowing through stone channels into collecting vats.

The transformation starts during the night. Four days thereafter, tiny bubbles emerge as if from creatures slowly releasing air. The juice ripples as if flexing its muscles. When this effervescence ceases, the wine is complete. Stored in waist-high amphorae that are coated inside with aromatic terebinth, it is unlike any other in the Galilee: sharp, biting, and cool.

"In this common transmutation lies a miracle," explains Hanina as they plug amphorae in his stone-walled storeroom. "A spirit enters the juice. When we drink, it slips into our soul. It's a benign ghost but sometimes it must be reminded of its place."

As they prepare sourdough loaves at his outdoor clay oven with yeast culled from grape skins, Hanina tells Yohanan, "A spirit also inflates our loaves before we bake them. Thus the special place of bread and wine in our Sabbath feast, which, as you know, is an invocation to benevolent Messengers. Bread and wine, unlike other foods of our feast, are transformed, and in turn, they transform us."

At night, Yohanan recreates the scroll he ruined in the Temple library. His pen atones for the sins of his eyes, his ink for his tears. Phrases he read thrice gush from memory:

I am black and comely, daughters of Jerusalem,
Black as the tents of Kedar, as the curtains of Solomon.

He also writes to his friends in the Temple, who copy and forward his thoughts to scholars in Judea and abroad, who in turn write back to Yohanan. Thus Yohanan becomes familiar, through scholarship, with men who share his passions in many lands.

Occasionally, working in the vineyard at the end of a hot summer afternoon, he sees a stranger walking up the path beside a donkey. The stranger's sandals, the hue of his skin, and the broad blue, yellow, and red stripes of his clothes place him as a foreigner.

Perhaps the donkey's bag bears a greeting from a scholar in Rome, or a comment on a comment from a citizen of Rome's eternal enemy, Persia. The missive may overflow with praise, its author expressing joy in the novel interpretation of a phrase or word, or even a character in an ancestral text. Or the note may give voice to its author's scorn, reflecting a passionate disagreement about the role of Shatan, the *adversary*, in the world; or denouncing the unholiness of a particular text. It may attempt to justify the distress of a small people, at the hands of powerful nations, as a form of redemption; or probe the deeper question: whose interpretation of suffering is more accurate, or apropos of today's circumstances—Isaiah's or Jeremiah's, Ezekiel's or Job's?

Yohanan's correspondents never refer to their spouses, children, or private lives, yet he feels a strong fraternity with them. What matters is communication itself, the flow of concepts across the surface of the world and through generations. For Yohanan, the written word seems the most precious form of love if only because it is mysterious and fragile, yet contains the essence of human experience, and transmits that essence to others, much as a perfume transmits the essence of a flower.

In these letters the most brilliant minds of his scattered nation search the words and phrases of their collective memory, known as the Tradition, for lessons regarding the human condition, with an emphasis on morality. How should people treat each other, other beings, and their world? How should such gleanings be codified into law? Yohanan thinks of this work, meditation and writing, as an extension of his soul into the world. He wishes he were able to place similar value on his physical labors in the vineyard, and on their results, but he feels powerless to compete in the cacophony of trade and boasting that is the bazaar of Arav. Entire days there pass without a customer. He is an unarmed soldier in a combat zone.

He allows his work of meditation to infiltrate the clamorous vacuum of the marketplace. Hunched over a leaf of papyrus, a small, sharpened writing stick in hand, he fails to notice the customers who approach his booth. Instead, he is walking in gardens with the Dark Lady of the *Song of Songs*, or witnessing Israelites dancing around a golden bull, or standing in the court of King David, who, weeping on Yohanan's shoulder, laments the loss of his son Absalom.

When a merchant or other resident of Arav, or of Nazareth or Capernaum, plans to travel south, word of his preparations spreads. Yohanan and others offer what they can, and the traveler carries their correspondence. He may return a month or a year later, or never.

❧

Yohanan's reputation grows. A teacher from Damascus visiting disciples in the Galilee stops at his booth in the marketplace to buy a jug of wine for the Sabbath. They discuss arcane details of the Law of Israel, an amorphous body of written and oral principles by which the Children of the Covenant distinguish their heritage of justice and worship from those of the Greeks and the Romans. When the visitor, impressed with this wine seller's knowledge, learns that he is talking with none other than Yohanan, son of Zakkai, he raises the wine seller's hand to his lips, a gesture of admiration and respect. "I read your epistles, some of them many times," he tells him.

One summer morning a woman, lean and tan, arrives in the market-place wearing a colorful tunic, a carved bracelet, and sandals. She stops near Yohanan's booth, brings her wrist to her long, tanned face, closes her eyes, and inhales. A maiden, carrying a jug of sheep's milk, notices. The woman smiles at her. "Come here." She displays her wrist. "This is a scent of healing," the woman tells the maiden, loudly enough that others can hear. "A blend of sandalwood, myrrh, and lily oil. I made this fragrance myself in a spacious, airy workshop near the shores of the Dead Sea. Do you live here in Arav? What brings you to the mar-ketplace?"

She digs in her satchel as the young woman answers.

"Try this. It will suit you. I have long experience matching people with scents." She extracts a small bottle. "We concocted this," she twists off the plug, "from citron zest and cedar oil." She applies a drop to the young woman's wrist.

The young woman smells her wrist. "It is lovely, but I'm afraid…"

"Don't worry," says the perfume vendor. "That single drop will last all day. Enjoy it and come back tomorrow for more. "I have traveled with these essences for over a year now, and they are as lively as on the day I created them. This will be the end of my path, however, as my stocks are low and I am weary."

Other women approach. She talks to each, assessing her needs and choosing fragrances suited to her complexion, eyes, and voice. One fragrance lends itself to meditation and prayer; another invites love; a third is useful in preparing for death.

By midday, her stocks are exhausted. Seeking to mark the end of her year's labors, she stops at Yohanan's booth for refreshment.

"You have an unusual way of reaching out to your audience," he tells her as he pours a cup of wine and sets out small dishes of roasted grain, goat's-milk cheese, and grapes.

"Your wine is delightful," she tells him. "Its flavor sweet and strong."

"Thank you," says Yohanan. "Unfortunately our sales are not so very strong."

She leans in. "It is not enough to have a good product. You also need a good story. Everything is a story." She asks him about Hanina's vineyard, whether the grapes are crushed in the morning or evening, about the composition of the soil, the drainage of the land, and Yohanan's scholarship. Then she carries her cup of wine into the crowd, rhapsodizing about galbanum, the rich earth of the Galilean hills, and sacred texts. She speaks to the villagers of weather and war, of children and cooking and long sunsets—all the while offering sips to the gathering crowd and weaving in the story of Hanina's wine.

❧

After morning ablutions and a meal of seeded bread dipped in vinegar and olives, Yohanan, Hanina, Shoshana, and Shlomo labor in the vineyard. In the afternoon they join stones with mortar and hang beams for a second building in a corner of Hanina's field. The evenings are spent in intoxicating discussions of literary chronicles, poetry, and law.

Shlomo entertains Yohanan with his garbled version of the Tradition, in which Babylon destroys the Temple prior to Joseph's descent into Egypt, and the Garden of Eden blossoms at the end of time. Shlomo's nonsense intrigues him.

One Sabbath eve, Shlomo speaks of *Pinkhas*'s "broken peace."

"You are referring not to a 'broken peace,'" Hanina corrects him, "but to the broken letter *vav* in the word *shalom*."

Yohanan finds meaning, though, in Shlomo's error. "It is not just a broken letter. It is a broken word. A broken idea."

The following morning Yohanan, Hanina, and Shoshana teach in the marketplace, building Arav's synagogue not of stone but of words and the peasants' hunger for knowledge. "Rabbi," asks a young woman. "We are required to travel to the Temple each year to offer a sacrifice, but I cannot leave my ailing father. What should I do?"

"For those who have no choice," says Yohanan, "study of the Tradition must take the place of sacrifice."

"On what authority do you Pharisees make such claims?" objects a man who calls himself Menakhem, son of Judas the Zealot. His thinning nutmeg hair, heftiness, and sonorous voice lend him an authority beyond his thirty years.

"Learning, as a substitute for sacrifice?" asks Yohanan. "This idea dates from the time of our exile in Babylon, when we had no Temple."

"Learning and interpretation form an endless maze, from which there is no way out," Menakhem objects. "What matters, in our time, is expelling the foreigners. If we fail, those Traditions of which you speak will be destroyed, and there will be nothing to discuss."

❧

Despite Yohanan's preconceptions, selling is not a matter of persuasion or duplicity, the perfume vendor explains. It is about spinning a melody of images and gustatory sensations, a lyrical flourish that buyers crave.

Her name is Miriam. The instability of her situation worries him. Like Yohanan, she has been roaming through the land. She has rented a small, windowless room off the marketplace but avoids spending time there, except to sleep. "I have a house of my own now," he tells her. "Hanina, Shoshana, and I built it near a fragrant orange tree. There is an extra room for you, if you would like it. Winter is approaching."

That night she accompanies him home. As they plod along the path that winds into the hills, she reveals fragments of her story. It is darker than Yohanan suspected. She rues her mistakes. Her teacher was crucified in Jerusalem. She fell in love with a foreigner and conceived a child with him. Before the child was old enough to speak, her husband stole him out of the country. She has searched for him everywhere, repenting and begging forgiveness of the Lord. Only recently has she accepted that her son is lost to her and Israel.

"When events beyond our control overwhelm us," Yohanan says, "we have little choice but to trust they serve a larger plan, a plan we may never understand."

"That is little comfort," Miriam replies.

He wishes he could wrap her in a mantle of solace. Although she smiles, Yohanan understands that the loss of her son has cast a shadow over her life. Though he navigates the multifarious words of the Tradition with ease, the heart of one mortal confounds him.

Miriam weaves grass mats. She naps under the fragrant bower of the orange tree. She cuts blossoms, grinds them with olive oil in a stone mortar, and daubs her neck with the ointment. With Hanina, Shoshana, and Shlomo, they share stories and laughter on warm Sabbath evenings.

One morning Yohanan studies her face over a meal of olives and goat's milk. "In my dream last night, you were filling a satchel with empty jars," he says. " You were going home."

"Home?" she asks.

"I pleaded with you to stay," he tells her. "I explained that your life and mine had mixed, like water and wine, no longer separable."

"Home is here," Miriam assures him, reaching for his hand.

Although she has not forgotten her mission, to avenge her people, neither has Aislin found the opportunity to fulfill it. The Roman sun has darkened her freckles. Her cheeks have lost their fullness as if manifesting the slow ebb of her spirit, her increasing solitude, the distance between her and the ruined villages of Albion. Her hair uneven and short, her tunic torn, she drifts through crowded streets and sleeps in malodorous alleys.

Her only companion is a scrawny gray cat she calls Nigellus. She first met him in a back street near the public park known as the *Horti Sallustiani*. At the time he was a mere kitten, no larger than two fists held together. A woman, cleaning her apartment by candlelight, swept him off her balcony and he scampered into a corner, not far from where Aislin was nibbling on fried anchovies, a marketplace vendor's leftovers.

She reached out. The kitten sniffed her hand and she clapped her other on his back. His little body shook as she raised his face to hers and looked into his yellow-green eyes. He hissed, spat, squirmed, and scratched her cheek. Admiring his spirit, she gave him the last morsels of her dinner and released him. He skittered away but later that night she woke to his warm body snuggling against her thigh.

❧

Much of her nourishment, Aislin steals. She runs nimbly, familiar with small footpaths and hiding places. Sometimes her pursuers catch and beat her. Other times she falls asleep hungry. Nigellus finds her as if by magic, rubs against her, and curls at her feet. Yet other times, a stranger reaches out to help. A man who sells sausages saves some for her, as does a baker of nut tarts. A little girl invites Aislin to her third-story flat for a meal of porridge and figs.

Aislin wonders how such honest, simple people can take pride in the empire that humiliated and obliterated her people. It is not that they do not know. Emperors boast of their conquests in Gallia, Germania, and Britannica. They tug vast ropes of chained warriors, braided tresses of human flesh, through the streets to vaunt their might. These slaves, who will toil in mines or fight elephants and lions in massive arenas, are the fortunate ones. The survival, however brief, of these few attests to the deaths of so many of their countrymen. Aislin wonders: *Do distant massacres matter less than near ones? Does a foreigner, who speaks an incomprehensible tongue, not suffer the same as a man or woman who converses in Latin? How can caring people cultivate such indifference?*

Sometimes, as she reflects upon the generosity of the Romans who have assisted her, these musings become intertwined and her path less clear. Would her mission of vengeance, should it ever be carried out, not inflict terrible suffering upon innocent people? The little girl and her mother, who offered her porridge and figs, were they responsible for the destruction caused by Vespasian's army? Could the sausage maker be held responsible for the death of Muirgheal? To what extent should she blame the people for the violence of its leaders?

Nigellus, meanwhile, grows into an extraordinary creature, lean and large, affectionate and vicious. He prowls, swaggers, and nudges. His yellow-green eyes catch Aislin's as he rubs against her legs. She picks him up, cradles him, and pets his belly. They gaze into each other's eyes. He raises a paw to her cheek. His purr is a deep, throbbing music, which she answers with her own, humming the tunes of her youth.

Winter wings away.
Daisies dot the dale.
Blackbirds babble.
Streams sparkle.

She holds him in her lap, retelling the stories of her childhood, tales of seekers, warriors, and lovers, of the Companions' antics and Bleiz's malice. How quaint and harmless Bleiz's escapades now seem, compared to the wickedness she has since experienced. She carries Nigellus into the park, where he scurries up tree trunks and pounces on blowing leaves. She calls him *my little one.*

Sometimes Nigellus disappears for a day or two. In the middle of the night he finds Aislin, paws her cheek, and releases a flood of guttural vocalizations, sounds he uses for only one purpose. Aislin shakes herself awake and discovers his offering, a dead bird, its head cocked to the side, a dash of blood congealing on its neck.

Or, rising early, Aislin finds a dead mouse at her feet and another convulsing in death-throes nearby. They are gray and nearly the same color as Nigellus himself, who sits watching. The dying mouse whirls in small circles, always to the left, getting nowhere. Perhaps a cat-bite to its neck has damaged its ability to move to the right. It rolls onto its back, claws the air with its tiny paws, and opens and shuts its mouth. Nigellus reaches out and gingerly paws it. On its belly, the mouse resumes chasing its tail. Only after the mouse stops moving does Nigellus commence eating.

At night, horses and carts stamp and clatter through Rome. Nigellus dashes between them, tempting fate.

❧

One morning Aislin discovers Nigellus at the roadside, his neck broken by a cart wheel, his long body stiff. In his favorite park, the *Horti Maecenati*, she locates a willow that he loved to climb. She kneels and paws at the damp soil. She sings to him. He was so young. As she lowers his corpse into the hole and caresses him one more time Aislin ponders an irreducible mystery. Big things—buildings and avenues—cannot simply disappear. How then can the largest thing of all, an oversized personality like Nigellus's or Muirgheal's, do so?

❧

On a gray afternoon Rome mourns the passing of its emperor Claudius—poisoned, it is rumored, by his wife—and lionizes the ascension of his great-nephew, stepson, and son-in-law Marcus Domitius Ahenobarbus, who now adopts the name Nero Claudius Caesar Augustus Germanicus.

A man, whose striped toga and three well-kept slaves identify him as a patrician, pushes toward the imperial procession. "Let us pass, miserable larvae! Let us pass!" His slaves try to shove the plebeians out of his way but the young emperor's zoological procession—which includes camels, bears, ostriches, and species whose names no one knows—causes the crowd to swell and tighten like the hot swirling bubble on the end of a glassblower's pole.

Although an imperial decree requires that all be present, Aislin did not plan to attend. She pays no attention to the whims of emperors. Lingering on the margins of the marketplace, she contemplates stealing a raw egg, a handful of olives, or a few salted and dried sardines. The crowd jostles her to the side of the bellowing aristocrat, whose purse catches Aislin's eye. She slips her hand within and seizes two large coins, but the horde jolts her. As she falls, her coins spill to the pavers.

"Thief!" the patrician cries, yanking her up.

Aislin kicks and screams as he hauls her down the street, cutting through the mob like the prow of a ship parting turbulent waters. In the commotion, few pay attention. No one will defend a commoner, let alone a thief, against a man of means.

Trumpets sound in the bustling street below and a courtier on a black steed cries, "All hail Emperor Nero Claudius, Son of the God Claudius, Emperor and Conqueror of the Germans!"

Hoisted aloft by slaves, who stand on the backs of elephants, the pudgy seventeen-year-old emperor seems to delight in the spectacle. He beams and sweeps his arms through the air gathering the love of the multitude. Swathed in a purple toga that only he can legally wear, crowned in laurel leaves, he has been waving and grinning all day throughout Rome, yet his performance rings like a bell resounding with overtones of sincerity and pleasure.

The patrician slips into a passageway. "You have a choice, gutter-snipe," he tells Aislin. "I can haul you before a magistrate or you can work off your debt in my home."

"What kind of choice is that?" she asks.

"The choice of your attitude," says the patrician.

"What kind of work? Who are you?"

"Call me Pallas. I recently lost a servant, about your age. Consider yourself fortunate."

"Bring me to the magistrate, then."

"Wrong answer." He slaps her, knocking her against the wall.

Aislin looks for an escape. His slaves block the passageway.

❧

Torches burn in cressets, illuminating frescoes that cover the walls in indigo and ocher. A tall slave with pale, waxy skin and ruby lips escorts Aislin to a room of plaster and wood, one of three torchlit chambers that open onto the main corridor at the front of the house. Linen togas sit piled on a wooden table near a terracotta bowl, in which peach-colored rose petals float on scented water. The slave pours her a glass of wine and invites her to drink.

The warm beverage tastes sweet, spicy, and...There is another flavor. Within moments she hovers above the ground. Thirsty, she sips again. She imbibes. She gulps.

"Remove your sandals and tunic." The slave extends his pallid hands. He has applied cimolian, a whitening cream, to his entire body. She thinks he may be a hermaphrodite, half-man, half-woman. His accent is...*slimy*, thinks Aislin. She slips off her tunic and unfastens her sandals. The slave washes her body with a towel dipped in rosewater and massages her with fragrant oil. "My master is entertaining this evening to celebrate the ascension of our new emperor. He would like for you to circulate among his guests."

The slave rubs a waxy substance into her face and neck, darkens her eyelids with kohl, and dusts her cheeks with powdered rose and poppy petals. He oils her back, buttocks, legs, and feet. Lastly, he trims her ragged, short hair, and applies fragrant oil to her scalp.

"You have such lovely hair. As blonde as sand. I'll bet men stare at you. Women, too, no?" He hands her a mirror of polished copper, and she gazes at her made-up face and hair. He drapes her in a tunic and guides her into a spacious marble-floored room.

Two bronze donkeys flank a table. Each carries baskets of food on its back: green and black olives, chunks of venison, dormice fried in oil and honey and coated with poppy seeds. Amphorae of wine and platters of breads, cheeses, and dried meat adorn the table.

Men and women lounge on sofas or wander through the rooms, holding plates of bite-size delicacies. A harpist, flutist, and drummer perform in the corner, and a wrestling match dominates the center of the room. The two fighters, long-haired and nude, grunt as they hold and twist each other, seeking positional dominance. Their muscular torsos glisten with oil.

As Aislin picks tidbits from the mule baskets she hears desperate gasping and croaking sounds. She turns to see one wrestler squirming atop the torso of the other, choking him, his erect penis thrusting toward the man's belly. Blue, gagging, the wrestler on the bottom attempts to slap his victor. An awed hush descends upon the room, broken by the jangling strings of the harp, as the man on the bottom expires with a rattling gurgle. Sweaty, panting, the victor rises to his feet. The guests break into applause. Pallas's slaves haul off the dead wrestler.

Towering over his guests, his gray-tinged hair wild, Pallas stoops to hear the patter of a man half his height, but he is looking at Aislin. She ignores him. The slave reappears at her side. "Follow me."

He leads her through several rooms, some long and rectangular, some small and square, some oval-shaped. Through porticoes, Aislin sees indoor and outdoor gardens and frescoes that resemble slabs of marble, lozenges, and circles. Others depict imaginary landscapes and detailed architectures. They reach a warm, humid room tiled in blue and yellow, with a pool at its center, the first chamber of Pallas's bath suite.

A young, dark-skinned female servant in a tight wrap, her braided hair piled high, emerges from the wings. "I am Chloe," she says in a foreign, musical accent. She steers Aislin into the pool.

"From where does this water come?" asks Aislin, who has never before experienced a warm bath.

"From under the house," says Chloe with a chuckle. "Slaves down there stoke a fire, all day and all night."

Aislin closes her eyes as Chloe washes her face, shoulders, and chest. It is the second time in one day that she has experienced cleansing, a great luxury. When she opens her eyes she sees Pallas leaning against the wall, watching. "I thank you for stealing my coins, Aislin," he says in a gentle tone. "Had you not done so, I might not have noticed you, and I certainly would have had no pretext to carry you into my house. But this is how the gods work their magic, is it not? Tell me, which savage forest produced such delectable fruit? Oh, but forgive me. I should express myself in words comprehensible to the primitive mind. Where were you born?"

"In a village," says Aislin. "Far from here."

"Tell me about that village."

Aislin describes her village, its beauty and magic and the cruelty of the Roman conquerors who eradicated it.

"Well, one thing is clear," he remarks. "Rome sickens you. Suppose, however, that I should endeavor to change your mind?"

"No one can do that."

He smiles. "I adore challenges."

Following her bath Pallas offers wine, figs, meats, cheese, and grapes. Although no longer hungry, Aislin accepts them.

❧

In the morning she awakes on a feather-stuffed bed with a throbbing headache.

Pallas's slaves drape her in a robe and serve her a copious breakfast, but the novelty of abundance is already wearing thin. She picks at a fig and salted seeds, sips apricot juice, and declares that she is not hungry.

Chloe appears in the doorway, her hair braided tight. Lapis lazuli beads encircle her wrist and neck and a silken sheath hugs her hips. "Let me show you to our chambers." She leads Aislin down a hallway, past storerooms and servants' quarters.

"You are not Roman," Aislin observes.

"No," Chloe confirms. She enters a modest room, takes a lamp, and lights the wall sconces. Aislin remains in the doorway. "You may enter," Chloe says. "This is your room, as well as my own."

Aislin sits beside her on the mattress. Chloe stretches an arm around her shoulder. "We are destined to be sisters," she says.

"Where are you from?" asks Aislin, distrustful. "What brought you here?"

"I spent my childhood in a Greek-speaking town in Egypt," Chloe explains. "We lived well at times, but when my mother died she left nothing but debt."

"And your father?"

"I have never met my father. Pallas purchased me in the marketplace."

"Where is Egypt?" asks Aislin.

Chloe fetches a wax tablet and stylus. She draws a map. "I learned geography by traveling through these lands." She draws Egypt, Judaea, Syria, and Cilicia. "Now I am going to teach you your first word in Greek, the language educated people everywhere understand. *Agapé.*"

"*Agapé,*" repeats Aislin. "What does it mean?"

"*Amor,*" says Chloe in Latin. Love.

❧

Chloe leads Aislin into the city, through small alleys to a stone-linteled doorway in the side of a hill. This is the hidden shrine of Isis, Chloe explains, the patron goddess of paupers, thieves, orphans, and maidens, a deity who reassembled the body parts of her murdered brother and husband, Osiris, and restored him to a full and rich life in the underworld. The goddess, painted in amber, sapphire, and ruby, and shrouded in incense smoke, radiates *agapé* from her outstretched palm. Chloe kneels and kisses the goddess's bare feet.

"Every year," Chloe explains, "Isis's tears flood the Nile. The annual rebirth of vegetation mirrors Osiris's death and resurrection. My deity is a goddess of compassion and salvation. She protects the dead and guides them to new life. She is also a goddess of magic."

"Are you a priestess of Isis?"

Chloe laughs. "Not a priestess. A devotee."

↊

During the first few days Aislin sleeps with no schedule, meanders through hallways, and stops in the kitchen when hungry. The other slaves acknowledge her with a courteous "*ave.*" She steps outside and rambles along the river. When a storm breaks she returns to the shelter of their bedroom and wonders whether Pallas has forgotten about her.

On the afternoon of the fourth day Chloe again pours her a bath. "Now you have tasted opulence," she tells Aislin. "If you leave, he knows you'll come back. They always come back, until he tires of them."

"Why does he tire of them?"

"None have been able to give him what he wants."

"And that is?"

"A son."

Aislin contemplates her situation while Chloe scrubs her back.

Pallas again slips in to watch. He has composed a poem that describes Aislin's girlish appearance, her long fingers and lilting dialect, her cropped blonde hair, her spirit and innocence, and the struggle between his desire to provide her with happiness and his fear of damaging her. He personifies this struggle as two evenly matched wrestlers, each determined to kill the other, and delights in descriptions of their ruses and physiques. Aislin cannot help admiring his verbal wizardry.

After the bath, Chloe hands her a short whip without explanation. She exits, closing the huge doors with a dreadful thunk.

"Are you comfortable here?" Pallas asks. "I have instructed the other servants to attend to your every whim. Are they doing so?"

"They are," Aislin replies.

Pallas removes his toga and tunic, revealing soft mounds of flab and fields of coarse, twisted hairs. "I am exceedingly and dispiritedly enamored of you, of your wild beauty, even the fire of your resentment. I fear I might be burned but that fear thrills me. If there's one thing I've learned in my long years, it's that no one can experience pleasure without pain." He spreads out his hands. "I know what we Romans did in Britannia to your people. Here is your opportunity for vengeance. Whip me, strike me, scream at me. Give me what I deserve, not just as a man but as a Roman."

"And you won't hurt me?" Aislin asks.

"I know when to stop. But as I said, there is no pleasure without pain. Despite appearances to the contrary, this rule applies to everyone. Those who enjoy the most exquisite thrills also endure the most suffering. Not even the emperor escapes this principle."

"You're speaking nonsense," Aislin protests.

"If you knew him and his family, as I do, you would understand. He is the most miserable of mortals."

࿎

Chloe shows Aislin a small upstairs room, where an open passageway offers a view of the Tiber's turbid waters and on clear nights, a splash of stars. With a pang, Aislin recognizes the heroes and ancestors that wended through the skies of Britannia. She points. "Look, there: a lass, washing her hair in a milky stream. Can you see that, Chloe, as I can? Her face, and some of the water."

"This bruise," asks Chloe touching her cheek, "tell me."

"He knows how much I can endure," says Aislin. "But I shall savor my revenge."

"You must not speak that way," Chloe warns her.

While she clings to fantasies of retribution, she cannot ignore the myriad ways in which Pallas spoils her. She has never lived as well as in this sprawling, luxurious domicile. She eats what she likes, when she likes, and sleeps soundly. Despite his propensity to violence, Pallas also delights in his ability to elicit a smile. When she perceives her sorrow, he offers her an amber bracelet or an amethyst intaglio brooch. He also provides her with what he deems the most valuable gift any Roman can bestow upon a barbarian: a rudimentary Greek education. Aislin is aware of his dream of improving her, of transforming her, of melting her innermost being in the crucible of his social class.

All of which she finds insulting, even degrading. She does not desire to become one of *them*. She finds Pallas's devotion to intense physical sensations repulsive. Still, she cannot help reflecting on her aunt Muirgheal and the rituals of warfare that enlivened each Albion spring. The primal thrill of beheading one's foes mattered to Muirgheal and to the warrior class that was once Aislin's destiny. In the end, though, what was the purpose of all that turmoil and bluster? Muirgheal now reposes in the same place as her enemies.

The abundance of food, the protection of Pallas's roof, and Chloe's companionship all come to seem indispensable to Aislin. The thought of returning to the streets fills her with dread. Despite her abhorrence of Pallas's philosophy of pleasure and pain, she recognizes a kernel of truth in it.

Although she sleeps in luxury, Aislin feels as if her abode were a fragile hut, constructed of leaves and branches, situated on an isolated hill, buffeted by opposing winds of emotion. Gusting from the west, a loathing of Rome and Pallas; and from the east, a zephyr of opulence and pleasure. These winds howl around her, rattle the branches, and blow off the roof.

❧

Aislin falls pregnant a second time. Delighted, Pallas hosts a reception. "I have been waiting all my life," he tells his guests, "to bring a young man into the world. A young man who will grow into the image of his father. No other woman could do for me what my lovely, resilient guttersnipe has done." He smiles at his ridiculousness and his guests smile with him, having heard similar words before.

Sitting on a gilded maple chair, bejeweled in carnelian and turquoise, Aislin feels her skin warm, the effect of Pallas's tainted wine. The warmth is a sheath, while her core remains empty. Chloe sings in Greek, accompanying herself on the lyre.

❧

As her belly swells, so does Aislin's morosity. She lies less frequently with her master and sits for hours under the willow in the *Horti Maecenati*, speaking to her unborn child, whom she imagines as a daughter with blonde hair and green eyes.

"You have two older siblings," she tells her unborn child. "Meitheamh, whom I buried in Brittania, and Nigellus, here at our feet. They're both in the underworld now but you must remember them. They were as innocent as you."

❧

One morning Pallas's pale-skinned, ruby-lipped servant appears in their room to announce that she and Chloe will have to move to separate, smaller quarters. A team of plasterers and painters, under the direction of a renowned slave-artist, will repaint their chamber in preparation for the baby's arrival.

During the previous months, Aislin has acquired the trappings of a woman of means. She wears a wool *peplos*, a tunic fastened on either side of the neck with gold pins, and her amber bracelet. She gathers her jars of face cream, makeup, and jewelry into trays as the laborers—slaves rented from other members of the patrician and senatorial classes—flow in and begin setting up planks and poles. Hurrying out, she catches sight of the fresco artist, whom she recognizes.

He wears a leather-belted cotton tunic and sandals. His face is shaven, his hair trimmed. He stops to survey the premises, his arms crossed. When his eyes catch hers, they crinkle in wonder. "Aislin! Aislin, is it you? And here, of all places!"

She observes that his condition has improved. *How could it not?* She remembers how he abandoned her at his sister's palace. But she also remembers that during their travels, despite their increasing intimacy, Septimus honored her wish not to be touched, except during the delivery of her stillborn child Meitheamh.

"Hardly a day has passed when I haven't thought of you, Aislin. When I realized you had left my sister's villa, I left, too. For two days I slept on the street searching for you." His face widens in a nostalgic grin. "But we were used to that back then, you and I, weren't we—sleeping under the stars."

At last, she smiles. It has never occurred to her that he might have looked for her, or that he imagined she exited Poppaea's residence of her own volition.

"He's good to you, your master?" Septimus asks, his eyes drawn to her belly.

"He's good to himself," she replies. "But you are an artist? And a slave? Who is your owner? Your sister?"

Septimus raises a finger to his lips.

"She is good to you?" asks Aislin.

"She is good to herself," says Septimus.

Pallas enters, places a hand on Septimus's back, and describes his vision for the baby's room. "Take your time," he tells Septimus. "This boy will be my heir."

Aislin slips out, feeling Septimus's gaze. Holding the tray of her belongings, she heads to her new chamber reflecting on Septimus's surprising bearing and attire. *Is it that I misperceived him, when my understanding of Latin was weak, or is he not the person he once was?* No longer the heir of a great aristocratic estate, no longer a failed soldier or a desperate deserter, he is now a proud slave—as is she.

Have I, too, changed? Aislin wonders. Is she still a child of Albion, or has Rome transformed her? And what future metamorphoses might lie in store?

❧

Aislin's second child slides into the world more easily than the first. This, however, is the end of his good fortune.

A boy born with the gift of physical beauty is one whom the gods cherish. If he is a citizen of Rome, he can excel on the battlefield and in the forum. For those who are denied honor, though, the gods mold bent noses and beady eyes, marks of their contempt. Such children are destined to fail in society.

Some cases are more complex. Upon Aislin's son, the goddess Venus bestows a broad forehead, a prominent chin, sparkling eyes, and rust-red curls. But the favor Venus grants, Hermes denies. From the moment Chloe hands the bathed infant to his mother, Aislin knows he is unusual. His arms and legs flop. He wails, inconsolable, as Aislin carries him. She names him Faolan, *Little Wolf* in her native tongue.

❧

When the infant is a few months old, Aislin brings him to his father. Pallas touches the boy's face, picks him up, coos at him. Shrieking, red-faced, his limbs drooping, Faolan appears unable to fix his gaze upon his father. Pallas slumps to a bench and hands the baby back. "There's a trash heap outside the city walls," he tells Aislin wearily. "Leave him there. It is the civilized thing to do."

Pressing the infant to her chest, Aislin shakes her head in horror.

"Aristotle tells us that the faculty of reason is what separates humans from animals," Pallas tells her. "That child will never be able to think like a human, therefore he is not human. But what do you know of Aristotle? We Romans discard defective progeny. This is how we maintain our strength as a collective. To consider only your feelings, or your child's, is to be dangerously—and I would add, willfully—selfish."

"He is your son, too, you twisted bastard," says Aislin.

"That animal is not my son," Pallas growls, and he slaps her, hard.

Clutching her baby, Aislin backs away, then ducks out the door into the courtyard, and from there to the crowded marketplace. Fearing Pallas might pursue her and kill her baby, she dashes between merchants who hawk jars of wine and olive oil; past coppersmiths, who bang on pots and pipes; and glassblowers, who inflate vases in reflective blue, red, and green swirls. She turns and escapes up a steep path between monumental *insulae*, wood, rubble, and brick apartment blocks five and six stories high, faced with columned loggias and covered in ivy. She passes fountains where bearded gods and small-breasted goddesses spill water into shell-shaped pools, where slaves fill buckets and naked children splash.

Aislin pauses to breathe, leaning against an alley wall. Blossoming passion-flower vines spill over wooden balconies where barefoot women in loose tunics string damp laundry between crumbling edifices. A peddler pushes his cart, advertising used household wares in a nasal sing-song. Aislin turns another corner and discovers the grotto of Isis, where Chloe brought her months ago. She hurries inside and, still clutching her whimpering child, drops to the stone floor facing the goddess.

"I have no right to ask for your protection," Aislin murmurs. "I am told, though, that you are a goddess of love. Undeserving of your compassion, I implore you: shelter me, Isis. Protect my child. Help us find a path out of wretchedness."

PART TWO: Circa 64 CE

Dozing in an alley near the theater of Marcellus, his unkempt ginger hair strewn across his mother's lap, Faolan appears at once bulkier and younger than most ten-year-old boys. Like his mother, he long ago learned to slumber through the grind and rattle of jubilation and dissent: generals' steeds prancing in glory after their battles against the Persians to the east or the Roxolanis to the north; news peddlers hollering of a devastating earthquake in Pompeii; a phalanx of plebeians decrying the emperor's murder of his mother, or of his wife; extravagant celebrations of his new marriage to an alluring ingénue named Poppaea. But on this morning, the tintinnabulation of hand chimes and the chanting of maidens awakes Aislin, who shakes her son out of sleep. "The Day of the Argei, Faolan! Come!"

They join a procession of priests, priestesses, and worshipers. The priests' incense burners exhale smoke as they snake through pathways and *viae*, stopping at temples to utter prayers and collect life-sized human effigies made of plaster-covered straw with painted eyes and lips. By the time they reach the *Pons Sublicius*, the crowd numbers in the thousands. The highest-ranking priest halts at the center of the bridge and speaks to each statue in turn as his assistant sets them on fire. "You have absorbed the impurities of the Esquilina, and we cast you into water." The burning wicker sculptures fly into the dark river, sizzling and sputtering, and bob away.

Faolan whimpers. Aislin strokes his head.

"You have absorbed the impurities of the Piscina Publica and we cast you away, into water."

Faolan whines more loudly. Aislin knows he is empathizing with the straw figures, and pats his arm. "This is how they purify the different neighborhoods," she explains. "We're all supposed to witness." Although Roman religion remains foreign to her in many ways, the rite of purification fascinates.

"You have absorbed the impurities of the Transtiberina," the priest tells a third statue, "and we cast you into water."

Faolan starts wailing. Aislin draws him away, into a narrow alley that coils toward a dismal, neglected area of the city that no one has ever bothered to purify.

❧

Faolan frequently wakes at night, and Aislin tries in vain to calm him. "They will never accept you, my beautiful son," she tells him. "Nor do they see me as fully human. We're like those straw people they threw from the bridge."

Faolan howls in terror.

"Oh, my Faolan, I didn't mean that." She strokes his hair. "Of course, they will not light us on fire and toss us in the water. Close your eyes, sweet one. Your mother is with you. Go to sleep."

She wakes to the shouts of two fourteen-year-old boys, sons of patricians, who have caught Faolan between them and are shoving him back and forth. Aislin has hardened to others' taunts and jeers. To wander through Rome with her son is to expose herself to mockery, as well as him, but Faolan takes no offense. When others tease, he giggles with them, savoring their merriment. Now, though, she rushes toward the boys, seizing the shorter one by the scruff of his neck and shaking him. "How could you do that to my child?" she demands.

Aislin shoves him down and kicks his stomach and face. The boy screams, covering his face with his hands. Retrieving Faolan, Aislin flees into the back alleys of Rome.

❧

As they pass through the city center one evening, Aislin recognizes the corpulent figure of a man who holds a young boy's hand, both surrounded by a number of slaves. Age and vice have whitened Pallas's curls and swelled his belly. Bending down, he whispers in the child's ear and both laugh. Revulsion and indignation whip Aislin like a cold wind, and she squeezes her son's hand. "Be careful now, Faolan. Make no sound."

As if blown through wide avenues and tangled alleys, they track Pallas to his home and the man and child disappear inside. Evening dims from lazuline to onyx. Servants light torches in their iron rests, naked boys in bronze, on either side of the door.

Aislin approaches the door and pounds it with her fist. One of the torches falls. She tries to reinsert it but molten tar spills, smoking and stinking and crawling down the door on blue and yellow fingers. Faolan screeches, flapping his hands like wings as he leaps, agitated, from foot to foot.

"Come, Faolan. We must run!" Aislin cries, seizing his hand.

Faolan resists her entreaties, seemingly transfixed by the growing blaze.

"Please, Faolan. They will kill us!"

Suddenly, he spins and darts away, and she loses sight of him in the gloom. She catches sight of him tumbling past an intersection and skipping around a corner. She calls for him as shouted commands, stomping feet, and clanging shields herald the arrival of the Praetorian Guard. Finally, she catches up with Faolan, who cowers in an arched doorway, trembling like a plucked harp string. She urges him within, kisses him on his head, and promises to return soon. Head bowed, shaking, he creeps into the shadows.

A few days have passed, or so she believes, for she has lost track of time. The old man chained across from her scratches his bald head, the whites of his blue eyes and his beard barely visible in the moonlight that filters through the narrow window high in their cell wall. "You are lucky," he growls, "they did not capture Faolan with you."

"But how can he survive without me?" she asks.

"You're also fortunate they did not kill you then and there."

"Fortunate?" She scratches her thigh. "They'll make an example of me. They'll strangle me on the Gemonian Stairs. I've seen it more times than I can count. Have you not? But you're not from here, are you?"

"Nor are you. I was born in Cilicia," says the old man. "In a city called Tarsus, at the eastern edge of the empire. But I've stumbled through a dozen city gates and slumbered under countless roofs." He wipes a bead of water from his glaucous, half-shut left eye.

"Perhaps you have a name?" asks Aislin.

"More than one," the man replies.

"What will they do to my son?"

"The best navigators can't predict where the wind will blow. It won't help you to ponder the worst."

"It's not up to me, what I ponder."

"Between hope and fear, you have a choice."

❧

The old man shifts his legs and his chains clink and rattle. "I occasionally have a dream," he remarks, "or maybe I'm imagining it. I sail on a sea of tears—the distress of all those who have suffered unmerited wounds, wounds that never healed—which is everyone. And this sea of tears speaks to me in a million tongues, like fingers that buoy my vessel and caress my face in a warm and soothing wind."

Aislin has rarely heard a man talk this way. The old prisoner is educated, a son of the privileged classes, yet he is humble, compassionate.

Aware of a ticking at her foot, Aislin twitches but fails to frighten the rat that snuggles there. She opens her eyes to the familiar stone walls, two parallel, two angled.

"Listen," says the old man.

Over the clamor of the forum, a girl sings, her lyric indecipherable, her voice redolent of innocence and sorrow. Behind it, the crackle of fire. Aislin closes her eyes. Memories glide past, Companions, familiar faces, strangers. "These flames," she asks the old man. "Do you smell them? This is what I started."

"Perhaps," he replies. "There are fires every day in Rome." After a moment he adds: "Like you, I have experienced the crush of sin. I carried it from land to land, hoping to slip out from under it, until...."

"Sin?" Aislin asks, perplexed.

"Errare. Being lost. Moral wandering. It sullies the soul. That is why you are here. To be cleansed. That's why we are all here."

"What will they do to my son?" she asks.

"Stand up. If you don't, you'll lose the ability. This is what my good friend Lucanus, a doctor, advised me. You will meet him. Go ahead and stand. Your chains are long enough, just."

They clank as she rises, raises her arms, and squats again. *Where is Faolan?* The question bounces off the walls of her mind like balls in a rattled box. *Where is Faolan?*

❧

The old man gibbers and wheezes in his sleep. Sometimes he utters anxious or tortured cries. Other times, he giggles. "This is how one slumbers in this hole," he grumbles upon awakening. "Intermittently, day and night. Dreams and reality, intermingled in a rich, piquant stew."

"What did you dream?" she asks.

"I dreamt I murdered someone."

"Have you?"

"In a former life," says the old man, "I participated in the killing of an innocent man."

"Is that why you're here?"

"Perhaps, in a roundabout way."

The girl sings again, or is it a different girl, and Aislin remembers her daughter Meitheamh in the soil of Albion, and Nigellus, the cat she loved like a son, buried in the *Horti Maecenati*. Now she has lost another son, Faolan, a misunderstood boy bursting with love and innocence. As a mother, she has failed. Smoke wafts through the high window, stinging her eyes. She coughs.

The Companions of long ago inspired her dream of revenge. She served as their instrument. They played her, as a mortal might play a lyre. If she has lost Faolan, she now wonders, where is the benefit?

❧

Through the high window the afternoon sun blazes. Smoke swirls. Dust motes dance in the shaft of light. Sporadic, frantic street sounds reach their ears, the rattle of cart wheels, the cry and clamor of anxious voices. "Sin," Aislin says. "Moral wandering." It is an unfamiliar concept, one that intrigues her.

"It is the universal condition," remarks the old man. "There is a moral standard that is known among my people as the Tradition. Against it, we all fail."

"That is a dark view," says Aislin.

"A dark view and a light one, all at once. You see, we're given the opportunity to redeem ourselves. Not because we deserve it, but because the God we venerate loves us, as a parent loves a child."

"Which god is that?"

"There is only one God."

"Is that what they believe in Cilicia?"

"No. I was born in Cilicia, but I am not of it."

"Tell me your story," she says. "What else do we have, now, but our stories? I know you have more than one name. What name did you go by in Cilicia?"

"Ah, but we are not talking about me," the man replies. "We are talking about the boy I was, before I was transformed. His name was Paulus, which happens to be my name as well. He was an adept wrestler. He wore a mask. He was so used to it, he hardly knew. His adversary, too, wore a mask."

"His wrestling adversary?"

"Yes."

Aislin closes her eyes. "Tell me that story."

❧

Tarsus was a wild and woolly outpost, a place where Judaean and Greek merchants rubbed elbows with African pirates and Roman soldiers. Paulus was fifteen but his wooden face appeared timeless. Smooth and white, it depicted the emptiness of one who has yet to receive wisdom. His wrestling foe, Sabinus, wore the mask of a player, frozen in a grimace of derision. Despite their pretense at anonymity, each boy knew his opponent and each despised the other. Their teacher encouraged such antagonism. "Through strife, we better ourselves. *Nikeses ho kratistos pais*," he instructed the boys before every match. "May the better one prevail."

They circled each other, arms extended, searching for a grip, seeking not only physical domination but moral vindication, as if attached to opposite sides of an invisible wheel that slowly spun one way and another. Their classmates barked and hooted from the sidelines.

In the eyes of other Cilicians, Paulus and Sabinus had much in common. They both attended gymnasium, studied rhetoric and geometry, resided in large homes, and enjoyed Menander's comedies. Sabinus, however, had inherited the myths and prestige of the equestrian class. His father served his country as a *publicanus*, a tax collector. His family worshiped the gods that had brought glory to Rome. Paulus's father owned a tent factory, with little prospect of social advancement.

Paulus lunged. Sabinus dodged, spiraled, and caught his forearm. Paulus's left palm met Sabinus's with a smack. Their fingers laced together and they held each other, orbiting an invisible, wobbling center, each searching for advantage. Sabinus lowered his head and drove it against Paulus's. They wrapped their arms around each other and stumbled backward and forward like a blind, two-headed creature.

Paulus reached for the calf of Sabinus's left leg and lifted it. Sabinus stumbled backward on one leg, wrenched himself free, got hold of Paulus's left leg and abdomen, raised him to a horizontal position, and fell on top of him. They grasped each other's hams and writhed. The Roman boy grunted, snorted, and stumbled and Paulus flipped him onto his back, pressing his forearm against his throat. "Beg for mercy," he gasped.

Sabinus responded by wrapping his legs around Paulus's and squeezing. He rammed his head into Paulus's face. He reached for the two-inch length of sheep's gut that covered Paulus's penis, hiding his mark of tribal affiliation, and ripped it off. The other students jeered and howled. Paulus attacked his adversary with renewed ire. "Violation!" Paulus croaked as they twisted in contentious embrace.

"Match over. You have won by default," their master affirmed.

Sabinus positioned himself—hands against the wall, feet apart—for a whipping.

❧

That night Paulus knelt at his father's bedside. In the dim light from the atrium his father's eyes shone. Perspiration glistened on his forehead. "This is hardly the first time I have been ill. It is a matter of atonement, my son. Go to the home of Judah, son of Nikandros. He lives near the house of prayer and knows the incantations of healing. Tell him to pray for me, that my soul may live."

"I will, father," Paulus assured him.

His father inquired about his day. Paulus spoke reluctantly of the wrestling match. "Sabinus pulled my covering, father. They saw."

His father stroked Paulus's hair. "You learn to ignore their taunts and jeers, my son. It is essential. This is why we placed you in the gymnasium."

Paulus kissed his forehead.

❧

Under a full moon, tile-roofed homes jutted into the streets, streaked in shades of rust, moss, chalk, and coal. Alleys sloped and wormed toward the river. Disorientated, for he had never before ventured into Tarsus alone at night, Paulus slowed his pace. Cart wheels clattered across uneven pavers in the distance. Somewhere an animal snorted and grunted. Ancient utterances passed through Paulus's mind, as if from a heavenly Messenger: *Dikaios oiktirei psychas ktēnōn autou.* The righteous soul takes pity on the beast.

"In the original scroll, the meaning differs," Narcissus, his slave-tutor, had explained. "The righteous man knows that by virtue of its in-breathed life, the animal is his equal. You see, in matters of virtue, to know is to feel."

Paulus followed the sounds of the beast toward the agora, which emerged in shadows of silver-blue luster framed by columned porticoes. To Paulus's right rose the Temple of Venus Aphrodite: pillars of polished stone, a capacious, shadowed chamber, and frozen within as if fished out of the stream of time and motion, a nude in marble. Near the Temple of Venus, a waterfall cascaded into the river Cydnus, its trajectory celebrated by flowering mandrakes and tumbling vines. Life, abundant and chaotic, sprang from water and dirt in tangled, moonlit blossoms and knotted, shadowed branches. Across the river the naked, vulture-pecked corpses of the criminals Rome deemed most pernicious, those who had openly opposed Rome's domination of Cilicia, drooped on crucifixes in orderly rows like hunched Messengers of death peering down upon the city. Paulus averted his eyes. Life was sacred; its negation, corrupting.

The Temple of Mithras stood before the river at the bottom of the agora, windowless and lightless except from a door that gaped open. Inside, the bull Paulus had heard was bellowing and men were chanting to the beat of a drum. Paulus descended a pink-marble stairway that opened to an arched chamber. Oil lamps affixed to the walls illuminated frescoes of phantasmagorical creatures beneath star-studded skies. Men and boys crowded the benches under the curved ceiling. Among them Paulus recognized Sabinus in the company of his father.

A priest, wearing a floppy blue hat, held a miter beneath a massive sculpture of a bull rising from a rock. A wrestler straddled the beast, pressing a knife to its neck; a dog yapped at its hooves. A snake circled the bull's ankle. A scorpion scurried over its back. Sheaves of wheat sprouted from the bull's tail. Two torchbearers framed this sculpture, one pointing his torch upward and the other thrusting his downward. Above the bull, to the left, the face of Helios, the sun, shone in a circle of rays. To the right, Luna, the moon, stared through clouds. A pillar joined to the sculpture depicted a man with the head of a lion straddling a globe. Two rays, forming a cross, intersected at its center.

As the priest and his congregation chanted hymns to their god Mithras, the bellowing reprised louder, followed by a thud. Blood drizzled from slits in the ceiling. Men and boys swarmed around the priest, waving their hands aloft as crimson rain sprinkled their upturned faces. The priest raised a stone bowl. "Our homeland is in the heavens, my brothers. When we were children, the elemental forces of the cosmos enslaved us. At the end of time, a great conflagration will destroy the universe. This is the bowl of death. Drink of it and you will have eternal life." He sipped. His congregants reached for the bowl and passed it from lip to lip, blood streaming over their shoulders and naked chests.

Paulus felt the *ruakh hakodesh*, the Holy Breath, blowing through that chamber, inflating those worshipers with joy and certainty, and he asked himself how this could be. Confused and dizzy, he hurried out and up the stairs. He spun left and right, up and down, until lost and breathless, he stopped. Gasping for breath, he thought he saw a great, colorful bird sailing through the night sky, but when he looked heavenward he found only the bright moon and a silvery wash of stars. He closed his eyes, thrust his arms skyward as if to grasp the feet of a passing Messenger, and prayed for forgiveness and guidance.

As the eastern horizon faded to lavender he wandered in an unfamiliar quarter. The palatial homes of the Roman overlords stretched behind walls that receded toward the dawn. Large pavers gleaming with dew clothed the street like clunky baubles on the gown of a wealthy harlot. Scents of honeysuckle and jasmin wafted from balcony gardens. A door yawned open, defined by the torchlight that quivered within. Convinced that a Messenger had led him to this place he removed his shoes and entered.

A passageway led to a wide, torch-lit atrium with mosaic floors, walls of polished marble, and busts of Graeco-Roman gods, their faces congealed in astonishment, anguish, or wrath. In the center of the atrium, a pool reflected shimmering torchlight.

A young woman prayed before an altar. With its painting of a man sacrificing a pig, slumped boys bearing wine vessels and crocks, and slithering snakes, the altar resembled a miniature Roman temple. Smoke rose from a bowl. The young woman finished praying, then crossed behind the water channel in the center of the room, where she stopped and looked at Paulus.

"Forgive me," Paulus told her. "I am lost."

She smiled graciously. "We are all lost, are we not? And yet we are where the gods want us to be. Come." She led Paulus past a water channel, where a burly slave stood guard, to a small chamber where couches of silk and carved walnut inlaid with gold and ivory hugged the walls around a low table. A fresco above depicted red flowers floating in an azure garden, disembodied heads, and inset portraits of reclining nude women. "Gaipor, bring us porridge with lard, figs, and a pitcher of wine, watered-down and sweetened with honey," she commanded the slave. "Please, sit," she instructed Paulus. "I am Tryphena. What is your name?"

"Paulus," he replied uneasily, wondering why a Messenger of The Name would have directed him to this pagan domicile, and why Tryphena was welcoming him so.

"My parents are in Rome," Tryphena told him. "We have the house to ourselves."

"But your gods..." began Paulus.

Tryphena tilted her head, her lips parted, and looked at him quizzically. "Our gods?"

"Do you not fear them, even in your parents' absence?"

"I'm afraid they're too busy with their own intrigues to worry about mine," she laughed.

"They don't concern themselves with human sin?"

"What is sin?"

"A form of impurity. A stain."

Gaipor lumbered in and set a tray on the table.

"Please," she gestured.

Paulus declined.

"You're not hungry?"

"Perhaps some figs."

She pushed the plate of figs across the table. "I begged the spirit of my great-grandfather to intervene with the goddess on my behalf," Tryphena explained. "If Venus grants what I desire, I shall sacrifice a pig at her temple."

"What do you desire?"

"A companion for the night. A moment. Something fierce."

"Why would you need Venus's help?" Paulus asked, feeling his cheeks warm. "You must know many young men."

"Everyone is the son of someone. They are all so predictable. How old are you, Paulus?" She filled her spoon.

"Sixteen," he lied.

"You're my age," she returned with a smile, a chestnut curl dangling on her face. Her expression darkened. "I am so sick of this place."

"Many would envy you."

"Not if they knew my family. The games my parents play. My father chasing boys. My mother toying with his friends. I don't believe we were put on this earth to hurt each other, do you?"

"I'm sure that is not why we are here."

"Do you think we were put here to comfort each other?"

"I don't know."

She looked him in the eyes. "You're not like other sixteen-year-olds."

He sighed.

"Have you ever even seen a girl naked?"

He rose. "I should leave," Paulus muttered.

"Why?"

"It's late."

"It's early." She stood and took his hands. "My bedroom is before the peristyle, on the right. You will come back tomorrow, will you not? I know you will."

"How can you know?"

"Venus sent you."

❧

Paulus leaned over his wax writing tablet, taking dictation. "The lips of the foreign woman drip like honeycomb," Narcissus recited, "but in the end she is bitter as wormwood. Drink waters from your own cistern and from your own well. Let your fountains spill over and your rivers fill the streets. May the breasts of your wife quench you always, and may you always be ravished with her love. Why would you be ravished, my son, with a foreign woman, and embrace the bosom of a stranger?"

Paulus wrote each word dutifully. He chewed on his wooden stylus, closing his eyes as he recited the passage by heart. "How did love enter our world?" he asked his tutor.

"There is more than one kind of love," Narcissus told him.

"The love between a young man and a young woman."

"In paradise, God created Earthling and Life. Adam, the Earthling, from *adamah*, earth or soil, and Eve, *Khava*, life. At first, their affection was that of a brother and sister. Lust had yet to enter the garden."

"Until the serpent came along."

Narcissus smiled. "The serpent, perhaps. But in the Teachings, literal meaning can be misleading. *Ha-nakhash*, the serpent, also means diviner or spell-caster. Keep in mind, these words are written without vowels.

Ha-nakhash, in consonants, inverts to *shekhinah*, the Presence of the Lord—a female presence. So the serpent can also be understood to mean *the opposite of the presence*."

"The absence?" Paulus tried.

"And this absence," confirmed Narcissus, "which is paradoxically a presence itself, offers *Khava* something exhilarating. Pure and innocent, she cannot identify evil. Her ignorance, you see, is her strength but at the same time her weakness. And so she accepts the gift."

"The fruit of the tree of the knowledge of good and evil."

"And after her eyes open, Adam feels separation and yearning. It is through that breach that carnal passions flow down to our souls, love as well as its opposite, hatred, and imprison us in the sublunary realm."

"I'm afraid you've lost me," Paulus sighed.

"The sublunary realm," explained Narcissus, "comprises everything within the sphere of the moon's orbit—the earth, its plants and creatures, the seas, and the lower portion of our skies. Beyond that sphere all is spirit, the stars, the denizens of heaven. Messengers, composed of thought—*malakhim* in Hebrew, *logos* in Greek—mediate between the earth and the skies."

"Is love the same for the Children of the Covenant, the Greeks, and the Romans?" Paulus asked.

"The Romans claim to have inherited the stories and gods of the Greeks," said Narcissus. "But Rome is not Athens. To subjugate us, the Romans make sport of our maidens. This is not what we call love."

&

His father's wheezing had not improved. "Did you find Judah?"

"I lost my way," Paulus told him. "Today I found his home but his door was closed. I shall try again tonight."

His father believed Judah's prayers would enable his soul to live, Paulus knew. But Paulus wondered whether his father's soul would indeed live after his body expired. The issue of eternal life was referenced only obliquely in the Five Basic Scrolls; but then, Narcissus had always emphasized that to read the Scrolls literally was to miss their point. The Secondary Scrolls of Daniel and Maccabees were more explicit, linking the survival of the soul to righteousness. Many, like Paulus's father, believed righteousness unattainable without prayer. Other writings Paulus had read, such as *Kohelet*, Gatherer, seemed to deny the possibility of eternal life, and most of the stories in the Holy Scrolls dealt with other matters—how to structure Israelite society, how to worship, and human emotions including fear, envy, and love between fathers, mothers, children, their rulers, and the Ultimate Ruler.

"Do you believe most pagans are evil, father?" Paulus asked.

"Who am I to judge? None of us is perfect."

"Do you believe they can work magic upon us?"

"They can conjure spirits and demons as well as we can, I suppose."

"Narcissus says that to be attached to hatred, or love, is to be a prisoner of passion."

"And what is so terrible about passion?"

"We are made of earth and life. Emotions belong to the realm of earth. Reason is of the realm of life."

His father stared at the black ceiling. "Narcissus is the disciple of his master in Alexandria. Learn what you can from him, but keep in mind he is a man. His master was a man. No matter what he claims, he does not possess ultimate truth. No man does."

"His master," Paulus objected, "learned these things from the Holy Books of Plato, who in turn learned them from the Sacred Scrolls of Moses."

"The Scrolls of Moses are indeed sacred," Paulus's father said. "Not the scribblings of that Greek."

"Both were inspired by the Lord, were they not?"

"I am not familiar with the writings of Plato. What I do know is that the Lord endowed us with feelings as well as reason. Why should we deny them?"

"You must rest, father," said Paulus, offering him a cup of water. "Tonight I shall visit the home of Judah, son of Nikandros."

As he walked that evening, he wondered how it was that the pagan seductress Tryphena had taken up residence in the dim, reverberant atrium of his soul, and how he could be so enamored of her, even as his father struggled to breathe.

He turned right where he had previously turned left and came upon a trapezoidal plaza, dominated by a tall synagogue. Beside it stood the home of Judah, son of Nikandros. A slave girl answered his knock, her head covered in a cream-colored shawl.

"I need to speak with your master. My father is ill."

"My master is not home."

"When he returns," Paulus said, pressing a coin into her palm, "please tell him that Benjamin, son of Isaac, the tent manufacturer, is ill and requires his incantations."

Half-deliberately Paulus retraced his steps to Tryphena's house. When she saw him, she kissed the statue of Venus.

"I fear your Venus is playing tricks on me," he told her.

She smiled and tousled his hair. "Will you share some porridge?"

"There is meat-fat in your porridge, no?"

"Do you not eat meat-fat?"

"When you sacrifice an animal to one of your gods," he asked her, "which portion do you give to the god and which to worshipers?"

"We eat the meat. The organs belong to the god."

"It is much the same with us. The organs, blood, and fat belong to our God, but we apply the rule every day, not just when we sacrifice."

"Why?"

"We are told to be a nation of priests."

She awoke her slave, Gaipor. "Porridge with honey and sheep's milk but without lard," she instructed him. Gaipor lit the triclinium as they sat down.

"We have six days," Tryphena said, placing her hand on Paulus's. "After that, we shall never see each other again."

"Why?"

"The strongest feelings strike when passion is doomed. Why do you think Venus sent you?"

"I don't believe Venus sent me."

"What do you know about Venus?"

"Not a great deal," he admitted.

"Then how do you know you're not her puppet?"

As Gaipor brought two bowls of hot porridge, Tryphena related the story of Venus and Adonis. "When Venus saw Adonis, she fell in love."

"Why?"

"Because she had been scraped, right here, on her breast, by one of Cupid's arrows. And so she longed to make love with Adonis, but he was not ready."

"Did you not tell me she was the most beautiful creature?"

"The very goddess of beauty and love."

"If she was divine, and he was mortal, perhaps he was afraid of her."

"Maybe," Tryphena agreed. "But his reluctance only increased her desire, for Adonis was foreign and mysterious. However, before anything could happen between them, a wild boar killed Adonis, and despite her divine powers Venus could not bring him back to life."

"Your gods are not omnipotent," Paulus remarked. *Of course*, he reflected, *with so many of them, they can oppose and limit each other.*

"But with the help of her father Jupiter, the most powerful god, Venus was finally able to revive Adonis in the form of a flower, the anemone, that dies young and is reborn every spring. And so, you see, Adonis attained partial immortality."

"Do Romans worship him?" Paulus asked, scraping the last of his porridge from the bowl.

"Some believe he is the most important god of all," Tryphena replied.

❧

A slave chanted Hebrew psalms in the corner of his father's cubiculum. Paulus knelt and kissed his father's hand.

"Did you find Judah?"

"He is traveling, but he will pray for you."

"I am feeling somewhat better, my son."

"Father, I spoke with my gymnasium master. A famous healer, reputed to be a righteous gentile, favored by the Lord, has arrived in Tarsus."

"A gentile?"

"A righteous gentile," repeated Paulus.

His father closed his eyes, breathing deeply. Paulus listened to the chanting of the Hebrew slave in the corner. "*Elay beni atah...*" "You are my son; today I have become your father. Ask and I will make the nations your inheritance, the ends of the earth your possession."

❧

The Temple of Healing emerged from the center of an orange grove, just beyond a stream that flowed over the faces of stone idols. Too weak to walk alone, Paulus's father gripped his son's shoulder for support. Apollonius of Tyana greeted them in the garden. Long haired and barefoot, the healer wore a linen tunic. He stopped and looked into Paulus's father's eyes. "You are Children of the Covenant. You are worried that I will coerce you into idolatry."

Paulus exchanged a glance with his father. How did this man know what he was thinking?

"We will wash you with pure water that has flowed over these sacred stone faces and invoke spirits to bless you," Apollonius said. "These are not gods. We do not pray to them. Do you deny the existence of spirits and demons?"

"Who does?" asked Paulus's father.

Apollonius led them into the miniscule, incense-filled temple. "We have healed many Children of the Covenant, including great teachers— *rabbis,* as you say—masters of your sacred and ancient tradition. We have visited your temple in Jerusalem. Be assured, we will not betray your confidence. Please, lie down." He indicated a stone bench.

Paulus had never met anyone who had visited the great Temple of Jerusalem, and he longed to hear Apollonius tell of it. He longed to touch him, smell him, and breathe through him any lingering fragrance of the incense that burned day and night there.

Apollonius felt Paulus's father's stomach and the contours of his organs. "All this seems strange to you."

"I will not deny that," said his father.

"Allow me to tell you a little more about our ways. Like your Nazirites, I neither cut my hair nor consume flesh. I am chaste and own nothing. At the Temple of Healing, we accept neither gold nor silver, though we do not refuse food, drink, and provisions." He wiped Paulus's father's brow with a damp cloth. "The gods provide, or, as you would say, the Lord provides."

❧

Paulus knelt at Tryphena's cot, listened to her breathing, and inhaled her lavender-scented hair.

"Tryphena," he whispered. He shook her awake.

"Where were you last night?" she asked. "I waited for you."

"I'm sorry."

"Did you think of me, at least?"

"If only I could think of anyone else, of anything else, Tryphena. I do not want you for only three more days. I want you forever."

"That is how I want you to want me."

"Even if it's impossible?"

Her lips curled in a smile as she sat up and the sheet fell off her body. "Especially if it is impossible." She drew him to her.

❧

On the third day of his father's treatment, Paulus returned to the Temple of Healing with his slave. His father trembled with fever, his breathing labored. "We worked through the night," Apollonius said regretfully, "but were unable to coax the demons out. These ancient spirits speak Aramaic and have resided in Judaea and Babylon since time immemorial. Perhaps this information will be of value to you."

Paulus offered a box of fig cakes, a sack of nuts, and a length of linen canvas.

"And I have something for you." From a box of polished olive-wood, Apollonius withdrew an ancient bronze coin. "This was given to me in Jerusalem by a priest, whose child I healed. It is a *prutah*, minted hundreds of years ago by the Maccabees, who re-purified the Temple after they overthrew the invaders."

He dropped the coin into Paulus's palm. On one side, there were squiggles and dashes in ancient Hebrew; on the other, a flower-like symbol. "All is not lost," Apollonius assured the boy. "Something good will come of your father's travails: knowledge and a path out of misery."

Looking at the beautiful coin that the healer had given him, a coin that had traveled all the way from the holy land, Paulus listened to the healer's words, taking them to heart.

❧

He lay beside Tryphena, her perfumed hair lulling him to a dreamscape where sin and redemption mingled and flowed like rivulets through a lush, dusky landscape. Before dawn, she stirred and kissed him.

"Our last night together," she whispered, her tears wetting his cheeks.

"You must not say that." He stroked her hair.

"You smell so sweet. You bathed and anointed yourself. Hold me in your arms. I want us to share a moment we shall never forget."

He took her in his arms. She felt lighter, fragile. They fell asleep.

At sunrise, she woke him with a kiss. "My parents will be home shortly. You must leave."

"And never see you again?"

"So it must be," said Tryphena.

"It cannot be. I do not live in that kind of world."

"But you do. We all do," she murmured, covering his face with kisses. "Do you not see? Everything changes and nothing lasts. The challenge is to embrace what will no longer be. And so I am going to close my eyes and kiss you one more time, with all the passion I can muster, but when I open my eyes, you must be gone."

"If I must leave, then come with me."

She laughed. "And give up all this?" She waved toward her opulent surroundings. "It is over. Go."

He caressed her head, nuzzled her neck.

"Gaipor!" cried Tryphena.

Gaipor appeared. He lifted Paulus off the bed, hauled him to the front door, and threw him into the street, dropping the latch behind him.

&

At home, his father's face was tinged with blue and his breath wheezed. "No prayers or incantations will persuade this demon to quit my chest," he rasped "That night in the Temple of Healing, I recalled things. Memories that were and were not my own."

"Father," began Paulus, but his father cut him off.

"We bear in our heart the perfidies of our ancestors, my son, who never properly atoned. Will you go to the holy Temple after I die, to pray for my soul and atone for our sins? Everything we possess, I have purchased with sin-money."

"What are you saying?"

"Your great-grandfather was little more than a pimp to the Roman triumvir, Marcus Antonius."

Paulus knew that Marcus Antonius had lived in Tarsus, where he had met and fallen in love with the pharoah Cleopatra, the most powerful woman in the world. Antonius had then divorced his wife, and a war had ensued. But Paulus had never heard that his family was involved with any of this.

"Your great-grandfather built Marcus Antonius a tent camp to facilitate his adultery," his father explained. "This in turn became the foundation of our tent-manufacturing enterprise, our family fortune, our standing in Cilician society, our Roman citizenship, everything. We have profited from sin, my son, and nothing can come of sin but death."

A slave appeared with a bowl of chopped figs and almonds mixed with lamb's milk and honey. Paulus coaxed the old man to eat, but his father pushed away the bowl.

૭

At the tent manufactory, at gymnasium, and during his studies with Narcissus, his spirit drifted between the springs of youth, where Tryphena, a Naiad priestess, offered herself, and the desert of death, where his father implored him to redeem him and their ancestors. Sensing his disarray, Narcissus tried to comfort him. "My master in Alexandria taught that the eternal soul and the mind are one," the slave reminded him gently. "The body and emotions are without value."

"I would like to believe what you say," Paulus replied, sitting against the wall in the garden, his knees to his chest. "But my thoughts and feelings are bound together like muscle and bone. Even if my father's soul survives as pure thought, that thought would differ from the person he once was—the man I have held in my arms, whose voice means as much as the words spoken, whose cheeks I have wet with my tears."

"The soul is a purer variant of ourselves, Paulus. To be anchored here in Creation, in corporeal form, is to experience only change, loss, and suffering."

"And yet that is where we reside. That is what we know and love."

"For the time being, just as I reside here with you. But that, too, will end." Narcissus's sixth and final year of servitude was to conclude in five months. The crushing debt that had led him to this station, this home, would be erased.

A chiffchaff warbled and flitted from the fig tree. Paulus's father's Hebrew slave stepped into the garden. "He is departed," he announced. "Blessed is the name of the Lord."

"Go to the synagogue," Paulus instructed the slave. "Tell everyone."

Within his father's cubiculum, Paulus gathered his still-warm corpse, wondering whether Judah, son of Nikandros, had prayed. He asked himself how he had allowed the pagan Tryphena to distract him during his father's final days. Amid his tears, and the weight of his grief and guilt, Paulus heard his father's voice. "Go to Jerusalem, Paulus. Pray for my soul and atone for my sins. Perhaps, if you do, my soul will live."

Overcome with fear that his father's unwashed soul might descend to the coldest depth of Sheol, there to dwell alone and cold, Paulus promised him through tears: "I shall go there, father, to sacrifice at the Temple and pray for absolution so that you may be gathered to your ancestors until the resurrection."

Narcissus brought a bowl of water and a jar of perfumed oil. Together they washed and anointed the old man's body, cut the fringes of his shawl, and wrapped him tightly within it.

D awn blushes the prison walls. Did you ever see Tryphena again?" asks Aislin.

"Years later," Paulus replies, "I returned to Tarsus a changed man, reborn, as it were. I attended services in the synagogue where my father had worshiped, and invited others to break bread with me. I told them of my messiah, Joshua of Nazareth, the Son of the Lord, whose sacrifice has been my salvation, and will be the salvation of the world. One Sabbath evening a widow attended the synagogue, and later traveled with me."

"Tryphena?"

"Tryphena, reborn," says Paulus, smiling. "And the moment of carnal love we had once shared, which was doomed, flowered into a different love that was both universal and eternal. We are no longer strangers, gazing at each other across a great expanse of language and traditions."

"We?" asks Aislin, confused.

"Tryphena and I." He smiles. "But, yes, you and I as well. Everyone and everyone. In the end, we are all merely human. And the good news? The end is now."

"My people," asked Aislin, "murdered on the soil of Albion—their memory annihilated—are the same as the Romans, their killers? Is that what you mean?"

"As I now see it," says Paulus, "through the infinite suffering of one individual who is, at the same time, every man, woman, and child—yes."

Aislin shakes her head at the absurdity of his words.

☙

A lanky man in a woolen gown, together with his slave, visits Paulus. "I brought nourishment, brother," he says, opening his satchel and drawing out a round loaf of bread and a bladder of water.

"You are a good man, Lucanus," Paulus tells him.

"I am striving, in the name of our Lord." He turns and gestures to his slave. "Puer, too, has something for you." Puer sets a three-sided writing desk over the old man's legs. Lucanus places a blank papyrus, a wooden pen, and a brass ink bottle on its surface.

Paulus passes Aislin a portion of cheese. "How did you get in?" she asks Lucanus.

"I brought gifts for the guards, too," he replies with a sly grin.

"Can you get them to free us?"

"Only the emperor can do that," Lucanus says.

"Suppose it happened," Paulus asks her as she eats. "Suppose someone freed you. What would you do?"

"I would hug my Faolan and never let go. We would dance in the Forum."

"The Lord loves the innocent and the helpless," says Paulus.

Aislin frowns. "From what I have seen of this world, no one cares for the helpless, neither God nor man."

"Your experience deceives you."

"Can you find my son?" she asks Lucanus. "Tell him I'm alive? Make sure he survives?"

"Where can I find him?" Lucanus asks.

"We were running up the *Vicus Fortunae Respicientis* and we stopped in an archway, the entrance to an apartment block. It was next to a shop that sells eggs, cabbages, and bread."

"Can you find that building, brother?" Paulus asks him.

"With the help of the Lord, one can achieve anything," Lucanus replies with a smile.

Yohanan has grown gaunt and tan; wrinkles line his eyes and nose, and his dark hair is scattered through with white. Two weeks before *Shavuot*, the Pentecost, he instructs his followers to spread the word: farmers should tie reeds around their first sheaths of grain or boughs of fruit, and load them across the backs of oxen with gilded horns and flower harnesses. On the first day of the celebration, surrounded by musicians and singers, they are to lead the oxen to the market square for a feast. And so Yohanan's congregation of Aravites will mirror the festivities of the holy Temple in Jerusalem.

At dawn on the day of *Shavuot*, Yohanan, Miriam, Hanina, Shoshana, and Shlomo bathe, dress in white, and set out for town carrying baskets of fruit, flowers, and two square loaves of bread. A storm is gathering and the scent of myrtle and sage mingle with the aroma of fertile, moist soil. As they near town, the celebrants' songs drift over the fields. "They may be illiterate, but look at their sincerity, their fervor," remarks Hanina.

Yohanan and he have argued endlessly about this question: what matters more, sincerity or knowledge? Rather than delve into it once again, Yohanan just looks at him and smiles.

Roman guards surround the town center, controlling the flow of pilgrims and oxen into the market square, where the dancing and singing continue. As Yohanan and his friends approach, some of the celebrants kiss the hem of their robes and shout, "Make way for our teachers!"

The town gathers around him, falling silent, and waits for him to speak. Yohanan describes Moses's ascension of Mount Sinai, the thunder and lightning, the voice of the Lord breaking through clouds, and the people's disoriented, terror-stricken recourse to idolatry.

"Your souls were present," he concludes. "Whether your ancestors traveled with Moses or resided in foreign lands. All Israel was present, including every unborn soul and every soul yet to arrive, through all time until the coming of the messiah."

A Roman guardsman, who has understood nothing of Yohanan's Aramaic, bends over, raises his tunic, and releases a long, ripping fart. To further mark the insult, soldiers on either side blow trumpets.

Outraged Aravites rush at the soldiers, who pummel them with iron clubs. Other Romans, disguised as Judaean pilgrims but holding bludgeons and short swords under their tunics, enter the fray. Unable to distinguish between friends and foes, the worshipers attack each other or try to flee.

"The insult of a soldier is meaningless!" Yohanan calls out. "By answering with blows, you're giving them an excuse to beat you!"

"We don't need Rome to protect us!" shouts a man, whom Yohanan recognizes as Menakhem, son of Judas the Zealot. "Let the Holy One shelter us!"

Menakhem's followers echo his sentiments. "We do not need Rome! Let the Holy One alone rule!"

Menakhem opens his ox bags. Instead of flowers and grain he has brought stones, which he distributes to his followers. They hurl them at the soldiers as thunder rumbles and rain begins to splatter the pavers.

"I concur, may the Holy One protect us!" shouts Yohanan. "That's no reason to fight, when fighting means our certain death! Our laws forbid it!"

The worshipers push and climb over one another, stampeding out of the market square. Abandoned oxen trample the fallen bodies. Lost children wail. Yohanan searches for Miriam, Hanina, and Shoshana. A club strikes his shoulder and head. He collapses. A stranger pulls him up. A little further, through rain and blood, Yohanan helps a staggering man to his feet. The side of his head smashed, the man expires in his arms.

When it is over, the market square weeps in hues of crimson, brown, and ivory. Most of the vendors' stalls are demolished. Hanina's wine puddles around pottery shards and seeps into the earth to blend with the blood of the ancestors.

Long after the crowd and soldiers have dispersed, Yohanan finds the crumpled form of Miriam. He closes her eyes, buries his face in her neck, and weeps.

A Roman soldier, his face bruised, the plates of his apron bloodied, crouches beside him and grips Yohanan's shoulder. They sit together, lost in grief, as the sun declines. Finally the soldier helps Yohanan lift Miriam's body.

Hunched under his load, Yohanan stumbles out of the marketplace. Deliberately, cautiously, he plods out of the city through dimming fields of barley and date palms. By the time he reaches Hanina's vineyard the sky has purpled; his feet and shins are caked with mud. He lays Miriam down under the blossoming orange tree. "My beloved," he tells her, his throat catching as he inhales the orange blossom scent she so savored.

A islin watches Paulus write. Hunched over his lap desk he seems oblivious to the outside world—the commotion, the flames, the screams. Occasionally he leans back, then resumes after a time. His temples crease in thought. He lets out a satisfied *Ah!* as he unravels a logical tangle. She remembers Septimus's ability to capture a landscape with a charred stick and a stone, removing himself from the horrors of Albion while distilling something of their essence. For hours on end she observes Paulus, admiring his sense of purpose—his absurd conviction that what he has to say, in this dank cell, while Rome burns around him, will change the world.

As evening weaves shadows on the ceiling, Lucanus returns with bread, water, and chamber pots. "Did you find Faolan?" she asks.

"I found the archway and a shopkeeper who knew your boy," Lucanus replies. "He wanted fifty sesterces. I had only a few in my pocket."

"Fifty?" asks Aislin in despair.

"He will get his fifty," the old man assures her. "Your son's life is holy."

"Holy?" she asks. She has heard this word, *sancta*, before, but has never heard it applied to a human being.

"The spark of life he holds," explains Paulus. "It is not of this world."

"My son is mortal," sighs Aislin. "For most, he's the least of mortals."

"Centuries ago," says Lucanus, "our King David proclaimed, 'Blessed are the meek; they shall inherit the world.'"

These men, thinks Aislin, *are dreamers.* But she enjoys listening to their dreams. *After all, what if they are right and I am wrong?*

It is impossible, though. She and Paulus will die in this cell and their dreams will die with them. As for Faolan...but no, she cannot even contemplate his situation. It is too painful. She would rather listen to Paulus's and Lucanus's dreams. She would rather eavesdrop on their intimate conversation, in which they plot the salvation of the universe. At the very least, it is a distraction.

After Lucanus leaves, she tries to sleep but thoughts of her son, Lucanus, and the shopkeeper torment her. She thinks too about the story the old man told her: Tryphena, how he could not control his thoughts, his father's death. "Did you make it to Jerusalem?" she asks. "To your holy Temple?"

"Yes, but matters did not unfold as I had anticipated," he replies bleakly.

"What happened? Is that where you killed that man?" Aislin asks.

"It was a group of us," he says. "The Synagogue of the Freed Slaves, we called ourselves; for my people are all freed slaves, you see, my entire people."

"You speak as if there were no shame in it," says Aislin.

"In being the descendants of slaves?" He smiles, shaking his head. "There is none, but there is shame in what we did. We were enforcing what we understood to be the law and we dragged a man called Stefanos before the High Council of Judaea, knowing the high priest would condemn him. This man—Stefanos—was denying the holiness of the Temple, you see. A direct affront under Greek law, and the high priest was trained in Greek law as well as Hebrew law. His duty to Rome was to enforce the former. Socrates, Anaxagoras, Phidias, Protagoras, among others, had all been found guilty of *blasphemia* of one sort or another. The council debated, but in the end it hardly mattered. The high priest held the power."

"What happened?" Aislin asks.

"For weeks after Stefanos breathed his last," sighs Paulus, "I heard his message. I saw his face, radiant like that of a Messenger. I heard his last words, 'Lord, forgive them.' I attended the atonement sacrifice at the Great Temple of Jerusalem, where I fell weeping upon the Goat of Azazel, the bearer of our sin. Remorse and sorrow poured through my hands into the beast, who moaned in acknowledgment as I implored the heavens."

This, Aislin understands: the idea of a goat absorbing sin and carrying it off into death. She has seen this idea enacted in the ritual of the Argei, although in that case the bearers of sins were not goats but straw effigies that represented the different neighborhoods of Rome.

The old man leans back against the wall of the Imperial Jail, staring at the arched ceiling. "Weary of myself, I sought a new place in the cosmos. At the eastern gate of Jerusalem, I met a group of travelers saddling up their camels for the journey to Damascus, three days through wind and sand. These men, like Stefanos, spoke of messianic expectation. I took this as a sign and accompanied them.

"As we set out, a strong, dry *khamsin* wind was gusting from the north. We tightened our cloaks, wrapped our faces, and set off into the dust. That night we slept near an oasis: a few palms, a handful of shrubs, a watering hole. I saw the black sands swirl around me, as if they were alive. As the *khamsin* howled, the stars brightened and congealed until their glow filled the desert. I heard a voice, as if a man knelt beside me whispering in my ear, his voice hardly distinct from the wind. *Paulus, Paulus, why do you torment me?*

"I called myself Saul at the time. This voice knew my childhood name. I wondered who had spoken but I knew the answer. The voice belonged to Joshua of Nazareth, said to have died on a crucifix above Jerusalem—the man Stefanos called the messiah, the Anointed One, the King who will save my people, and all the world."

"That is what they call the emperor," comments Aislin. "Nero. Savior of the World. Son of the gods."

"We are all children of God," says the old man. "But as you know, the emperor is not the Savior of the World."

"What did he look like, this Joshua of Nazareth?" Aislin asks.

"He came to me as a blinding burst of light and a voice, assuring me that my sins and the sins of all people could be forgiven, even the sin of murder. Bathed in his love, I was renewed. I felt an inner rejoicing that has never abated. Having flailed in a sea of sin, I now floated under a warm radiance, and wherever I go, this sense of freedom and love accompanies me. After I recovered my sight, partially...."

"You lost your sight?"

"How could I not, facing Him? You see, my left eye is damaged to this day." He points to the corner of his watery eye. "After I partially recovered my sight, as I was saying, we continued to Damascus. For two years I harangued the Judaean community there, telling them of my encounter with Joshua in the desert. I tried to explain that the forgiveness of sin is not achieved through Temple ritual but as a result of divine love; not through good deeds, as the rabbis claim, but through faith alone. If I, sinner that I am, am eligible, then everyone is."

Aislin hears the passion rising in his voice. She sees it in his eyes and in the way he holds his hands before his face, as if protecting himself from the divine radiance.

"Stefanos's messiah," Paulus continues, "this paradoxical incarnation of eternity, offers a mediation with God that no priest, nor even any Messenger can provide, precisely because Joshua of Nazareth is entirely human and, at the same time, entirely divine."

She is skeptical of his story, but his seriousness and his way of elevating compassion above other human sentiments is moving. "I have never heard a man speak of love the way you do," she tells him. "Although my friend Chloe spoke similarly of her goddess, Isis, and of *agapé*."

"To experience love, one must abandon control of one's identity, even of one's destiny," observes Paulus. "Most men, especially those who value power, are terrified of doing this."

"If only it were true," she says. "If only there were such a god or goddess, surely the world would not be as it is," Aislin says.

"This world, perhaps, but this is not the only world," Paulus tells her.

"If only I could believe that, too."

"What choice do you have? How can you inhabit a moral universe that makes no sense?"

"I was not given the choice," says Aislin.

Night settles. The scent of burning wood thickens and a red glow lights the walls. Soot floats through the high window on the evening breeze. Bells ring in the distance, summoning fire carts. Women scream and babies wail in an aural mural of confusion and pain. "This blaze will kill us all," says Aislin.

"I have been waiting for it," says Paulus. "We've all been waiting. The righteous will live."

❧

The gate creaks open and Lucanus steps in carrying a lantern. "They're all gone. The palace is empty." He kneels before Aislin. "Your son is alive. He is safe; he is with my wife."

She sighs and smiles, tears pooling in her eyes. She grips his hand. "Thank you," she whispers. "Thank you."

"Now come," Lucanus urges, holding up a key. "The guards have fled. The palace is wide open. Everyone is fleeing. We must go."

"Take me to my son," says Aislin as Lucanus releases them from their fetters.

Shimmering, sweltering flames streak the Forum yellow and red. Smoke blackens the sky. The heat is stifling. As the trio shelter beneath an overhanging roof, the marble façade of the Temple of Castor and Pollux crashes to the ground, its wooden support disintegrating into burning embers and ash. Beyond, the Domus Transitoria and the palaces of the Palatine and the Esquiline Hills feed the flames that are devouring the world. There seems no way forward.

"The pit beneath the cells," says Lucanus. "We can access it from the hallway; it will take us to the river. Quickly, there is no time," he urges them, returning to the prison. Lucanus and Aislin pry the floor grate loose and descend the iron-rung ladder into the darkness below.

At the bottom, the air is cool and moist. A dull luminosity filters through an open window four feet off the ground. Lucanus hoists himself up to the ledge and peers down. "Can you swim?" he asks as he reaches to pull Paulus up.

"I've survived more than one shipwreck," Paulus growls. He mutters a prayer and jumps.

Aislin scrambles up after him. Below, the Tiber flows black and thick, reflecting flames. Burning and smoldering timbers drift with the outgoing tide. Again, Aislin recalls the burning effigies on the day of the Argei, the ritual cleansing of Rome.

She flails, gulping smoke and water. She hears intermittent screams, shouts, and whooshing sounds. The city spins in gurgles and bubbles. She coughs and chokes but continues swimming.

Gasping, she climbs onto the muddy bank and flexes onto her back. In the moonlight, she sees a flood of Romans pushing their way out of the city, tugging donkeys and goats that are fitted with rope sacks; the bags bulge with silver candelabras, brass vases, and stone statuettes of gods and ancestors. Fire bells clang and *insulae* glow along their seams, belching dark smoke. As one building crumples, the adjoining sections lean inward, sway, totter, and disintegrate in spitting embers. Wooden poles and beams, pulsing in red, yellow, and black-veined orange, shoot flames and crash to the pavers. Other buildings combust in a flurry of sparks that spin like swarms of radiant bees. Cinders settle like expiring flies.

Paulus drags himself through the mud nearby, coughing and hacking. His hair drips. His tunic clinging to his emaciated form, he pulls himself to his feet. Lucanus takes Aislin's arm and the three of them wander cross-current through the carbonic mist into the crowd. A man leaps from the fourth-floor window of a burning building. A patrician woman runs shrieking through the street, her stola and hair aflame. Babies wail and dogs bark. The "eternal capital" dissolves to ashes as if the gods, speaking clearly for once in tongues of flame, were castigating Rome for its presumption and hubris. In the hot, sooty breeze Aislin feels the presence of her aunt Muirgheal, her grandfather, and her ancestors. They are watching, their thirst for vengeance finally slaked.

Paulus and Lucanus guide her around the center of the city, past the rectangular Temple of Portunus, the god of keys and livestock; the circular Temple of Hercules, protector of olives; and the towering grain warehouses, illuminated by the fires within; to the *Forum Boarium*, the cattle market, where milk cows bellow and yank on their chains behind burning gates.

They cross the Fabricius Bridge to the Tiberine island, in the middle of the river, and across the *Pons Aemilius* to the Etruscan bank and the eerily calm Trastavere district, inhabited by Syrians and Judaeans. Here the streets are empty and the river mirrors flame-lit, undulating walls. They climb to Lucanus's apartment, where he parts a beaded curtain and escorts Aislin and Paulus into a spacious room. Wooden niches line walls filled with glass bottles: green, blue, yellow, violet, some with long necks, others short and squat, blown off-center. In each niche, three lamps illuminate these bottles from behind, providing all the light for the room. Surgical instruments—knives, hooks, pliers, files, and spoons—hang on pegs. Tightly rolled scrolls fill hollows in the opposite wall. "Where is Faolan?" Aislin asks.

Puer appears from another room, leading Faolan by the hand. The boy moves with an awkward gait, his left arm bandaged. When he sees his mother, Faolan's pace quickens. He hugs her with his one good arm, whirling her about with so much strength she can hardly breathe. He howls with untamed delight.

"A gang that organizes beggars took him," Lucanus explains. "They smashed his left arm to elicit sympathy. We purchased his freedom and dressed and bandaged his wound, but it will take time to heal."

Even in this closed room, the smoke stings Aislin's eyes. Or is it the salt of tears? She tastes a drop and knows.

"He may not be able to express his feelings in our language," comments Lucanus, "but he has a bigger heart than anyone I've known."

"And that, in the end, is all that matters," adds Paulus.

"Are you happy?" Faolan asks his mother.

"You've been teaching him!" Aislin exclaims with delight, kneeling before her son.

"Certainly not!" Lucanus laughs. "Puer, perhaps."

Puer smiles.

"Are you happy?" repeats Faolan.

"More happy than I have been in a very long time," Aislin tells him. "In the imperial jail," she tells Paulus, "when you spoke of miracles, I had no idea what you meant. Now I understand."

❧

Aislin and Faolan reside with Lucanus for four days while fire consumes Rome. At night Faolan curls beside her, frightened by the crackle of blazing tenements, the crash and thunder of collapsing buildings, and the yelps of starving hounds. She and Paulus, Aislin reflects, have traded one smoke-filled jail for another. At the same time, she feels protected and wonders why Paulus and Lucanus pamper her so.

"We do have a purpose for you," admits Paulus as if guessing her thoughts. They stand at the balcony looking over the devastated capital. "But for now," continues Paulus, "try to find contentment within Lucanus's home. Gangs roam the city, looting whatever is left. Buildings that appear stable could collapse. You might enter and climb to the fourth floor, only to feel the stairs give way as the edifice bursts into flames. Rome is finished and the world, transformed."

"Then why are we still in Rome?"

"Patience," advises Paulus.

To Lucanus, Paulus narrates the history of his sect and of the conflicts he has endured. When he describes Stefanos's trial, he refers to the High Council of Judaea by its Greek name, *Sanhedrin*.

"One thing we must keep in mind," Lucanus advises him. "Judaea and the Galilee are enemies of Rome. As you know, open rebellion has broken out."

"And why must we keep this in mind?" asks Paulus.

"If we want the world to sympathize with us, we must tell the story it wants to hear."

Paulus agrees. Having addressed congregations in many lands, he has learned that while absolute Truth is universal, the way people can perceive it varies from one locality to another.

"I will tell your story in a compelling way that Romans will understand," Lucanus assures him.

While occupied with Faolan, Aislin listens to Paulus's conversation, immersing herself in his recollections and philosophy. She learns of Joshua of Nazareth's mission, of his disciples' and kin's misunderstandings, and of the quarrels that arose between Paulus and the leadership of the Synagogue of the Way.

❧

Two years after he went to Damascus, Paulus tells Lucanus, word of his preaching reached Stefanos's congregation. Their teacher, Jacob of Nazareth, or Jacob the Righteous One, as his followers called him, sent a courier to Damascus with word he wished to speak with Paulus. As far as Jacob knew, Paulus had never met his sibling, Joshua, and therefore had no authority to preach in Joshua's name.

They sat on the floor of Jacob's synagogue. "I first heard of you, if I am not mistaken," Jacob the Righteous One told Paulus, "in connection with the murder of my beloved friend Stefanos, may he walk forever in the glades of the righteous."

Paulus lowered his eyes. "That person," he said, "the person who participated in that murder, called himself Saul. I call myself Paulus. I am returned to my self and am renewed."

Jacob leaned back on his hands.

"I am reborn," Paulus added, "by the grace of the Lord, through the love of your brother Joshua, the Messiah, who was reborn before me. We, the Synagogue of the Freed Slaves, saw Stefanos's error as an opportunity to affirm our righteousness. I report none of this with pride, but in disgrace."

"To affirm your righteousness—through an act of murder?" asked Jacob incredulously.

They sat in silence, listening to each other's breathing. "I begged the

Lord for forgiveness," Paulus said at last, "and It granted forgiveness. Following my encounter with your brother, in the midst of the desert," Paulus began again, "I realized that Stefanos had been right, that salvation could not come to us alone through the corrupt Temple leadership but must come *through* us to all mankind. Just as we need the help of the Lord, so It needs *our* help to save the world. If ultimate destruction is imminent, as so many preach, then we must bring as many souls into the light as possible before the cataclysm."

Jacob cocked his head. "And how do you propose to accomplish this?"

"By instructing them in the Truth. In the Way."

"And aligning the gentiles' practice with our practice?" Jacob asked in a tone of disbelief. "The dietary commandments? Circumcision? The covenant?"

Paulus averted his eyes. "The gentiles are assured of a place in the *olam haba*, in the World to Come, if they are righteous," he explained.

"My brother Joshua never preached to gentiles," said Jacob. "He avoided the Greek cities, as anyone who really knew him would tell you."

"Of course," said Paulus in a conciliatory tone. "It had to start here— in Judaea, in the Galilee, in the ancient Land of Israel—as the prophets foretold."

Jacob rose to adjust the sputtering wick in one of the oil lamps. "My brother urged his followers to respect the Teachings. Word has it, you do not."

"I respect the Teachings," Paulus assured him. "But if salvation is to come to the Nations, we must not place impediments before them."

"This is where you depart from our tradition. There is danger in your approach."

"You knew Joshua in life," Paulus told Jacob the Righteous One. "I did not have that privilege. I encountered him only after his death. As the first of us to pass into the World to Come, the Joshua who preached and drew spirits from the ill here in Judaea and in the hills of the Galilee metamorphosed into the Joshua whose blessings shine on every land, the Bringer of Peace."

Jacob said nothing as he replaced the oil lamp in its niche.

Both men understood that neither would convince the other. In

Paulus's view, the Joshua of Jacob the Righteous One's memory was provincial. But in the view of Jacob, Paulus's messiah lacked an identity. Jacob's messiah was flesh; Paulus's was spirit. Both men knew they would remain at odds, two competing visions of a man whose purpose had been to bring harmony.

Paulus decided to change course. "I possess a coin," he told Jacob, referring to the *prutah* that Apollonius of Tyana had given him, "minted by the first generation of Maccabees, a coin that commemorates the purification of the Temple." He suspected this coin would interest Jacob the Righteous One. It represented liberation, for which both men yearned.

"I should very much like to see that. To hold it in my hand. That would give me hope," Jacob the Righteous One confirmed.

❧

What fascinates Aislin most is Paulus's preoccupation with the well-being of the weak, the crippled, and those who feel shunned. The concept of a God of compassion, a supreme Deity that has garbed Itself in human flesh and suffered as a man, affects her with increasing power as her days in Lucanus's home increase. Without the help of such a divinity, she suspects, children like Faolan cannot hope to survive. Surely, at the end of time, there must be justice for the innocent, the truly righteous, like Meitheamh and Nigellus.

Other aspects of Paulus's story confuse her. "What happened to Joshua of Nazareth *after* the resurrection?" she asks him. "Did he die again? Does he still wander the earth?"

"He is still with us," says Paulus.

"I could meet him, just as you did?"

"We will all meet him one day."

On the sixth morning the fire lies down to rest in a smoldering, sighing heap, and Aislin begins to ponder her future and that of her child. In a devastated city, devoid of inhabitants, it seems unlikely anyone will worry about an escaped prisoner. She could return home, to Albion, but discards the idea. She has heard rumors of a rebellion led by a female warrior named Boudica. The Romans demolished her army, laid waste to the land, and captured tens of thousands of slaves. There is nothing for her and Faolan in Albion now.

"I have a task for you," Paulus interrupts her musings, holding out a bronze coin, ancient but recently burnished so that its surface glows while the characters inscribed on it, dashes and squiggles, and the obscure figures on the obverse, seem etched in black. "This is the coin that the healer Apollonius of Tyana gave me in Tarsus. I want you to take this coin to Jerusalem and deliver it to Jacob the Just, the brother of my savior and leader of the Synagogue of the Way. I will pay you as I would any other courier. Judaea will be the best place to be when the Kingdom of Heaven arrives, which will happen imminently. Can you do this for me, Aislin? It would be a great service." He folds her hand around the coin. "It will be a gesture of healing," Paulus tells her.

Her eyes meet his. "For you, Paulus, I will go," Aislin tells him.

❧

The following morning they bid one another farewell in the desolate street. Puer has prepared a cart piled high with provisions. "Puer will accompany you to Ostia," explains Lucanus, "where we have booked you passage on a merchant ship."

Paulus embraces Aislin, then Faolan, lifting him off the ground as they laugh together.

"Do you intend to remain here, Paulus, amid these ruins?" she asks.

"I am needed elsewhere," says Paulus.

As they make their way through the devastation that is now the once-grand city of Rome, Puer describes the world that awaits her in the Holy Land. "Lucanus has taught me of the cult of Joshua of Nazareth," he says. "When the Kingdom of Heaven arrives, a golden light will pour down like rain and wash away the regrets and sorrows of the followers of Joshua, and their righteous ancestors will rise from graves to greet them. Will you stay in Jerusalem after your task is completed, or return to Albion?" he asks her.

"A snake does not crawl back into its skin," says Aislin as they pass through the ruined gates of Rome. "Come Faolan," she encourages her son, who is distracted by a mouse or rabbit he has seen scurrying in a field that stretches toward the Tolfa Mountains.

❧

It is the season of the Neptunalia, when Romans sleep in huts of laurel branches and pray to the god of the waters. Bonfires burn along the shore as refugees dance and sing. No one knows whether the emperor has survived, or whether Rome can endure this calamity.

Having arrived in Ostia, Aislin and Faolan prepare to board the boat that will carry them to Caesarea. The vessel is small, its space taken up with crates of grain and amphorae of wine. The stern sweeps upward like the tail of a great, fantastical magpie, and the prow juts forward like a beak, behind which lapis-blue and gold-leaf eyes survey roiling waters. The wooden planks creak as the ocean rises and falls like the chest of a sleeping giant. At the horizon, so close she can almost touch it, a blue-gray, watery murk blots out the boundary between sky and sea. The voyage will be hazardous—of that Aislin is certain—but it feels like destiny.

Nations are separated by a change of tongue, a range of mountains, a wide river. The sea, however, is not only a barrier between worlds, but a demarcation between phases of her life: her childhood in Albion, her captivity within the walls of Rome, her years of slavery in Pallas's domicile, and finally the *carcer*. She traveled to Rome to fulfill a task that the Companions and the spirits of her grandfather and Muirgheal had conferred to her in madness and dreams. Rome has burned and another world awaits.

Seagulls circle squawking above the port of Carthage, which reeks of brine and tar. In curtained booths between painted columns, vendors show off their wares: linens, silks, and wools, folded in open crates; incense; pottery; salted fish; copper hand mirrors; carved ivory; phials of perfume. Red, yellow, and blue brocade panels rustle and snap in the sea breeze. In an open-walled warehouse across from the wharf, a bearded Greek auctions slaves. Sailors haul the wealth of Africa—crates, amphorae, an ape in a wheeled wooden cage—into the wide bellies of docked ships.

Flanked by soldiers and advisors, Titus Flavius Vespasianus, proconsul of Africa, follows a courier toward a square-rigged *liburna* that is painted yellow, green, and black. He dislikes traveling in the company of so many guards and sycophants, but remembers what the philosopher Seneca once told him: "It is the curse of high achievement. One is courted by the merely covetous, and for protection from those whose envy is malicious, one is obliged to surround oneself with thugs."

That kind of success, Vespasian never sought. Many of the wealthiest and most powerful men in Rome he holds in contempt; nor does he hesitate to express his disdain. He has never chased advancement as an end in itself, but to return to Rome its republican strengths. During the Republic, a man's worth was measured not only in terms of wealth but by his devotion to the common good, the bonds of loyalty he formed, and his ability to act on his convictions. Since the demise of the Republic and the rise of the Empire, Rome has lost its moral bearings. The *virtu* of Rome now resides in the person of its emperor, a madman.

For his victories in Britannia, Vespasian won a series of lofty but symbolic administrative positions. He was miserable as a politician in Rome, but his brother, Sabinus, thrived in that environment, where social affiliations mattered more than character. Vespasian watched Sabinus ingratiate himself with superiors, even going so far as to bed the emperor's wife and, if rumors were to be credited, the emperor himself.

Careening drunk through the streets of the Palatine late one night six years ago, Sabinus lectured his younger sibling: "Your half-mythical Republic is long dead! And so much the better. The Gods themselves have little respect for this republican *virtu* you rant about." He clapped Vespasian on the shoulder. "We have achieved far more than your Republic ever did. We've built an empire! We're wealthier than ever." He tripped on a loose paver. Vespasian, who had hardly tasted the wine at that evening's feast, caught him. "People prattle about you," Sabinus concluded. "They say you're self-righteous and judgmental."

"Yes," admitted Vespasian, "Caesar built an empire, the wealthiest the world has known, on the ruins of the Republic—yes, yes—but I assure you, Sabinus, if we ourselves aren't convinced of its moral purpose, this empire cannot endure."

"The pursuit of prosperity and pleasure," riposted Sabinus, "is that not a worthy purpose? Is it not what our gods themselves spend their eternal lives doing?"

When Vespasian's consulship expired, the new emperor, Nero, dispatched him to the provinces, not in recompense for any accomplishment but in retribution for a failure. He had failed to applaud loudly enough at one of Nero's lyre performances. At the same time, the new emperor promoted Sabinus to the powerful position of consul of Rome.

One of Sabinus's responsibilities is to ensure the continuous supply of millet. The government distributes this grain free of charge to citizens. Upon it the vast majority of Romans depend for daily nourishment. Most of the millet ships from Carthage in quantities that reflect the census count in the province of Africa, now under Vespasian's charge. If a ship sinks, the older brother tasks the younger with making up the difference. Vespasian and Sabinus thus work closely, corresponding monthly, but Vespasian is grateful for the sea that separates them.

The ship's captain, wiry and young, salutes. "Hail Caesar!"

"Hail Caesar," echoes Vespasian. "What word from my brother, the consul?"

"The word is not encouraging, my lord," replies the captain rubbing his hands together. The captain conducts him onto the deck, pulls open a trap, and leads Vespasian down a rope ladder into the dank, lead-lined hold. Vespasian's eyes adjust and he recognizes the contents of his apartment in Rome: his desk, his cot, his dining table and chairs, a multitude of crates. He purses his lips, perplexed. "What does this signify?"

"A fire has destroyed much of the capital. The prefect, your brother, lost everything, but the flames didn't reach your neighborhood. Brigands have taken over the city. The prefect instructed me to save what we could."

"How did this happen?"

"They say it began in the quarter of Judaean exiles. From what we understand, they pray for the end of the world. This fire is the first fruit of their prayers."

This is not the first vexing report Vespasian has received regarding the Judaeans, whose province even the most ruthless Roman governors have considered unmanageable. Tens of thousands of Judaeans live in exile in Vespasian's province of Africa and in neighboring Egypt and Libya, displaced generations earlier from their homeland by the Ptolemies. Even now they refuse to worship the Roman gods, behaving as if their invisible God were superior to Roman deities despite ample evidence to the contrary. Of all the subject nations, the Judaeans are reputed to be the most obstinate.

"A Judaean leader named Chrestus is claiming to be the true emperor," the captain says, "and may have started this fire himself."

"Is Sabinus safe?"

"He's fled the capital along with the rest of the government and almost all the citizens. Rome is now a city of wind, spirits, and bandits. All its granaries are in ruins. That is what the consul asked me to tell you."

Vespasian considers this. If he is to replenish Rome's grain stores, he will need to double the flow of millet. The Africans in his province will despise him and Rome even more than they already do, and while their rancor scarcely fazes Vespasian, their loyalty, sincere or not, remains indispensable.

ֆ

The palace of the proconsul, glazed marble and tall Corinthian columns, curves around a plaza that overlooks the Mediterranean. In a room decorated with fading blue and pink frescos, Vespasian confers with the Census Taker and the Chief Tax Farmer of the province of Africa. "The peasants are already giving all they can," the Chief Tax Farmer tells him. "They hardly retain enough to survive."

"That is true for most crops," says the Census Taker. "However, we did have a bumper crop of turnips last year."

"Indeed." The Chief Tax Farmer leans forward in his chair, his gray beard brushing his collarbone, and tells Vespasian, "Here they feed turnips to pigs."

"This is not about whether Africans like the taste of turnips," says Vespasian.

"There is a rate of taxation, lord," says the Chief Tax Farmer, "beyond which people lose hope. Mere grumbling turns into revolt."

"If the Africans loved Rome, the Rome that built this great city, as I do," the Census Taker chides the Chief Tax Farmer, "the thought of revolt would not cross their minds."

"Built this city?" The Chief Tax Farmer scratches the tip of his nose with his little finger. "Forgive me for lecturing you," he tells the Census Taker, "but peasants, too, are proud, and their memory is long. Before Rome built Carthage, Rome destroyed Carthage." He turns back to Vespasian. "And while the burning of Rome saddens me, lord, many will see poetry in it."

Vespasian clasps his hands under his chin and regards the Chief Tax Farmer, whose courage he has always appreciated but whose audacity sometimes veers to insubordination. "Rome does not wantonly destroy great cities," he reminds him. "Carthage was threatening Rome. Do you imagine that Hannibal, had he prevailed, would have been kinder to Romans than Rome was to his people?"

"As the Carthaginians see it, Hannibal sought justice, not domination."

"They may see it as they like," retorts Vespasian. "But history is history. Rome won."

જે

Vespasian spends the next three days in consultation with tribal leaders, Berbers and Egyptians as well as Carthaginians. With the assistance of the Chief Tax Farmer, he drafts a speech intended to move the Africans to sympathy. Although he lacks confidence in his speaking ability—he is, after all, the scion of a rustic equestrian clan; he grew up on his grandmother's farm, nor did he excel in rhetoric—he sends out criers to rally the residents to the semicircular plaza under his second-floor balcony.

In solemn, clipped phrases he describes Rome's conflagration, the losses and repercussions for the empire, and the suffering endured not only by citizens of Rome but by non-citizens as well, including thousands of Carthaginian expatriates. He is prepared, he announces, to make personal sacrifices, donating furniture from his Roman apartments for use in Carthage's public buildings and paying his share of taxes. He calls on the people of Africa to demonstrate their loyalty by providing Rome with even more grain, for the good of all.

"If we give Rome the last of our grain," calls a man in the crowd, "what shall we eat?"

"We had a bumper crop of turnips last year," answers Vespasian.

As if on cue, the crowd pelts him with turnips, which they have hidden in their cloaks. Vespasian covers his face, as much in humiliation as for protection. As he turns to the other officials on his balcony, he notices his Chief Tax Farmer avert his gaze. He realizes that the content of his speech has been leaked; how else could the African peasants and the Carthaginians have known to bring turnips?

The proconsul issues orders for the arrest of his Chief Tax Collector, who will be charged with *maiestas*, treason, and thrown to lions in the amphitheater. It thrills the populace to witness a mauling, Vespasian knows, especially if it involves a tax collector—even one who has defended the perspective of the common people.

❧

"We have built aqueducts, sewers, and amphitheaters," Vespasian complains to his Chief Census Taker. "I have not lived extravagantly or arrogantly, but have tried to demonstrate the great republican virtues of piety, self-sacrifice, and courage. Yet even while accepting all we offer, they reject our leadership."

The Chief Census Taker replies, "What they crave is dignity. Every time they nibble from your outstretched hand, it erodes their pride."

"Why do they refuse to see merit in Rome's greatness? We all share in it, do we not?"

"You cannot force them to rejoice in Rome's accomplishments," says the Census Taker. "The best you can do in that regard would be to instill a fear of Rome."

"My colleague Pontius Pilatus tried that in Judaea," observes Vespasian.

"As you recall, he was hauled back to Rome in chains, charged with greed, corruption, and brutality."

During the ensuing months, Vespasian spends his personal savings on administrative travel and taxes himself at the same rate as his subjects. To lead by example, to teach virtue by *being* virtuous, is a novel and worthy experiment that suits his temperament.

He consults with his astrologer and promotes the Census Taker to the position of Chief Tax Collector. Together they plan a tour of his province, to plead with community leaders for increased grain production and to ensure that the provincial head-count, the basis for taxation, is accurate.

In a mountain village Vespasian witnesses an ancient ritual. A priest sacrifices a six-month-old infant to the fires of Ba'al Hammon, a terrifying and generous god who reminds Vespasian of the Roman Saturn. The priest places the baby on the burning altar. The winding sheets and the boy's hair catch fire first. His garbled wails fade behind the curtain of flames. His flesh smokes as it melts. The priest holds up his hands to receive the flames' radiance, then displays his palms—now inexplicably stained red—to the assembled villagers.

That a village prince would sacrifice his own child to his principal god, as a proof of devotion, moves and appalls Vespasian. This particular flavor of death, voluntary and communal, differs from any he has encountered in warfare.

In exchange for this proof of mortal devotion, the priest explains, Ba'al Hammon will provide rain and fertility. "For your participation in our most holy festival," he tells Vespasian through a translator, "Ba'al Hammon will bless you with equanimity in affliction and victory in battle." The priest escorts him deep into a lamp-lit cave in the mountainside, the shrine of Ba'al Hammon, a place so austere and silent that the proconsul can hear the earth itself breathe. A gate of gold blocks entrance to a smaller passage. Still reeling, Vespasian asks what lies beyond the gate. His host refuses to answer, insisting on the priestly right of inscrutability.

Later, descending the road from this village, Vespasian asks the Census Taker for more information. "It is said that in the Temple of Ba'al Hamon there lies a repository of all the gold given to the chief Deity of the Africans since the founding of Carthage, thousands of years ago," the Census Taker tells him. "When the Roman general Scipio defeated Hannibal, he sent scouts to find this cave but the Africans filled its mouth with dirt and rocks and planted grass and trees. I am shocked that the priest led you there. He senses in you a man of great integrity."

That evening, as they make camp at the base of the mountain, two envoys deliver a second message from Sabinus.

To Titus Flavius Vespasianus,

Titus Flavius Sabinus sends greetings.

The emperor has returned to the capital and by means of his unique genius we have found gold in the ashes of horrific destruction. We will appropriate a large swath of land in the center of the city, where all the buildings burned to the ground. There we will construct a great palace, more than a mile long, replete with a revolving, perfume-misted dining room and an automatic mechanism that will release thousands of rose petals from a ceiling that opens to the stars, and closes to the sun. Needless to say, the emperor is thoroughly absorbed in this project and consults with me and others throughout the day. Architects, stonemasons, painters, and a thousand craftsmen (who have of late been underemployed) will be laboring for years to come. Nor have we neglected to exact painful vengeance, as a lesson for all Romans, upon the Judaeans, who follow the rabble-rouser Chrestus—whom the people unanimously blame for this catastrophe. Seeing the reward that we shall mete upon them, no Roman will ever again dare to call their emperor weak or effeminate. Of course, all this building will require support in the form of increased taxation throughout the provinces.

Be healthy.

In his reply, delivered orally to the couriers, Vespasian congratulates his brother on his fruitful collaboration with the emperor and reports that he has levied his own income at the same rate as the Africans', and lacks the means to continue touring his province. Regretfully, he must borrow money if he is to continue pursuing the case for increased taxation. He closes his letter with the salutation: *May the gods guard your safety.*

As they leave the mountain behind, one of Vespasian's mules sprains its ankle in a gopher hole and the proconsul is obliged to kill it. He deploys a scout to locate a mule breeder, while his men redistribute food and supplies.

The next day a gregarious mule breeder fawns upon Vespasian and his entourage. Apologizing for the modesty of his estate, he serves them gruel and a bubbly beverage of fermented honey while an enormous hog roasts on a spit above a stone-lined pit. When they depart the following morning, the mule breeder insists they choose not one but three of his best animals, refusing remuneration. Vespasian vows to remember this honest, hard-working peasant.

∂

Returning to Carthage, to a palace now largely denuded of furniture, Vespasian receives yet another communication from Rome.

> To Titus Flavius Vespasianus,
>
> Titus Flavius Sabinus sends greetings.
>
> We are most distressed to learn of your circumstances and agree to lend you one year's living wage, to supplement your earnings as proconsul of Africa. To secure this loan we demand for collateral the farm you inherited from our grandmother as well as your apartment in Rome. The loan will accrue interest at twenty-four percent per annum over a period of two years and will need to be paid back at the monthly rate of one-twenty-fourth of the total debt. Upon failure of payment, ownership of said lands and apartment will devolve to us.

Sabinus, who has married into a wealthy family, has no need for more property, and Vespasian understands the terms proposed as a reprimand.

Rather than borrow from his brother, he muses, he could requisition the gold that lies idle in the Temple of Ba'al Hamon. Pilatus did something similar in Judaea, but Judaea rebelled. It is not impossible, in this light, that the fire in Rome was caused, if indirectly, by the zeal of one of Rome's provincial governors.

Deciding not to betray the trust of the Temple priest, and of all the generations of Carthaginians who have offered the fruits of their labors to their god, Vespasian devises another strategy. The emperor will need to quarry vast quantities of marble from Tibur and Carrara for the construction of his palace. Thousands of African mules will be needed. Vespasian sees opportunity in this—not only for himself, but for the humble mule breeder. His jaw clenched, he writes back accepting his brother's terms.

A head of schedule, the proconsul now known to Africans as *Vespasian the Muleteer* finishes reimbursing his brother. A month later, in the palace that remains sparsely furnished, he receives a singing courier costumed as Hermes, playing a hand-held, gilded harp:

> From the living God, Nero Claudius Caesar Augustus Germanicus, to his adoring worshipers, bounteous affection and greetings! The Mighty Vulcan has made his thunderous voice heard! Shall we not raise ours too, answering Him in choral exuberance? Let us honor Vulcan's power with the most magnificent festivities ever offered the God of Volcanoes and Conflagrations, culminating in the performance of an Original Hymn to Vulcan by the Divine Emperor of Terra Firma, Nero Claudius Caesar Augustus Germanicus.

The harpist concludes his song with a question: "Shall I report back to the Living God, the Emperor of the World, that you will attend?"

Aware that a refusal might end his career, Vespasian answers curtly: "We shall attend."

"Wonderful! You are directed to come in costume to the New Golden Palace, where the Divine Emperor will perform for a select group of his most ardent worshipers."

Vespasian wonders how many *aurei* the emperor disbursed to send this singing courier, and hundreds like him, to government officials throughout the empire, and how many years of back-breaking peasant labor funded such frivolity.

As a slave shows the courier out, Vespasian turns and sees his wife, Domitilla, draped in a cornflower-blue robe that covers much of her hair. Unlike Sabinus, who married into a powerful family, Vespasian has tethered his destiny to the former mistress of an obscure African soldier. Behind her stretch the painted and curtained columns and gardens of the palace. "So we are finally off to your beloved capital," she remarks.

"It cannot be helped," Vespasian mutters. "Besides, my term will soon end. Make the necessary arrangements. I shall consult with my astrologer, who will determine the propitious day for our departure."

His last stroll through Carthage takes place at dawn, alone. The city is quiet and misty, its air scented with decay. As he trudges through its empty streets, a sense of failure embraces him. He has maintained the peace well enough, but the provincials obstinately fail to see themselves as beneficiaries of a greater civilization's tutelage. Their resentment, Vespasian knows, so unlike the admiration of Rome vis-à-vis its Greek mentor, will curtail their potential.

❧

For five weeks Vespasian tosses on the sea with his wife and two sons, tracing the coasts of Africa, Judaea, Syria, Asia Minor, Greece, and Italia. When they reach Ostia, they travel five hours up the Tiber to the urban diadem of the world. As dusk settles over the *Forum Romanum*, Vespasian bears witness to a nightmare of charred, half-destroyed temples; buildings reduced to rubble and ash; blacksmiths' anvils ringing for the god of metallurgy; free men and slaves disguised as satyrs, nymphs, beasts, gods, and barbarians, blowing pipes and horns; a partially built palace of extravagant proportions; and looming above it all, torch-lit in the twilight, a one-hundred-foot-high bronze statue of the emperor clutching a golden lyre as he contemplates the heavens.

A crowd surrounds the site of the original Temple of Vulcan, a place regarded as the heart of Rome during the republican centuries but which Julius Caesar demolished when he redesigned the Forum. A priestess dressed as the goddess Fortuna plunges her hands into a wood-and-brass bucket, pulls out a handful of tiny, shimmering fish, and flings them onto an open-air altar. As the fish sizzle, the priestess shovels incense onto the coals, which spit sparks and clouds of scented smoke. Thus the god Vulcan savors a symbolic victory over Neptune, fire vaporizing water, death defeating life.

As he crosses the forum toward the New Golden Palace, a man disguised as a pig stomps on the hem of his toga—a deliberate affront. "What kind of costume is that?" oinks the pig-man, taking hold of Vespasian's shoulder to stabilize himself. "Careful I'd be, if I was you."

Vespasian understands his drunken reasoning. Rome strictly regulates the clothing of its citizens and its hordes of non-citizens. Each class is assigned a tunic or toga of specific design, denoting its rights or lack thereof. The proconsul's *toga praetexta*, with its bold crimson band, denotes high rank; and to attire oneself beyond one's rank is a serious crime.

"Off me, pig-man," orders Vespasian, "or I shall have you flayed."

The pig-man backs off, oscillating back and forth. "Ah, so it is real, is it? And you are what you pretend to be?" With a cloven fore-hoof he impudently scratches Vespasian's toga. "Then you're violating a different edict! All Romans are to be costumed, by imperial decree. You dare defy the emperor?"

"Who are you, knave, to address me this way? Out of my sight." Vespasian steps away but the pig-man coggles after him, falling upon him when he stops. "I meant no harm! Just brotherly advice!"

Vespasian pushes him down. The pig-man falls, kicking out his hooves and tripping the proconsul.

Vespasian rarely loses his composure but this man deserves a beating. He throws himself on top of him and tries to twist him onto his stomach but the pig-man, despite his inebriation, proves an aggressive tussler. Vespasian wraps his arm around his neck and yanks back his opponent's mask.

His brown hair matted, a three-day stubble covering his chin, Vespasian's older brother, Sabinus, grins at him. Vespasian releases his grip but Sabinus pulls him close, embracing him. Vespasian shakes his head in chagrined amusement. "I should have known."

Sabinus laughs. Trumpets blare in the New Golden Palace. "We must hurry." Sabinus jumps to his feet. "Take my mask. You really must disguise yourself."

"And you?"

"My cloven hooves and pink belly will have to do. As brothers, we complete each other. Some may find it clever."

Arm in arm they stride to the palace, Sabinus's uneven gait no longer suggesting drunkenness but swagger. Recognizing him, the palace guards admit them to the rambling courtyards, where Rome's elite stroll with wives and lovers in elaborate costumes. Some lie together in the grass or on marble benches, honoring Vulcan with grunts and moans.

Sabinus shepherds his brother through torch-lit, colonnaded walkways that smell of damp plaster and paint, toward an inner compound, explaining in rapid, hushed tones that Nero has hired a team of architects, unsurpassed in talent, and that they are witnessing the birth of an eternal monument.

All through the city, jugglers and mimes conclude their performances. Anvils still and singers hush to pay tribute to the appearance of the emperor, although none other than the small crowd gathered in the New Golden Palace can actually see him. Two rows of sputtering, reeking, naked human torches—men, women, and children impaled on poles, covered in pitch and ignited—illuminate the marble stage.

It is human sacrifice on a massive scale, although Vespasian is aware that most Romans would not recognize it as such. While Africans sacrifice their children to negotiate with their gods for rain, Nero sacrifices to illuminate his own divine power.

Vespasian is not one of those who glamorize warfare, but death by immolation does not equate with death by war. In combat, opposing parties fight over land or ideology, whereas ritual killing involves no contest of ideas, technology, or property, nor does its victim pose a potential threat to the state. Instead, it presupposes a bloodthirsty god who requires constant affirmation of mankind's subservience.

"They are Judaeans, followers of Chrestus," Sabinus whispers, nodding toward the burning figures to explain that what they are witnessing is not sacrifice at all, but collective punishment.

A chorus of maidens rings tiny bells as the emperor glides onto the stage, lyre in hand. His naked body is painted gold and adorned with tendrils, berries, leaves, and a spiked crown.

Vespasian knew Nero's father, a scoundrel who was charged with incest and treason by Tiberius, a previous emperor. He always thought Nero an unlikely ruler, even after the teenager asserted his intention by murdering the heir-apparent, his half-brother. It was Nero's mother, in the end, who engineered his ascension by poisoning Nero's stepfather, the emperor Claudius. She paid the price for her power-lust when, five years before the Great Fire, Nero had her strangled.

A sole individual, the new empress Poppaea, occupies the first five rows before the stage, her isolation ensured by an intervening rank of guards. Gold filaments, intermingling with loose curls, tumble from her elaborate coiffure and down her back. Vespasian has seen her once before, at a party hosted by her second husband. Scandalously, she and Nero retreated to a bedroom for the duration of the evening. After which, mad with lust for Poppaea, the emperor charged his first wife and stepsister, Claudia Octavia, with adultery, divorced her, banished her to the island of Pandateria, and tortured her loyal maidservants to death. Outraged citizens paraded through the streets, hoisting garlanded statues of Octavia, demanding her return, and leaving Nero no choice, in his view, but to have her executed. In a delicate gesture of imperial concupiscence, he instructed her executioner to deliver Octavia's severed head to Poppaea. Two weeks later, the emperor and his mistress wed.

On stage, Nero raises his lyre, gazes at the stars in imitation of the statue of himself that soars above him, and starts singing in a pinched, trained warble a hymn to the god of metallurgy and flames. Vespasian prefers the vigorous songs of peasants to the epic poetry of Rome's aristocracy. Stifling a yawn, he searches for something redemptive or worth his while, other than his reunion with his brother, in this festival of ostentation. He finds it, surprisingly, in the attitude of sincerity, the apparent lack of guile, in the twenty-eight-year-old emperor's adipose face. Clearly, as a god himself, Nero feels more at ease addressing Vulcan than conversing with the humble mortals who jam his half-built palace.

❧

Following the emperor's concert, Sabinus escorts Vespasian into an adjacent atrium. In the center of a glistening marble floor, surrounded by torches, scaffolding, plasterers, and painters, Nero dons a simple gown and basks in the afterglow of performance.

"It was magnificent, Caesar. Your voice was divine, as always." Sabinus prompts his brother with a glance.

"Yes, magnificent," agrees the proconsul, holding the pig's mask under his arm.

"Was it?" The emperor, extending his arms to allow a slave to wipe the gold paint from his hands, glances pointedly at Vespasian. "The audience seemed quite overwhelmed, as if my voice floated above you all and winged away into the heavens, where I suppose it belongs."

When called upon to engage in rituals of flattery, Vespasian's language fails him. "So it does, Caesar," Sabinus interjects. "So it does. And yet, gazing up at your voice, as at a wondrous bird, we can hardly fail to perceive its ethereal beauty, much like diminutive sparrows twittering at dusk."

"Diminutive sparrows?" The emperor arches an eyebrow.

"Or rather, soaring falcons," Sabinus corrects himself with a smile and a slight bow of his head.

Nero leans toward his servant, who wipes the makeup off his cheek. "Still, they adored our recent performances in the province of Achaea even more, did they not?" Nero turns his face to allow the slave to clean his other cheek.

"Adored them? Caesar, they crow about those performances to this day."

"If only Rome possessed the fine sensibilities of Greece," sighs the emperor. "Ah, well. Perhaps one day, with sufficient instruction from enlightened leaders like myself."

"Speaking of the provinces," Sabinus prompts him, "I believe there is something you wanted to discuss with my brother."

The emperor presses his hand on Vespasian's chest. The general resists the urge to recoil.

"This pesky people," says Nero, "the Judaeans, who burned down our beautiful capital, and whose chief city lies north of the region you so recently governed, they reject Rome's rule and attack our representatives."

"They have ceased offering sacrifices to Caesar," explains Sabinus.

"We moved the Twelfth Legion in from Syria to quell their insubordination," resumes Nero, "but it was a bloodbath. These deranged Levantines cut down our Twelfth Legion, and now they're proclaiming that this victory proves their God's superiority over ours. Over *me*. What should be done about it?" he demands of Vespasian.

"Send in massive forces. Take the smaller towns first. Punish them. Give Jerusalem the opportunity to relent. If they refuse, make an example of the capital."

"My thinking precisely," says Nero.

While they have been talking, Vespasian's eyes have caught those of a palace decorator, who crouches at the base of a pillar painting flowers. Candlelight illuminates his concentrated expression.

Decades have passed since Vespasian last saw the soldier Septimus, whom he left for dead in the forests of Albion. Glancing up, the artisan meets Vespasian's gaze.

"Are you up to the task, proconsul?" Nero demands.

"I would be honored, Caesar," Vespasian replies, averting his gaze from Septimus.

"Good. Your first duty will be to rebuild the Tenth Legion, *Fretensis*, who so bravely contributed to our effort to quench the fire, and whose numbers were thus tragically reduced."

"I shall take on that task at once, with eagerness, Caesar."

The young emperor turns and ceremoniously departs with his retinue.

Sabinus grins, as if to say *You see what your brother has done for you?* Then he follows Caesar, together with the remaining courtiers.

☙

Septimus kneels on a brocaded cushion, designing wreaths, garlands, columns, and inset scenes that illustrate pivotal moments in the lives of gods and heroes. Years have passed since anyone has recognized him in the capital. With Poppaea's ascension to the imperial throne, worlds opened to Septimus. She built an extravagant summer home in Oplontis, where Septimus mastered his craft. Patricians in nearby Pompeii perceived brilliance in the painted fantasies of the empress's favorite slave-artist and competed with each other to procure his services. By the age of thirty-one, Septimus had saved enough money to purchase his freedom.

That was the happiest moment of his life. Born an aristocrat, he had never felt privileged as a child. Free, though not wealthy after ten years of bondage, he was reborn. Still, a voice within nagged him. Had he advanced so remarkably, so rapidly, as an artist, or had others' appreciation of his work improved as a consequence of his sister's seduction of the emperor?

When he discussed this with Poppaea, she laughed. "Don't torture yourself. What you *are* is what others perceive. If they see you as brilliant, then that is what you are; if they later decide you utterly lack talent, that you never had any in the first place, then history reverses itself. We're nothing but mirrors, brother, of how others see us."

Despite his misgivings, Septimus derived great satisfaction when his work was admired. Visitors and clients exclaimed over his technique, his use of light, and the ways in which he wove disparate scenes together. The future appeared bright and prosperous. Work was plentiful and he had fallen in love with a freed slave.

After construction began on the *domus aurea*, the philosopher Lucius Seneca, seeking to ingratiate himself with Poppaea, hired Septimus to decorate the rooms of the new palace. Seneca rose before dawn and wrote by the light of a small flame until the affairs of state required his attention. Occasionally his work and Septimus's coincided, and sometimes they conversed.

"I sense you are not unhappy, though you are hardly wealthy," Seneca told the painter.

Septimus, painting Hippomenes's golden apple, paused in his work.

"What is the nature of your contentment?" pursued Seneca. "Is it due to your vocation? Your family?"

"I believe we are happy to the extent that we feel loved," Septimus opined.

"You do feel loved, then?"

"I have loved three women." Septimus put down his brush. "The first didn't love me in return, though perhaps she thought she did. In any case, I was blissfully unaware of her feelings. I was only aware of my fantasy about them."

The philosopher nodded.

"The second...well, I didn't know I loved her until I lost her. With the third, I'm finally experiencing a moment of shared emotion, or an illusion of shared emotion—it hardly matters, does it?"

"So you believe love is to be measured by how we experience it?" Seneca queried.

"How else are we to measure it?" asked Septimus.

"I would propose that love is to be measured only by what we do for the other," said Seneca. "Otherwise, we are at the mercy of forces beyond our control. But tell me, Septimus, why do you, as a skilled practitioner of art, believe that people feel an urgent need to mirror their world in painting, poetry, and music?"

"I cannot claim to know," said Septimus. "One can, after all, become a skilled practitioner without understanding such mysteries."

"But where does the artistic inclination come from?" Seneca

wondered aloud. "Do you believe it comes from the god, or from your own mind?"

"*Which* god?" asked Septimus, stepping down from his ladder.

"In my view there is only one god, ultimately—Jupiter, the deity of lightning and thunder. The other so-called gods are merely his attributes."

"Does the emperor also hold this view?" asked Septimus.

"The emperor is an actor. This role was thrust upon him. He plays it as well as he can."

Septimus approached Seneca's table and sat down opposite him. "I have heard of this philosophy of monotheism," Septimus acknowledged. "My sister took an interest in the philosophy of the Judaeans for a time, even attended their meetings here in Rome. A singular god, all-powerful, beneficent, who can inspire specially endowed human beings, or even appear as a man. It makes no sense to me. With such a simple god, a god of peace, how do you explain a world like ours that is so complex and full of conflict?"

"I will not defend the god of the Judaeans," said Seneca. "If indeed they worship Jupiter, perhaps they misunderstand him." He picked up his pen. "But I must return to my work, and you to yours."

∂°

Septimus regards his exchange with the philosopher as a rare privilege. Seneca is celebrated, brilliant, and powerful. Their discussion has illuminated, for Septimus, an exquisite, ragged symmetry in his pursuit of his craft and his quest for love.

His life is revealed to him as an epiphenomenon, an unintended consequence of uncontrollable forces. For this reason, when Titus Flavius Vespasianus recognizes him in the Domus Aurea, Septimus does not consider fleeing.

"I never expected to see you again, Septimus. You will recall," Vespasian reminds him, "that I swore by Quirinus, the God of my ancestors, that if I ever met you again, I would kill you."

"My life is in your hands, general."

Vespasian would rather spare him, but Septimus twice betrayed Rome: once when he abandoned his post as night watchman, endangering the camp; a second time when he returned to Rome despite his promise not to do so. By returning to Rome, Septimus risked exposing Vespasian's leniency and undermining his authority. The general has no choice but to reassert that authority and to honor his pledge to Quirinus by executing the delayed sentence.

"I keep my promises," he tells the artist. "Kneel."

Septimus falls to his knees before Vespasian, who wraps his massive hands around the artist's neck and squeezes, his thumbs pushing against the night watchman's windpipe. The artist gasps and collapses backward. Vespasian falls upon him.

Septimus beholds his own shadow, half-illuminated by flickering torchlight, in the general's pupils. The shadow fades.

In a dissolving reverie, as if from a hilltop at dusk, Septimus surveys the passions, frustrations, and joys of his mortal existence: his first loves, his inadvertent betrayal of his country, his subsequent enslavement by his sister. His life has been a precipitous fall, but it afforded him a view of the world from an unsuspected angle. Slowly he climbed out and for a moment, he danced in freedom and sunlight with the last woman he loved.

As his spirit takes leave of the world, he reflects, these sentiments will endure only in his murals, echoing through the ages in the minds of those who contemplate them, as long as the walls he has painted remain, as long as there are eyes to behold them.

&

Only after Septimus expires does it dawn on Vespasian that he has just killed the empress's brother. Miraculously, it appears the atrium is deserted and there are no witnesses to his deed. He offers a silent prayer of thanks to Quirinus, whose work he has just performed, and strolls out of the room.

Leaving the palace, Vespasian reminds himself never to look backward. There is no cure for regret, guilt, or compunctions other than time. Even time, he sighs, may not heal them. Perhaps it merely buries them.

We forget. That is a blessing. If we were unable to forget, the cruelties of our mortal existence would overwhelm us.

Ten summers have ripened Hanina's grapes and ten autumns have fermented their juice. Miriam is gone and the winters have been lonely. Although Yohanan's Sabbath interpretations of the Tradition attract crowds in Arav, Capernaum, and Nazareth, he lies awake at night, wondering why the Lord hides Its face, no longer speaking to men through prophecy or miracles.

"Although we must trust that the Lord has a plan," he tells his congregation, "and that doing what is right matters, we must act as if we were entirely responsible for our own destinies. In our time, we must not expect miracles. To proclaim, as Menakhem, son of Judas the Zealot, does, that a tiny, occupied nation can throw off the shackles of an empire, that Israel can rout Rome, is tantamount to claiming knowledge of the Lord's mind—or, even more presumptuously, trying to impose our will on the Lord."

The poem about Solomon's love for the Queen of Sheba still soothes him. The *Song of Songs*, he now understands, is about seeing beauty in what is foreign and strange. As spring approaches, a series of dreams unfurls like embroidered sails in the oneiric gusts of his sleeping mind. Stones glisten at the bottom of a stream, a rising wind causes the river to boil, and the stones to turn to dust. Gathering a handful of the dust at the parched riverbed, he examines it and is struck by the realization that it is composed of miniscule Hebrew letters. The breeze blows it away. The letters jumble.

He meanders through Jerusalem near his family home; he meets people who speak a variety of languages, but recognizes nobody and understands nothing of what they say. He encounters a woman staring up at the dark, cloud-filled sky. He speaks to her, but she does not seem to hear him.

He awakes and sits up on the mattress. A breeze wafts through his window, which overlooks a corner of Hanina's orchard. A flock of geese wings southward across the cloud-flecked heavens, in a formation that reminds Yohanan of the broken Hebrew letter *vav.*

He strolls along the hillside in a harsh wind, describing to Hanina his dreams and the dread they engender. "The stones represent the people of Israel," Yohanan tells Hanina, "who crumble into the letters of the Tradition. What is a people but the stories they tell? And what are stories but words, made of letters?"

"And the water?" asks Hanina. "And the south-blowing wind?"

"The water is the cosmos," says Yohanan. "The stars, the air, the earth. The wind is time." Yohanan reflects upon the paths he has wandered and the people with whom he has shared moments of communion. He feels as if a circle were closing, or a spiral were looping back upon itself.

"Passover is approaching," he tells Hanina. "I feel the tug of the season." Yohanan notices small butterflies cavorting above the vineyard, twisting and tumbling through the air and then vanishing.

❧

The springtime month of Nisan sprinkles the Galilean hills with grass and forget-me-nots. The *kedem*, a hot wind, gusts from the east. Groups of pilgrims dot the roads, trekking across the land of their ancestors with sheep, donkeys, and camels. Most are poor, many destitute, but all imbued with the mad hope that this Passover will bring liberation. Yohanan meets travelers who sit on boulders sharing bread and water, as they are required to do during the season of Passover.

On the third day of Yohanan's descent from the Galilee, rain begins to fall. As he pitches his tent he sees a woman, drenched and shivering, her arm around a young boy's shoulder. A goat trots behind them. The woman's hair, he notices, is the color of wet ibex fur, her eyes the dusty green of olive leaves. The boy clings to her ragged tunic with his good arm. The goat nestles against his thigh. "Are you in need of shelter?" Yohanan asks. "Please, warm yourselves by my fire and share some soup."

She assents, speaking a Latin that yields to Greek, and Yohanan leads them to his tent. He sets down a basin of water and proceeds to wash the boy's feet. The boy giggles as the woman looks on, fascinated, as if she has never before seen a man wash another's feet.

Yohanan spoons out portions of lentil-barley soup, which his visitors devour. When they are done, the woman whispers something to her boy, who proceeds to hug Yohanan, pressing his face into his side.

In the candlelight, Yohanan examines the goat. They have found an animal without blemish, he notes, which will make an apt sacrifice for the Passover.

"*Yerushalayim?*" he asks the woman. "*Pesach?*" Jerusalem? Passover?

"*Nai,*" says the woman in Greek. Yes.

Yohanan fills a bowl with water. "*Mayin,*" he says in Aramaic, offering her the bowl.

She sips, her gaze one of suffering but not resignation.

As Yohanan busies himself with provisions for his guests, the sky darkens. When he returns to their side the boy moans and raises a finger, gawking. Yohanan looks where he points. The full moon, heavy and amber-hued, has risen into retreating clouds, partially hiding its face as if behind a veil. Citrine rays shoot out above and below, filling a portion of the sky with a brilliant, diffuse glow. It seems so close, like a great eye watching the world, signifying something important in a language Yohanan cannot read.

That night, he lies awake listening to the breathing of the woman and the boy. He wonders where they came from and why they are traveling to Jerusalem, whether indeed to honor the Passover or for another purpose. He chants songs he learned in the Temple, softly so as not to wake his guests, but the boy does wake and snuggles beside him, pressing his ear to Yohanan's chest.

❧

The goat trots beside the boy, occasionally bleating. The boy speaks to it in squawks, honks, and taps. The woman seems absorbed in her thoughts and in contemplation of the landscape. The goat sleeps curled like a dog. The child snuggles beside it.

At the end of a fifth day of travel, Yohanan lies awaiting sleep, listening to the rhythmic chirp of crickets, inhaling the aroma of salt and mud, acorns and flowers, aware of the nearness of his companions. The woman slumbers beside her son, her arm holding him close. An oak tree leans over them, a breeze rustling its leaves. Other pilgrims' tents dot the hills beyond the River Jordan.

Near the town of Yotapata a redolence of ash and cinders fills the air. They round a hill and see the town on a distant elevation, aflame, its walls breached, Roman soldiers streaming in. Yohanan hears shouts, cries, and the brattle of steel. The woman sinks to her knees, her expression one of intense grief. Yohanan wants to comfort her but she waves him away.

He walks further. In a broad field, thousands of slain Roman soldiers repose in pools of congealed blood. Overwhelmed, yet captured by the sadness of the place, Yohanan steps into their midst.

Young men, all. Most, clean shaven. Astonishment and anguish contort their mouths and eyes. Perhaps it never occurred to them that Galileans could kill Romans. Others appear to be sleeping. He kneels to close the eyes of a freckle-faced, boyish fighter.

To wash away the stench of death they bathe in a pool fed by tributaries of the River Jordan, amid tamarisk shrubs, lotus trees, and saltbushes that bend like mothers over their infants. Yohanan slips out of his sandals and tunic and gestures for the boy to remove his but the boy shrieks and flaps his uninjured hand like a stunted wing. He dresses again and the woman hurries over. She kneels before the boy, cups her hands, dips them into the water, and sips. She offers him some but he screeches louder, waving his hand frantically. Finally, she trickles water onto his hair. He shakes himself like a waterfowl and the two of them collapse laughing and tickling each other, shadows of leaves playing on their faces and garments.

❧

Yohanan observes how she reaches for the boy and how the boy in turn caresses the goat, as if passing along a message of kinship. Sometimes they sit together, the boy stroking the beast's head, mumbling. When Yohanan or the woman separates them, the goat bleats plaintively and the boy whimpers in protest. On fine afternoons, the boy and the goat skip through the fields until both are weary. In uncanny mimicry, the boy, too, takes to bleating.

At night they lie on their backs gazing up at the stars. The woman tells Yohanan her name and the boy's. Yohanan holds Faolan. The goat snuggles at their feet. The woman points out the constellations, describing them in Latin. Yohanan understands none of what she says, nor can he discern the pictures her fingers trace. While he would recognize the names of the Roman zodiac, these are not the names she pronounces or the patterns she traces.

She turns her face toward his and he understands that it is his turn to speak. In Aramaic he tells her what he knows of cosmology: that the earth is either an immobile sphere at the center of the turning spheres of the heavens, each of which holds stars, as the Greeks claim; or a flat disc floating on water, as the Persians maintain. Some constellations, such as Kesil, Kimah, and Ash, are Messengers; while others—Nisan, Iyar, Sivan, Tammuz—correspond to the Hebrew months. The bright planet that appears near the horizon at dusk is *Meleket Hashamayim*, Queen of the Heavens, he tells her. The sun, moon, and planets revolve through the heavens in cycles of varying lengths. To investigate these patterns is a holy pursuit, tantamount to studying the mind of the Creator.

≈

Yohanan's voice soothes Aislin like water lapping the shore of a lake. Most men, in her experience, either seek to lord it over others or bitterly accept their tyranny. Vying for position in the social hierarchy preoccupies the strong, while the effort to endure abuse exhausts the weak. Paulus described an inverse society where the meek triumph and gentleness holds sway over force. This society will take form in Jerusalem and spread from there. Aislin suspects Paulus is a dreamer. He described an Israel filled with dreamers. When the whole world shares the same dream, perhaps it will be transformed. Or maybe, muses Aislin, the world will never share one dream, but will learn to share an infinity of dreams.

She observes Yohanan playing with Faolan. He lifts him onto his lap, points at various features in the landscape, and pronounces Aramaic words, *tree, stream, hill*. Watching them caper with the goat, Aislin remembers Elisedd, the lamb she loved before the troubles began in Britannia. It occurs to her that she is reliving her travels with Septimus following the destruction of her village decades earlier, both slowly learning to trust each other, she mastering his language as they journey to the capital. But this is a different land, Jerusalem a different capital, and she and Yohanan, different people. Time is neither straight nor circular but bends back upon itself as it ascends.

At a roadside fruit stand, made of tent poles and palm fronds for the benefit of pilgrims, Yohanan purchases three pomegranates and juggles them for Faolan. The boy falls to the ground, writhing with laughter and braying. Yohanan laughs, too.

On the seventh day they crest a hill where fragrant narcissus flowers bloom, honeybees alighting on their petals. The walled city of Jerusalem emerges under a glowing, stippled sky. The travelers can discern the Temple esplanades, overlooking dense residential areas and palaces; the Roman theater and the Healing Pool of Bethesda; the sheep market and the gardens.

With its buildings of white marble and yellow sandstone and its rooftop gardens, Jerusalem is much smaller than Rome. Masses of pilgrims crowd every street and public space within and without the city walls. Yohanan, Aislin, and Faolan watch the sun set in the east, reflecting mirror-bright off the silver- and gold-clad Temple doors. Torches and lamps glow throughout the city and bonfires in the valleys and hills, mirroring and magnifying the constellations.

In the morning they pass through the Shechem Portal into the holy city. Well-wishers throw anemone, white rockrose, and crocus flowers from rooftops and balconies, shouting greetings to the pilgrims in the streets below. Aislin is reminded of a Roman *triumph*, a parade honoring a victorious general, but here, at Passover, the festival of freedom, every man is his own leader, his own general. The Roman despots find the notion of freedom threatening. This is why, on Passover, soldiers line the rooftop of the Antonia Fortress and all the major streets and gateways.

They reach a plaza where musicians scrape and blow on timbrels, flutes, and drums. Children, women, and men dance. Faolan squirms, laughs, rolls his eyes, and hoots. A boy pulls him into the children's circle. Faolan whirls and brays, giggling as the children spin around him. Dizzy, Faolan stumbles and falls. A dark-skinned boy pulls him to his feet. Another imitates his halting, unsure way of moving and Faolan cackles in delight.

&

Aislin sips diluted wine on the moonlit rooftop home of Yohanan's sister, Hannah, among Aramaic-speaking strangers. Torch-bearing revelers parade through the streets below, chanting hymns. Hannah touches Aislin's elbow. "You speak Greek?" she asks.

"A little," says Aislin.

"You are from Rome, no? This is my brother's impression."

"Yes," confirms Aislin, glancing at Yohanan, who is engaged in conversation with a group of men. "I learned Greek in the home of my former master."

"You are a freed slave, then?"

"I was once a servant," Aislin confirms. "And you? How do you come to speak Greek?"

"My husband, a merchant, grew up in a Greek-speaking home, and conducts much of his business in Greek. But tell me, what brings you here from Rome? Does Jerusalem please you?"

"Yes," Aislin says. "So far I am pleased."

"Of course you are happy here. We're humans, not beasts."

"And Romans are beasts?" asks Aislin.

"Perhaps I misspoke," says Yohanan's sister. "They are not animals. To call them animals is to insult so many wonderful creatures like your son's friend."

"Some Romans have been kind to me," says Aislin, "despite my foreign birth and poverty."

"They can be kind," concedes Hannah. "But as a nation they are rotten and deserve to die for the evil they do, just as they bring misery and death to so many others."

Hannah translates for Yohanan, who is astonished to hear Aislin's thoughts. It is as if he has previously viewed only her back and hair and can now see her face. "I once thought every Roman carried the guilt of his nation," says Aislin, "but I no longer believe this to be true."

"What brought about this change?" asks Yohanan.

"Not *what* but *who*. A man I knew in Rome. In jail."

Yohanan learns that Aislin, too, spent her childhood in a land violently subjugated by Rome, but unlike the Children of the Covenant, her people relied upon oral traditions alone for the preservation of their stories. When the Romans exterminated their bards and warriors, they erased Albion's past and future.

Aislin confides that she believes she started the Great Fire, influenced by her people's Companions. She speaks, too, of her jailmate, Paulus, whose philosophy appears to represent a blend of Israelite traditions, emphasizing the moral purpose of Creation, with others that memorialize the death and regeneration of an incarnate god, a Mithras or Adonis. She speaks, too, of Paulus's faith in a god whose love for humanity is so powerful that It was willing to sacrifice Its only son.

"This concept of human sacrifice, of death as redeeming, I cannot abide," says Yohanan. "What your Paulus preaches is not our faith. But this is to be expected from a man who grew up in Tarsus, a land known for its jumbled beliefs and practices."

"Are the people of Judaea less confused?" Aislin challenges him. "According to Paulus, no two men agree on anything here, yet all are passionate in their convictions."

"Then why did you travel all this way?" he asks.

"I'd rather live in a land where people argue about what is true, or what is good, than an empire where a madman's will is the only measure of both. I also travel to deliver this coin to the Synagogue of the Way," she explains.

Yohanan examines the coin. An ancient Hebrew script covers the obverse; on the front, a haut-relief depicts bull horns, or a twin candelabra, and a pomegranate. "I will take you there," he says, returning the coin.

Other visitors gather about Yohanan, asking about his travels, the struggle against the Romans in the Galilee, and points of law. They call him "teacher" and request his blessing. Exaggerated reports of his gentleness and erudition and of the miracles he supposedly performs have preceded him to the capital.

"These people treat your brother with respect, even veneration," Aislin says to Hannah. "They regard him, it seems, as a great teacher, or a healer. What is the philosophy he preaches?"

"Ask him," Hannah replies. "In the morning. For now, you need rest."

Before retiring for the night, Aislin asks Yohanan, "Is it true that you are a healer? Can you heal Faolan?"

"I'm afraid it's the other way around," Yohanan tells her gently. "Faolan has been healing me. I had quite forgotten that such innocence still exists in the sublunary realm."

The love between the boy and the goat reminds him that in the ability to feel and express joy, love, compassion, and sorrow, humans are in no way superior to beasts. The Greeks, the Romans, and the Hellenized Judaeans, with their elevation of reason over emotion, have made a fundamental mistake. Reason and emotion, Yohanan muses, are like a husband and wife, often striving against one another but frequently compatible. For those like Faolan, whose capacity to reason is weak, there is no inner strife. His life, more pure than others, is all the more holy.

Aislin nods. *"Ayn"* — yes, in Aramaic.

❧

In the morning they make their way through crowds of pilgrims toward the Synagogue of the Way, pausing before the towering, gold-leafed Genath Gate, where pilgrims, raising their leader in a gilded chair, chant, *"Mashiakh, mashiakh, hosanna, hosanna!"*—Hooray, hooray, our anointed one has come! Yohanan recognizes their bearded, grave messiah: it is Menakhem, son of Judas the Zealot. Despite the Romans' decimation of his followers in the *Shavuot* massacre, their numbers have increased. They carry him to the center of a great square, flanked by royal palaces and a theater. Roman soldiers guard the palace gates, beyond which Agrippa II—known as Herod, after his great-grandfather—meets with emissaries from Rome, Syria, and the Judaean population over which he rules. It is an audacious place for any Galilean to sermonize, but for one who calls himself *king* to do so is *laesa maiestas*, a capital crime. The group lowers the gilt chair to the ground and forms a circle around Menakhem as he addresses them.

"We have journeyed from the Galilee," Menakhem tells them, "where we have witnessed horrors worse than any you have seen in Jerusalem. Israel has always paid dearly for its sins, have we not? We labored in Egypt two hundred years; Babylon dragged us out of our land in chains. One liberation begets another bondage but the final liberation still awaits us!"

Some in the swelling crowd cheer. The Roman soldiers watch, impassive, either not comprehending Menakhem's Aramaic or failing to perceive its import.

"We live in a time of darkness," Menakhem continues. "The Lord no longer dwells in Its Temple, and evidence of this is foisted upon us daily. The high priest performs illicit sacrifices and traitorous genuflections, but few are fooled. So we have lost the protection of our Father. And what do we get in return?" His voice rises: "Rome widens our aqueduct! Yes, Jerusalem gets more water, but who pays for this so-called marvel? Where did the money come from?"

"Our taxes!" shouts a man.

"Not our taxes," Menakhem corrects him. "Our taxes finance their chariot races and gladiator matches. They stole the money for the aqueduct from our sacred *korbanot*, the Temple Treasure—from the very hands of our Heavenly Father. This is the source of our water, with which we purify ourselves! The offense will not go unpunished," Menakhem bellows. "And in the end, the righteous will triumph, as in the day of the Maccabees."

"What you preach, Menakhem, son of Judas, is folly!" shouts Yohanan.

"Why do you say that, Yohanan, son of Zakkai?" he asks.

"Lo ratzakh," says Yohanan. "Thou shalt not murder. What you advocate is not merely wrong, it is suicide."

"Killing is permitted in defense of our land," counters Menakhem. "It is not suicide if the Lord is with us. The Maccabees proved that."

"The Maccabees were misguided," Yohanan protests. "Yes, they prevailed for a time, because the occupiers were busy on other fronts, but look at the consequences! Their descendants grew dissolute. This was to be expected, because their victory was not a victory of prayer but of violence. Rome conquered Jerusalem and installed the Herodian dynasty. This is the legacy of the Maccabees."

"You say the Maccabees were not justified," says Menakhem. "But I tell you, the story of the Maccabees does not arise from nowhere. It comes directly from Scripture. It is a flowering shrub that sprouts from the ancient soil of the text *Pinkhas*."

"You wish to discuss *Pinkhas*?" Yohanan challenges Menakhem.

"I will gladly do so, Yohanan, and in public. Let us discuss *Pinkhas* the night before Passover, at the base of the Temple stairs. And after I convince you, I hope you will join us to reclaim the pride and independence of Judaea."

Yohanan and Aislin reach the Synagogue of the Way, to find a deserted building, its walls defaced with scribbles that refer to incest, cannibalism, and atheism. Yohanan steps outside, where a young man pulls a cart up the street.

"The Synagogue of the Way?" The young man frowns. "Their leader feared that the fighting in the Galilee would spread to Jerusalem. They all fled. Some say they journeyed to Pella; others insist they simply scattered."

Looking at the coin that Paulus gave her, Aislin appears flustered, as if her voyage has suddenly lost its purpose. Yohanan pats her shoulder as if to say, something good will come of this.

That night as he lies on a mattress on the roof of his sister's house, Yohanan contemplates his upcoming debate with Menakhem. It is a contest for the hearts and minds of his fellow Judaeans, many of whom feel sufficiently angry and confused that they might embrace a dangerous and desperate philosophy. He recites a portion of *Pinkhas* aloud, searching the text for nuances and ironies. He senses it cannot mean what most assume it means, but falls asleep before he finds what he is seeking.

Word has quietly spread that Yohanan, son of Zakkai, has returned after years of travel. In the morning a priestly messenger in colorful silk robes arrives at Hannah's door with a message from the new high priest, Mattathias, son of Theophilus, who summons Yohanan to the Temple.

The messenger leads him through the city and up the long path toward the Temple. Flat-roofed, two-story stone houses, shops, and synagogues border the path, which opens onto a plaza at the base of one of the Temple staircases. They climb three flights to the Plaza of the Nations, where vendors sell food, gifts, and sacrificial animals and change money. They cross through the Golden Gate and the Plaza of Women, where men and women are dancing, and turn before reaching the altar. The messenger and Yohanan proceed down a path to an inconspicuous building next to the Plaza of Israel. He enters an unadorned room, raw stone walls with a lattice window that casts shadows across a marble table.

Mattathias, son of Theophilus, corpulent as a student but now tall and thin, rises to embrace him. He instructs his attendants to fetch a platter of cheese and a jug of wine, and the two men settle on the benches to talk.

"I need to know what you have seen, Yohanan. You must understand, I cannot often leave the Temple and our sources of information are...."

"Roman?" Yohanan suggests.

Menakhem smiles. In the hour that follows, Yohanan describes his travels, the widespread resentment of Temple leadership, and the poverty and destruction he has witnessed. The high priest rests his chin on his fingers and stares off into the courtyard reflecting. "I thank you, my old friend, for this news. There is indeed much work to be done. May I ask one additional favor of you?"

"Of course, my lord."

"My niece is ill. Would you offer her your blessing? I would like her to attend our Passover feast. Naturally, you will be paid."

"It will be my honor," offers Yohanan. "Nor will I accept compensation, but if you would grant me an hour or two in the Temple library, I will be most grateful."

"Spend as much time there as you like."

The high priest's assistant escorts Yohanan to the library, and as he walks between its pillars and under its candelabras, he remembers his first reading of the *Song of Songs* and his encounter with Kayafa the night he learned of his mother's death.

He locates the scroll *In The Desert*, unrolls it on a marble reading stand, and studies the section known as *Pinkhas*. He finds the broken *vav* and meditates upon it, recalling Shlomo's observation that the broken *vav* represented a *broken peace*.

☙

The high priest's niece resides in the palace of Mattathias's youth, where Yohanan and Josephus once witnessed a Roman soldier kissing a Hebrew slave. He recognizes the statues, the fountains, the fresco of a bird perched on the edge of a bowl, but the colors have faded, the marble has dulled. A manservant escorts Yohanan to the girl's door.

The plump eight-year-old girl sits cross-legged on the floor, holding painted dolls, one astride a wooden mule. Yohanan hesitates, surprised, for these are toys devout Hebrew parents deny their children, preferring playthings such as marbles, cubes, or wagons. To fashion a living being, even in sculpture or painting, seems to Yohanan an act of arrogance and a usurpation of holy power. As he enters, the girl looks up.

"Who are you?" she asks.

"A friend of your uncle's. He tells me you are not feeling well."

"I'm sick."

Yohanan sits down. "You don't look sick."

She holds the female doll in front of him. "How dare you talk to me this way! I should slap you."

Yohanan moves a bearded doll forward with the mule on which it is seated. "Go ahead," his doll tells hers. "Slap me!"

She positions her doll closer to his, raises its articulated arm, and swipes it across his doll's swarthy face. Yohanan's doll falls off its mule, lies stunned on the tiled floor, then raises an arm and props itself to a sitting position. "That didn't hurt at all. You know why?"

"Why?" squeaks the girl's doll.

"Because I'm made of wood. See?" Yohanan uses the doll's hand to slap its own cheek and then its other cheek, knocking itself down again.

The girl cackles. "Stop it!"

He looks her in the eyes. "I'll tell you a secret if you'll tell me one."

"What kind of secret?"

"Anything you want to know. Just ask me and I'll tell you. But only one thing, and you can't tell anyone else."

"Fine," she agrees.

"What do you want to know about me?" asks Yohanan.

"Why are you so strange?"

"One is never strange in one's own eyes. If I seem strange to some, it is because they want to see me that way."

She frowns. "Why would they want to see you that way?"

"That makes two secrets," says Yohanan, "but I'll answer anyway. Some people say others are strange because they think it makes them seem better. Now, my question."

She leans back on her hands. "Go ahead."

"Why don't you want to attend the Festival of Freedom ceremony?"

"I can't stand the smell," she admits after a moment.

"Sizzling meat? Most people like that smell."

"It makes me think of the animals they had to kill."

"I can't ask you a second question," says Yohanan. "But if I could I would ask, why don't you just tell your uncle that, instead of pretending to be sick?"

"He wouldn't understand."

Yohanan nods. "Let me take care of this." He rises. "I promised your uncle I would bless you. Lower your head."

She does so. He sets his palm on her head and pronounces an ancient benediction, not in Aramaic but in Hebrew: "May the Lord bless you and keep you. May the Lord make his face shine upon you and be gracious to you. May the Lord turn his face toward you and give you peace."

"What will you tell my uncle?" she asks.

"I'll tell him you are not ill but that you have good reasons for not wanting to attend the Temple ceremony, and that your uncle should respect them."

Dimples light her face as she grins.

As the high priest's assistant accompanies him back to the inner precincts of the Temple, Yohanan reflects that he has done what he can for the high priest. If Mattathias, in turn, agrees to speak frankly with the people, perhaps there is still time to save Judea.

આ

On the evening before Passover, Messengers of Freedom fly over the rooftops of Jerusalem and through windows and doors. At the foot of the Temple stairs, the plaza fills with pilgrims who carry baskets of flowers and fruits, eagerly anticipating a fierce disputation between celebrated minds. Menakhem, the Zealot, and Yohanan, son of Zakkai, stand on the stairs, their faces lit by flickering torches.

"Why are we here tonight," Menakhem begins, "on this evening before one of the holiest days of the year, our Festival of Freedom? I cannot speak for you, Yohanan, son of Zakkai, but I am here because I believe, as our Holy Scrolls instruct us, that we are meant to be free."

The crowd erupts into cheers. Menakhem raises his hand to silence them. "I am here to tell you, Yohanan, son of Zakkai, and you, citizens of Jerusalem, that with the help of our Lord, little Judea, the smallest of provinces, can take on the vast empire of Rome and win."

When the acclamation again subsides, Yohanan begins to speak. "'With the help of our Lord,' you say, Menakhem, son of Judas the Zealot. And so I ask you, what gives anyone, in our day, the right to speak for the Lord? How can you stand before Jerusalem and state with confidence that in our holy texts, which so stress the importance of charity, love, and peace, you find justification for violence?"

Hannah translates for Aislin.

"When the Children of the Covenant returned to the holy land, after two hundred years in Egypt," asks Menakhem, "did they not kill the people they found there?"

"That event was an anomaly," answers Yohanan. "Nowhere in the writings is there any suggestion it should be repeated."

"No?" asks Menakhem. "Well, that brings us to *Pinkhas*. For those unfamiliar with the story"—Menakhem gestures toward the gathered crowd—"it is quite simple. A man of Israel brings a Midianite woman, a pagan, into his tent. While they lie together, another man, Pinkhas, drives a spear through their bellies. What does the Lord do? The Lord rewards Pinkhas!" roars Menakhem. "The Lord is pleased with him, which proves that killing in the name of our Father can be appropriate."

Yohanan waits for the cheers to die. "Except it is not that simple," he tells the crowd. "To read the Scrolls of Tradition in such a narrow, literal way is to do them a grave injustice. You see, Tradition tells us that Pinkhas is heir to two identities—the grandson of Jethro, a pagan, on one side, and of Aaron, the first high priest of the Israelites, on the other. His name, Pinkhas, is not a Hebrew name, but an Egyptian one. The Judaean man and the Midianite woman represent Pinkhas's own two selves—pagan and Israelite. And notice that the two lovers are not named until *after* Pinkhas murders them. What do you think this signifies?"

Yohanan scans his mystified audience. His gaze meets that of Aislin, who stands with Faolan and Hannah. "Humans have names, no?" he pursues. "Objects, which do not possess souls, lack proper names. So people without names, you see, are like mere objects. And this is what these lovers are, to Pinkhas. It is his inability to see his victims as fully human that empowers him to kill."

Faolan yelps.

"In killing them," resumes Yohanan, "what does Pinkhas attempt to destroy? *The intermingling of different storytelling traditions.* He is trying to eradicate what he hates most about himself, his split nature."

"If what you are saying is true," Menakhem challenges him, "why would the Lord reward Pinkhas?"

"Does the Lord reward him?" queries Yohanan. "When the Lord confers upon Pinkhas his *covenant of peace*, Pinkhas may indeed seem to get his wish. He loses his complex identity, becoming the pure heir of one set of grandparents—the first priest, Aaron. But look at the text. You'll notice something odd. The word *shalom* in the phrase 'my covenant of peace,' spoken by the Lord, is written here, and here alone in all the Holy Scrolls, with a broken letter."

Faolan brays, calling for his goat.

"Can someone do something about this child?" shouts a man in the crowd.

"Faolan, your goat is at Hannah's house," Yohanan calls. "You will see it soon, I promise."

Hannah whispers in Faolan's ear and points to Yohanan, but Faolan's braying turns to wailing. The crowd's attention is now on the boy.

"Excuse me," says Yohanan. He approaches a member of the audience, asks permission to remove three lemons from her basket, and steps back to his place, juggling them. Faolan ceases bawling and watches Yohanan, his eyes wide and his mouth half-open.

"What does this mean?" Menakhem demands over the crowd's laughter. "A broken letter?"

Yohanan tears his eyes from the anxious boy and answers, slowing his juggling. "The letter, *vav*, pronounced *o* in the word *shalom*, meaning peace—" one of the lemons almost falls, and he lunges to retrieve it, "—is written in an unusual way in this passage, and only in this passage, but in every copy of the scroll of *Pinkhas*. It is a broken letter!"

"We can hardly verify that here and now, can we?," objects Menakhem. "But broken letter or no, the Lord rewards Pinkhas for what he does! And please stop that juggling!"

"The Lord rewards him, in a manner," agrees Yohanan, returning the lemons to their owner, "but for *helping the Lord overcome Its own jealousy*. This is explicitly stated in the text."

"How can the Lord be jealous?" Menakhem asks skeptically. "And how could a man help the Lord? Are you saying that the Lord is imperfect?"

"That is exactly what I am saying," says Yohanan. "The Lord is not complete. It is *becoming*. What does It tell Moses to call It? *Eyeh asher eyeh*. That is the Lord's name, *I shall be what I shall be*. The Lord is a process and It depends on us."

The crowd responds in confused mutterings.

"And furthermore, let us be clear," adds Yohanan, "the reward that the Lord offers Pinkhas is a strange one. Rather than make him a great military leader, a position to which a man of his violent sensibilities might aspire, the Lord confers upon him a *covenant of peace*. It transforms him. And within this irony, as I just pointed out, there lies a further irony. The peace—the *shalom* that the Lord bestows—is broken, imperfect. If this is a reward at all, it is a highly qualified one."

"Despite your convoluted reasoning," Menakhem interjects, "to be offered the priesthood is clearly a prize."

"It may seem like a prize," insists Yohanan, "but only if you regard the priesthood as inherently good or virtuous, an assumption that Israel's history undermines. Remember, Moses's brother Aaron, the first priest and Pinkhas's grandfather, betrays the Lord by allowing the Children of the Covenant to fashion a golden calf to worship, out of ear- and nose-rings. The priesthood is not a reward, but a responsibility, and the holiness associated with it is a power that can be used for good or evil."

"I believe the simplest interpretation is best," says Menakhem. "Your take on *Pinkhas* is far too complex, Yohanan, son of Zakkai. My head spins when I try to make sense of it. You will see the truth when we, or our descendants, sit on the throne of Rome wearing the garb of holiness and ruling the world." Over the crowd's rising enthusiasm he shouts, "I ask you, Yohanan, son of Zakkai, how could Rome, which prays to chiseled lumps of marble, prevail over the chosen people of the almighty, invisible Lord?"

The crowd erupts into a roar for their bearded, self-proclaimed messiah.

"This arrogance could well be our undoing!" Yohanan shouts back, but few hear him.

❧

In the morning Hannah accompanies Aislin to the women's ritual bath. When Aislin returns, Faolan reaches up to stroke her hair, asking, "Are you happy?"

"Very," says Aislin. "Happy and proud. And you?"

"*Ayn*," says Faolan.

Aislin laughs. It is the first time Faolan has answered his mother's question in any tongue.

Yohanan, Aislin, and Faolan lead the boy's goat to the Temple, the culmination of their long journey. Hundreds of white-robed priests collect offerings from the crowd. Yohanan lifts the little goat into his arms and hands it to an approaching priest, who offers a blessing as Faolan watches, mouth agape. The goat returns his gaze and bleats. The young priest deposits the goat on the pavers, ties a rope around its neck, and pulls it away. Faolan follows him through the thick crowd and into the aisle reserved for priests.

"No, Faolan. This is our gift," Aislin tells him, tugging at his hand.

The goat breaks into a trot toward the Plaza of the Israelites. The rope slips out of the priest's hand and he chases it past other priests and worshippers. Faolan bolts after them, with his uneven gait, into the Courtyard of the Priests. Yohanan pursues them.

Silver trumpets blast, announcing the Levite choir that begins to chant Psalms. Hundreds of officiants transfer the blood of the slaughtered in bowls of beaten gold and silver to the foot of the altar.

Through the music of the Levite choir, the timbrels, and the harps, Yohanan hears Faolan howl in agony. The boy has pushed his way through the gate, into the sacred Courtyard of the Priests, and has witnessed the sacrificial rite.

Two priests seize Faolan and drag him back as the boy yelps and calls for his goat. A third priest tugs the goat away, but it stops and emits an unearthly plea, combining an aching bleat with a plaintive howl. Faolan echoes the goat's wail and a hush falls over the congregation.

The cry jolts Yohanan. He has heard it before. As he turns his eyes from the sacrificial beast—fawn-colored, with black stripes on its legs, back-swept horns, and large oval eyes—to Faolan, and back again, he wonders if it is conceivable that this is the very goat, burdened with the sins of Israel, that he led years ago to the chasm of *Duda-El*. If so, how has it returned to the realm of the living, and what could its miraculous return portend? Did the Lord reject Israel's expiation? Does the fact that he has petted the sacrificial animal mean that the sins of Israel have been transferred back to him, and, through him, to everyone he has touched? And through those he has touched to all Israel, perhaps even to the nations? What would transpire if the people of Israel were to sacrifice this goat anew during this Festival of Freedom?

With these questions whirling in his mind, Yohanan hurries to the gate and tells the guard that there has been an error; one particular goat must not be sacrificed. The guard answers that no goat consecrated to the Lord can be returned alive to men.

"On what basis do you make this claim?" Yohanan demands.

"It is self-evident," says the guard.

"If the Law were self-evident," Yohanan replies impatiently, "we would not need our scrolls. We would be like Rome, where the whim of the emperor is all that matters."

Faolan's wailing and kicking have increased. Mattathias, son of Theophilus and high priest of Judaea, notices the commotion. He confers with the Captain of the Temple, before returning to his duties.

The Captain of the Temple approaches the guard who is detaining Yohanan. "What does this man desire?"

"He wants us to return that goat—a beast consecrated to the Lord— to that boy, who charged into the Court of the Priests."

"Do as he asks," the captain replies. "This man is a *tzaddik*, a holy man."

The guard returns the goat to Faolan. Yohanan empties his pockets of the coins he has saved for a donation. "Please see that these find their way to the Temple *korban*, the Treasure."

Nervous and excited, the goat bolts away, darting this way and that, finally carving a path through the crowd down the monumental stairway and into the steep, narrow streets of the city. Hooting, Faolan bounds after it. Yohanan chases, shouting, "Stop them!" Several worshipers try to comply but the excited goat proves stronger and faster than most imagine.

Yohanan loses sight of both boy and goat. He and Aislin push their way through the crowds in search of them. Increasingly frantic, they race down side streets, shouting Faolan's name, asking all they pass if they have seen an unloosed, wild goat or a wobbly, sprinting boy. Finally they return in sorrow to Hannah's home, where Yohanan's students are to meet for a meal of herbs, unleavened bread, and consecrated lamb.

Hannah is busy in the cooking area, while others carry platters up to the rooftop. "We cannot find Faolan," Aislin tells her, biting her lips to fight tears.

Yohanan climbs to the rooftop and rallies his disciples. "We'll have to forgo our Passover feast," he tells them. "Aislin's son, Faolan, is lost, and we need you to scour every street and building for the boy and his goat. If you find the goat, Faolan will be near. Ask everyone you meet to keep their eyes and ears open. And may the Lord watch over Faolan and the goat."

Yohanan divides his disciples into groups, assigning them different quarters of the city. They disperse and as word spreads, the search party swells to thousands. Passover in Jerusalem takes on an unexpected significance but by dusk they have found no trace of the boy, nor even a tuft of the goat's hair. Hannah packs a mule basket with supplies.

Yohanan and Aislin search beyond the city walls. They travel over hillsides and through valleys. That night, and for four nights thereafter, they sleep on oak-covered hillsides and in the desert. They speak little. They listen to the wind. Finally they reach a cliff overlooking an abyss. "This is Duda-El, the deepest chasm in the world. It is the repository of our sin," Yohanan tells Aislin as they prepare for sleep.

When Aislin awakes the next morning, she sees Yohanan sitting on a rock overlooking Duda-El, weeping. She joins him and holds his hand.

❧

At the conclusion of Passover, Levites parade through the city, calling the people of Jerusalem to assemble for an announcement by the high priest. Citizens pack the torch-lit square before Herod's palace under Roman soldiers' watch. Menakhem the Zealot stands before the high priest at the front of the crowd, backed by four rows of disciples. Priest-musicians blow silver trumpets and beat tambourines.

Mattathias, son of Theophilus, the high priest, wears a white wool outer garment, tasseled at the corners, a prayer shawl draped over his head, and leather sandals. He speaks in a voice both strong and gentle. "I have never stood before you as a fellow citizen of Jerusalem to discuss my concerns about my people, about all of us." He clasps his hands at his linen-sashed waist and gazes at the faces. "We are broken," he admits. "We used to speak one language, our holy tongue. Today some speak Greek, as I do with Herod and Rome." He glances at the guards. "Others speak Aramaic and know not a word of Greek. Some pray in a language we are forgetting."

The crowd listens, spellbound. "A people's language is its soul," continues the high priest. "Our language holds our memories. When we stopped speaking the same language, that marked the beginning of our travails."

He allows the people a moment to reflect on his words. "Unfortunately," he resumes, "that wasn't the end of it. Our worldly, urban ambition so often conflicts with our tribal, nomadic roots. Speaking the language of the occupiers not only separates us from our tradition but aligns us with another tradition that provides a ready path to wealth and power—a wealth and power that is national as well as personal, as exemplified in the buildings and esplanades that surround us. This alternative tradition, however, this accumulation of wealth and power, also inures us to the suffering, poverty, and powerlessness of those who lack such advantages. And so we have twice cut ourselves off."

A man coughs. A woman whispers to her neighbor. No one has ever heard a high priest confess this way.

"My predecessors may have erred," continues Mattathias, "wrongfully executing popular heroes, who were perceived as threats. For that, many of you despise us. I vow to you that such crimes shall not occur under my watch. Nor will I blame the occupation. Rome has done magnificent things for Judaea. Look at our Temple on that hill—one of the wonders of the world—and at Herod's Theater. Every night that theater fills up with Greek-speaking Judaeans, eager to see the comedies of Gaius Maecenas Melissus. Some of you might protest that this is not our Tradition, that this is a pollution."

"So it is!" bellows Menakhem. "As a result of this Greek filth, our people will lose its character, little by little, until we no longer exist!"

"That is, indeed, the challenge," the high priest affirms. "But violence is not the answer."

"Who appointed you?" asks Menakhem.

"You know who appointed me. Herod."

"And who appointed him?"

"You know that, too. Caesar."

"What then gives you the right to call yourself our high priest?" demands Menakhem. "Are you a descendant of Aaron, the brother of Moses?" Menakhem turns to the crowd. "Of course, he is not! His very position represents a defiance of the Lord and a defilement of our Temple! You are a sham and a blight upon Israel."

With that, Menakhem rushes upon the high priest, pulling a dagger from his cloak, and strikes him repeatedly in the chest. The high priest collapses to the ground and Menakhem turns, holding up his bloody hands for his agitated spectators to see. "Like the Maccabees we must reclaim our Temple and kingdom!" he yells.

The crowd's goodwill dissolves as outraged citizens, loyal to the high priest, scuffle with Menakhem's followers. The throng engulfs the Zealot messiah and swallows him alive. When it is over, Menakhem, son of Judas the Zealot, lies trampled and lifeless beside the high priest he murdered.

❧

Word of the deaths reaches Yohanan and Aislin in the main square of Bethlehem as they journey home from Duda-El. "Madness has gripped our land," laments Yohanan. "How can so many find inspiration to iniquity, even in our lore? They believe they serve the Lord but they sow ignorance."

They have rent their garments and mourned Faolan's disappearance, which feels like an amputation. Now they have another loss to contend with—the death of a dear friend, a high priest, the first in generations to offer hope.

"In a dark world, Mattathias and Faolan were stars on the horizon," Yohanan laments.

"I would like to think that Faolan finally obtained what he desired most during this Festival of Freedom, to be with that goat," Aislin reflects.

"He understands that animal," says Yohanan. "He has that gift."

"And it understands him. It is as if they were meant for each other." Aislin smiles, wiping away a tear. "I need to go to Pella," she adds.

"For how long?"

"As long as necessary."

"I will travel with you," he offers.

"Thank you, Yohanan, but I will need to be alone."

❧

A long stroll into the wilderness, Aislin tells herself. *A time to reflect, to pray, to shed tears. Then I shall return.* She pauses at a spring to drink. She stops in Jericho to purchase bread, nuts, cheese, and pomegranates, and to ask the way. She carries Paulus's ancient coin.

She dreams of her aunt's divining stones, of Companions beckoning her in a forest; of Muirgheal, expiring on a battlefield; of Meitheamh, five years old, with long blonde hair, playing in a field of flowers; and of Pallas, all flesh and hair, masturbating in a bath.

She hikes through fields and olive groves three more days, barely eating or sleeping, conversing with her lost son. She tells Faolan how much she misses him. She admits that caring for him has sometimes been a burden and that she always feared others' reactions, their uneasy solicitude, their feigned indifference, their callousness and cruelty.

During her years with Faolan, she realizes, shame and envy shadowed her: shame for who he was and envy for what he would never become. She asks him to forgive her. Faolan has been a blessing. She accuses herself of failing to protect such a precious, vulnerable gift. She sobs and calls to him. She hoots and brays. Only the wind answers. She chants his name until sleep overtakes her. Faolan, my Little Wolf.

She arrives at the gates of Scythopolis, known in Hebrew as Beit-She'an. An older woman with uncovered black hair and crossed, tired eyes regards her with caution. "I heard that hyenas tore you limb from limb, two days after you left Pella," she says in Greek.

"Have I met you before?" Aislin asks.

The woman cocks her head. "You look like her. Except the accent. Seeking a room, are you?" She leads Aislin through the wealthy city, past the amphitheater, well-appointed stalls, and gated homes. Clean-shaven, Greek-speaking Syrians in embroidered tunics conduct business beside bearded Children of the Covenant in blue-fringed tunics. The old woman turns a corner where a Judaean sits begging. She spits, curses him, and crosses the street.

"In Scythopolis," she tells Aislin, "Judaeans and Greeks live, work, and pray side by side, but we do not like each other." By *Judaean* she means anyone who speaks Aramaic. The Judaeans' identity resides in their language and all that remains deeply encoded in the sounds of that language, memories and legends. By *Greek*, she means Syrian. Her father prayed not to Ba'al, Astarte, or any of the old gods, but to Aphrodite and Adonis.

The old woman escorts Aislin to a small stone house near the center of town and serves her wine. "Scythopolis has always been Greek," she tells her. "Dionysos himself founded the town. We commemorate his death and rebirth every year with a festival of wine and bread. The Judaeans believe their invisible God will restore their kingdom, but an invisible God is a powerless God. A boulder endures far longer than a breeze."

"Even so, I am looking for a community of Judaeans," Aislin says.

"The Synagogue of the Way and Jacob the Righteous, brother of Joshua of Nazareth, the messiah. Have you heard of them?"

"There are so many synagogues," says the widow. "So many messiahs. If they lived in Pella, they are dead. My husband died, brave and fierce, fighting for Rome. The Judaeans, those savages, killed him. They should all perish. The world would be better without them."

The next morning Aislin crosses the Jordan River and follows a path to the ruined city of Pella. The desolation and the oppressive silence remind her of the destroyed village of her youth. Houses gape empty and dark. She enters one. Wooden toys, an earthen pot, a fruit basket perched on a shelf, overturned furniture. She sits on a blanket, closes her eyes, and chants an Aramaic prayer for the dead, which Yohanan taught her outside the destroyed town of Yotapata. It wanders into a Celtic melody from her childhood and ends with a lament for her son Faolan.

❧

From Pella, she travels two days to a cliff that overlooks the sea. She dreams of her son transformed, a vision both reassuring and frightening. *Faolan, love of my heart, where are you?* She reaches to touch him but he vanishes.

Standing high over the waves she invokes her jail companion. "I am so sorry, Paulus. I promised to deliver this coin to Jacob the Just. He and his people are no more." She looks at the coin in her hand. "So I shall give it to the world."

She throws it. A breeze catches it and carries it some distance over *Mare Nostrum*, Our Sea. As it flutters to the water it whirls, catching flashes of light like a winking eye.

A large bird, with yellow and green wings, alights on the branch of a nearby tree. It stares at Aislin, opens its beak, and sings a melody that Aislin recognizes from an ancient memory or a dream.

❧

By candlelight, while Jerusalem sleeps, Yohanan smells the ink and parchment of a rare scroll. He examines the handwriting and contemplates the story it narrates, a tale of passionate longing.

Aseneth, the daughter of an Egyptian priest, falls in love with Joseph, the Hebrew patriarch. He spurns her, convinced that her family traditions, her very identity, render her unfit to bear his children. A heavenly Messenger, carrying a magical beehive, arrives to comfort her. Bees swarm around. Some ascend to heaven and others die, and Aseneth is transformed.

A person's inheritance of memory, Yohanan reflects, need not imprison that person. Rather, people are vessels that can be emptied of one tradition and filled with another. People do not live within their traditions; traditions live within people.

His mind skips, as so often these days, to Aislin. He worries that she might not find her way back to Jerusalem, or that her grief over Faolan's disappearance might overwhelm her.

He never intended to grow attached to her. Like the Queen of Sheba, of the *Song of Songs*, Aislin is a stranger. He understands little of the land of her youth or the stories that nurtured her soul, but he feels her absence as a dull ache, an unanswered question. Her foreignness, her resilience, and the depth and inscrutability of her experience have captured his imagination. He wants to believe they share something important and meaningful, but he cannot deny that they are both ultimately alone. Perhaps that is what they share: a sense of isolation.

He pours himself a cup of water, rises, and opens the door to peek out. Dawn is breaking. His students will soon await him at the steps of the Temple.

❧

Thousands of Zealots parade through the great avenues of Jerusalem, shouting, "Menakhem is dead! Long live the revolt!" They no longer fear the Roman guards. Not only do they outnumber them; they now have weapons. Since the death of the high priest, thousands of rebels from destroyed towns and villages north of Jerusalem have sought refuge in the capital. Some mutinied against Roman taxes or the imposition of Greek gods in the Galilee or Idumea. Others became entangled in the violence despite their earlier indifference to wealth, power, or eschatology. Hard rebel leaders named Yohanan, son of Levi, and Eleazar, son of Simon, commanding hungry, battle-scarred fighters, have marched into Jerusalem with ragtag armies after defeating Roman contingents in their Galilean towns. They seized valuable booty and weapons, then fled the ensuing massacres, abandoning their townsfolk to the Romans' ruthlessness. Like Menakhem before them, they clamor that the Romans can be defeated and insist that with the Lord on their side, they are poised to overcome an empire. Another self-appointed Savior of Judaea, Simon, son of Giora, leads a group that calls itself the *Sicarii*—the Dagger Wielders. They are desperate, violent men from Hebron and the desert region of Idumea, whose motivation is the apocalyptic conviction that Jerusalem, indeed all of historic Israel, will soon be liberated—or annihilated in the attempt.

Each of these Zealot leaders recruits and trains thousands of followers in Jerusalem, and soon their troops are fighting each other as well as Rome. They battle for control of the granaries, the Temple, and the royal palace. When they lose fighters their determination increases, along with their recruiting efforts. Most Jerusalemites, like Yohanan, understand that the competition between these militias is undermining the cause they are fighting for—the cultural unity of their people. While only a small contingent of Roman soldiers, with Herod's assistance, has hitherto been sufficient to control the capital, the competing Zealot armies recklessly murder Romans and Herodians alike.

Despite the danger, or rather because of it, Yohanan, son of Zakkai, teaches every morning on the steps of the Temple, never relenting in his insistence that only study of the Tradition can bring redemption, and that internecine conflict and war with Rome are inconsistent with Judaean law. Strands of gray now twine through his long black hair. "Listen to the voices of our prophets," he implores his followers. "We are redeemed by caring for one another, not through violence."

"What about the Maccabee warriors?" one of Menakhem's followers asks.

"This is an unholy story," Yohanan insists. "The Maccabees gave us the Hasmoneans, and the Hasmoneans gave us Roman domination. Where in this chain of events do you find salvation? It would be preferable to forget the story of the Maccabees."

"So you believe it is the Lord's intent that Rome continue humiliating us?" asks another.

"Who am I to speak for the Lord?" asks Yohanan.

"And where has your approach, the approach of the Pharisees, gotten us?" asks a third. "All you have are questions."

"We are a small people," Yohanan reminds his listeners. "We always were a small people among the nations. Our challenge is to endure, to strive to be righteous, and to pray for a better day."

While hundreds still gather to hear Yohanan speak, a growing number of Jerusalem's frustrated, angry youth finds his words passive and less inspiring than the swords of Yohanan, son of Levi; Eleazar, son of Simon; and Simon, son of Giora. Some consider Yohanan the most eminent of traitors, but dare not harm him due to his reputation as a sage.

His wealthier disciples—priests, merchants, tax collectors, and Judaean functionaries—offer provisions and a narrow two-story home below the Temple that leans on poles like an old man on a walking stick. He takes up residence there and the first floor becomes a synagogue, where scholars and students can gather to discuss the holy texts and the ebb and flow of history.

Aislin's absence troubles him. He struggles to comprehend his feelings. He does not understand her the way one might understand a sister or a distant cousin.

He remembers arriving in the Galilee, how relatives whom he had never met embraced him, how their speech and postures seemed strangely familiar. Yohanan appreciated their openheartedness and generosity but distrusted his temptation to settle with them. His world was larger than their home or community.

At the same time, his world view is not that of Athens or Rome, a fantasy in which all storytelling traditions dissolve into one, under Greek or Roman domination. He has seen the damage that such fantasies cause.

His father, Zakkai, Yohanan realizes, must also have struggled with the tension between the desire for the comforts of home and a longing to *go beyond*. Perhaps Zakkai fell in love with a foreign woman, drawn to the mystery of her otherness. Perhaps her temperament matched Zakkai's needs better than the soft-spoken moodiness of Yohanan's mother. Zakkai's decision to abandon his family must have been excruciating. It was wrong, though, not because *going beyond* was evil but because in so doing Zakkai caused pain and confusion to those he loved.

Aislin, Yohanan senses, is a woman condemned to wandering, who yearns for rootedness. Yohanan has always felt anchored to the land and its lore, but long ago learned to question the restrictive, narrow confines of any one neighborhood.

"And so it is with the stories of the Tradition," he tells his disciples, "which must be seen as flexible, yet specific to a place, a language, and a set of customs." Both Aislin and Yohanan struggle with such contradictions, refusing easy solutions. Is this why her absence feels like an emptiness? Or is there another explanation, one he will never understand? Yohanan decides to travel to Pella to ask after her. He leaves a brief note for his sister and his students and departs before dawn.

Six hours into his journey, he climbs down a mountain to a plain of orchards, primarily date palms. He reaches the ancient town of Jericho and the home of a respected scholar, which serves as a synagogue, to ask about Aislin. The scholar, who has been studying Yohanan's writings for years, invites him in. "Why are you asking about a foreign woman, Yohanan, son of Zakkai?"

"The Tradition teaches us, 'You shall love the stranger who sojourns in your midst as you love yourself, for you were strangers in the land of Egypt,'" says Yohanan.

The scholar hands him a cup of diluted wine, clasps his hands together, and lowers his gaze. "There is indeed talk of a foreign woman like the one you describe, who ventured alone into the hills and was torn apart by hyenas."

"When?" Yohanan asks.

"Not three weeks ago."

Yohanan tears the fringes of his tunic in a gesture of mourning and lowers his face into his hands.

❧

Aislin thinks incessantly of Faolan. She whispers to him: "I know you're out there. I hope you can see me." She visualizes him sitting on Yohanan's lap, watching the moon. "I know how much you loved Yohanan. You cherished his voice, his manner, the way he looked at you. I hope, wherever you are, these memories serve you. We finally found a place for ourselves in the world, didn't we?"

Aislin smiles, recalling Yohanan's juggling act during his debate with Menakhem, Faolan's wide-eyed astonishment, and his doleful screeching dissolving into laughter. She knew good men and women in Rome, people who saw her as a fellow sufferer rather than as a stranger, who provided her with food and shelter on occasion. She never thought of living with any of them, except as their slave. Now, however, she finds comfort in the thought of spending the rest of her days in the company of Yohanan.

Their surprising sense of kinship, she believes, springs from the ways their lives, though separated by thousands of miles, have mirrored each other. They have both wandered, searching for ways to put together pieces of puzzles that fell apart long ago. Both have learned a great deal but more than anything else, they have learned about the limitations of what they can know.

Yohanan has never inquired about her beliefs. If he were to ask, she would be at a loss. Aislin believes in everything and nothing—in a compassionate God and in no God; in Companions and Messengers and in their absence.

When Aislin looks up at the stars, she asks herself what forces guide their paths, why she alone survived the Roman destruction of her village, and why destiny extricated her from such a small world and thrust her into such a vast one. Aislin weighs the teachings of Chloe's Goddess of Compassion, Isis, and all she has learned about the God of Israel from Paulus, Hannah, and Yohanan. Although these philosophies differ in important ways, they all emphasize compassion and decency, rejecting the notion, so prevalent in Rome and Greece, that supremacy in this world—the ability, even the legal right, to plunder and murder—reflects blessings bestowed by divine beings.

Like the Roman and Greek gods, Isis is one among many and her powers are limited. But she looks out for the most vulnerable: thieves, maidens, and paupers. Paulus's and Yohanan's teachings postulate one Divinity, infinite and invisible; that life derives from It, and is therefore holy; and that we must forever hope for a day when respect for life and peace will be universal.

Aislin does not doubt that Paulus encountered an incarnation of this God, a mediator between the human and the Divine who lifted his burden of sin. The faith of Israel, as she learned from Paulus, is the cult of the weak against the strong, of David against Goliath, and of Egyptian slaves against their oppressors.

She understands that Yohanan sees these matters differently. For him, the concept of faith is not central. He thinks about his people, their mission, and their history in terms of a covenant, a body of literature, and a sense of moral purpose.

But like the bottles in Lucanus's parlor, which imbued candle flames with dark hues, an awareness of sin colors Yohanan's world no less than Paulus's. Both men are Pharisees, after all. For Paulus, sin is universal and prefigures worldwide redemption. For Yohanan, sin is multi-layered, like the skin of an onion—individual, national, and human—and although one can pray for absolution on behalf of oneself, of one's people, or of the nations, the degree to which remission from sin is achievable remains uncertain. Sin trails us all as ineluctably as a shadow in the glare of the divine radiance.

Aislin re-enters the holy city through the Eastern Gate and follows now-familiar streets toward Hannah's domicile. Hannah answers her knock and draws her into an embrace. "My brother was worried about you and went off in search of you. But come in. You must be hungry."

Aislin helps Hannah care for her children, particularly her youngest, who lies ill, shaking and sweating, on his straw mattress. Hannah teaches Aislin the rudiments of Aramaic and how to pray with her to the God she addresses as *Abba*, or Father.

Six days later, Yohanan returns to Hannah's home, his face smeared with ash, his tunic dirty and torn, his feet bare. Wearily, he recounts what he learned in Jericho.

"This is terrible!" says Hannah. "I am so sorry to hear that a blonde-haired, foreign woman died in such a dreadful way. But it wasn't our Aislin. Aislin is at the market, buying vegetables with my little one."

Yohanan takes hold of her shoulder, steadying himself as his heart floods with relief.

❧

Over a simple dinner that she has prepared in Hannah's home, Yohanan asks Aislin to take him as her husband. "You and I are orphans," he says, "survivors of a shipwreck. We are also each other's companions."

"There's much you do not know about my life," Aislin replies quietly.

"I do not need to know who you were," says Yohanan. "I know the person you are. Nor am I better than you. Knowing all I have experienced, my wanderings, my failures, how could you trust me?"

"You are a seeker, a thinker," says Aislin. "What failures?"

"My people are committing suicide," says Yohanan, "and I haven't been able to stop them."

Aislin takes his hand. "No man alone can stop this madness."

"Does that mean you will be my wife?" he asks with a smile. It is an unusual way of proposing, but then again, they are no longer young.

"Let me answer your question with a question of my own," Aislin says.

"What do you want to know?"

She smiles. "Why did you wait so long to ask?"

Yohanan considers replying, *I used to wonder whether the mixing of story-telling traditions was not unwise.* Instead, he says simply, "I never imagined myself worthy of such a beautiful wife."

⇛

Their marriage is Judaea's last exultation. Hannah dresses Aislin in robes of red, blue, yellow, gold, and silver and helps carry her through the streets on a colorful litter accompanied by musicians and singers. When they reach Yohanan's house, he yanks open the door and invites her in with a flourish. He is dressed exquisitely, his hair braided and perfumed with oils, his dark eyes dancing.

She steps down from the litter and crosses the threshold as the men and women of Jerusalem, filling the street and alleys, sing and dance. Thus Yohanan and Aislin consecrate an unlikely union, one that no one, least of all they themselves, could have foreseen. No one, that is, except perhaps a Messenger or two.

⇛

The followers of Yohanan son of Levi, Eleazar son of Simon, and Simon son of Giora battle in the streets of Jerusalem, not only against each other but against those who oppose armed conflict with Rome.

Although the Zealot factions despise one another, they agree on the necessity of murdering or chasing out of Jerusalem anyone affiliated with the Roman leadership. The *Sicarii*, under Simon, son of Giora, distinguish themselves in their ability to sidle up next to functionaries or soldiers, slip their daggers into their backs, and disappear before the bodies hit the ground. The followers of Yohanan, son of Levi, recruit adherents who ambush and massacre Roman and Herodian guardsmen.

Eleazar's band robs the homes of wealthy priests and functionaries, tortures them, kills them, and thus takes for themselves entire neighborhoods of the ruling class.

The brutal and rapid success of these rebel groups astonishes Rome. King Agrippa II, who has inherited the title "Herod" from his grandfather, flees with his armies to join forces with the Romans, who call in legions from neighboring provinces. Each of the rebel leaders claims to control the Judaean capital as the Roman armies encircle Jerusalem.

Having subdued the Galilee in the north and Idumea in the south, three legions construct their camps on three sides of the capital. Citizens flee Jerusalem at the risk of their lives. Commerce slows to a trickle. Zealot fighters infiltrate the Roman camps at night, set fire to their wooden structures, fell guards, and slaughter soldiers. From atop the city walls, Zealots shoot legionnaires using bows and flaming arrows.

Then one morning, the gates of the city no longer open. Zealots guard them from within, Romans from without. No resident or merchant, no wagon or mule, enters or exits. The siege of Jerusalem has begun.

৵

Aislin's path, she realizes, has led her into the heart of a people, a nation, that dares assert and maintain its ancestral Traditions in a peril-fraught defiance of Rome. The disagreement between Yohanan and the Zealots is not over the importance of maintaining these Traditions; it is about how to do so. Within the scheme of Aislin's life, Israel's apocalyptic dream answers Albion's doomed innocence like an antiphonal choir. While she adopts the customs of her husband's people with fierce conviction, she fears the consequences of overt rebellion.

Yohanan no longer meets his disciples at the Temple stairs—that would be dangerous. Instead, he invites them into his home. Flaxen rugs cover the stone-tiled floors. Cushioned benches run along the walls. The hungry find sustenance here, a bowl of leek soup or a round of bread sprinkled with olive oil and thyme. Those with plenty bring lentils, nuts, dates, and lemons. Wives and neighbors assist Aislin in feeding their extended families. Since her son's departure Aislin's eyes have deepened, her cheekbones have become more pronounced, and her forehead has acquired new lines. With a glance, she says, *What we are doing here together matters more than anything.* Or, *You have no idea how much you mean to me, oh daughters of Jerusalem*, for in them she has found, at long last, a second family.

On the evening of the Sabbath, scholars and disciples buzz in like fireflies eager to entangle themselves in a web of scribblings and utterances that stretches to the corners of the universe. Temple priests, millers' sons, and pilgrims come to discuss the hidden implications of passages buried deep within the Scrolls of Tradition. Should priests wear sandals while blessing the people, or not? (Yohanan thinks not.) Was Job pious because he loved the Lord, or because he feared It? (Because he feared It, Yohanan argues.) How is one to visualize the immensity of the heavens, the domain of the Infinite? (One must try to extend one's imagination beyond the limits of thought.)

A man asks for counsel. "Rabbi, I am a stonemason. My family once lived well enough but now we are poor and often go without supper. My two youngest have died, and my oldest son has joined the Zealots. He eats what he can steal. But I am not here for that. I come because I killed a man. A fellow Judaean. We fought over an amphora of grain."

Yohanan listens, as much to the pain in this man's voice as to his words.

"Day and night," says the man, "sleeping and awake, I carry with me the knowledge of my deed. If I pray, will the Lord forgive me?"

"I cannot withdraw that knowledge from your soul," says Yohanan. "Nor would I do so if I could. Prayers will not erase your deed. The destruction of a life is the greatest sin. It is the annihilation of a universe, and it affects the lives of all who remain. But even though we cannot wipe away the past, the Lord has provided us with a way of compensating for it."

"What is this way? Where can I find it?" the man asks.

Yohanan leads him to the edge of the roof, where they look out over the city and beyond, to the armies of Vespasian that enclose the city in a tightening fist. "You already have the way," says Yohanan. "It is the future and it is precisely the opposite of the past—entirely uncertain and full of possibility. We stand poised between the inalterable and the unknowable. Is that not a beautiful symmetry?"

"How does it help me?" the man pleads.

"It means that while in a sense we are prisoners," says Yohanan, "in another, we are free. Although mired in evil, we can still do good. You cannot undo your deed but you can devote the rest of your life to performing acts of loving kindness. If possible, direct them toward the family and friends of the man you killed."

"If they saw me, they would kill me," the man says, gazing at the Roman campfires, which flicker like fallen stars across the dark hillside.

"Think of King David," says Yohanan, "and his murder of Uriah, the husband of the woman he covets. While this curse hangs over him, he creates poetry that has comforted so many over the centuries. His legacy is tangled and knotty, as is each of ours, yet we venerate his memory as a leader of our people."

The man, like so many who seek Yohanan's guidance, appears puzzled and unsatisfied. Yohanan believes, with utter conviction, that his approach to life and to the Tradition—nuanced, complex, non-linear, flexible but never formless—more closely resembles Truth than the alternatives; but as he learned in the marketplace of Arav, he is not a good salesman. Although many recognize his genius, few understand it.

❧

Famine blows through the capital like a wind storm roaring in alleyways, raising the dust of a nation's dreams and scattering it to the desert and the sea. For ten miles out from the city walls, the Romans have felled olive trees, pines, and shrubs. Foot-high stumps stud the hills like legionnaires' cleats.

One forest remains: the crucifixes that now sprout not only from the hilltop known as Golgotha, but from every field and hillside around Jerusalem. Ten thousand roods bear rotting, sagging corpses like abstractions of the human form, feet rooted in the earth, heads jutting heavenward, arms outstretched toward the horizons as if to embrace one last time all of Creation.

These crucified men, women, and children who gaze down at the city in sorrow and impotence, pecked by winged scavengers, behold in their dying moments an image of limestone-hued serenity, alleys snaking between box-like houses, the colonnades and tiled roofs of Upper City villas, and hovering just beyond, like a Messenger with open wings that echo the embrace of the dying, the plazas and arcades of the gold-and-silver-clad Temple.

The Zealots, who have unleashed these calamities upon their people, believing the Lord would support their folly, now join the ranks of the emaciated, the weak, and the desperate. They kneel not in supplication or prayer but to chew grass and even dried dung or to search the folds of corpses' garments for crumbs of stale bread. They roam from house to house in bands, killing for half a jar of olives, roasted grains, or a crust of cheese that a starving mother has been saving for her infant. Refusing to admit their error, to capitulate to the forces of Vespasian while there is still hope some might survive, the Zealots murder Roman sympathizers, any who resist their methods, and, finally, members of competing Zealot groups. Vying for the title of messiah, they burn each other's storehouses, assault each other's disciples, and impale anyone who tries to escape. Believing their martyrdom will hasten the general resurrection, they fear nothing. Death, they look upon as a blessing.

Corpses pile in the streets. Those who would have avoided touching the dead, for fear of dishonoring them and sullying their souls, now tread carelessly upon rotting cadavers. Brothers steal food from their sisters' mouths. The man who manages to scale the city walls undetected finds himself in the Roman camp, where he is flailed, gutted, and thrown into a ditch. The slightest breeze, whether from north, east, or south, carries the stench of decaying flesh.

᷒

Looking back, Yohanan reflects with a wince that it is fortunate Faolan has left them, and perhaps the realm of the living, when he did. The Jerusalem in which he tasted happiness lies in its death-throes. Faolan might have survived another few months in the capital but not much longer. Despite their professions of sanctity, the Zealots provide no refuge for the weak.

The air within the home Yohanan shares with Aislin diffuses memories of yeast, spices, and conversation, but today no scent of bubbling stew wafts out the door. His black hair sprinkled with silver, as close-cropped as his beard, the scholar discusses recent events with his surviving disciples, how Judaea has squandered its inheritance, and what hope, if any, remains. "Perhaps the rebellion was inevitable," Yohanan tells his congregation. "The Roman administrators of Judaea—Pontius Pilatus, Gessius Florus, Porcius Festus, and the others—were the most corrupt and abusive in the empire, and Judaeans the most recalcitrant of subject kingdoms. But what began as a cry for justice has devolved into wanton murder.

"Every people needs a functional government," he says, reminding his students of the early Israelites' demand that their prophet Samuel appoint an earthly king to rule over them. "The Zealots," he adds, "are not a government. They are thugs who seek not justice but power. In that pursuit they inflict violence not just upon Rome, or each other, or the people of Jerusalem, but upon the Lord Itself. In mocking all that is most sacred and defiling the terrestrial home of the Lord, they shear themselves of any legitimacy they might once have claimed. Despite this, these murderers and thieves dare call their leaders *Mashiachim*, or Anointed Ones.

"Their fatal error, however, is that they believe the Lord will demonstrate Its preference for one faction by granting it military victories," Yohanan says. "But the Lord abhors nothing so much as the spilling of blood. I know, I know," he says, holding up his palms to quell the tired objections. "They read our Holy Texts otherwise. Their reading is grounded not in knowledge but in ignorance, not in love for the Lord or their fellow man but in a quest for domination.

"When a man dies in the street today," continues Yohanan, "who pauses to recite a prayer for him? Unless he is a revered teacher, and they fear he will retain unusual powers even in death, the Zealots dump his body in a pit in violation of our sacred laws. We are all going to die. I only pray that when you find Aislin and me in our coffins, the Zealots and the Romans will allow you to carry us out of Jerusalem, as they have permitted other scholars."

He asks his students to help him saw off the second-floor balcony of his home. The boards have to be cut, nailed, and fitted with metal locks, adapted from the doors of empty homes and designed to open from within, so that when Yohanan and Aislin rise from their graves, as they expect to do, they will have no trouble climbing out.

❧

Two weeks later, beating their breasts in the streets and squares of Jerusalem, Yohanan's followers announce their master's death. "Woe unto Jerusalem! We have lost yet another of the few torches that lit our path.

Woe unto Israel, for Yohanan, son of Zakkai, and his beloved wife have been taken from us!"

As dawn breaks, passersby drag carts laden with amphorae of well water or rags pilfered from corpses. They pause in the street to listen and reflect. By mid-morning, mourners fill the paths between the stone houses, and as the sun nears its zenith, the Zealot leaders join their ranks. These rival rebels bow their heads in tribute to the learned and pious scholar who despised them.

The cortège swells to thousands, seemingly the entire surviving population of the city. Hannah's two daughters lead the procession. Yohanan has taught that because man introduced death to this world, women should be accorded the privilege of leading processions out of it. Musicians who have not picked up their lyres, flutes, finger cymbals, or drums for months pluck and blow lively dirges, while singers chant ancient hymns. Many weep and beat their breasts as the summer sun wilts the few surviving fig and olive trees. Rome waits silently outside the city walls, crouched like a leopard.

The Zealots have sent word to Roman sentinels, who permit ten men under guard to carry the coffins past the gates to the burial ground on the Mount of Olives. There, with a view of the Temple, the resurrection of all righteous men and women will commence. The disciples lower the caskets into two shallow graves, toss loose soil onto the boards of weather-worn pine, and trudge back to the city to await their own deaths.

❧

Yohanan feels for the latch inside his coffin, pushes up the lid, sweeps the dirt from Aislin's coffin, and helps her climb out. They stand a moment together, hand in hand. The Temple looms before them, darker than Yohanan has ever seen it, no longer lit by torches. Beyond lies Jerusalem, the city that so many clans, tribes, kingdoms, and empires have fought over for so many centuries, whose name derives from *yarah* and *shalem*, meaning *foundation of peace*.

So recently, the capital crackled and buzzed with torches, music, and dancing. Life, that spark within the created universe that mirrors the creative fires of the heavens, abounded in Jerusalem as nowhere else. Now the Antonia Fortress, to the right of the Temple, is a smoldering ash-pit. Other than the whine of a starving dog and the creak of a door, the city slumbers in moribund silence.

To the right and left of the Mount of Olives, on this side of the city walls, stretch the Roman encampments of the *V Macedonia*, *X Fretensis*, and *XV Apollinaris* legions, as well as the Syrian army and Agrippa II's regiments. To the north, beyond the land of the Samaritans, lies the Galilee, where the flame of revolt first flared. Yohanan remembers its grassy hills and villages, its slow pace, and the vineyard of his friend Hanina son of Dosa. The Galileans' towns now stand empty or filled with Roman colonizers. Surviving residents have been dragged off to Rome and other parts of the empire to toil and expire as slaves or gladiators. Others have fled to Jerusalem, their minds bursting with apocalyptic imagery.

For all these reasons, Yohanan will not return north. To the south lies the desert; to the east, the now inhospitable realms of the Pereans and Nabateans. If any hope remains, it resides in the west, along the coast, but traveling without Vespasian's permission would be foolhardy. Approaching Vespasian's camp, Aislin and Yohanan step out of the shadows and wait before the fence of sharpened trees that bars their way.

"Who goes there?" shouts a sentry.

Aislin replies in Latin that her husband is a scholar, a Pharisee renowned throughout Judea, the Galilee, and all of Israel, and that he wishes to speak with the Supreme Commander of the Roman Forces in the East, the general Titus Flavius Vespasianus. As she pronounces his name, her voice wavers.

The night watchman, a young man with an angular face and short stiff hair, laughs. "You think I can abandon my post, march into the general's tent in the middle of the night, give him your message, and survive? But tell me, how is it you speak Latin so fluently? Are you a Roman?"

"No," says Aislin. "I am a human."

An hour later Yohanan and Aislin enter a spacious goatskin tent where they rest until dawn, when four soldiers escort them through a grid of dirt streets to the general's quarters. Commander Vespasian's tent, no larger than those of the soldiers, is furnished with an oak and brass desk, a collapsible chair, a cot, and a long table of fresh Judaean pine. At the table sits a richly dressed Judaean, who appears familiar to Yohanan. Vespasian, now a massive, balding man with a clean-shaven, protuberant chin, rises to his full height and assesses Yohanan and Aislin.

Aislin has anticipated this moment with a sense of dread and fatalism, but now feels as if she were spinning into the distant past, a descent as vertiginous and terrifying as her jump with Paulus from the carcer of Rome into the Tiber as the city burned around them. Long-ago moments resurrect themselves with vivid clarity—the filtered daylight on dusty goatskin walls; the faint odors of tanning oils, fish sauces, and sweat; the patina on the brass fittings of the folding desk and cot. All that transpired between this moment and the destruction of her village, decades earlier, now seems to her an illusion, as if she had somehow remained trapped within these goatskin walls. Her gaze comes to a rest on the brown skull that rests upon the table. It is her grandfather, the last bridge to Albion, to her people.

To Yohanan, the general poses two questions in Greek that the Judaean translates. "Who are you and what do you want?"

"I belong to a group of Judaeans known as Pharisees," Yohanan replies. "We maintain that the essence of our Tradition resides in the letters of our Sacred Scrolls, a view that our high priests and the Zealots dispute. It is the Zealots who have desecrated our city and Temple and who challenge Rome. While Rome will doubtless take the city, I ask only that you allow us to preserve our remaining heritage, our words, for future generations. These stories are the memory of my people."

"And by what right or duty do you take responsibility for these stories?"

"My uncle was the guardian of the Treasure that your prefect, Valerius Gratus, removed from our holy Temple to fund the widening of the principal aqueduct of Jerusalem. I was named after this uncle and have spent my life searching for that Treasure," Yohanan says. "Only slowly, little by little over the years, did it dawn on me that the Treasure lies not in gold or silver, but in our words, in our stories, and in our minds and hearts."

"Frankly, it is this arrogance," says Vespasian, "this glorification of your stories that has landed your people in so much trouble. I fail to see how your invisible god differs so greatly from our chief deity, Jupiter. Both command thunder, no? Both have ultimate power."

"Your gods are created in the image of man," says Yohanan, "for us, man is created in the likeness of the Lord."

Vespasian frowns. "How can that be, if your Lord is invisible?"

"That is the point, Your Excellency. Life itself is invisible," says Yohanan.

With a flick of his hand, Vespasian dismisses Yohanan's argument. "These are mere word games," he says derisively, glancing at Aislin. "Why have you brought a woman into my tent? It is a violation."

"Ah, but who has violated whom?" asks Aislin in agitated Latin, her heart pounding. She feels as though her aunt Muigheal has come alive again within her heart, and is speaking through her.

Vespasian frowns, astounded that anyone, let alone a woman, should address him in such an impudent manner.

"Let us be honest, general," said Aislin. "This is hardly the first time you've had a female in your tent."

"And what do you know of my personal habits?"

"More than I would like," replies Aislin, looking at her grandfather's skull on the table.

Vespasian turns to see where she is looking.

When he turns back, she nods. "*That* belongs to me."

Still frowning, Vespasian says, "Impossible." But his voice is hardly louder than a whisper.

"Tell me, General, does he speak to you after all these years?"

Only now does Vespasian recognize the fiery contempt in her eyes and the braided blonde hair that peeks from her scarf. He remembers the combative girl from Britannia biting, kicking, and insulting him over a morbid family relic. "Does he speak to *you*?" he asks Aislin skeptically.

"He will always speak to me, even if he says nothing."

Vespasian strokes his chin.

"I gave birth to your child, a beautiful girl," says Aislin. "She is buried in the soil of Albion."

"Albion no longer exists, as you well know," he corrects her. "The land where you spent your miserable childhood is called Britannia."

A courier enters to hand Vespasian a scroll sealed with the imperial insignia. Vespasian scans the scroll. "Keep them alive," he instructs an aide, gesturing toward Aislin and Yohanan. "Josephus," he says to the Judaean, "see what you can learn from them."

Josephus. Yohanan looks at the translator. Josephus nods at Yohanan, a gesture of acknowledgment and recognition.

"Carry on with the morning sacrifice to Quirinus," Vespasian instructs his entourage. "I shall join you shortly."

❧

After Yohanan and Aislin leave the tent, escorted by the translator Josephus and guards, the general gazes into the empty orbits of the age-darkened skull. It is the only relic he has retained from the dawn of his long career: an empty face that has witnessed his fears and failures as well as his costly victories.

The woman claimed he fathered her daughter. He wonders how many other women have given birth to his battlefield offspring. He remembers the young Aislin and marvels that she has survived, learned to speak Latin, and ended up here, like him, in this craggy, untamable hell. "What are the odds of that, old man?" he asks the skull. But the skull does not speak to him. It has never spoken to him.

Outside, a squealing pig bolts through the camp. Soldiers pursue it with whoops, cries, and shouts of laughter.

❧

Josephus, Yohanan, and Aislin sit under guard on the floor of an empty tent. "I heard about Mattathias," begins Josephus.

Their eyes find each other and for a moment Yohanan detects a whiff of a past, the scent of the room where priestly students slept in the Temple, the breath of Josephus and Mattathias sleeping beside him. United in sadness, they say nothing.

"So, like me, you have given up on Jerusalem," says Josephus, finally.

"Not on the idea of Jerusalem," says Yohanan.

"And therein lies the dilemma: *whose* idea?"

"If you don't know the answer to that question," says Yohanan, "we did not study in the same Academy, under the same teacher, the revered Gamaliel."

"Tell me, Yohanan, are you one of those who blame Rome for everything that has happened in Judaea? You may speak freely. The guards don't understand a word of Aramaic."

"It is lazy and dishonest to blame the occupiers," says Yohanan. "We have brought this upon ourselves."

234

"And those who remain in Jerusalem? Do they agree with you, or have the Zealots won them over?"

"The Zealots remain a minority. Most residents despise their ideology and methods, but the messianists are ruthless. When you believe the end of the world is at hand, reason flies out the window."

Josephus nods. On this much, they agree. "I am not abandoning my people, Yohanan," he says. "My people have abandoned me; or should I say, my people have abandoned themselves, their principles. In the end, what is right? To survive long enough to explain who we are. That is what matters. Isn't that what our people have always done, chronicling our hopes and struggles?"

"I agree with many of your words," allows Yohanan. "But to aid those who are killing my brethren—that I cannot condone."

"As you yourself attest, Yohanan, your people—my people—are killing themselves. While, undoubtedly, some of the Roman governors were corrupt, there were ways of dealing with such matters other than taking up arms. And, yes, sometimes one must suffer injustice in silence. Sometimes people die needlessly. Allow me to enquire a little further about your project," continues Josephus. "You say you wish to preserve the heritage of Judaea. I sympathize—I more than sympathize—but how do you propose to do this? A Sadducee will not agree with an Essene or a Zealot—not to mention, with you—on many of the details."

"Unlike the Sadducees, who collaborate with Rome, we Pharisees are not guilty of alienating the common people," explains Yohanan. "At least, most of us are not," he adds pointedly. "We empower the people by welcoming discussions of our Holy Texts. We encourage interpretation. And, unlike the Zealots, we do not advocate violence. As for the Essenes, their manner of living—ascetic and monastic—as well as their mystical beliefs, isolate them from most men."

"Nevertheless," observes Josephus, "you run the risk of narrowing the self-definition of Israel, do you not? I ask this as a Pharisee, myself."

"My aim is not to squelch debate. On the contrary. But for now, our focus must be on survival."

Again, Josephus nods, peering quizzically at his childhood friend.

&

Later that morning, Josephus is summoned by Vespasian. Upon his return, he bears welcome news. "General Vespasian grants your request to found an academy. He will provide you with a facility at Yamnia, on the coast."

From whom was it confiscated? wonders Yohanan.

"Further, General Vespasian has agreed to arrange funding for your venture, for which we wish you the best of fortune. But I would like to ask for your assistance with a particular matter," continues Josephus.

"It would be my pleasure, Yosef, son of Matityahu," says Yohanan, reverting to Josephus's Hebrew name.

Josephus hands him a writing tablet and a stylus. "Write a note for your followers. Tell them to gain admittance to the Temple, howsoever they may, to remove as many of the Holy Scrolls as possible, and transfer them to the guards on the Roman side. I will do my best to ensure your instructions are relayed to your disciples."

Yohanan hesitates. Sounds of jubilation outside the tent distract him. Soldiers beat their swords against their shields and call out, "Vespasian Caesar!" and "Vespasian Imperator!"

"You must trust me, Yohanan," adds Josephus. "My purpose is to save the scrolls."

Yohanan writes the instructions and returns the clay tablet to Josephus. "What is happening out there?"

"The emperor, Vitellius, is dead. So is our commander's brother, Flavius Sabinus, the consul of Rome."

"What I hear does not sound like mourning," remarks Yohanan.

"Sabinus supported Vitellius," explains Josephus. "With both of them gone, and with the backing of his troops and allies in Africa, Vespasian has the strongest claim to the throne."

"How did Sabinus die?" asks Yohanan.

"A mob murdered him," Josephus replies, lifting the tent flap to let them leave. Armed soldiers pack the streets of the camp, clamoring for a speech from their leader.

As the furor subsides, Yohanan, Aislin, and Josephus hear Vespasian's stentorian bellow: "This has been a difficult year for all of us, and a bloody one for Rome."

The soldiers rattle their swords and shields in response.

"Three incompetent emperors have ascended to the imperial

throne—Galba, Otho, and Vitellius—and three have perished. I never sought the throne, nor do I now."

The soldiers hiss and jeer, stomping their feet and banging their swords on their shields.

"But if Rome calls upon me to clean up this mess," Vespasian roars, "by Jupiter, by the spirits of my ancestors, and by all that is sacred, I stand before you, ready to serve!"

As the soldiers' shouts echo off the hills of Judaea, Josephus takes his leave.

Yohanan asks Aislin about the skull and about her Latin conversation with the general. He tells her he saw the emotion in her eyes. He heard it in her voice, and in Vespasian's.

She refuses to discuss it.

Nevertheless, Yohanan realizes that if his plan succeeds—if Yamnia becomes a refuge for the Tradition, until better days arrive—he will owe its success not to any of the thousands of men trained to preserve the Tradition, and loyal to it, but to a foreign woman with whom the Roman general seemed strangely familiar—and to a traitor, Josephus, who is desperate to find redemption.

☙

Vespasian leaves Judaea without another word to Aislin or her husband. There are many things she would have liked to tell him. She would have explained the true value that resided in her grandfather's skull, the only remaining connection to her people. She would have expressed her feelings about the Roman way of life that Vespasian so vigorously promoted to her aunt, before murdering her. She might even have tried to forgive him.

It will have to be enough, she tells herself as she and Yohanan trudge away toward their future with a letter of passage and a mule laden with food and coin.

At the age of sixty-seven Paulus is once again doing what he has always done best, voyaging through the empire preaching about the imminence of the general resurrection and urging repentance. The crossing is difficult, the seas choppy, the roads few and often unpaved. Brigands abound. He is frail. He is alone.

A young man meets him at the gates of Tarraconensis. "Surely you've heard about the sorry events in Jerusalem, lord."

"I have heard," answers Paulus. "The Temple was destroyed. So they say. I pray it is not true. But no one has been able to tell me—" He slips and almost falls. The young man holds him. "—the Synagogue of the Way," resumes Paulus. "No one seems to know."

"Oh, master," says the young man. "I am so sorry."

They approach a modest white building at the side of the dirt road, with arched windows and a tiled roof. Inside, a small group awaits them, standing. The young man leads Paulus to the far wall. He turns and looks at the faces watching him, eager for knowledge: a wrinkled old man, several women, the young man who escorts him. *These are the faces of the future,* he tells himself.

"The fire in Rome, the destruction of Judaea, this is just the beginning," he tells them all in a voice hoarse with fatigue but at its core still confident and determined. "It is all part of a plan and the Author of that plan is the Lord, the God of this sacrificed people."

"Are rebels against Rome to be counted among the righteous?" asks a philosophy student with long, dark hair and a small beard. "Would an all-powerful God, the God of the entire cosmos, you say, allow His Temple to be destroyed, or His Son to be murdered? If that God exists, it is a perverse one and one I would have difficulty praying to."

"At the core of our faith," replies Paulus, "is the concept of sin. Unless you understand that concept you cannot understand our God. The order of the universe is a moral order. For those who wash themselves in the love of the One God, death is an illusion."

"Must we avoid eating certain foods," asks an older man, "or spend one day a week in idleness, or mutilate our bodies, to be deemed worthy?"

Paulus knows he is referring to the dietary laws, the Sabbath, and to circumcision, all of which the Greco-Roman world abhors. "We can all share in the blessings of Judaea," says Paulus, ignoring the irony that others perceive in this formulation. "What matters is that we accept the rule of the One Invisible God, which is a rule of love. We are all sinners but when we are forgiven, we become righteous. We die and are reborn. In the end, all that matters is the love God bestows upon us, although none merits it."

"But how can we pray to a God we cannot see?" asks a woman whose blush-colored shawl drapes her shoulders and wraps around her left arm and waist.

Feeling a sharp pain in his chest Paulus closes his eyes and struggles to breathe. After a pause he resumes. "It is true. We cannot visualize the Lord. That is why he sent His own flesh and blood, our Savior Joshua of Nazareth, to walk among us and show us the path that leads beyond death. A man who suffered and died: that you can visualize, no?"

He closes his eyes again, dizzy and nauseated, his jaw clenched, and waits for the pain to subside.

"For years I have traveled through the nations telling His story in the hope that others can march with the righteous of Judaea into the World to Come, a place where piety, honesty, and compassion will at last be rewarded. Now I invite you, too, to join me there."

As a fog creeps into the hills and valleys of the landscape that is his mind, he slumps forward falling into the loving embrace of the Father who awaits him. From beyond the horizon he hears voices, faint, and a commotion:

"Is he well? Are you well, my lord? Someone, please!"

"I am well," murmurs Paulus inaudibly. "I am more than well. I am forgiven."

At the eastern edge of the Campus Martius, the Field of War, ensconced in an open, gilded chariot, his breath and that of his four horses steaming in the autumn chill, Titus Flavius Vespasianus closes his eyes and silently mouths a prayer to the God who has watched over him, Quirinus. Amulets affixed to the side of the chariot—eyes, hands, and animals—ward off evil spirits. Soldiers line up at the front of the field. The staff and bodyguards of the Roman Senate direct thousands of cavalry troops and Judaean captives to their starting positions in the Triumphus, the victory parade that will culminate with the investiture of Vespasian as Caesar, Princeps Senatus, Pontifex Maximus, and Imperator of the Roman empire.

He enjoys the support of the armies of Syria, Egypt, and Germania but Vespasian remains uncertain whether the people of Rome will accept him. He was not born into the patrician class, nor is he a descendant of Julius Caesar. No emperor before him lacked these dual qualifications.

His brother Sabinus, who excelled in every endeavor and who would likely be sitting in this gilded chariot had he survived, is no more. Nor was Sabinus's demise inevitable. It was a symptom of the moral decay rotting Roman society. The task Vespasian will accept on this solemn day, in honor of his brother's memory, is to address that moral erosion. He will mourn Sabinus in decrees and battles, not in tears.

Twelve musicians lead the procession into the city through the Porta Triumphalis. Thousands of chained Judaeans tote booty including a solid gold candelabra as tall as two men, ropes and fabrics of silver, and vibrant tapestries in rare hues, the richest haul ever seized in a single Roman battle. Behind the prisoners march the ranking politicians of Rome: senators, priests, consuls, praetors, aediles, and their bodyguards, garbed in red and holding laurel-wreathed staves.

In his chariot, clad in a purple, gold-embroidered toga and a laurel crown, Vespasian leads tens of thousands of cavalry and marching troops past cheering crowds along the Via Triumphalis to the Circus

Maximus, through the Via Sacra to the Forum, and finally to the Temple of Jupiter on the Capitoline Hill. There, incense burns; musicians pluck, hammer, and ring bells; the high priest sacrifices an unblemished white bull with gilded horns.

As he prepares to address the leaders and people of Rome, his audience packs the plaza below the Temple and the adjacent streets all the way to the horizon. Only a few hear his shouted words, which echo, blended with cheers, off the Temple of Juno Moneta and the Tabularium, a voluminous edifice that houses the state archives, which miraculously survived the Great Fire.

The Academy in Yamnia: three long buildings of unpolished sandstone surrounding a grassy courtyard. The doors remain open to admit light and air. Twelve students, calling themselves The Remnant of Israel, dwell with Yohanan and Aislin. In a field behind the Academy, they have planted a garden.

Jerusalem, a two-day hike east, lies in ruins. The Temple of the Lord has been reduced to a pile of rubble. Vespasian's troops, led by his son Titus, have cast asunder the massive stones, carted away the gold candelabras and silver-clad doors, and dragged the surviving residents off in chains to fight bears and lions in arenas throughout the empire. In that vast ruined plaza, Yohanan understands, the Romans are erecting an altar to Jupiter.

Flames have consumed the scrolls *Enoch* and *Jubilees*, the *War of the Sons of Light against the Sons of Darkness*, the *Testament of Abraham*, and countless other parchments lovingly, and in many cases controversially, preserved in the Temple library. The verbal heritage of Yohanan's people has been reduced to a small collection of texts that his followers spirited out of Jerusalem, and for which Josephus arranged conveyance to Yamnia—and one copy of the *Song of Songs*, which Yohanan penned from memory in the Galilee.

Yohanan is an explorer and a student, not a prophet. The Lord has never spoken to him, except perhaps in dreams mediated by Messengers. All he can do is to look at the realm of man and attempt to discover the best path forward that does not involve abandoning his inheritance, Israel's inheritance.

❧

In sailing to Judaea, Aislin had hoped to flee the grime and strife of Rome, but she has learned there is no escaping from the past. She rinses garments in the academy fountain, reflecting that the apocalypse predicted by so many—from Daniel to the Essenes and Joshua of Nazareth—has occurred in her lifetime, though not in the way its prophets had envisioned. The apocalypse began with the destruction of Britannia and spread to Rome in a fiery blaze that engulfed much of the city. It culminated in the devastation of Jerusalem. The messianic age that will follow, she feels, will not be bestowed upon mankind but will be earned, an effort that may take years, centuries, or even millennia.

The Name of the Lord, Yohanan has taught her, is *Eyeh asher eyeh*, I will be what I will be. The Lord is an ongoing act of creation, as will be Its messianic age.

She shares these thoughts with her husband. "And one other thing," she adds, her voice dipping. "I saw him. Faolan. In a dream." She leans forward and clutches Yohanan's hand on the table. "He is here, with us."

"Here? In this Academy?"

"In the realm of the living."

He looks into her eyes.

"I know, I know. But he is somewhere among us, in our realm," she repeats. "And he has...He has changed."

Yohanan caresses her cheek. "How?"

"He can reason! He can speak. Brilliantly. And..." She chews a morsel of bread, searching for words.

"It troubled you, this dream," says Yohanan. "Of course."

"Yes. It was him and it was not him," she says, remembering her vision. "Not my little Faolan anymore. A Faolan with power." She looks beyond her husband, lost in thought. "Like a spark, fiery and bright, among ashes. The power of hope amid devastation."

❧

The next evening, in the leafy courtyard of his academy, Yohanan discourses with his twelve disciples. An oil lamp burns in their midst. "We have been through this before," he tells them. "The Babylonians ransacked Jerusalem, exiled our leaders, and burned our first Temple. How did we survive? What did we do in Babylon? We told stories to our children. And what happened? Even after our world was destroyed, it endured. We endured. The *olam haba*, the world to come, rises not from a graveyard but from the pages of sacred texts and in the mouths of storytellers. And if, once again, the Lord has allowed men to destroy Its Temple, what is left? Our memory, our lore, our philosophy. Our stories."

"What are stories?" the sole survivor of a once-powerful family asks. "Mere words, consisting of breath and air, invisible and insubstantial."

Yohanan reveals a brass coin with an effigy of the emperor. "What is this but a scrap of cheap metal? It's the story, the fiction we create around it, the credence we give to that fantasy—this is what imbues this coin with importance. We understand our world through such stories. No, my friend, stories are not nothing; without them, we are nothing.

"However, we must abandon two ideologies. First, our belief that by virtue of our Traditions, we are morally superior to other peoples. The Zealots, with their violent certainties, put an end to that illusion. The best of us are sinners; the worst, hypocrites. We are who we are, our traditions are our traditions; that is the most we can say, and that will have to be enough. And second, just as in the time of Abraham we ceased sacrificing human children to the Gods, so now, deprived of our Temple, we must forsake the spilling of blood in the name of our Lord."

"Without our Temple, we are nothing," objects an elderly man.

"A man can leave the home of his father," replies Yohanan, "and remain a man. Only if he loses his memory does he lose himself."

"But why has the Lord allowed this to happen?" asks a third.

"The Lord did not allow this to happen," says Yohanan. "We allowed this to happen. Since the last time the Lord spoke directly to man, in the generation following King David, we have been responsible for our destiny. We allowed corrupt leaders to guide us, leaders who claimed to possess a privileged access to the Lord or the gods of Rome."

He is thinking of Kayafa, remembering the Day of Atonement and the High Priest's quiet confession.

"We are on our own," continues Yohanan. "That has been made abundantly clear to any who dare listen to the voice of history, which is the only voice through which the Lord now speaks to us. To the world. Our freedom from direct divine intervention, our spiritual independence and the responsibilities it entails, are a blessing, but a weighty one."

"You say our continuing claim to existence resides in our literature," objects a young woman, the niece of his friend, the late high priest Mattathias son of Theophilus. No longer chubby or spoiled, she has grown into a taciturn, dark-haired beauty. "But that literature prescribes rituals we can no longer carry out, sacrifices led by a priestly caste that no longer exists, in a Temple that is now no more substantial than a memory."

"Then our memory will be our Temple and we will have to be a nation of priests," says Yohanan, "as it is written in the Scroll of the Exile. Instead of a bull or a lamb, we will have only words as offerings—prayers, with no expectation of a response."

"A nation of priests, perhaps," remarks another disciple, "so long as we do not resemble those who dwelled in the Temple."

"I grew up in the Temple," reminisces Yohanan. "I saw and breathed and lived the excesses. They were not insincere. They were sure of their views. In that respect they resembled their enemies, the Zealots." He absently rubs his earlobe. "If we are to survive, perhaps we must never be too sure of anything. Perhaps the lack of a Temple will help us in this way. "

"The lack of a Temple will only isolate us," objects a fourth disciple.

Yohanan asks him to expound upon this.

"The Romans sacrifice to their Gods," the young man pursues. "So does every other people. Isolation is a curse but you ask us to isolate ourselves yet further."

"Isolation," says Yohanan, "may indeed be a curse, but it is not the worst of fates."

"What is the worst of fates?" asks the disciple.

Yohanan takes a moment to formulate his response. His disciples, it seems to Yohanan, stand at a crossroads. He thinks of all the pious Judaeans who suffered and died through no fault of their own. He thinks too of Josephus. "The worst of fates," he says finally, "is to do evil in the hope of earning the love of the misguided."

෪

At night Yohanan lies next to his wife, remembering his nights at the Temple as a young man, when the entire world stretched before him like a dark abyss. He remembers the secret text, discovered deep in the Temple library.

> *Behold the winter is past; the rain is over and gone.*
> *Flowers appear on the earth, the time of singing has come,*
> *and the voice of the turtledove is heard in our land.*

The fig tree ripens its fruit. The vines are in blossom.
They give forth fragrance.

He wakes at dawn and drapes an arm over Aislin's sleeping body. Without waking, she clutches his hand in hers. It is like reaching across a universe and touching the unknowable.

In the depth of Duda-El there is no breath of wind, only the odor of moist stone. For more than eight hundred years I dwelled in darkness. Since the day I remanded that little goat to the surface, I have spent my time praying that the Lord would reverse Its decree, providing me with the opportunity to help cleanse and stitch the wounds that scar the face of the world, wounds that I and my followers inflicted.

When the goat returned, gingerly descending over flinty stones and accompanied by the man-child Faolan, I felt a spark of happiness for the first time in millennia, since well before the hulking race of Nephilim issued from the union of my Messenger brethren with the mortal women of the earth.

As an incorporeal spirit, I might hope to inspire dreams, but as an embodied life, I could participate in the construction of history. I longed for Faolan's innocence even more than for his corporeal sheath.

Wrapping my wings around him, I conveyed a knowledge of who I was and what I desired. I intended to possess him but, unlike the demons that prowl the forests and highlands seeking vulnerable travelers, I did not wish to do so without his consent. I promised Faolan a sound mind and warned that in exchange I would need his heart. He wanted only to please me. I pressed the entirety of my being into his and felt his experience mingling with mine, like blood with the water of a muddy stream. I felt my veins warm and the curse of the Lord fall away, like chains slipping off my ankles. I fell to my knees—to Faolan's knees—and uttered a hymn of gratitude to the Lord of the universe.

The goat led us toward the mouth of the chasm. For two days we crawled up to the scalded desert, which we finally reached at night under a sliver moon and a star-splashed sky, our knees scraped and bloody but our spirit floating. Exulting in the sting of human injury, we proceeded into the unbounded night. When mortals looked upon our countenance, they beheld the sublunary envelope of Faolan.

I have lost my ability to perceive time *ab extra* but have gained the one power I longed for above all others. I now see the Earth and all upon it as mortals do, in vibrant evanescent colors, the interplay of shadow and light striking me with the fresh impermanence of morning dew. When I close my eyes, I feel the air caress my skin and fill my chest with breath. I know it will be a long, arduous journey, perhaps lasting centuries or millennia, until the end of time, but that hardly matters. The healing has begun.

ACKNOWLEDGMENTS

I owe a debt of gratitude to a number of friends and scholars, with whom I consulted and who read the manuscript of *Into The Unbounded Night* at various stages. To name just a few:

First, my marvelous publisher, Jaynie Royal and her ambitious and idealistic venture, Regal House Publishing—for believing in this book and helping me improve it.

My wife Annie's advice and counsel are invaluable. She is my sounding board, the reader whose instincts I trust more than anyone else's, and my first editor. I don't know how I could do it, or whether I could do it, without her.

The immense knowledge and assistance of Professor Dale Allison, New Testament Chair at Princeton Theological Seminary, cannot be overstated. Not only was Dale willing to discuss any and every question I put to him, he also steered me in the direction of primary texts that shed a fascinating light on the period. In the process, my family grew close with Dale's family, whom I count among my most cherished friends.

Samuele Rocca, an Italian/Israeli historian and archeologist who specializes in the first century, kindly read and commented on my first draft.

Lillian Klein Abensohn, university professor, retired, associated with the University of Maryland and American University, read and commented on more than one draft, and provided insights that helped guide my thinking on a number of issues.

Marc Kramer has always been there for me with valuable and sensitive advice, including feedback on my novels. My dear friend Adam Becker read an early, incomplete draft, and offered generous and intelligent comments. My friend and fellow historical novelist Sherry Jones also read and commented on the book during one of our delightful, rambling phone conversations.

In the early stages of planning this novel, I enjoyed a number of rambling conversations with Rabbi Alex Greenbaum, of Beth El

Congregation, Pittsburgh, during which we looked at Biblical and other texts and discussed details such as the structure of the Second Temple.

Following the publication of my first novel, *By Fire, By Water*, I developed warm relations with a number of novelists, often based on the simple fact that we all know what it's like to live this life—what we go through, why we do it. I count all the members of the Fiction Writers Co-op and Historical Fiction Authors Facebook groups among these friends, as well as my fellow authors in the Mt. Lebanon Writers group. I am grateful to all, and love more than one, but the camaraderie—dare I say, kinship—that I felt immediately with fellow historical novelist Stephanie Cowell and Mary Burns has been a special joy and consolation. Both read an early draft of this novel, and I thank them warmly for the comments and emotional support they offered.